"YOU DON'T WANT TO KISS ME?"

"Kissing you is all I've been thinking about for the past few days. I vowed the next time it happened I wasn't going to go about it like some hormone-driven teenager trying to get to second base."

"Second base?"

"Eloise, don't look at me like that."

She worried her lower lip. "Like what?"

"Like I'm the only man you've ever kissed."

Her eyebrows drew together as she asked, "Is that bad?"

He sighed. "Not bad. Just—"

"If you say 'different' I swear I'm going to stomp so hard on your instep you'll need a cane to walk out of here."

"Okay, okay." He thought before he spoke. "Not different. But I think I've figured out your secret."

"Secret? You think I have a secret?"

"I know you have a secret. Several, in fact."

Other books by Judi McCoy

I DREAM OF YOU

(Waldenbooks Bestselling
Debut Romance of 2001)

YOU'RE THE ONE

SAY YOU'RE MINE

HEAVEN IN YOUR EYES

Published by Zebra Books

HEAVEN SENT

Judi McCoy

ZEBRA BOOKS
Kensington Publishing Corp.
http://www.kensingtonbooks.com

ZEBRA BOOKS are published by

Kensington Publishing Corp.
850 Third Avenue
New York, NY 10022

All Kensington titles, imprints and distributed lines are available at special quantity discounts for bulk purchases for sales promotion, premiums, fund-raising, educational or institutional use.

Special book excerpts or customized printings can also be created to fit specific needs. For details, write or phone the office of the Kensington Special Sales Manager: Kensington Publishing Corp., 850 Third Avenue, New York, NY 10022. Attn. Special Sales Department. Phone: 1-800-221-2647.

Zebra and the Z logo Reg. U.S. Pat. & TM Off.

First Printing: October 2003
10 9 8 7 6 5 4 3 2 1

Printed in the United States of America

This book is dedicated to my Wicked Sisters:
Barbara, Jeanne, Jessica and Leah

And my Texas angels:
Kerrin, Sandra, Sherry and Tracy

As always
to Helen Breitwieser,
more than an agent: a dear friend

Prologue

"I see you've been promoted." Eloise stood in front of Milton's white marble-topped desk wearing a cool smile on her impossibly lovely face. "Congratulations."

"Thank you," Milton said, arranging a stack of papers he'd been studying. This discussion with Eloise was his first order of business since he'd been assigned as special-angel-in-charge, a sort of group leader of the *guiding* angels, and he knew for certain it wasn't going to be pleasant.

She'd dressed a bit more sensibly today, most likely in honor of their meeting. Holding a huge purple-and-white-striped umbrella, Eloise wore a bright yellow rain slicker and matching hat. The fact that she reminded him of a little girl dressed to the nines and sent to play in the rain by a caring mother was ironic. To the best of his recollection, this heavenly being didn't warm up to children or their mothers, or most any human. It was for those very reasons she stood before him today.

Twirling the umbrella, she lifted a leg to admire her dark purple knee-high vinyl boots with tiny yellow ducks imprinted on the sides. She could be a charmer when it suited her, he'd grant her that.

"So, why am I here? A new assignment?"

"In a manner of speaking."

Eloise twirled the umbrella playfully, but Milton got the impression it was only for show. He gestured and a plush cloud in the shape of a chair appeared behind her. Relief washed through him when she took a seat.

"Eloise, this is one of the most difficult things I've ever had to do."

She folded the umbrella and set it on his desk, an impatient-looking pout marring her perfect features. "I see." Leaning back in the chair, she raised a brow. "I suppose I'm in trouble for being so difficult about that silly scheme you concocted involving Tom and Anne McAllister. Well, you needn't worry. I've taken Tom back, as promised, and they seem to be doing just fine. He and Annie are in love; they're having a baby"— she made a sour face —"and all that *blah-blah-blah*. If you ask me, it's just too gushy for words."

Blah-blah-blah? Too gushy for words? "Those comments are exactly why I needed to speak with you. To answer your earlier question, yes, you are being reassigned."

Her face drained of all color. "I'm being demoted."

Milton's exasperated sigh fluttered the papers resting in the middle of his desk. "Try to understand, Eloise. It's the duty of every guiding angel to be compassionate and giving. Above all else, they must want the very best for their charges. It's important they agree to stand by the souls in their care through thick and thin, high and low, love and despair, and never give up hope their charges will succeed."

"I am giving . . . in my own way," she said defensively. "Not everyone plays by your rules, Milton."

"This isn't about *my* rules, and it's definitely not a game. It's about your attitude, which has come under some scrutiny from upstairs."

"So that's what this is about." She sniffed. "I'm being punished because my success rate isn't as high as yours."

"It isn't a punishment, but you have pink-slipped more souls than any other angel on record. Your success rate has dipped to an all-time low, and too many of your ex-charges are walking earth without guidance or support. *He* doesn't like the numbers, and you know what that means."

Eloise closed her china blue eyes and, for a second, Milton thought she might cry. Angels rarely shed tears, so the idea of this cynical, unforgiving heavenly being doing so shocked him. Was it possible he'd been wrong about her?

"It isn't my fault I keep getting stuck with foolish, sappy, brainless humans who can't make decisions, don't use common sense and think love is the answer to all their stupid problems."

Pushing his sentiments aside, Milton cleared his throat. Her words and the emotions they conveyed were downright annoying. "Love *is* the answer to all their problems, at least it is most of the time. That's why *We* have reached this decision." He tapped a finger on his desk. "Your time has come, my dear."

"Excuse me?"

"Allow me to make it a bit clearer. The Big Guy has decreed that it's time you took a refresher course in compassion and love—human love—in the most personal of ways. He's giving you a chance to experience life on earth firsthand, and to decide if being an angel is really your appropriate path and begin anew. Getting a handle on the three most important virtues might be a good place to start, by the way. Faith, hope and love are the reasons humans were created. Until you experience those virtues personally, He's convinced you will continue to fail with your current assignments."

Her mouth formed a surprised little O. "You can't be serious."

A gavel appeared in his hand, and Milton rapped it smartly on his desktop. "Hear me, Eloise, angel of the Most High. As put forth in rule sixteen seventy-seven, subset twelve, of the Guiding Angels' Handbook, from this day forward you are remanded to earth for whatever length of time it takes you to learn the virtues of faith, hope and love."

Before Eloise could speak, he whacked the gavel a second time and she disappeared.

Milton shook his head. He was under strict orders not to reveal any more than was absolutely necessary to the guiding angels singled out for *the choice*. He'd been so enthused that his first one was Eloise. It showed she was being given a chance to reach her full potential. But he doubted she'd understood a word he'd said. Eloise could be very stubborn when she felt wounded or misunderstood.

It wasn't his job to decide where the angels who were being reassigned to earth went, but he couldn't help wondering about his recalcitrant little friend. Wherever she was, she would be unhappy and uncooperative until she learned her lesson.

And when the time came for her to make *the choice*, he only hoped it would be the correct one.

One

"Why do I haf'ta go back to school today, Daddy? I like being at home with you and Grammy, honest I do."

Nathan Baxter tucked the white paper napkin firmly in place under his five-year-old daughter's chin, then poured milk onto her cereal. "Because Thanksgiving vacation is over, and things have to get back to normal around here. Grammy has her yoga class and a bridge game this afternoon. And I'm due at the precinct in,"—he glanced at his watch—"less than an hour."

Phoebe's lower lip trembled and Nathan's heart did the same. "What's the matter, punkin? I thought you liked kindergarten."

Checking her reflection in her cereal spoon, Phoebe's nose wrinkled as if the milk he'd just poured was spoiled. She touched the tangle of pink ribbon hanging over one dainty ear and quickly changed the subject. "You did my pigtails all wrong again, Daddy, not like Grammy does them. I want Grammy." She stared through accusing blue eyes. "She has'ta come do my hair! Right now!"

He sighed when her last words came out in a petulant wail. Since Janet's death, he'd been a minor success at every phase of parenting except his daughter's hair. Was he ever going to get it right?

"How about you eat breakfast, and I'll call her? If she comes downstairs and helps me fix it before her yoga class, will you promise to go to school without a fuss?"

Sniffing, Phoebe shrugged. "I guess so."

"That's my girl." He tapped a finger to her nose and she giggled. Their truce established, he pushed back from the table and walked to the phone mounted on the kitchen wall. His fifty-two-year-old mother had her own apartment on the top floor of his three-story town home, which many would consider a convenient arrangement for a widower with a small child. Rita Mae didn't always agree.

Crossing his fingers he dialed her number, relieved to hear her cheerful greeting on the second ring. "Mom? It's me. Can you come downstairs and give me another lesson on how to fix Phoebe's hair? She won't go to school unless you do."

Though given lovingly, Rita Mae's answer was short and to the point. "I have about fifteen minutes before I leave for yoga, and I've yet to drink my morning tea, so beware. Oh, and Nathan, do try to pay attention this time."

Hanging up the phone, he raised his gaze to the ceiling. Sometimes he wondered if there wouldn't be less fuss every morning if he simply took Phoebe to his barber and had him cut her curly mop to an inch all over. Then again, this entire single-parent business would be a whole lot easier if she'd been born a boy. Boys didn't demand sneakers that matched their dresses, or socks that matched their underwear or the ribbons in their hair. And they didn't usually—

"Daddy?"

Nathan wanted to take the hasty thoughts back the second he heard his daughter's singsong voice. He wouldn't trade Phoebe Marie for a dozen sons, not ever. If she reminded him of Janet, he had to remember it was his deceased wife's best parts that shined so brightly through their child. Intelligence, humor and an adventurous spirit were major components of Phoebe's joyful personality.

"Daddy? Are you daydreaming again?"

He walked to the stove and turned on the heat under the kettle, then went to the cupboard to hunt for a tea bag. "Just thinking, sweetheart."

"Is Grammy coming?"

"Yep. Now finish up. She'll be here in a few minutes."

He set the tea bag in a mug and, when the kettle whistled, added hot water. The rear door opened and Rita Mae walked in like a ship under full sail. Carrying a short mink jacket and matching hat, her diminutive form was dressed in name-brand sneakers, a bright red sweater and black stretch pants. Artfully arranged auburn hair and tastefully applied cosmetics made her look ten years younger than Nathan knew her to be. Floating past him on a cloud of pricey-smelling perfume, she snatched the cup from his hand and glided to the table.

Phoebe gave her grandmother a face-splitting grin, then stuck out her lower lip and fingered a drooping wad of curls. "Look what Daddy did to my hair."

The little traitor. This morning when she'd gazed in her bathroom mirror, Phoebe had pronounced his ham-fisted efforts perfect. Of course, that had been an hour ago, when the pigtails were tucked neatly into their elastic bands and tied with bright pink ribbons. Right now, they listed unevenly at half-mast, one ribbon trailing like the broken tail of a kite.

Nathan furrowed his fingers through his own dark brown curls. How the heck was he supposed to keep her rippling waves in those fussy little-girl styles when he couldn't even control his own hair? Maybe he was the one who needed to get shorn like a sheep, or—

"Nathan." Rita Mae dunked the tea bag rhythmically, then removed it from the cup. Taking the hairbrush in hand, she said, "Get over here, if you please."

He sighed, but did as he was told. Arguing with his too-smart-for-her-own-good mother always made him feel as if he were ten years old again. Not the best self-image for a homicide detective with twelve years on the force.

Raising his eyebrows, he held the brush in one hand and an elastic band in the other, and made like a surgeon preparing to operate. "You ready, sweetheart?"

"Ready."

His mother gave a drawn out *tsk*. "Honestly, I just don't understand this mental block you have about doing Phoebe Marie's hair. Now pay attention. Take hold of the brush correctly, and use your right hand to pull up from the bottom while you keep the elastic band in your left. Then slip your left hand under the ponytail and brush back from the—"

He cringed when his fingers stiffened like overcooked hot dogs and behaved just as uncooperatively.

"Ow! Ow! Ow!"

Aw, jeez. "Sorry, punkin," he said, refusing to look at Rita Mae. "Let me try it again."

Phoebe whimpered and his insides turned to pudding. Slowly, carefully, he wielded the brush a second time, amazed at how soft her white-blond hair felt as it slid like coiled silk through his clumsy hands.

"That's better," his mother pronounced. "Now slip the band under and around, loop it again . . . again. That's right. Pull the hair gently to tighten the band, then tie the ribbon."

Nathan heaved a strangled breath. *One down, one to go.* The torture, to both himself and his daughter, was over in another minute. Rita Mae nodded her approval, then pulled out a chair and sat next to her granddaughter.

"So, what's this nonsense I hear about you not wanting to return to school?"

Phoebe raised a shoulder and set her chin in her hand. "Miss Singeltary isn't coming back to teach us, because she's gonna have a baby."

Successful at ferreting out the real reason for the little girl's angst, Rita Mae shot her son a triumphant smile. "I see. And who's to be your new teacher?"

"I don't know. But Billy said he bet she'd be mean, like the sea witch from *The Little Mermaid.*" Phoebe scraped the last of her cereal from the bowl. "If Miss Singeltary got a baby for Thanksgiving, then I'm pretty sure we're gonna get one for Christmas."

"Oh, and what makes you think that?"

" 'Cause I asked Santa when Daddy took me to see him on Saturday, and Santa said I would get one, 'specially when I told him a baby would be somebody for me to play with when Daddy went to work."

Another quelling look from his mother had Nathan racing from the room. Next year he was going to think twice before he took Phoebe to see one of those mall Santas, or any white-bearded fat man in a red suit, for that matter. The bozo had probably thought it was a kick to promise children things he knew their parents could never deliver.

He rounded the upper landing and stopped in his tracks when he glanced in Phoebe's bedroom. Shortly after his wife's death, about eighteen months ago, he'd carted most of her things to a women's shelter in the District. Then, on the advice of his mother, he'd filled a bottom drawer in Phoebe's dresser with a few of Janet's things. Jewelry, scarves, old photos, an almost empty perfume bottle—anything he thought Phoebe might like to play with that would remind her of her mother—to enjoy whenever she wanted.

Right now, the drawer was open, a scarf dangling onto the floor, which told him she had already spent time sifting through the jumble. Was this the reason she seemed so glum?

Nathan tucked the scarf back into the drawer, shut it tight and headed for the private bath adjacent to his bedroom. He needed to shower and change out of his jogging gear before he took Phoebe to school and got to the precinct.

After stripping out of his sweats, he stepped into the stall and let the steamy water clear his brain. It was becoming glaringly apparent that Phoebe missed her mother, even though she was barely old enough to remember her. Since she'd started school he'd thought that combined with Rita Mae, Miss Singeltary would be an adequate mother figure, but with the kindergarten teacher now out of the picture, Phoebe was facing another loss. Just what an already insecure five-year-old needed.

Times like this, it really nagged him that he hadn't been able to fill the void Janet's death had left in his daughter's heart. He was the one who'd wanted Phoebe in the first place, not his wife. He was the one who had fed and walked her most nights, calmed her fears and soothed her colicky stomach. Janet had lost interest in their daughter soon after Phoebe's birth, and had never really gotten involved. Expensive jewelry, designer clothes, tennis lessons at the country club and any extravagant trapping she could buy with the money she'd inherited from her father had all come before her child.

After Janet's tragic death, he and Rita Mae had talked plenty about Phoebe, each taking an equal part in deciding what was best for the little girl. His mother had happily curtailed her own active social calendar to baby-sit until Nathan worked out an acceptable schedule at the precinct and arranged child care. Luckily, they'd agreed on the basics: the best private schools, piano lessons when she was ready, horseback riding or gymnastics lessons if Phoebe showed an interest—anything within reason that would give her a varied and fulfilling life.

Only one sticking point in Phoebe's upbringing remained. His mother had been adamant in thinking that, after an appropriate length of time, Nathan find a new wife.

He had been just as adamant when he'd said no.

Eloise sneezed three times in rapid succession. The force of the strange sensation made her eyes water and her teeth ache. Automatically, she blinked before shifting her bottom. Then she realized she was sitting on a chair—not the soft comfy one Milton usually provided—but a very hard chair that made her fanny hurt.

Sneeze! Teeth? Fanny!

She opened her eyes and stared down onto the top of a plain oak desk upon which sat a dull green blotter with a variety of items lining the perimeter. A plastic replica of a potato wearing ears, glasses and a hat, a blue-and-yellow-striped ball, a stack of books, a dried rose tied with a droopy red ribbon, pencils and pens standing in a bright orange mug . . .

Raising her head, she gazed at a veritable sea of furniture. Tiny desks and miniature chairs, all neatly aligned in rows, faced her as if listening for words of wisdom.

Confused, she stared at the sunlight streaming into the spacious room through a row of large windows limned with silvery white frost. Stunned by the glittering light, she shifted her gaze to take in the opposite wall, which had a closed door in its center, a row of hooks and shelves to the right and stacks of cubes to the left. The wall of cubes continued halfway around, then came a filing cabinet, a standing cupboard, a large overflowing bookcase and a watercooler. The room was painted a soft and cheerful yet comforting yellow, one of her favorite colors.

Sitting back against the torturous chair, she sighed as she drummed her fingers on the desk. It was coming back to her now, the reason she was in this room.

Milton.

He had banged that stupid gavel, zapped her from heaven and stuck her here on earth before she'd had a chance to defend herself. The pompous so-and-so had nerve, judging her and meting out punishment as if he were the Almighty. How nice of him to get a promotion and immediately start throwing his weight around. Just her luck he'd decided to pick on her first.

Fisting her hands in her lap, she closed her eyes. Once she got back to his office, she and Milton were going to have words. Important words.

Words no angel should ever have to speak.

Opening her mind, she envisioned heaven and all its splendor, and waited for the rush of cool sweet air that always accompanied her travels. She cringed when a blast of odiferous heat tickled at her ankles, and for a scant second feared she'd been sent to . . .

Looking down, she spied a covered, rectangular hole cut in the floor. Heating vents, meant to warm human being's homes, churches, public buildings—

Almost fearful to look, she pushed away from the desk and stood, intent on inspecting her person. Staring down, she could see that she was a tall and, as best she could tell from the mounds sticking out of her chest, well-formed human female. A drab purplish brown dress with plain black buttons marching down the front shrouded her from her shoulders to past her knees. Laced-up black shoes with big chunky heels covered her feet, and her long legs were encased in dark brown fabric she knew went all the way up to her waist. Ugh! She felt as if she were an oversize plum stuffed into a grape-size skin.

Milton would pay, she vowed, for turning her into a human fashion disaster. She was not going to take this humiliation lying down.

A jolt of terror gripped her and she gasped. Holding her hands to her face, she tried to intuit her features. What if he'd stuck her in a body that was ugly or disfigured? Worse, what if she was ancient, a dried-up old prune? None of the angels she knew had been unattractive or physically flawed, though some did seem a bit . . . interesting looking. When they appeared to humans, it was usually in a form their charges could relate to, not one that would frighten them.

She took another sweeping gaze around the room, but before she found a mirror the door opened. A young boy, little more than a toddler, poked his head through the door frame, then ducked from sight.

Eloise held her breath as reality struck in a great crashing wave. The reason for the desk, the dull, ordinary clothing and her ridiculously hard chair suddenly became clear. She was in a school. The Lilliputian-size furniture was meant for children, the cubes their storage area, the books their curriculum. In seconds this room would be filled with tiny human beings, looking to her for guidance, knowledge—all manner of instruction.

She was a teacher.

The irony of the situation welled up in her throat and threatened to swallow her whole. Milton knew how she felt about children, or at least he should. He had to know how much she disliked guiding the miniature humans, how uncomfortable she was in their presence. It was one of the reasons she rarely got involved in her charges' lives until they were teenagers.

The rules were simple and straightforward, and she'd always done her best to follow them. God created souls and gave them life. When the time was right, He willed them home. As an obedient servant, she honored His wishes without question.

But deep down inside, she'd never been able to accept the death of a child. Ever since she'd stood helplessly eons ago and watched as the first child in her care was called back to heaven before he'd reached his third birthday, she'd been filled with sorrow.

How was she supposed to teach them and care for them day after day, when she knew they might be taken from her at any moment? Milton thought she lacked compassion and maybe, with adult humans, she did. But he was wrong about the little ones. When they left, she was simply too despondent to say good-bye.

Shuffling feet and the sound of whispers teased her ears. Struggling to suppress a whimper, she ran her hands over her hair and hoped she was presentable. It wouldn't do to frighten the little creatures, at least not at their first meeting. But what was she supposed to tell them? Had she been their teacher all along, or was this her first day in the classroom? What city was she in? What was her name?

A round of giggles filled the air. Two heads peeked around the door. Silently, Eloise said a prayer, asking for strength. Later, when the day was over, she would have a talk with the Almighty and get this mess sorted out.

One by one, a river of bodies streamed into the room. Some of the children were wide-eyed and solemn; others pushed and shoved at one another with abandon. Most stared while they shuffled toward the wall pegs and shelves; took off coats, hats, mittens and boots; and hung them on a hook or set them on a shelf. Moving in waves, they walked to their desks and sat at attention, their curious gazes never leaving her face.

Smiling, Eloise swallowed her fear.

A little boy with carrot-orange hair raised his hand.

"Yes?" she asked, too tongue-tied to say more.

"Are you our new teacher?"

When she got hold of Milton, he was going to be one sorry heavenly being.

"I am."

A chubby girl wearing denim overalls spoke next without raising her hand. "What's your name?"

"Um . . . I'm Eloise."

The girl snorted out a giggle. "That's a funny name. Are we supposed to call you L-oh-wheeze, 'cause Mz Singeltary, our last teacher, she said we had to call her *mzzz?*" The youngster stretched out the lone syllable until she sounded like a raging bumblebee.

"How about Miss Eloise?" But if they decided to call her *crazy,* she would certainly understand.

A flurry of hands shot to the ceiling and she rolled her eyes. What more did the little imps need to know?

Before she could speak, the door opened and a woman wearing huge round glasses and a dress very similar to Eloise's own unattractive purplish brown sack stuck her head in the room.

"Good morning, children."

"Good morning, Ms. Hewitt," they answered in chorus.

The woman smiled warmly at Eloise. "And good morning to you, Miss Starr. Sorry I wasn't here earlier to welcome you formally to the Hewitt Academy and introduce you to your class, but I had car trouble. How are you and your charges getting along?"

Miss Starr? How very unimaginative of Milton, but it did answer one of her questions.

"We're fine, thank you, Ms. Hewitt, but . . . um . . ." Eloise felt her face warm. She certainly couldn't tell the woman she needed to ride the next express cloud to heaven without sounding like a fool.

Ms. Hewitt walked to the desk and lowered her voice. "I understand completely. First-day jitters and all that. The women's lavatory is down the hall to the right. Take your time while I chat with the class."

The simple suggestion of performing a very basic human function forced Eloise to slap her knees together. Not only did she have to tinkle—she liked that word more than any other for what she needed to do—she was in the throes of something she'd heard humans talk about whenever they were confused or unsure of their current situation.

She was having a nightmare.

"Thank you," she murmured, rushing to the door.

Completely overwhelmed by the day's activities, Eloise sat at her desk with her head in her hands. How could such tiny creatures find the energy to ask so many questions, make so many surprising comments and create such utter and complete chaos in a short seven hours?

Not fifteen minutes into the morning, Billy Humphrey had gotten his left index finger stuck inside the pencil sharpener and it had taken Ms. Hewitt, the school janitor and a can of something called WD40 to extricate the screaming child's digit.

Shortly after lunch, Missy Jenkins had spewed the contents of her stomach—potato chips, chocolate milk, a peanut butter, honey and banana sandwich, and a cup of lime Jell-O—not only onto her desk, but all over the back of Miles Arthur, the boy who sat in front of her. Both of them had to be sent home with their respective nannies, while the same harried janitor mopped up the disgusting mess.

Someone—she was still suspicious of a child named John Ecklestein who swore he had no idea how it happened—had tipped over the watercooler, which luckily was almost empty. But it made a puddle that required a third visit from the now-furious janitor, who swore he wouldn't return to her classroom again until the following week.

In between catastrophes the children had hopscotched from topic to topic with every manner of personal question known to heaven.

"Miss Eloise, are you married?"

"No," she'd answered, sincerely hoping it was the truth. Milton wouldn't have dared to be that foolish, would he?

"Why not?"

"Because. Now who has to go to the rest room?"

It was their fourth trip in two hours, and it didn't deter their invasive curiosity one iota.

"Miss Eloise, where did Ms. Singeltary go to have her baby?"

"A hospital, I would imagine," she'd answered, thinking that would be the end of it.

"Was it a boy or a girl baby? And what did she name it?"

"I have no idea," she'd responded, vowing to ask Ms. Hewitt at her earliest convenience.

"Where do babies come from anyway?"

A serious-looking girl with soulful brown eyes and black horn-rimmed glasses had quickly informed the class, "The stork, silly. My mother said so."

"Nu-uh. Babies grow from seeds the daddy plants in the mommy's tummy. My gramma told me, and she knows everything."

"Santa said he would bring my daddy and me a baby, and we don't even have to plant a garden," said a pretty little girl with a pensive smile.

"Miss Eloise, do you have a baby?"

"No!" With that, she had jumped from her hard-as-granite chair and announced it was time for a story.

"Are you going to get one?" Amber Morris asked, before Eloise could retrieve a book from the shelves. "Because my cousin Ashley got one, and she wasn't married."

The ultimate insult had come some time after the peanut butter–and–banana fiasco, when Adam Taylor, a boy with lots of freckles and a curious grin, had stared at her feet as if she were wearing canoes instead of shoes. "Miss Eloise, where did you get those shoes? My grandma has a pair just like 'em and she's *really old."*

That comment brought on a raft of new observations.

"How old are you, anyway?" Lucy Chin had asked through narrowed eyes. "My mother is twenty-seven and you look lots older than her."

"You probably don't even have a boyfriend, 'cause there's no engagement ring on your finger."

"She already said she wasn't married, silly. Besides, she's a teacher. Teachers don't get married."

"Ms. Singeltary wasn't married, and she had a baby."

"My mom says teachers are old maids, who shouldn't have kids of their own."

"You're not a thespian, are you?" Felicia Rathbone, a child with a supercilious expression, had told Eloise that her father was a diplomatic attaché to some high-ranking British official here on a series of highly secret negotiations.

"No, I'm not an actress," she'd answered, her head swimming.

"That's good, because my dad says *homaseptuals* are the most disgusting people on the planet."

Eloise had cringed at the statement, not daring to correct

the child's comical pronunciation for fear of opening an entirely different can of worms.

Now, at just past three o'clock, the school day was officially over. Earlier, she'd been reminded by Ms. Hewitt that as part of her teaching contract, she was expected to stay an extra hour before she called the homes of the children who had yet to be collected by nannies, chauffeurs and doting parents. Apparently, the Hewitt Academy catered to an elite group of families who were either rolling in money, had political clout, or both.

"Mith Elohweeth?"

She raised her head at the sound of lisping and gazed at the two children still waiting for their rides. Mary Alice Murphy, or was it Mary Anne Murphree? Between the little girl's speech impediment and Eloise's aching head, it was difficult to remember.

She dredged up a smile. "What is it?"

"Ith's three-thirty. My mother isn't usually thith late."

"Is that tho—er—so?"

The girl nodded through a well of tears. "I'm worried thse won't be here in time to get me to my tennith lethon."

Before Eloise could answer, the pretty girl with the pensive smile, a plethora of pale blond hair and enormous eyes the color of the sky on a bright spring day, stood and walked to Mary Alice. "It's okay. She'll be here."

Mary Alice sniffed, then wiped her nose on her rumpled sleeve. "How do you know?"

"'Cause she's your mommy. Mommies never forget their kids," the child pronounced sagely, patting her friend's shoulder.

How sweet, thought Eloise, *and how very not true.* She'd lost count of the number of mothers who took their children for granted and sometimes forgot about them completely. This little girl obviously had one of the good ones.

Just then, a woman dressed in tailored yellow slacks and a coat of black cashmere ran into the room. "Mary

Alice, why aren't you dressed? Get your things—it's time to go."

Eloise stood and walked to the frazzled woman, holding out her hand. "Hello, I'm Mary Alice's new teacher, Eloise Starr."

The woman whirled in place. "Did we get a memo about you?" She tugged her daughter from her chair. "Come on, we're late."

"Mary Alice was worried that you wouldn't be here, Mrs. Murphy," Eloise said, thinking the woman should be made aware of her daughter's concern.

Mrs. Murphy fluffed up her dark, curly bob as she watched her daughter reach for her coat. "That's ridiculous. I was at the hairdresser and Jean-Claude likes to take his time. Mary Alice knows I'll be here . . . eventually."

Biting her tongue, Eloise merely nodded. Besides the fact that she felt like a molting Emperor penguin standing next to a well-dressed chickadee, she didn't like the woman's cavalier attitude. When she got back to heaven, she was going to have a stern talk with Mrs. Murphy's guiding angel.

"Mary Alice drew a lovely picture today," she offered, trying to sound positive. "Would you care to see it?"

"I don't have time for that right now," Mrs. Murphy said as she pulled the child, who was still struggling to button her coat, toward the door. "It was nice meeting you, Ms. Barr. Come along, Mary Alice."

Eloise sighed and the other child, who had an oddly old-fashioned name she didn't remember, sighed with her. Swiveled in her seat, the girl continued to gaze at the door.

"I wish I had a mommy."

Eloise felt a flutter in the pit of her stomach. The pronouncement was the perfect ending to a very *un*-perfect day. "You don't have a mother?"

The girl turned to gaze up at her. "Nu-uh."

The flutter grew as Eloise studied the child's classic features more closely. Wildly curling, white-blond hair, bluer-than-blue eyes, a tiny turned-up nose and cupid's bow lips all melded perfectly. Even her rounded chin with its strangely familiar dimple tugged a cord deep inside. It couldn't be . . . could it?

"What happened to her?" Eloise asked, fearful she already knew the answer.

"My daddy says the angels took her to heaven, but I know the real story."

Eloise closed her eyes and willed herself gone from the room. This was not happening to her, not now when she was still reeling from the rigors of her first, and hopefully last, taxing day as a human. Holding her aching stomach with splayed fingers, she asked, "And what's that?"

The child swung her slender legs under her desk as she stared at the pencils aligned in a row next to her notebook. "A bad man shot her."

Closing her eyes, Eloise mouthed a desperate prayer. *Please, God, I'll be a better angel, honest I will. I'll even learn the things Milton said I must. Just tell the relocation department to put me in another city and give me a different kind of profession.*

But when she opened her eyes, nothing had changed. She was in the same schoolroom, standing in front of the same little girl, with the same pain writhing deep inside.

"What was her name?" Eloise asked through her frozen lips.

"My mommy's name was Janet. Janet Marie Baxter."

Two

Eloise squeezed out a breath as a ripple of awareness tripped up her spine. Raising her gaze, she saw a man in the doorway appraising her and the little girl, whom she recalled was named Phoebe, through narrowed eyes. Wearing dark jeans, a white dress shirt and black leather jacket, Nathan Baxter looked just as she remembered him, only better. Tall with a dimple in his square chin identical to his daughter's, he wasn't exactly handsome, but there was a compelling aura of masculine charm enhancing his rough-hewn features.

While Phoebe's words made her shudder, his expressive eyes and powerful build spoke to her in a primitive way no angel should ever dare ponder.

"Sorry I'm late, punkin," he said, focusing his gaze on the child beside her. "Something came up at the precinct. You about ready to go?"

"Daddy!" Her face joyous, Phoebe danced in place. "I have to go potty."

Grinning, Nathan stepped into the room and walked to the wall pegs. "Do you need help?"

"Nu-uh, I'm a big girl." She skipped into the hall. "I'll be right back."

He watched Phoebe leave, then turned and took down her dark purple coat and matching hat and set the items on her desk. "So you're the new teacher," he stated bluntly, acknowledging Eloise's presence with a wary smile.

Eloise set a hand over her heart to calm its frantic beating. This was not only an unfair punishment Milton had meted out; it was downright criminal. And when she saw him again, she was going to tell him so. Right now, she had to gather her composure and hold a sensible conversation with a human being she'd thought of far too often—in all the wrong ways—over the past several years.

Nathan Baxter had never been one of her souls, but his wife had. And although she had done her best to encourage Janet Baxter to behave in a manner befitting a dutiful mother and loving wife, Eloise had failed. She'd pink-slipped Janet only a month before the woman's demise, a fact that had weighed heavily on her conscience ever since she'd done the deed.

A pang of regret crept into her heart, and she pushed it aside. "And you're Phoebe's father."

He held out his hand. "Nathan Baxter. Thanks for waiting. Ms. Singeltary wasn't always so cheerful about staying."

"Eloise Starr," she answered, hating the breathless tone her voice had taken. Her heart stuttered in her chest and she willed her hand not to tremble as she shook his. "It's in our contract. We have to stay."

"Yeah, but you don't have to chat with the kids or listen to their concerns. Phoebe's a worrier, and she hates to be rushed. My job sometimes causes me to work odd hours. I try to get here on time, but it can be difficult."

Pulling her hand away, she took a step back. "You're a policeman."

"Phoebe Marie told you," he said, easily accepting her simple description of his often-complicated job. "Actually, I'm a homicide detective. I've been working flexible hours since my wife died, but I got stuck today, which is the reason I'm late."

Telling herself it was a lie of omission, because Phoebe hadn't once mentioned her father's occupation, she nodded.

"I couldn't help but overhear what the two of you were discussing before I walked in the room."

My charge, your dead wife and, according to Milton, another one of my failures.

Eloise hardened her heart. Milton could take his opinion of the way she handled her souls and fly them straight to the moon. To her mind, Janet Baxter fit perfectly into the category she'd declared vain, smug and self-absorbed. Too self-absorbed to do what was best for her husband and child.

"Phoebe seemed to need to tell me. I didn't mean to pry."

Stuffing his hands into the pockets of his jeans, he paced to the windows and stared out at the darkening afternoon sky. "Ms. Singeltary knew about Phoebe not having a mother, so I guess you should too, just in case it causes a problem."

"Problem?" The breath caught in her throat. "What kind of problem?"

Shrugging his broad shoulders, he faced her. "She gets anxious sometimes, and she can be a little insecure when the discussion turns to parents. If the school plans any mother-daughter outings or luncheons, Ms. Hewitt said you would send a note home ahead of time, so I could rearrange my schedule or let Phoebe's grandmother know. I don't want her left out of anything."

"Has she . . . been left out of anything?"

"Not yet. Then again, school's only been in session for three months. The class project for Thanksgiving was turkey-shaped centerpieces. I assume there'll be ornaments or Christmas presents for the moms and dads. I think the school does a Mother's Day thing, and you probably make stuff for Valentine's Day and Easter. Maybe when you do the gifts for the mothers, Phoebe can make something for her grandmother instead."

"Um . . . sure, no problem," Eloise stammered, overwhelmed by his litany. Ornaments? A turkey centerpiece?

Milton expected her to choreograph arts and crafts projects like some kind of Martha Stewart clone running a summer camp for midgets?

"So, what did Phoebe tell you?"

"Tell me?"

"About her mother. I heard her say Janet was with the angels, but I didn't catch the rest of it."

"Oh, that." With no intention of answering his question, she walked to her desk and picked up a stack of papers. Earlier in the day, she'd asked each child to draw their version of heaven, and a few of the results were startling. By the time she tacked the fifth one to the bulletin board, she could sense Nathan standing behind her. Close behind her. Ignoring the strange sensation in her midsection—she imagined butterflies tap-dancing in her stomach—Eloise sidled away from him and rested her back against the blackboard.

"That one is interesting," he offered, looking over an unusual rendition of an ancient church complete with winged gargoyles and a little girl perched at the very top.

"It's Amelia Santiago's idea of heaven. I think the fact that she was born in Spain, and misses her homeland explains it quite nicely.

"Could I see Phoebe's?"

"Certainly." She flipped through the drawings until she found what he asked for. It wasn't one picture, but a series of vignettes: Phoebe and a brown-haired woman sharing a picnic on a cloud; Phoebe and the same woman picking flowers in a field; Phoebe and the woman dancing together on a bigger cloud; and finally, a house three stories high with Phoebe, a tall, dark-haired man and a faceless woman standing next to a baby carriage, all assembled on the steps.

Nathan took it from her and studied it carefully. His eyes grew dark as he ran a hand through his hair. "Shit."

Despite his rough expletive, she bit back a smile. "It's pretty clear what she was going after, don't you think?"

He shook his head. "I'll say. The kid's about as subtle as a hundred-pound canary."

"Daddy? I'm ready."

They turned in tandem to find Phoebe dressed in her coat and mittens, struggling to tie the strings of her hat under her chin.

"Do you like my picture? I made it so all my heavens would be on one piece of paper."

"It's terrific, punkin." Nathan handed the drawing back to Eloise. "I still want to hear what she told you," he said in a low voice. "And I'd like to go over a little more of Phoebe's history. Can I call the school office for an appointment?"

"An appointment?"

"You know—one of those parent-teacher conference things."

"With me?" *Of course, you, dummy.* "I suppose so."

"Great. Thanks." He crossed the room in long, hulking strides and swept Phoebe into his arms. "Say good-bye to Miss Starr. We're getting pizza for dinner."

When he tossed her over his shoulder, Phoebe shrieked with glee, then raised her head and, hanging on to her hat, flashed Eloise a brilliant smile.

After Phoebe and her father left, Eloise found a full-length dark brown winter coat and a beret, muffler and matching gloves hanging on a peg at the back of the room. Underneath the coat was a large black shoulder bag, and inside the bag a variety of female paraphernalia. Assuming all of it was hers, she donned the clothing and hoisted the satchel over an arm. Moments later, Ms. Hewitt stopped by to say good night and offered her a lift home mainly, she said, because she hadn't seen any other cars in the parking lot.

Eloise said yes, positive Milton wouldn't have been so dim-witted as to entrust her with one of the dangerous vehicles. And she was fairly certain he wouldn't have been so heartless as to set her on earth without shelter. More than likely, she had a house, or apartment, or room somewhere nearby. All she had to do was find her address and Ms. Hewitt would chauffeur her home.

Once they were seated in the woman's ancient but immaculate automobile, it had been easy enough for Eloise to fumble through the bag and find a wallet, which held a driver's license she used as a reference for her address. That was how she learned she lived in Washington, D.C.

After saying a polite good-bye to Ms. Hewitt, Eloise climbed the steps of a five-story apartment building in a presentable neighborhood within walking distance of the Hewitt Academy, and stared at the locking mechanism of the glass-paneled front door

Digging deep in the bottom of the bag, she found a chain holding three keys, slid one of the larger keys into the lock and opened the door. After stepping into a tiled foyer, she appraised the row of shiny brass mailboxes lining the wall. Ten mailboxes and five floors told her the building was comprised of two apartments per floor, probably one on either side of the wide central staircase. She scanned the mailboxes and found her name, E. Starr, affixed to the box labeled 1-A.

Using the smaller key, she opened the mailbox and peered inside. Surprisingly, she had mail. The thought filled her with an unfamiliar quiver of delight. Why would anyone want to contact her about anything? What earthly treasures awaited her attention? Who else but Milton and the Almighty even knew she was here?

But after reading the names printed on the envelope, her joy quickly turned to disappointment. Everything was addressed to someone named Occupant. Okay, so the mail wasn't for her personally, but there might be something of interest in one of the letters. Tucking the envelopes in her bag, she walked to her right, used the third key to open the door marked 1-A and stepped into a welcoming foyer with a narrow table and coatrack situated against a side wall. After setting her bag on the table, she removed her hat, gloves and muffler and placed them next to the bag, then took off her coat and hung it on the rack.

Initially, she'd thought to let herself in and use the privacy to iron out her problem. Now that she was inside the apartment, she decided to explore. God and heaven would always be there for her, but the experience of having a human body might not. As soon as she got her bearings, she was going to have that long talk with the Big Boss she'd promised herself earlier. Right now, it might be fun to see how far Milton's fertile imagination would stretch.

She turned at the first door to her right and walked into a cheery white kitchen, accented with dark green counters and tile. Other than a teakettle on the range, there was little else in view. She opened cupboards and pulled out drawers to take inventory and found the kitchen fully equipped. The pantry was stocked with canned goods, boxed dinners, dried foods and paper supplies; the refrigerator with milk, fruit, bread and condiments; the freezer with frozen vegetables and ice cream. Eloise's stomach started to rumble, reminding her of another necessary human function—eating.

She'd studied enough of her charges while they cooked to feel confident she could do the same. The first thing that came to mind was a hot, fluffy baked potato. She took one from the pantry, washed it and set it on a shelf in the oven, then turned the temperature to a middle setting. Thinking this business of being human was a lot easier than so many of her whining charges made it out to be, she moved from the kitchen into a small eating alcove complete with a table and chairs.

From there, she made her way to a charming room with a plush rose-and-gold-patterned area rug, a comfy-looking sofa and matching chairs spaced evenly around the perimeter. There was even a small television on a table in a corner of the room, as well as a wall of books and a window with shelves that held dozens of flowering plants.

Leaving the room through an archway, she found herself at the far end of the hall. Entering another door, she walked into what she assumed was her bedroom. The delicately designed chest of drawers and dresser were made of dark wood, the oversize bed adorned with several large pillows and a pink, white and green flowered coverlet. Alongside the bed was a night table holding a cut crystal lamp and telephone, and next to that a dainty tufted chair.

Thinking the place adequate, she decided there was no need to explore further; she wouldn't be here long enough to settle in. The sooner she had that talk with the Almighty, the sooner she would be back in heaven, leaving Milton to scout out another human to teach those frightening kindergarteners and eat that darned potato.

Eloise sat on the edge of the bed and closed her eyes. Thinking of heaven, she willed her thoughts straight to God's ears, frowning when she didn't receive a reply.

Wondering if maybe she should be a little more humble and a bit less demanding, she knelt at the side of the bed and prayed.

But her heart remained a void.

Frustrated, she changed her plea from a prayer to a call. Surely Milton realized that she'd had enough time to consider her predicament. If nothing else, he should be willing to negotiate her time here. He'd banged that gavel like a superior court judge. Plea bargaining had to be a part of the process.

"Milton, get your sorry angel self down here this minute. I have a bone to pick with you."

Sadly, the room remained still and dark. Heaving a sigh, she rose to her feet, flicked on the lamp and plopped into the chair. "Milton? This isn't funny. I demand you bring me back upstairs. I mean it."

She closed her eyes again and waited, but she could tell nothing had changed. Thirty seconds later, her demand became a humble plea. "Milton, please," she whispered sincerely. "I need some help, and you're the only one who can give it to me."

When nothing happened again, she leaned back, grabbed a fistful of hair at each temple and tugged, stopping just short of tearing out her curls. This was too frustrating for words. How was she supposed to plead her case if there was no one to listen? Granted, the Big Guy was always there, but He had a busy schedule. Surely someone was hovering who could give her a hand or—

Of course. Why hadn't she thought of it before? Since she was now human, it stood to reason she had her own guiding angel. Maybe Bernice, a kind and gentle grandmotherly sort she'd spoken to on numerous occasions. Or Frances, a lovely angel with a wonderful sense of whimsy. She'd even take a nerd-head like Norbert and forgive his bad puns and wisecracking ways. Right about now, she'd take any heavenly being who decided to pay her a visit.

Anyone.

"You rang?"

Eloise snapped up her head and locked gazes with a short, chubby angel adorned with black spiky hair and the round, baby face of an adolescent. "Who are you?"

The heavenly being stuck out his chest and grinned. "I'm Junior. What can I do for you?"

Junior? Peachy, just peachy. Her eyes narrowed. "I don't believe we've met. Are you a guiding angel?"

Junior thrust out his chin and tucked his thumbs behind

his suspenders. "I am now. On probation, of course. But I have a regular roster of souls in my care."

"What do you mean, *on probation?* I've never heard of such a thing," Eloise countered. He couldn't be a day over ten millennia, and what kind of a name was Junior for an angel, anyway?

"Didn't Milton tell you?" He strutted across the room, opened the door to her closet and stared as if taking inventory. "Interesting wardrobe. Got to admit, if the Big Guy decided it was time you were sent to earth, this is a pretty nice place to be living."

"Listen, Junior," Eloise began, sitting at attention, "I don't know what you think you're doing, spying on me and poking your nose in my . . . stuff . . . but I want you out of here. Now. Go back upstairs and tell Milton I want to see him on the double."

Junior turned from his inspection, his brown eyes wide and smiling. "Don't get your panties in a wad, El. Milton's the one who sent me. He said I should answer your questions, 'cause he ain't got the time."

Sauntering to her dresser, he opened a middle drawer and pulled out a filmy, pale pink nightgown. "Very nice."

Eloise jumped to her feet and snatched the wisp of satin from his hand. "Stop going through my—those things." She stuffed the gown back in the drawer and slammed it shut for good measure. "And stop talking as if you were an extra on the set of *The Sopranos.*" She pointed to the chair. "Sit!"

Ignoring her command, Junior held a pudgy hand to his chest. "I am deeply wounded. Believe me, I've come here with only the most honorable of intentions. Besides, Milton made you one of my charges."

"Excuse me," she shouted, not willing to believe her ears. "Are you trying to tell me you're *my* guiding angel?"

His face turned bright red as he stared at his day-glo orange high tops. "Um, not exactly."

"What's that supposed to mean?" she asked, feeling only marginally better.

"The roster of souls he put in my care is your old one. I'm on probation with your charges until whatever is supposed to happen does. In the meantime, I'm in training. I report directly to Milton—he's the new special-angel-in-charge upstairs, ya know."

"I'm well aware of his position. I still need to speak with him as soon as possible."

Junior shook his head.

"Tomorrow then . . . or the day after that?" Surely she could handle those five-year-olds for another day or two?

"Sorry, kiddo, it just ain't gonna happen."

Staggering to the chair, Eloise dropped like a stone. Though inconceivable, she realized it was true. All of it was true. She was human, and she was going to stay that way until she did whatever it was that Milton had sent her here to do.

She remembered him mentioning something about faith, hope and love, but she'd been so surprised, so taken off guard she simply couldn't recall. Worse, she had to report to this third-rate angel fresh from the nursery until she satisfied only God knew whom. Too bad humility hadn't been one of Milton's directives because she was in the throes of learning that charming virtue at this very moment.

She raised her gaze and found Junior peeking in the top drawer of her dresser while whistling like a teakettle on the boil. "What do you think you're doing?"

He turned, innocence personified. "Who me?"

When she didn't dignify the silly response with a reply, he shrugged and closed the drawer. "So, you got anymore questions?"

Just a bizillion! But she might as well start with the biggest. "Explain all of this to me again . . . please. I . . . um . . . didn't quite get it the first time."

"Sure, sure." He tugged at his lime green bow tie. "Milton gave you a directive, right?"

Eloise raised a brow.

"Okay, he did. He told you he was sending you down here to learn the three most important human virtues: faith, hope and love, right?"

Oh, the shame of it all. Not only to have this upstart as her guiding angel, but to have him know she'd fallen short of God's expectations. "Right," she said softly.

"Okay, so once you learn the lessons, you're gonna find out what's next. The faster you learn, the sooner you're gonna go back." He winked. "Pretty neat, huh?"

Eloise slouched against the chair, trying to absorb the insurmountable-sounding task. "I wouldn't put it exactly that way unless I'd already tried it."

Junior had the decency to look sympathetic. "Oh, but I did. I learned my lesson a long time ago . . ."

"You? How old were you? One millennium? Two?"

He sat on the edge of her bed. "Don't let this baby face fool you. I'm older than you think. Believe it or not, I've been around the block more often than you."

"Then why are you on probation?"

"That's personal."

Like what was happening to her wasn't? "So how about telling me what you've been doing all this time?"

His face reddened as he again concentrated on his sneakers. "Polar ice-cap duty," he mumbled.

"What?"

His exaggerated sigh echoed through the bedroom. "I've been on polar ice-cap duty, making sure the darned thing doesn't melt."

It was all Eloise could do not to laugh out loud. Polar ice-cap duty was a joke among all level of angels—rumored to be heaven's version of Siberia. It was thought the angels who drew ice-cap duty were deemed too irresponsible—or was it too stupid?—to do much of anything else, at least in the eyes of other heavenly beings. Until this moment, she'd never thought anyone was actually remanded there.

"Yeah, well they are," Junior countered before she could voice her thoughts. "And I'm going to squash that lack-of-brains and responsibility misconception, if it's the last thing I do." He thrust out his chin. "Now, is there anything else I can do for you before I get back to my . . . your . . . our charges?"

Staring at her black chunky shoes, Eloise ignored his question. Her insides felt as if they were breaking into tiny jagged pieces. How bad of an angel had she been that Milton would think this brand-new, iceberg-guarding angel could do a better job of caring for souls than she had?

Her mind overflowed with just about every negative emotion known to humans: frustration, despair, anger, bitterness, even jealousy at the thought that Junior had already been given his lesson to learn, while she hadn't known such a thing existed.

She concentrated, recalling Milton's last words, and heard his command exactly as Junior had explained it. She had to learn the virtues of faith, hope and love; then someone was going to decide what to do with the rest of her existence. The Almighty had decreed it and Milton had carried out the sentence. She had no choice but to obey.

"El?" said Junior in a somber tone.

Finally, she replied, "Yes, there is something you can do for me. Promise you'll take good care of my souls. Don't let them do anything dopey while I'm away."

Nathan set the pizza box on the kitchen table, then took off his leather jacket and hung it on the back of his chair. Phoebe watched him carefully, imitating his movements, which reminded him that his jacket should be hung properly on a hook on the wall in the mudroom. Children learned by example, a fact of which he was well aware. He did his best to set a good one with most things, like keeping his clothes off the bedroom floor, not drinking from the milk or orange juice carton, and eating vegetables at most of the meals he shared with his daughter. It was tough always being in the hot seat.

Mentally patting himself on the back, he took their jackets from the chair back and hung them where they belonged. "So, besides getting a new teacher and drawing that picture, tell me what you did in school today?"

Phoebe brought a stack of napkins from the pantry to the table, climbed onto a chair and stuffed them into the holder. Then she took knives and forks out of a drawer next to the sink and set them in place at the table. "Ms. Eloise told us a story about a bunny rabbit. Then she asked us to draw a picture of heaven. She told us she isn't married. She didn't like it when Missy threw up all over Miles. She said it was *dee-kus-ting*. What's that mean, Daddy?"

Nathan took down plates and glasses, poured milk for the two of them and carted it all to the table. The last thing he needed was to have his daughter home with a stomach virus or worse. Why couldn't parents act responsibly and keep their kids in bed if they were ill, instead of allowing them to contaminate classmates?

"I think the word is disgusting, sweetie. It means . . . yucky. Did Missy say her tummy hurt before she got sick?"

"Nu-uh. I think it was her lunch. She had peanut butter and green Jell-O and chocolate milk, all at once."

Nathan shuddered, relieved to see Phoebe's wrinkled nose, which told him she felt the same. He'd never been one of those Renaissance men who went in for gardening or needlepoint or puttering in the kitchen. He was lucky they shared simple food favorites: baloney sandwiches on white bread with mayo, macaroni and cheese, canned fruit cocktail, pepperoni pizza and those bags of frozen broccoli drenched in butter and cheese sauce.

Give them both toast and a bowl of cereal for breakfast, a bag of microwave popcorn for a snack, some chocolate ice cream or a package of Ring Dings and they were set.

Phoebe settled at the table and wrestled with the unwieldy pizza box top. He let her fend for herself until the slice of pie she chose threatened to splatter all over the table.

"Here, let me help with that." Deftly, he slid her plate under the gooey slice and caught the drippings. "Do you like your new teacher?"

Phoebe chewed thoughtfully. "I think so."

"She seemed nice to me." And a damned sight better looking than Ms. Singeltary. Too bad that drab cotton dress had her so buttoned up she'd reminded him of a nun. It looked like she might have nice hair, but it was hard to tell because it had been scraped back in a bun, and she had pretty eyes— a deep, dark turquoise—like Phoebe's. He'd always wondered how he and Janet, who were both brown-eyed, managed to have a daughter with such lovely blue eyes. Rita Mae, who also had blue eyes, said it was a recessive-gene thing, and she was probably right.

"But Ms. Eloise said she's not goin' to stay with us long," Phoebe muttered through a mouthful of stringy cheese. "How come she's gonna leave, like my mommy and Ms. Singeltary did?"

Nathan stopped in the middle of swallowing his milk. *Great, just friggin' damn great!* The woman hadn't said word one about this being a temporary position. She'd even agreed to a parent-teacher conference. How the hell was Phoebe supposed to adjust to life if the adult females in it kept bouncing in and out like tennis balls?

First Janet—well, it hadn't exactly been Janet's fault, he conceded. Fate had simply put her in the wrong place at the wrong time. How often did a person stop to fill their gas tank at two in the morning and run smack into the middle of a robbery? Still, if Janet hadn't been on her way home so late from that charity thing she claimed she had to attend, it might not have happened. Then again, if he'd gone with her instead of letting himself get drawn into a case he could easily have turned over to a fellow detective—

Sometimes he wished he could turn back the clock to before his investment banker father-in-law, Archibald Breakwater, had died, and tell the man they didn't need his money or his fancy house in Georgetown—that they could live just fine on a detective's salary. Maybe if he'd done that, he and Janet wouldn't have fought so much about her newfound wealth or gone in different directions after Phoebe had been born. Maybe they would still be a family, and Phoebe would have that brother or sister she'd asked Santa for.

Damn Janet and her snooty high-society causes. How many times had he asked her to lay off the Junior League events and do something really important, like help the Police Benevolent Association and their crusade to get kids off drugs or volunteer at one of the police and firemen's causes. He'd known Janet came from money when he'd married her, but until her father had died and left her a veritable fortune he'd always thought they'd be able to work things out and—

"Daddy? I asked if you could talk to Ms. Eloise and ask her to stay."

"Aw, punkin. What makes you think I'd have any pull with Ms. Starr? I just met the woman."

Phoebe licked pizza sauce from her fingers and he handed her a napkin. "But you're a policeman. Everybody's got to listen to you, don't they? Policemen can make people do all kinds'a stuff they don't want to do. You said so."

Oh-boy. He *had* said so, but that was when he'd caught a couple of neighborhood nasty boys torturing a stray cat. It had been a simple task to walk outside with Huey, Dewey and Louie at his heels and give them a lecture on how to treat defenseless animals. Of course, reminding them that the three German shepherds took a personal dislike to anyone participating in cruelty to animals hadn't hurt his cause.

"Ple
teache

Nath
woman
ment, s
planne

Twea
grin. "I

Three

Eloise pulled her head out from under the pillow and stretched muscles she hadn't known existed. Opening one eye, she peered at the dim light peeking through the blinds and groaned. Rolling onto her back, she stared at the ceiling and listened to the sound of footsteps tapping overhead. A horn blared, then a door slammed. She heard a flurry of men's and women's voices, more horns . . . a baby's cry.

The alarm clock on her night table beeped and she jerked upright. She couldn't recall setting it, but she didn't remember much of anything she'd done last night after Junior had left. Meeting him and trying to make sense of her new life had sent her into shock. After eating her baked potato, she'd fallen into bed and slept a dreamless sleep. Still at odds with the idea of being human, she had no clue what she was supposed to do to learn her lesson and get back to heaven.

The beeping alarm drilled into her brain and she shivered. Swinging her legs off the side of the bed, she slapped at the rectangular black box until the jarring noise subsided. From the way her head was pounding, this sleep business wasn't as wonderful as people made it out to be. When angels needed revitalization, they landed on a fluffy cloud and floated on a breeze, or visited a mountaintop and contemplated their tasks. Why couldn't humans do the same?

Coming fully awake, Eloise shook her head. Now that she was in this distasteful state, lazing on a cloud wasn't an option. Instead, she had to handle all the chores required to live on earth. Things like eating and bathing and taking care of what she regarded as nasty *personal* functions were her primary concern. She would worry about the easy stuff—earning a living and relating to other human beings—later.

Which suddenly brought her to another earthly revelation. She had a job. She was a kindergarten teacher and she was expected to report to the Hewitt Academy in an hour.

Yawning, she padded to the bathroom. After taking care of the tinkle thing, and the shower thing, and the toothbrush thing, she figured she was ready to get dressed—until she took a good look at herself in the mirror.

What a mess. Her hair was a wet tangle of curls, her face looked pale as a cloud and her body— Well, she didn't want to think about all the crazy twists and turns it seemed to take, but she would need clothing to keep it properly covered. When she'd been an angel, wearing earthly garb had been fun—something to give her fellow angels a good laugh. Clothing also reminded her of humans and their vanities, for very few of them were ever satisfied with their appearance.

She stared at her large breasts and curvy hips and legs. Suddenly, she longed to wear all the frills of a real woman—high-heeled shoes, pretty underwear, flattering dresses—and nothing remotely resembling the depressing sack she'd been stuck in yesterday.

Fortunately, she'd spied on enough of her female charges to know that a proper hairdo came first. Squatting down, she found one of those hot-air machines in a cabinet under the sink, plugged it into a wall socket and turned it on. The warmth felt good against her skin as it dried the droplets of water she'd missed with her towel. Raising her arm, she aimed the contraption from above and watched her long, white-blond hair swirl around her head like leaves in a tornado.

Wow! What a whirlwind. What a do. What a pile of hair.

She reached for a brush and dragged it through the coiling locks, trying to tug the curls into submission, but like a pot of boiling rice they just kept growing . . . and growing. Pretty soon, even she was impressed by the size of her head, which had doubled, or maybe tripled in height and width.

She turned off the machine and checked the medicine chest, hoping to find something to tame the mass. Inside the cabinet was a shelf full of stuff to spray, pat or work into the strands, along with dozens of bottles of earthly concoctions. Besides Tampax and a variety of female necessities she didn't dare ponder were nail clippers, tweezers, bottles of pain relievers for stomach cramps, headaches and backaches, fungus creams, Band-Aids, corn pads, lotions for sunburned skin, dry skin, bumpy skin, scraped skin—.

Overwhelmed, she shook her head. Was she really expected to use all this stuff? She sincerely hoped not, because either Milton or Junior had stocked the cabinet with enough emergency medical aids to scare her witless.

She spied a small zippered bag and opened it slowly, fearful of what was inside. First she pulled out a gold-colored tube, then a longer silver one, then a plastic case containing perfect circles of color. One of the cases held powder, a big fluffy brush, something labeled an eye pencil, and more colorful circles. It was a veritable artist's palette for the skin.

Heaving a breath, she took another swipe at her hair, then set to work painting her face, just as she'd watched so many of her female charges do. Nothing too garish, but a little of the pretty blue powder on her eyelids, some of the red stuff in the tube for her lips and a brush or two, make that three, of the bright pink powder on her cheeks seemed to make a difference.

She turned her head from side to side, still amazed at the size of her hair. She'd seen worse in her travels, she thought, raising her now-darker eyebrows. It would simply have to do.

She walked back into her bedroom and opened a drawer, where she found several different styles of undergarment, all in plain white cotton. After slipping into a bra and panties, she checked herself in the mirror over the dresser. Although the dips, curves, and bumps hadn't disappeared entirely, they were molded into a more pleasing shape.

When she opened another drawer and saw a dozen packages of the body-strangling stockings she'd worn yesterday, she shrieked out loud, then tossed every one of the plastic wrapped packets into the trash.

No more of those detestable pantyhose for her. Ever.

At the bottom of the pile she spotted a few packages that looked different from the rest. Curious, she read the label—thigh-highs—and opened the plastic. Inside were individual stockings, much more silky and less constricting than what she'd been stuffed into yesterday.

She slid her toes into the first stocking and tugged it over her calf, knee and up her thigh, then did the same with the other one. Satisfied she could spend at least part of the day in comfort, she walked to the closet to check out her wardrobe.

To her dismay, every single article of clothing reminded her of funeral wear. Drab brown, colorless gray, dismal black or stark white seemed the order of the day. Sighing, she pushed the hangers aside and tried to find something that didn't look forbidding, finally settling on a gray skirt, white blouse and plain black jacket. Boring, boring, boring.

Returning to the dresser, she searched every drawer, then stomped her foot. There wasn't a single thing—not a scarf or a belt or a piece of jewelry—to make the utilitarian outfit less depressing.

Milton. He had to have been the one who'd set up this apartment and everything in it. How typical of him to want her to resemble a refugee from the *Mayflower*. Even Junior would have had a better sense of style, more imagination, more flair, more . . . everything.

Back at her closet, she gazed at her choices of footwear, the chunky, boxlike shoes she'd worn yesterday or a pair of black flat-heeled slippers, and realized her last chance at looking decent was gone. No wonder Adam Taylor had told her she reminded him of his grandmother. She would have said the same if she'd had an ancient female human somewhere in her past who'd worn these things.

But until she found the time to shop for more appropriate clothing, she was stuck. Resigned to her dreary wardrobe, she slid her feet into the flat-heeled shoes, then walked to the front hall and put on her coat and gloves—somehow, her hat had gotten too small to fit her head—and set out for school.

"What happened to your hair?" Amelia Santiago stood at Eloise's desk, her gray eyes round as saucers.

Smiling hesitantly, Eloise ran her fingers through the tangled strands. "What's the matter with it?"

Amelia put a hand over her mouth to hide a grin. "It's kind'a . . . big."

"Big?" She pressed down on the top, which felt about twenty inches higher than the rest of her body and frowned. "It's just full. I have a very *full* head of hair."

Miles skipped into the room, stared at her, then Amelia, and burst into a fit of giggles. The girl raced to his side and the two children whispered conspiratorially.

Eloise drummed her fingers on the desktop. The little heathens had absolutely no manners. She had taken great pains to look her best. On her way to the school she'd gotten cheerful nods from people she passed on the street. Even the policeman from whom she'd asked directions had smiled broadly and stared with admiration.

She stood and marched to the back of the room, only to be greeted by a stream of arriving children, who took one look at her and began tittering in wide-eyed amazement.

"What is so funny?" she demanded when they finally stopped hooting like demented owls.

"You look silly," blurted Lucy. "Kind of like the lady I saw once in a Frankenstein movie."

"Yeah," chimed Zeman. "Your face is made up like Ms. Rutherford's was at our Halloween party. She came as a clown."

A clown! A wave of heat flooded her face. She could handle wearing clown shoes—but a clown face? Turning, she stormed out the door, straight to the ladies' room. The pint-size troublemakers could take care of themselves while she ran a more thorough inspection of her person.

Once inside the bathroom, she stood in front of the mirror above the sinks and stared. Then she shuddered. In the bright light streaming through the rest room windows, she was a fright. No wonder people had smiled at her this morning. She'd been nothing more than an amusement, an entertaining jump start to their day. She was lucky that police officer hadn't arrested her for defacing the scenery or creating a public nuisance. Tugging at her hair, she grew furious. How cruel that not one person had stopped to tell her she looked ridiculous. And how very human of them to laugh at her instead of helping.

Humiliated, she ran warm water into the sink, pumped soap into her hands and began to scrub. The face paint turned into a smeary swirl of blue, pink, black and brown, covering her cheeks, nose and mouth in an oily sheen. Sighing, she tore off a wad of paper towels and rubbed at the colorful mess.

"It's not so bad now," said a small voice from the doorway.

She turned to see Phoebe Marie studying her through solemn blue eyes.

"It's awful." Eloise dragged the paper towel over her mouth. "I look stupid, and silly and . . . and . . . dreadful."

Phoebe stepped into the room and let the door close behind her. "Can I help?"

Eloise gurgled out a snort. "I don't see how. Besides the fact that you're down there and I'm up here, you're a child. I'm an adult, and I'm not having any luck."

Phoebe stood on tiptoe next to her at the sink. "Maybe if I came up there and did what my daddy does, it would help."

She couldn't imagine what trick Nathan Baxter used to erase a clown face, but it was worth a try. Bending over, she hoisted up the little girl, sat her on a sink and handed her a paper towel. Quicker than a lightning strike, Phoebe spit on the paper and began to rub at her cheek.

"*Ee-uuu!* Stop!" Eloise ducked out of reach. "That is so disgusting."

Phoebe's lower lip trembled. "But Daddy does it to me, and he always gets my face clean." As if to prove her point, she stuck her nose in the air. "See?"

Hating that she'd almost made the child cry, Eloise gave the cherubic face a quick inspection, then retrieved a clean towel, dabbed on more soap and continued to scrub. "Somehow," she muttered between swipes, "I find it hard to believe your father's spit will ever be marketed as a cleaning solvent." She winced, thinking if she rubbed any harder, she was going to need a few of those soothing lotions she'd found in her bathroom cabinet to take the sting away. "Soap is clearly the way to go."

Phoebe wrinkled her forehead. "Maybe you should try the stuff Grammy uses. It's white and creamy and comes in a jar."

Eloise reexamined her face. Certain her skin was never going to recover, she folded her arms and raised a brow. "White and creamy sounds nice."

"What are you gonna do about your hair?"

That, she thought, was a tough one. "There's nothing wrong with my hair. It's just a bit—"

"Gi-gundo?" Phoebe giggled for emphasis.

"Full," Eloise corrected with a sniff. Then she frowned. Who was she kidding? She was so inept at this *human being* business, she couldn't even fool a five-year-old. "I'm afraid I don't do hair very well."

"Neither does my daddy," Phoebe said, running a hand over her head of flyaway curls, half in-half out of twin pony-tails.

Eloise studied the mass of ringlets, very close to her own pale blond color. Phoebe's entire head looked as if it had been styled with a broken egg beater. "Your father did that to you?"

"Grammy keeps trying to teach him, but he's not so good yet. My mommy did it better, but she's dead."

A fist of guilt squeezed Eloise's heart. "So you told me." She cleared her throat. "Tell me, besides spitting on your face and doing a half-baked job on your hair, what else does this wonder-daddy do that's so great?"

Phoebe slid off the sink and began hopping in a circle. "He buys me pretty clothes and gives me bubble baths and reads to me at night before bed. Sometimes he lets me help him cook dinner. He even let me name the German shepherds and he—"

"Dogs? You own a dog?"

"Uh-huh. We got three. They stay with us when they're not helping the policemen. I love 'em almost as much as I love my daddy and Grammy."

Animals had never been one of Eloise's strong suits, though she knew most humans doted on them. She vaguely remembered a few comments about Nathan's dogs when Milton had hoodwinked her into helping him with Annie and Tom. It didn't matter, since she would never have to meet them, but it sounded as if Phoebe really cared for the beasts.

"What did you name them?"

"There's Huey—he's the biggest, but he's kind'a dumb and he slobbers a lot. And there's Dewey—he's the smartest. I can put a cookie on his nose, and he won't eat it until I say he can. Louie is my first favorite, 'cause he's a big baby. He likes it when I scratch his tummy, and he tries to crawl under the covers with me when I go to sleep at night."

"Charming," Eloise said, continuing to fuss with the haystack on top of her head.

"You want me to try and fix your hair?"

"*Hmph.* What makes you think you can do a good job?"

In a gesture of infinite patience, Phoebe set her hands on her hips. "I practice on my dollies. When I grow up, I'm gonna be a *booty* lady and work in a *booty* parlor. Grammy said I could."

Grabbing a comb from the shelf under the mirror, Eloise tapped it on the sink. "You really think you could do something with this?"

"Uh-huh. But you got to get closer."

Positive the blow-dryer contraption had fried her brain, she handed Phoebe the comb and knelt on the linoleum. "This had better work, kiddo, or I'm flunking you."

"That's okay," Phoebe said, grinning. " 'Cause then I'd get to stay in kindergarten and have you teach me for another year."

Eloise had no intention of being on earth that long. She'd be gone from this place by Christmas, New Year's Day tops. Crossing her fingers, she leaned forward to give Phoebe better access and was rewarded by a volley of painful tugs.

"Ow! Hey, take it easy."

"It's snarly," Phoebe pronounced, maneuvering the comb more carefully. "Duck down some more."

Eloise did as she was told, and was rewarded with another round of painful yanks. "Yeow! What are you, a sadist?"

Phoebe giggled. "Are there any hair pins or 'lastics on the shelf?"

Eloise ran a hand over the ledge above the sink, but all she found were two clips with large, pink, nylon butterflies glued to the top. "Will this help?"

Working diligently, the world's littlest hairdresser didn't answer. Long seconds of agony ticked by while Eloise thought she'd be snatched bald by the time the child was finished. Just as Phoebe pinned the last butterfly clip in place, the door to the rest room swung open and Mary Alice Murphy rushed inside.

"Mith Eloweeth! Mith Eloweeth! Come quick! Billy stuck hith finger in the penthil tharpener again."

Sighing, Eloise rose to her feet and followed the girls from the room.

"I can only assume it was a momentary lapse of common sense," Ms. Hewitt said, pacing in front of Eloise's over-laden desk. "Here at the Hewitt Academy, we pride ourselves on never putting our charges in jeopardy. It's important you remember that, Miss Starr."

Eloise bit her tongue as she pushed away from her desk. Walking to the windows, she gazed at a large group of children, most gamboling on the playground like lambs in a meadow. Though late November, the temperature was a balmy seventy degrees, warm enough for the students to spend part of their lunch hour taking in the fresh air.

"I was just down the hall in the rest room. I came as soon as Mary Alice told me what happened." *I was not derelict in my duty,* she fumed silently.

"It doesn't matter where you were or how quickly you responded when alerted to the emergency. Small children are as slippery as eels in a vat of oil. Fifteen five-year-olds—"

"Fourteen. Phoebe was with me."

"Fourteen children were left unsupervised in your classroom. Anything could have happened."

"But it didn't.

"Billy's unfortunate fascination with the pencil sharpener could be disastrous. I think you should place the machine out of reach of prying fingers or—"

"I already took care of it," said Eloise, focusing on the top of the bookcase at the far side of the room.

Following her gaze, Ms. Hewitt nodded approvingly. "Fine. Well, then—"

"Is there anything else?"

Ms. Hewitt inspected her through thick, owl-like lenses, which Eloise thought was a pity, because the headmistress had lovely eyes the color of amber. Standing stiffly under her scrutiny, she took in the woman's peaches-and-cream complexion, her thick dark hair coiled in a bun at the nape of her neck and her impressive Amazonian form. Was it possible that underneath her spinsterish exterior lurked a young, attractive woman?

"It's your hair."

"Pardon me?" Eloise muttered, returning her attention to the matter at hand.

"I don't mean to criticize, but it's a bit . . . wild. And those clips are somewhat . . . immature." Her narrowed eyes skimmed over Eloise a third time. "We at the Hewitt Academy uphold a strict code of dress and personal hygiene."

Eloise raised a brow. If she didn't know better, she'd think Ms. Hewitt had been the one to stock her closet. "I don't remember being given any specifics on how I was supposed to wear my hair when I interviewed for this position," she bluffed, knowing full well there had been no interview. "One of the children gave me these clips. It would have been impolite to refuse them."

With a thoroughly perplexed pucker on her face, Ms. Hewitt waited a beat before answering. "I didn't—you weren't—" With drooping shoulders, the principal stared down at her own unflattering outfit. "To be honest, I don't recall much of your interview. I was overcome by the fact that Miss Singeltary had declared herself pregnant and given formal notice. I don't even remember running an ad for the position." She frowned. "You did say you answered my advertisement in the *Washington Post,* did you not?"

"How else would I have known about the job?" Eloise

countered, pleased she hadn't needed to lie outright even once during the discussion.

Ms. Hewitt seemed to gather her mental armor. "Forgive me. I've been under a great deal of stress lately, for a variety of reasons. I don't want us to get off on the wrong foot." She smiled, showing even white teeth. "I had hoped we could be allies in our common goal of bringing knowledge to young impressionable minds."

Whatever, Eloise thought. She gazed at the clock over the door. "The children will be here soon. I have to get ready for their afternoon lessons."

"Oh, yes. Of course." The headmistress smoothed the skirt of her own fashion disaster, a black-belted sack of dark gray wool with black buttons and collar, and held out a second flag of truce. "I'd be happy to give you a ride home later this afternoon."

Eloise returned the smile. "Thank you, but it's a lovely day and I enjoy walking. I may take you up on the offer if the weather turns unpleasant."

"I'm frequently here for several hours after school has ended, but if we happen to be leaving at the same time, it will be a pleasure. I only live a few blocks from you." Ms. Hewitt sidled from the room, turning when she reached the door. "Do you like your apartment?"

"It's . . . adequate," Eloise answered. Would the woman never leave? And why was she being so friendly?

"Georgetown is lovely. Several of our students live in the neighborhood. Some of the town homes come with their parents' high-profile government positions, but many families own the buildings outright. The Hewitt Academy has a long history in this city. Some of our graduates have gone on to do great things in the world. Foreign countries recommend us to the families of their attachés and diplomats, as well." Voices in the hall alerted her to the end of lunch hour. "I'll be in my office if you need me. Have a good afternoon."

At the rear of the room, Eloise waited while her charges filed in the door. It was a few minutes past one o'clock and she had no idea how she was supposed to entertain them for the remainder of the day. Perhaps she needed to take home the book labeled *lesson plans* she'd found in her desk drawer and study it in detail. From the sound of her conversation with Ms. Hewitt, the woman was going to be watching her carefully until she was certain Eloise could be trusted to do a proper job.

Before she could make a decision, the children had lined up behind her like chicks following a mother hen. Turning, she found them staring expectantly.

"Are we going somewhere?" she asked of no one in particular.

"Today's Tuesday. We have computer lessons on Tuesday and Thursday afternoons," answered Shawanna. The rest of the chicks, er, children nodded in agreement.

Computer lessons? "Oh, sure, of course." Thank goodness someone would be taking over for a while, because she really needed a break. Stepping to the side, she said, "All of you go ahead and I'll follow."

Obediently, Shawanna led the line into the hall. Eloise closed the classroom door and brought up the rear. Maybe she could sit and think about her predicament while the computer professional taught class. Except for turning on a light switch or making a phone call, she didn't know the first thing about modern technology. Since she had no intention of staying human any longer than necessary, there was no reason for her to learn.

Four

Eloise shoved wisps of hair from her forehead, grateful the afternoon was over. She wanted to smack Ms. Hewitt for not telling her that as the teacher, *she* was the one who had to conduct the computer lesson for the kindergartners. Between trying not to blow up the evil machines and properly shutting them off, she'd answered dozens of questions incorrectly, or so she'd been told by Adam, Zeman and John.

Now back in the classroom, she did a quick head count, just in case someone had taken the opportunity to wander on their way back from the computer science lab. When she realized there were only fourteen bodies, she counted again, fearful another lecture from Ms. Hewitt was lurking around the corner. Still one child short, she worked to fill in the missing name. Drawing a blank, she walked into the hall, but all she saw were older students already dressed to leave the building.

Angry that she'd allowed herself to get so distracted, she'd actually *lost* a child, Eloise ordered everyone to sit in their seats so she could take roll call. Caretakers would be arriving shortly to collect their charges. If she didn't find her fifteenth student soon—

"Please raise your hand when I say your name and keep it raised until I figure out who is missing."

"Aw, that's easy," Billy said, saving her the trouble. "It's Sebastian. He always manages to get out of computer lab."

"And why is that?" she asked the class in general, relieved at least part of the mystery was solved. Sebastian Beauchamp was a quiet, dark-eyed boy with an engaging smile and a propensity for dressing much too formally for a five-year-old.

"I'm waiting." Propping her bottom against the desk, she tapped a foot on the floor. Blank faces stared back at her.

"Don't know," Adam finally said, shrugging. "But he's prob'ly in the bathroom. Want I should go find him?"

Eloise thought a second. "All right. But take Billy with you, stay together and come right back if he's not there."

Both boys scrambled from the room while the children began collecting their things. Moments later, drivers, nannies and parents arrived to escort their charges from the classroom. Just when she thought she would have to find Billy and Adam, the boys returned.

"Sebastian won't come out of the bathroom. He's afraid you're gonna yell at him," pronounced Adam, putting on his coat. A woman she recognized as the boy's mother stuck her head in the door and Adam called out a cheery "See ya" as he left.

Eloise put on her best teacher's smile as the rest of the children walked out with their respective rides until finally, only she, Phoebe and a towering, stern-faced man dressed in a navy blue suit and turban, were in the room.

Hesitantly, she asked, "Are you Sebastian's father?"

He folded his arms and answered in a clipped French accent.

She heaved a sigh as she remembered her orders from Ms. Hewitt, then took Phoebe by the hand and waggled her fingers at the man, hoping he would get the hint and tag along. He frowned mightily, but did as she indicated. At the lavatory, she pointed and said clearly, "Sebastian."

The man nodded and went inside.

"He's scary lookin'," said Phoebe. "Do you think he'll hurt Sebastian?"

Hurt Sebastian? "I don't think so," Eloise said, but the man did have an angry look about him. Just when she thought it might be a good idea to peek inside the men's lavatory door, the woeful-looking little boy stepped into the hall, the larger man's hand firmly on his shoulder.

Eloise dropped to her knees and gazed into Sebastian's downcast eyes. "Are you all right?"

He threw a wary gaze at his tall, turbaned escort before answering, "Yes, ma'am."

"And is this gentleman your ride home?"

Sebastian nodded. "He's my father's driver."

"Then you'd better go with him. But don't think you're going to hide on me again. You and I are going to have a serious talk very soon. Is that clear?"

"Uh-huh." Sebastian sniffed. "I got to go with Ulimar now."

Eloise watched the fearsome chauffeur and teary eyed child leave the building. Then she and Phoebe walked side by side down the hall.

"Is what Billy said about Sebastian true, Phoebe? Does he have a problem understanding the computer lessons?" she asked as they rounded the corner.

"I think so," Phoebe answered. "He says he can't figure out how to make the programs work like the rest of us can. Billy tries to teach him once in a while, so does Zeman. Sebastian always snuck outta the room when Ms. Singeltary taught us, but she didn't care."

"I see." *And I sympathize,* she thought to herself.

Seconds later, they arrived at their classroom and found Nathan Baxter pacing at the windows, a dour expression marring his chiseled features.

"Where were you two?" he asked, sounding just short of annoyed. "I was getting worried."

Phoebe answered simply, "We was helpin' Sebastian outta the bathroom."

"You took her into the boys' lavatory?"

Eloise wanted to tell him to take a chill pill, but thought better of it. The man wore a scowl almost as big as the guy who'd picked up Sebastian. "No, I didn't. We waited outside."

"Oh, well, it's time to go home." Nathan handed Phoebe her coat, then asked her another question. "I need to schedule that conference we discussed as soon as possible, Ms. Starr. I was hoping we could meet tonight."

Eloise swallowed when her stomach did that infuriating flutter thing again and sidled to safer territory on the opposite side of her desk. She hated the way her attention always seemed drawn to Nathan Baxter's expressive brown eyes or his well-formed physique, even when he was rude and cocky. And she detested the way her breath hitched whenever he came within twenty feet of her. It had been difficult enough ignoring him as an angel; her physical body and the mind that accompanied it seemed to have no sense of decorum or control whatsoever.

"I don't think that's a good idea."

He squared his shoulders. "Mind telling me why?"

"I have to study up on this week's lesson plan." *Not a lie,* she told herself. She did have that book she'd found in the desk drawer to read. "And I have reports to look over."

He stepped closer and lowered his voice. "Phoebe told me you might not be staying at the Hewitt Academy much longer."

"I think I mentioned it," she muttered, straightening the already neat pile of papers on her blotter. "I haven't made up my mind."

"The news upset Phoebe, Ms. Starr. If you won't meet with me, I'll have to schedule a talk with Ms. Hewitt. Perhaps we could discuss your decision and—"

As much as Eloise disliked the idea of Nathan giving the headmistress another reason to put her under scrutiny, she disliked even more the thought of being alone with him. Unfortunately, if she truly was doomed to live on earth until she satisfied the Almighty, she was going to need this job.

"Maybe later in the week?" she offered. By then she hoped to be back in heaven, making their meeting a nonissue.

"With my schedule, afternoons are tough. Unless my mother is free, I need time to find a competent sitter." He glanced over his shoulder and checked on his daughter, who was engrossed in a book. "How about dinner tonight? Since I don't think we should talk in front of Phoebe, I'll ask Rita Mae to baby-sit. When I get called out, she usually makes supper for the two of them and brings Phoebe upstairs. Since you and I both have to eat, we might as well do it together."

I can't be alone with you when I have all these strange feelings tumbling around inside of me, she wanted to shout. Instead, she said, "It would be unprofessional to see you in such a familiar setting."

Nathan shrugged, a glimmer of challenge in his eyes. "Okay, then you pick the time and place. But make it soon, Miss Starr. My child's welfare is something I don't take lightly."

With that he clasped Phoebe by the hand and strode from the room.

What in hell was wrong with the woman? Nathan wondered, guiding Phoebe out of the building and to his car. He'd only been trying to make things easier on both himself and the kindergarten teacher by setting up a friendly meal. Instead, he felt as if he'd been sucked into a confrontation.

When Eloise Starr had first walked into the room and found him standing at the windows, she'd looked as startled as a cat in a cloudburst. After he'd asked about their proposed meeting, he could almost see her back arch and her hackles rise. By the time he'd invited her to dinner, she looked ready to run screaming from the room.

He knew his six-feet-two inches could be imposing, a definite plus in his line of work, and Rita Mae always told him he had a bad habit of scowling when he was lost in thought, but Ms. Starr was no delicate flower of a woman. Besides, she dealt with a room full of five-year-olds every day. That had to be more frightening than one perturbed dad.

Nathan didn't realize he'd been dragging his daughter across the landing and onto the stairs until Phoebe tripped. Glancing down, he saw that her shoelace had come undone. "Sorry, punkin. How about I give you a second to tie your sneaker? Or should I do it for you?"

Shaking her head, Phoebe handed him her backpack. "I can do it myself." She set her foot on a higher step and began to work at the shoelace.

Pleased at his daughter's independent nature, he watched as she carefully attended to the task. Before Phoebe finished, he heard someone call his name. Raising his gaze, he spotted Eloise Starr trotting in their direction.

"Mr. Baxter? Mr. Baxter! Wait!"

Now what? Folding his arms, he dug in his heels. The contrary woman could damn well come to him if she'd changed her mind.

As soon as Ms. Starr realized she had his full attention, she stopped in her tracks. He tamped back a smile when she tugged the hem of her dowdy jacket, then smoothed her flyaway hair and continued down the stairs as if preparing to brave a den of lions. As she got closer, her determined march slowed to a falter. Finally, she stopped a step above the one Phoebe was using to tie her shoe, which put them at eye level.

Nathan took in her flushed face and lush lips, now set in a thin line. Aware he was staring, he raised his gaze to her tangled mass of white-blond curls, a far cry from the tightly coiled bun she'd sported yesterday, and did a double take. What the heck did she have dangling from her hair? Trying not to gape, he wondered why he hadn't noticed those goofy butterflies when he'd been with her in the—

"I don't appreciate being blackmailed, Mr. Baxter."

"Excuse me?"

"Just a moment ago, you threatened to tell Ms. Hewitt something personal I mentioned to the children in passing. It sounded like blackmail to me."

Jeez. Didn't she realize she should have mentioned her plans to Ms. Hewitt before she'd said a word to the kids? She jutted her chin, and the sudden desire to grab Ms. Starr and kiss the color right out of her sassy, rose petal lips overwhelmed him.

Tightening his grip on Phoebe's backpack, he ground out, "Now wait just a darned second. Who said anything about blackmail? I wasn't trying to—"

"I'll have dinner with you tonight, if the offer still stands," she said, taking the wind out of his sails. "But no more threats."

He refused to think about how long it had been since he'd had the urge to haul a woman against his chest and kiss her senseless. Too long, if he went by the reaction this woman had on him. Attempting to lighten the mood, he said, "It's only dinner, not an invitation to a mud-wrestling match. Just two concerned adults sharing a meal while they discuss the needs of a child."

She crossed her arms under her breasts and he swallowed down another, more lustful urge at the way the buttons on her plain white blouse drew taut over her bountiful chest. God, he was pathetic.

"What time?" she asked, dropping her arms when she saw where his gaze had strayed.

"What time what?"

"What time do you want to meet for dinner? And where?"

"Oh . . . uh . . . where do you live?"

"Here in Georgetown, not far from the school. As a matter of fact, I'm on my way home now."

"I thought you said you had to work on your weekly

lesson plan tonight?" he quipped, noting her lack of study materials.

"I was gathering my things when I decided to take you up on your offer."

"Phoebe and I live a few blocks from here. Why don't you go inside and retrieve your books and we'll give you a ride home? Or I can drop Phoebe off and we can go straight to dinner from here."

Her complexion lost all color and he again thought she might bolt.

"That won't be necessary. Just give me the name and address of a restaurant and I'll meet you there."

"Chinese or Italian?"

"I beg your pardon?"

"Do you like Chinese or Italian food?"

She nibbled on her lower lip, and he groaned inside. The woman was his daughter's teacher, for cripes' sake. What business did she have sporting a hairdo that made her look as if she'd just left a man's bed? He was a professional, not a pervert.

"I didn't mean it to be that difficult of a question, Ms. Starr."

"Chinese," she blurted out, definitely not happy with the way he pushed for an answer.

"Fine. How about The Golden Dragon at seven? It's two blocks south of here, on M and Thirty-third. You know where that is?"

"I'll find it." Taking a step backward up the stairs, she turned and headed for the building.

He was still staring when he felt Phoebe's tiny hand inch its way into his palm.

"Why was Ms. Eloise actin' so funny, Daddy? Doesn't she like you?"

Like him? If Ms. Starr could read minds, she would have slapped him.

Sighing, Nathan recalled her eye-popping figure, those

kiss-me-now lips and the oddly seductive butterflies dangling from her sexy, tousled hair. "I wish I knew, punkin. I really wish I knew."

Eloise gave herself a final inspection in the bedroom mirror. Even though she'd spent time working out most of the tangles, her hair still tumbled to her shoulders in a mass of unruly curls. Though it wasn't any less attractive than some of the styles she'd seen on a few of her charges, she was sure Ms. Hewitt would think it immature and in need of professional assistance.

She gave thanks that she wouldn't be in the headmistress's company tonight. Tomorrow morning would be soon enough to try and emulate the bun Ms. Hewitt seemed to prefer for herself and the other female teachers.

She still wore her dark gray skirt, stockings and flat shoes, but she'd exchanged her dowdy white blouse and boring black jacket for an oversized turtleneck sweater in a demure shade of gray, which she hoped would keep her full breasts hidden from view. The last thing she wanted to experience was the flush of heat that had bubbled through her veins earlier, when Nathan Baxter's chocolate-colored eyes caressed her from across the school steps.

One thing was certain, there would be no more private meetings with the man after tonight. The overbearing brute had insisted he hadn't blackmailed her into this dinner, but she hadn't been fooled. So many adult humans were self-serving and manipulative or plain outright lied, it was a wonder any of them made it to heaven.

Eloise furrowed her brow, trying to remember the kind of marriage Nathan and his wife had shared. Guiding angels had rules, and one of them was not to push their way into a spouse's or significant other's conscience. If their charges were having relationship problems, all an angel could do was open the soul's mind and help them see both sides of the situation. As a last resort, they could initiate a dialogue with the partner's guiding angel, as Milton had done when he'd tried to help Annie.

She'd been so busy guiding Janet away from earthly excess and on to the more humane activity of nurturing her daughter, she couldn't remember which angel was Nathan's, or exactly how he had reacted when Janet had begun her final plunge into self-indulgence. How hard had he worked at keeping their union intact? What part had he played in his wife's downward spiral?

Almost from the day Janet had met Nathan, Eloise had suspected a marriage between them wouldn't last. Guiding angels were always given a list of their charges' soul mates, and neither had been first or even second on each other's roster. She'd done her best to ease Janet into situations where she would meet more suitable life mates, but Janet had set her sights on Nathan Baxter and would not be deterred.

Eloise shrugged into her coat and hat, and grabbed her bag. Once outside, she gazed up at the sky, hoping for a sign, something that would tell her she was on the right track in her own earthly existence, but the stars twinkled down on her exactly as they did on every other person walking the street. She was definitely on her own.

She drew in a sharp breath. She'd always been a resilient sort of angel. She could handle being a human alone. All she had to do was think and act the way the better ones did, and she would be able to accomplish her goal. Once she learned about faith, hope and love, she'd be transported back to heaven where she belonged.

It was obvious she'd been sent to earth as a kindergarten teacher because the Powers That Be thought it was the place for her to learn her lesson. So what did those little creatures know that she didn't? What could they possibly teach her that she couldn't learn by doing something else—like being a movie star, or a race car driver, or a lawyer? She would have been better suited to any of those professions. There had to be a reason she was where she was, doing what she was doing.

She turned a corner and spied an awning imprinted with the words *The Golden Dragon*. Since she'd eaten nothing but baked potatoes for the past few meals, she wondered what Chinese food would taste like. She took the stairs to the basement level, opened the door and walked into the waiting area. Immediately, her senses were teased by all manner of exotic scents. Pungent, spicy and sweet aromas surrounded her, and her stomach began to make that funny rumbling noise she'd come to learn meant it needed to be filled.

Taking the time to compose herself, she sidled back into the entryway and hung up her coat, then peered around the door. Engrossed in reading a menu, Nathan sat at a table in a far corner. Even from this distance she could tell that he'd changed his shirt and shaved. Though he wasn't handsome in the classically beautiful way that caused female hearts to flutter, he exuded a purely masculine quality that telegraphed his commanding self-control and no-nonsense approach to life.

Right now, the sight of him brought a fizzy sensation welling up from deep inside of her. If this was the way human females felt when in the presence of an attractive man, no wonder they walked the planet like so many addlepated idiots.

She pushed the memory of how she had trembled inside when he'd gazed at her at school to the back of her mind. Now was not the time or place to deal with unsettling emotions. When she'd been Janet's guiding angel and she'd experienced the same strange tinglings, it had been disconcerting. In her present form, the feelings were downright tumultuous.

Mentally bracing herself for a few hours of torture, she inhaled and headed into the restaurant. She was positive

Milton had staged each and every one of her strictly human reactions to Nathan just to show her how little she understood of the physical and emotional difficulties her charges had to suffer. He was purposely making her feel this way to prove she was oblivious of the souls in her care.

Well, he wasn't fooling her one iota. She was fully aware of how fragile and frightening human emotions were. She also knew the feelings she was experiencing were wrong—very, very wrong.

Unfortunately, she didn't have a clue what to do to make them stop.

Five

Nathan spotted the puzzling Ms. Starr the second she walked into the restaurant lobby. Looking more than a little unsure of herself, she'd taken one glance inside the dining room and skittered backward like a scalded cat. It was the same timid demeanor she'd had on the school steps, right before she'd accused him of blackmailing her.

Was Ms. Hewitt aware of the fact that her new teacher blew hot and cold at the drop of a hat? He'd met plenty of people with personality quirks in his line of work, but he wondered if anyone with such obvious mood swings should be allowed to teach small children.

Then again, the woman had been pleasant enough at their first meeting, and Phoebe did like her. His daughter had related enough horror stories about upchucking classmates and pencil sharpeners in the past twenty-four hours to last him a month. Who knew how sane he would be, stuck in a room full of troublesome five-year-olds his first day on the job.

Ms. Starr peered around the corner a second time and Nathan feigned interest in the restaurant's offerings. She'd done a fair job of taming her sex goddess hair, but it still looked suggestive as hell. The baggy dull-as-dirt sweater she was wearing did nothing to hide her generous bustline and hips. Reaching deep into his vocabulary, he decided voluptuous was the perfect adjective to describe her tall, curvy body.

She spoke to the hostess, and the woman led Ms. Starr to the table. The moment their eyes met, her face settled into a prim, almost pinched expression.

"Mr. Baxter."

He stood, pulled out her chair and reminded himself to be *charming*. "Ms. Starr. Thanks again for agreeing to meet me."

Unfortunately, her raised eyebrows told him she was still thinking *blackmail*.

The waitress brought over a second menu and glass of water, and he grinned. "So, what's your favorite Chinese dish?"

Without adding a word to the conversation, she stared at the plastic covered pages as if they were written in the restaurant's native tongue.

He cleared his throat, fearful of giving her a suggestion. He'd bet his last nickel she was the type of woman who wouldn't tolerate a man taking charge of her meal. He was about to tell her what he'd decided on, just to help her make up her mind, when her eyes shot open and her complexion turned as white as the tablecloth.

"They serve chicken here . . . and beef . . . and pork."

Rolling his eyes, Nathan gazed at the ceiling. She sounded shocked and horrified at the same time. Great. Didn't it just figure she'd be one of those fruit-and-nut-loving vegetarians. He wouldn't be surprised to learn it was the lack of protein in her diet causing a chemical imbalance in her brain that made her cranky as all get-out.

"This is a regular Chinese restaurant, Ms. Starr. If you wanted vegetarian, you should have mentioned it."

"I didn't realize . . . I mean I know most people partake of animal flesh, but I . . . don't." After laying the menu flat on the table, she rested her head in her hands and stared. "Just give me a minute, please."

The waitress came to take their order and he sent her

away. Time ticked by while he held his tongue, until finally he said, "Do you like it hot and spicy?"

Ms. Starr's head shot up and her cheeks flushed the color of an overripe tomato. "Hot and—"

Open mouth; insert foot, thought Nathan, mentally kicking himself. "What I meant was do you like your food on the hot side or more bland?"

"I'm not sure. This is my first time in a Chinese restaurant."

He tried not to let his surprise show as he reached across the table and pointed to a list on the far side of a page. "They have plenty of meat-free selections, including a vegetable and tofu stir-fry. It's only my humble opinion, but personally I think tofu tastes like candle wax. I've heard this place spices it up to give it more flavor."

She focused on the column he indicated. When the waitress returned, she asked for the stir-fry along with a cup of vegetable soup.

Nathan gave his order and leaned back in his chair. "Ms. Starr, I don't mean to be rude, but why did you pick Chinese? We could have gone to any of a dozen restaurants that serve meatless dishes."

Not quite meeting his eyes, she placed her open napkin on her lap. "I've lived a . . . sheltered life. Chinese sounded like fun, so I thought it might be time I tried it. I'm sorry about the meat thing. I simply forgot."

Relieved to see that she wasn't quite as disagreeable as she'd been at the school, he nodded. "So tell me, where was it you lived this sheltered life?"

She paused with her water glass halfway to her lips. "Excuse me?"

"What city do you come from? It doesn't sound like you were born around here."

"Come from?"

"I was born and raised in Alexandria. After I became a

cop and married my wife, we lived in Maryland. We moved to the District when Janet inherited her father's house."

She scrunched up her forehead, her expression confused. "I've been lots of places, but no one city for very long."

"A military brat? I hear that's a rough life, following your parents from one base to the next. How long have you been in the D.C. area?"

She drummed her fingers on the table and Nathan got the distinct impression he was treading on forbidden ground.

"Mr. Baxter, I thought we came here to talk about your daughter?"

Fighting the urge to kiss her sassy mouth, he folded his arms. The woman jumped from polite to pugnacious faster than a felon looking to cut a deal. Dare he ask if she'd remembered to take her medication this morning? Or her Midol?

"We did. I was just trying to keep the evening friendly."

Ms. Starr's shoulders sagged, then lifted. "You're right. But I think we need to stay professional at the same time. Now, what was it about Phoebe you wanted to discuss?"

Nathan swallowed hard. When she batted those baby-blue eyes and asked so sweetly, it was all he could do not to reach across the table and—Annoyed that his thoughts were again wandering into dangerous territory, he straightened in his chair. At least the woman had lost her crabby attitude—a definite step in the right direction.

"I have several concerns, the most current of which is that you told the class you might not be at the Hewitt Academy much longer. Phoebe's already lost two women who played an important role in her life. Losing a third could devastate her."

She moved her fork from one side of the place mat to the other. "Children are resilient. Eventually they learn to accept things and move on."

Accept things and move on? The paper lantern cast a pale glow over their table. Nathan wasn't sure whether Ms. Starr was blushing, but she should be. For a person who was supposed to be a specialist in the education of children, it didn't sound as if she understood what kind of damage the sudden loss of a loved one might do to them.

"I agree that kids are resilient. But they also have fragile psyches," he began, spouting an edited version of the lecture Rita Mae had given him after Janet died. "Like most people, each of them reacts differently to tragedy or triumph. As an education professional, surely you realize that."

"I didn't want to lie to the children. It would have been wrong to mislead them, then disappear from their lives."

Okay, she had a valid point. Maybe she wasn't as thoughtless as he'd first imagined. "All right. But you could have held off mentioning it until you knew for certain." They ate in silence, until their server removed the bowls. "I'm curious. Why are you thinking of leaving when you just started the job?"

He picked up his chopsticks and pulled them apart. Ms. Starr ignored his question and did the same, but when she separated the sticks the two pieces fell from her trembling hand.

"Here, let me show you." He held his own set correctly and used them to snag a crispy noodle.

Still fumbling, she bit at her lower lip and tried to emulate his technique—until one of her chopsticks jumped from her fingers, slid across the table and landed in his lap.

"I . . . oh . . . I'm so sorry."

Nathan picked up the slender utensil, reached over and grasped her right hand. When heat and a faint tingling tickled his palm, he pushed the weird sensation aside and manipulated her fingers until she held both of the sticks properly.

"Don't get discouraged. Eating with chopsticks is an art. There, now try it," he said, ready for her to bite his head off.

Instead, she snapped the chopsticks together and managed

to successfully capture a noodle. Smiling as if she'd just snared a diamond, she held up her prize. "I can't imagine eating breakfast cereal this way, or ice cream, or anything slippery."

Her childlike enthusiasm had him grinning. "I brought Phoebe here once and she thought they were a kick, too. Don't worry, you'll get the hang of it."

The waitress served their main courses. Gamely, Ms. Starr balanced a square of tofu and a snow pea pod, brought the food to her mouth and slipped it between her lips. He tried not to laugh when she picked up her water glass and drained it in one long swallow. Fanning her face with a hand, she began to cough.

"Are you okay?" He signaled the waitress for more water.

"I—I—I—" she rasped between gasps of air.

"Try some of the rice. It might help."

Still gasping, she nodded as she stabbed at the bowl with her chopsticks. Quickly, he grabbed his fork, scooped up a pile of rice and shoved it into her gaping mouth.

Though her nose was cherry red and her eyes were streaming tears, Ms. Starr chewed valiantly. Nathan suddenly realized where his fork had been. Well, hell. The last thing he needed was for dinner to turn into the eating scene from *Tom Jones*.

Smoothly, he exchanged their silverware. "Feeling better?"

She dabbed at her eyes with the napkin, then gave an unladylike sniffle. Her voice squeaked when she asked, "Do you think I could try something a little less—?"

"Sure. Hang on a second." He called the waitress over and asked for the same meal—minus the hot sauce.

Her demeanor subdued, Ms. Starr blotted at her bright blue eyes. "Thank you."

Nathan nodded, confident he was gaining her trust. "No problem." Sitting back, he waited for the waitress to bring her a replacement dinner. "Phoebe thinks you're a great teacher, by the way. Even better than Ms. Singeltary."

"She's a very perceptive little girl." Ms. Starr's stern expression softened. "I like her, too."

"She needs a woman in her life."

Their waitress placed the new entrée on her place mat, and she picked up her fork. "I believe you both mentioned a grandmother?"

"My mother lives above us in a third floor apartment, but she has a very full social calendar. Phoebe needs someone younger—someone more like you."

"Like me?"

"You know, someone who's fun." He set down his chopsticks and mentally crossed his fingers. "I'm asking as a concerned father for you to consider staying the entire year. Phoebe—and the rest of the kids—need you."

Her lips feathered up at the corners as she raised her gaze to meet his. "You think I'm fun?"

"Come on. What teacher who wears pink butterflies in her hair wouldn't be fun? Besides, you stayed late without a complaint. I'd imagine the parents and children noticed that."

"If you're worried about Phoebe—"

"I won't be worried if you agree to stay. Now let's get back to my original question. Where did you come from, before you moved here?"

Eloise walked at Nathan's side, careful not to let her coat, handbag or any part of herself brush up against him. Throughout the evening, she'd been supremely conscious of his presence. Sitting across the table from him had been difficult; watching his chiseled lips turn up in a smile or grasp a bite of dinner was an almost painful experience that hurt someplace deep inside.

Now on their way home from the restaurant, her uneasy awareness hadn't lessened. They'd finished their meal with her talking about Phoebe while Nathan doggedly tried to steer the conversation back to her private life. So far, she'd managed to avoid most of his clever ploys, but he'd never been put off for long. Even now, as they approached her apartment, he continued to plague her.

"Where did you get your teaching degree?"

"I'm sure you wouldn't know the school."

"Try me. I know lots of institutions of higher learning. Northwestern? Harvard? Benny's Diplomas by Mail?"

"Why do I get the feeling you're grilling me like one of your suspected felons?" she asked, positive that was the case.

"Maybe because I am? Come on, Ms. Starr, give a little. I've told you more about myself than I've told anyone in a long while. It's only fair for you to do the same."

"And I've told you this relationship has to stay strictly professional. What time does Phoebe go to bed?"

"Eight-thirty on school nights, nine on the weekend. Did I tell you I'm an only child? What about you? Have any brothers or sisters?"

They reached the corner of her block and she came to a standstill. When Nathan realized he was the only one moving, he spun around to face her. "Don't tell me you're actually thinking of answering one of my questions?"

"Of course not. I'd just feel more comfortable if I walked the rest of the way alone."

Shrugging, he returned to her side. "You can't be serious?"

"I don't think it's right that you know where I live, or anything else about me. I'm supposed to interact with the children, not their parents. And I don't feel comfortable revealing my private life to a stranger."

"Let's be honest, Ms. Starr. You've managed to reveal precious little of a personal nature tonight. And a stranger wouldn't have treated you to dinner, even if I did have to strong-arm the check away." He snapped his fingers. "I just figured out our problem—we're still doing the Mr.–Ms. thing. How about you call me Nathan, and I'll call you—"

"Ms. Starr?" She hoisted her bag over her shoulder and made to push past him, still angry over the way he'd insisted on paying for her dinner. "If you'll excuse me, I think it's best we say good night. You go your way and I'll go mine. Alone."

He shook his head, his expression determined. "Sorry, no can do. I'm a cop. It's against my nature to let a woman walk home unescorted at"—he checked his watch in the light from the street lamp—"nine o'clock at night."

She frowned at his sensible explanation, then tossed out one of her own. "I live about four buildings down. You can stand right where you are and watch me climb the stairs."

Propping himself against the lamppost, he shook his head. "You drive a hard bargain, Eloise, but okay."

She almost said Ms. Starr again, then thought better of it. Beside the fact that she liked hearing her name pronounced in his deep rumbling voice, getting her point to penetrate his thick skull was about as easy as pounding a nail into cement. "Fine, and I'll remember what you said about Phoebe. Good—"

"Then you're staying?"

She thought about her choices and remembered that earning a living had always seemed to be a major concern of her charges. Milton had been insightful enough to drop her here with a viable means of support. She'd be a fool to throw away the opportunity all because of one obnoxious human.

"For now. Good night, Mr. Baxter."

"Good night, Eloise."

Eloise walked briskly, climbed the stairs and let herself into the building. She didn't need eyes in the back of her head to know Nathan was following her with his penetrating gaze. Once in her apartment, she raced into her bedroom and peeked out a window at the street lamp, but he'd already left his post.

Just as her pulse slowed to a bearable tempo, she felt a presence in the room and whirled in place.

"Have a nice time tonight?"

"Junior! You scared me to death."

He grinned, his round cheeks a ruddy red. "Sorry. Didn't mean to startle you. How are you doing?"

She set her hands on her hips and gave him the schoolteacher glare she'd practiced earlier in her bathroom mirror. "I'm stuck in a room with a gaggle of nosy, boisterous five-year-olds all day. How do you think I'm doing ?"

"El, El, El." He shook his head. "You're not seeing the big picture here."

"Is that so?" she snapped. "Then how about you be a good sport and enlighten me?"

Junior sauntered to the side of her bed, sat down and bounced. "Nice mattress. Not as comfortable as a cloud, of course, but it'll do."

Eloise placed her fingers on her temples, hoping to ease their throbbing. Suddenly, a frightening thought prompted her to ask, "Is there a problem with one of my charges?"

He tapped a knuckle on his apple-dumpling chin. "Hmm. Nope, I don't think so."

"Claudine Withers? The last time I checked, she was seriously considering a divorce. What did she decide to do?"

"She's staying with her husband. I got her to see the light."

Snorting her disbelief, she pushed for more answers. "Max Streeter? He'd been thinking of cheating on his wife. Please tell me he changed his mind?"

"He did."

"Lillian Wu? Richard Barrett? Little Danny Kulakowski?

There was a kid at Danny's grade school trying to get him to do drugs, and I—"

Junior held up a hand. "Trust me. They're all doing fine. A few have passed over, but that's to be expected. Most of them are surviving and staying on the straight and narrow fairly well without you."

The idea that her charges didn't need her hurt more than Eloise thought it would, but Junior had probably already figured that out. She eyed him suspiciously. "So why are you here?"

He swiped his palms on his thighs. "I kind of got the idea you were confused."

She removed her fingers from her temples and ran them through her hair. It didn't take a genius to know that confused was putting it mildly.

"I thought so," he said when she nodded. "Figured I might be able to help you work things out."

Plopping into her chintz-covered bedroom chair, Eloise stuck her legs straight out in front of her. "Go ahead and figure. I'm too tired to think."

"Did you have a good time tonight?"

She raised a wary brow. "What does having dinner with that man have to do with my predicament?"

Junior's gaze wandered to the window, her dresser, the bedside table—anywhere but her face. "Quite a bit, actually."

Not thrilled by his evasive body language, she sat up pin straight in the chair. "What, exactly, are you trying to say?"

"Hey, don't get mad at me. I'm not the one who decided you needed to be here, remember? I'm just supposed to help make it clear if you're not getting the message. I have to let you know that Baxter and his little girl are somehow interwoven with the reason you were sent here. They're the tie-in to your faith, hope and love lesson."

Nathan Baxter, Phoebe Marie? And her? Good gravy, she

wasn't being given a choice—she was being given a personal flogging. Lips quivering, she found the breath to ask, "Who told you that?"

Junior had the decency to blush. "No one. I figured it out all by my lonesome."

"Oh. Well, then."

"Want to know what else I figured out?"

Positive the apprentice angel's frightening theory about her life as a human was wrong, she said, "Sure. Go ahead and tell me what else you *don't know*."

"You're holding back, and that's not good." He hunched over and rested his elbows on his knees. "The whole reason you were sent here was to become a female human. You've got to let yourself go, dive in feetfirst, so to speak, and feel, live, think and act the part. Open your mind and heart to everything they experience; do what they do, just as spontaneously as they do it. Until you manage that, you'll be no better than a hamster in a cage spinning your wheels and going nowhere."

Let go? Dive in? Think and act the part? If Junior had added *make a total fool of yourself,* she just might have believed him. "I take it you're speaking from experience?"

His gaze was encouraging. "Except for the fact that I had to do it from a male perspective, you got it right." Leaning back on his elbows, he stared at the ceiling. "It's easy, once you get into the swing of things."

Eloise wrinkled her nose at the distasteful idea, then stood and began to pace. "Isn't it enough that I've been forced to suffer all the unpleasant personal things humans are stuck with like body odor, belching and using the bathroom? Next you'll tell me I have to experience toenail fungus or dandruff, or go to the dentist for a root canal. Worse, I'll have to visit the gynecologist and get one of those humiliating exams, or have sex or—"

"Uh, El?"

"What?"

"You're getting warm."

She opened and closed her mouth, too shocked to say more.

"Good. Great. You got my drift."

With her hand on her throat, she shook her head. "What? No!"

In true cowardly fashion, Junior glanced at his naked wrist. "Oops! Gotta go. Time for my weekly powwow with the new boss."

Though he disappeared from sight, his parting words lingered. "So long, kiddo. And good luck. I'll be in touch."

Nathan tiptoed down the hall toward the back stairs leading to the kitchen. Phoebe was tucked in safe and sound, just as his mother said, but he always felt better after checking for himself. A parent couldn't be too careful these days, even if the house was equipped with a state-of-the-art security system. Had the dogs been visiting, he would have been less worried, but the guys at the precinct had needed them tonight. He shook his head. Phoebe was so in love with the dopey mutts, she'd probably never want a pet of her own.

Stopping at the top of the stairs, he thought about his evening. After seeing to it that Ms. Starr got safely into her building, he'd gone the long way home, adding several blocks to the normally straightforward route he would have taken if he'd walked directly from The Golden Dragon. Right now, there were so many half-baked ideas rolling around in his brain, he was having a hard time keeping them all in focus.

His analytical side told him the only way to handle a problem was to confront it head-on. Since there was no other way than to say it, he had to voice the words. It didn't matter that he was a single man with needs—make that urges—most normal men found a way to satisfy on a regular basis. It didn't matter that he was a cop, one of a group of people expected to hold themselves to a higher standard. And it definitely didn't matter that he was a father with a child who had to come first, second and last in his life.

I have the hots for my daughter's teacher.

The shocking, almost unbelievable idea had him more appalled than angry. He was a policeman, an authority figure and role model for children. Instead of holding his thoughts in mental lock-down, he'd let them run amok. No doubt about it, Eloise Starr was dynamite to look at, and when she let her guard down, she had a weird, almost childlike manner that had him intrigued, but still—

Running a hand across the nape of his neck, he started down the stairs. Even now, the mere thought of her sleepsexy hair and bountiful curves had his nightstick at attention, but it was more than her physical attributes that had him yearning to get to know her better. She had a good sense of humor, when she chose to let it show, and she had an endearing quality that brought out his protective side.

For the first time in a long time, he was thinking about getting involved with a woman and for him, that was a truly frightening idea.

He'd been a play-by-the-rules kind of guy his entire life. Thanks to his staid insurance salesman father, he'd learned to be responsible and do the right thing. Good grades had come first; then a sport—his had been baseball—which had enabled him to get into a brand-name college. After that, he'd found a useful, solid profession and begun the kind of life that went with it: marriage, children, a home and a pension plan.

He and Janet had met in college and, like that old saying, she'd chased him until he'd caught her. She'd pushed for a quick wedding and they'd gotten married, bought a little house and began to argue on a weekly basis. After Phoebe was born, they'd fought almost daily. By the time Janet's father became ill, they were practically sleeping in separate bedrooms. He'd tried to get her to agree to marriage counseling, but then the old man died and she became distraught. At that point, he'd become too fed up to care that they only spoke to each other for appearances' sake.

It hadn't been a perfect life, but it had been his, and he'd vowed to make the best of it . . . until Janet had gone through a total transformation and decided the life of an heiress was more enticing than that of a wife and mother and started mentioning divorce.

Some nights he told himself he'd done everything he could to be a good husband; none of the bad feelings had been his fault. On really ugly nights, when the guilt ripped him apart, he was pretty certain Janet would still be alive if he'd tried harder to make things work.

Here he was at age thirty-three harboring impossible fantasies about his daughter's kindergarten teacher as if he were a horny adolescent. Worse, the woman acted as if she didn't want to talk to him, much less get to know him. If she had an inkling of the hot-as-a-pistol visions that kept leaping into his brain whenever he thought of her—

He had to be out of his mind. Or he had to take things in hand—so to speak—and work off the crazy urges before he did something really stupid, like pursue Ms. Starr in earnest.

"How was your date?"

Nathan didn't realize he'd made it into the kitchen until he heard Rita Mae's question. Spoken in her usual intuitive tone, he'd swear she'd just read his thoughts.

"I already told you, it wasn't a date. It was a parent-teacher conference." He walked to the refrigerator and took out a beer. "More like a business meeting."

"Hmm." Dressed in a cream-colored sweater, with every hair in place, Rita Mae looked as cool as the late-November night.

He sat down across from her and played dumb, something he should do more often if he wanted to stay out of trouble. "What's that supposed to mean?"

Rita Mae rested an arm on the table, the hint of a smile lifting the corners of her red-painted mouth. Reaching across with her other hand, she picked up his beer bottle and took a healthy swig, then set the bottle back down in front of him. "Phoebe tells me her teacher is young . . . and very pretty."

"Phoebe's exaggerating," he said, much too quickly. And if he wasn't careful, he was going to be struck by lightning at any moment. "The woman is passable at best."

Her smug expression shifted to the one she used when he'd been a kid and she'd caught him in a lie. "I believe she described Ms. Starr as blond haired and blue eyed, with the face of an angel."

"Blond hair and blue eyes do not an attractive woman make." Nathan ignored the clap of thunder sounding ominously in the distance. "Besides, most of the time she's as grumpy as a cat with its tail caught in a wringer."

"According to Phoebe, Eloise Starr has a stern but gentle nature. She's not afraid to let the children teach her a thing or two," Rita Mae continued, as if she hadn't heard him. "Just because she's immune to your charms—"

"She's probably shell-shocked, cooped up in a room full of five-year-olds all day," he corrected, wincing at a crash of thunder so loud it rattled the windows.

Rita Mae hissed air from her lungs like a blown tire. "Then you won't be seeing her again?"

An image of Eloise Starr, her wildly curling hair spread across his pillow, writhing under him while he explored every satiny inch of her sex goddess body slithered across the mirror of his mind. He'd be *seeing* her all right—in his daydreams, in his nightmares, in his every waking moment.

Ticked at his lack of self-control, he leaned into the table. "Not unless I need to speak to her about Phoebe." He took a sip of his beer. "Ms. Starr and I are worlds apart, Mother, and I'm not interested, so you can put your matchmaking wand right back in the cupboard alongside your broomstick, and lock the cabinet door."

This time, the clap of thunder was accompanied by a bolt of lightning so shattering Nathan felt the jolt to his very core.

Six

Eloise sat at her desk, squirming in her seat as she flipped through the book of lesson plans she'd found yesterday before leaving school. Last night, after Junior spouted his mind-jarring hypothesis and abruptly disappeared, all thoughts of reading up on what she needed to teach her students had flown from her head.

Truth be told, she'd forgotten to breathe for several minutes while the guiding angel's ridiculous suggestions had sunk into her brain.

Between reliving every moment of her dinner with Nathan Baxter at least a dozen times, and hearing Junior's voice repeat over and over like a trite golden oldies refrain, she'd spent a near-sleepless night. Just knowing there were more unsavory things she had to experience in her new life sat like a huge lump in her stomach. Worse, the idea that she was expected to have an intimate relationship with Nathan made her pulse pound and her palms sweat, almost as if she were suffering from some strange incurable malady.

After waking at dawn, she'd gotten ready for work in a numb stupor, not bothering to do more than run a brush through her tangled hair and slip into one of her many unflattering dresses. It wasn't until she was halfway to school that she realized the dress was composed of a fabric so abrasive it made her itch all over. She'd arrived at the Hewitt Academy an hour ahead of schedule with no thought to the rest of her day except how she was supposed to control her scratching.

Now, she decided, might be the perfect time to focus on her job. If Honoria Hewitt found a reason to fire her, she would have to come up with another way to earn a living, a task Eloise didn't like thinking about on any level.

Before she got any further in her musings, the head-mistress knocked on her door and charged into the room. As usual, she wore her scraped back bun and black horn-rimmed glasses. If Eloise didn't know better, she'd think the woman slept at the school most nights instead of going home.

Ms. Hewitt skidded to a stop and stood stiffly, her hands folded at her waist. "Ms. Starr. How nice to find you're an early riser, as am I."

Early riser, my halo, Eloise almost snapped, scratching at the neckline of her dress. She was so tired she was ready to fall asleep in her chair, but there was no way she would confess such a thing to her superior.

Honoria's chipper gaze rested on the lesson planner. "I came to remind you that practice for the Christmas pageant begins today in the auditorium, promptly at one-thirty, but you're probably already aware of that since you're reading the kindergarten planning guide."

"Christmas pageant?"

"It's there in your notebook under December events. I assume you've assigned the children their parts?"

Eloise opened and closed her eyes, wriggling in her chair when a place it wasn't proper to scratch in public began to plague her. If the overflowing medicine cabinet in her bath-room had something to cure a rash, she might be able to get a good night's sleep, provided she could stop thinking about—

"Ms. Starr?"

"Umm . . . oh . . . yes, that was going to be my first task of the day," she said, trying not to scratch.

"The kindergarten, first and second grades always do the pageant, with the honor of reenacting the nativity rotating among them. This year the second-graders will be in charge of the gift exchange while the first-graders sing the carols. When Mrs. Nelson heard I was allowing a new teacher to tackle the play, she jokingly suggested that she might challenge you to an arm-wrestling contest."

Eloise hid behind a thin-lipped smile as she envisioned herself in a pair of tights, flowing cape and body-hugging leotard. If need be, she could fake a losing match just as convincingly as any of those WWF contenders did.

"If Mrs. Nelson wants to arm wrestle for the privilege, I'll do my best not to hurt her."

Ms. Hewitt cleared her throat, apparently unimpressed with Eloise's attempt at levity. "Are you feeling all right? You seem . . . distracted."

"Me? Distracted? No, of course not."

The headmistress sidled backward down the aisle. "Very well. Just remember to be culturally sensitive when you award the parts. The Hewitt Academy caters to all ethnic backgrounds, but it's difficult with Christmas being such a national event." She stopped just short of the door. "I'm counting on you to assign the roles properly."

Eloise waited until she disappeared, then plopped an elbow on her desk and rested her chin in her hand. What in the name of heaven was the woman talking about—assign the roles properly—national event? Didn't she realize that Christmas wasn't a sports competition like the World Series or Super Bowl, but a joyous, all-encompassing celebration of the most important birthday in the history of the planet? Though many adult humans had lost sight of the true meaning of Christmas, she would be dealing with children. Surely they understood the enormity of the day.

Heaving a sigh, she ignored a particularly virulent itch that had taken residence under her left arm and thumbed through the planner until she came to the December schedule. After skimming over a list with the daunting heading of Suggested Gifts for Parents, she found what she was searching for— three pages entitled "The Christmas Pageant."

Thinking she would peruse the roster of possible presents in her apartment—where she could remove her dress and have the privacy to scratch to her heart's content—she read through the play's cast list. She needed a boy and girl to take the parts of Joseph and Mary, a few to be shepherds, and three students to play the Wise Men, plus a group to be a chorus of angels and one to play Gabriel, the angel who had announced the wondrous birth.

No sweat. Nothing she couldn't handle.

Dividing up the characters on scraps of paper, Eloise made sure there was a part for each child, then mixed a few of the shepherds and angels into each pile. Since there were eight girls in the class and only seven boys, she decided the angel Gabriel would be played by a female.

If nothing else, the pageant would take her mind off Nathan Baxter. She might even avoid him altogether, if she did as Junior suggested and dived into teaching feetfirst. Then again, the guiding angel had insisted she was supposed to interact with the man in the most personal of ways. If Junior knew what he was talking about, and Eloise had a sad suspicion he did, she was going to be having more contact with Nathan than she'd ever imagined.

She thought back to the years she'd been Janet's guiding angel. Coveting—no—admiring the woman's husband from afar had been a mere flutter in her mind, a tiny impossible thought about what it would be like to be cared for by a man such as Nathan. Was this the punishment she deserved for simply wondering about him, when she should have been concentrating all her efforts on counseling Janet?

Out in the hallway, older children sauntered to class in groups, their almost-adult voices sharp and knowing. She heard a series of childish giggles and smiled, mentally bracing for her students. The little creatures weren't such a bad lot, nor were they as frightening as she'd first thought. When she regained her heavenly connections, she might even drop by and check on them from time to time, just to be certain their angels were doing a competent job.

As she was thinking and doing her best not to scratch, Felicia Rathbone trotted into the room, a superior smile gracing her patrician features. British in the extreme, she stated loudly, "My father says I'm to be treated with gentle hands today, because I have a sensitive nature. I don't have to do any written work if I don't want to, nor do I have to answer questions."

Biting her tongue, Eloise gazed at the ceiling and resisted another urge to wriggle. Felicia's haughty statement only proved what she'd suspected all along: there was nothing wrong with children that couldn't be cured by a good rap to their parents' empty noggins. Mr. Rathbone would probably need to be whacked with a baseball bat in order to see the light.

"All right, if that's what you want," she said to Felicia. "But we're choosing parts for the Christmas play this morning. Since I'm not allowed to tax you, you'll just have to accept whichever role is left over."

"But my father—"

"Isn't in charge here. I am."

Sebastian, John and Miles tumbled into the room in a tangle of arms and legs. Pushing and shoving at one other like playful puppies, their boisterous camaraderie mercifully drowned out Felicia's sputters of protest.

"Hey, Ms. Eloise. I got a baloney san'wich for lunch today," said John. "You can have half, if you want."

"An'I got ham and cheese to share," offered Miles.

Not to be outdone, Sebastian added, "I don't know what Cook made, but I'm sure there's enough for both of us."

Eloise swallowed down a groan. For the past two days she'd forgotten to bring a lunch, and it sounded as if the children had noticed. Unfortunately, when she thought about the slaughter of all those helpless chickens, cows and pigs, there was no way she could accept what they offered.

Before she could politely turn them down, the rest of the students filed in, ready to begin what she was certain was going to be a very long day.

Nathan paced the worn linoleum in front of his captain's desk, his conscience divided by the latest speed bump cluttering the road of his career.

"I'm sorry, Nate, but that's the way it has to be," said Joe Milligan, raising a manila folder in the air. A tall man with salt-and-pepper hair, the captain had a dignified and quietly authoritative manner on the job and a fun-loving swagger when he dropped his guard. "With O'Hara and Waters on sick leave and a half-dozen others on special detail, I really need you on this case."

Nathan ran a hand through his already rumpled hair, unsure how to react to the surprising decree. "I thought we had a deal. I was supposed to be assigned grunt work so I could have more time with my daughter. If I'm in the field, it'll mean spending nights on the street."

Milligan continued to hold out the file as if it were a prize. "It's been over a year. I don't mean to be insensitive, but I need you to come off amended duty and take on a full workload again."

Unclenching his fingers, Nathan accepted the manila folder. He'd always meant to return to his regular job as soon as Phoebe felt secure enough to know the remaining adults in her life would never leave her, but he couldn't help wondering if his daughter was ready.

"Look, I'm grateful for the downtime, but Phoebe's still in kindergarten. I'd hoped the lousy hours wouldn't catch up to me until she got a little older."

Narrowing his steely gray eyes, the captain rested his hands on a pile of files stacked in the middle of his overladen desk. "Sorry, but there's no longer any way I can justify keeping you off the streets—unless you're willing to tackle that job as line commander. I know how much you hate the idea of sitting at a desk all day, but you're still my first choice. I've been dragging my feet about naming a candidate because I'd hoped to convince you to take it before the big brass pushed me into making a decision."

A few months ago, when Captain Milligan had first offered him the desk job, Nathan had held off accepting it because he loved working the streets. If he agreed to take the position he'd be stuck with it for the rest of his career.

"I was just hoping for a few more months of light duty, maybe over the summer, so I could take my time easing Phoebe into the situation and find her a competent sitter."

Milligan brought his body to attention. "What about Rita Mae . . . um . . . I mean your mother . . . Is she still living with you?"

Nathan recalled that the captain had asked Rita Mae out to dinner a time or two with no success. Though Milligan was only five years her junior, his mother had told the both of them she wasn't the type of woman who robbed the cradle. From the hope-filled expression in the man's eyes, it looked as if her refusal had done little to cool his interest.

"Yeah, but she has her own life," Nathan confided, not adding that Rita Mae thought keeping herself an unwilling sitter would force her son into finding another wife. "I don't want to take advantage of her good nature."

"The desk job comes with a big raise."

"I don't need the money. I need the time."

The captain nodded at the file. "Sorry, I just don't have anyone else I can give the case to. Romero is too new to go it alone, but you can teach her the ropes and maybe she'll free up some of your time."

Nathan tucked the folder under his arm. At the door, he turned. "I've been meaning to tell you how much I appreciate everything you've done for me, Captain." He tapped the folder against his palm, taken with a new idea. "And I'd like to show my appreciation by inviting you over some night when Rita Mae is fixing dinner. I'm not making any promises, but you never know what might happen . . . "

Leaning back in his chair, Milligan grinned as he rubbed a hand across his broad chest. "Why not. A night of family fare has got to be better than the pepperoni pizzas I've been downing for the past three months. Damn things give me heartburn. I'm up for a home-cooked meal anytime."

His mind a kaleidoscope of emotions, Nathan sauntered to his desk. A detective's life usually wasn't in as much danger as a patrolman's, but things still got hairy on the street—something Janet had never failed to remind him of. On the night she'd been shot, he'd been on volunteer assignment primarily because he wanted to show her that she couldn't boss him around where his career was concerned. Her death had uncovered a wellspring of guilt that sometimes caused him to feel like a drowning man going under for the third time.

Nathan thought about his daughter's future and the several million bucks sitting in a trust fund waiting to be claimed on her twenty-fifth birthday. At that time everything, including the house they lived in, would officially belong to her. He was trustee of the account, and as such was allowed to take a monthly stipend as well as debit the trust for all items pertaining to Phoebe's care. It galled him that he had to use a portion of the money to pay the taxes on the house in Georgetown, but no way could he afford them on his salary. Other than that, he hadn't touched a penny, not even for the house he was building at Lake Mary.

After Janet's death, he'd made a promise to himself—one he intended to keep. He was Phoebe's father and he was going to be the person financially responsible for her upbringing. He paid the hefty fee at her private school and he was going to fund any college she was intelligent enough to attend. He wanted her to grow up with a sensible approach to her wealth, but not be ruled by it.

He heard a knock on his desk and raised his head to meet the golden-eyed gaze of Detective Isobel Romero. The petite, dark-haired woman nodded smartly. "Looks like it's you and me today, Detective Baxter. You ready to roll?"

Nathan handed her the folder. Grinning, her eyes rested on the picture frames mounted on the wall behind him. "I still can't believe I was lucky enough to draw you for my first assignment. Word around the precinct is you earned every one of those commendations the hard way."

Nathan felt his face warm as he rose from his chair. He kept meaning to take the certificates home, or at least hide them somewhere, but every once in a while when he wasn't looking, some smart-ass pulled them out of his desk drawer and hung them up. The last thing he needed was a partner with a bad case of hero worship.

"I'm a real sweet guy, all right," he growled, hoping to change her mind. "And just to show you how sweet, I'll drive."

Eloise noted the time on the wall clock as she watched Miles skip from the classroom alongside his family's chauffeur. It was just past four and she was exhausted. Doling out roles in the Christmas pageant had turned into a free-for-all of gigantic proportions. All but a few of the children were happy with their parts. Between the tears and shouts, it was a wonder Ms. Hewitt hadn't barged in and fired her on the spot.

Except for Phoebe, all of the children had been picked up. If someone didn't come for the little girl soon, Eloise would have to explain the situation to Ms. Hewitt and let the headmistress take care of things. She didn't want to be here when Nathan strutted through the door, late and unapologetic, as so many of her other students' *uncaring* caregivers did.

"I know my daddy's gonna be here." Phoebe's voice echoed in the nearly empty room. "He never forgets about me."

Their first rehearsal for the Christmas pageant had drained Eloise of patience, while the dress she wore had turned her body into one massive rash. All she wanted was to go home, toss the offending garment in the trash and find a product in her overflowing medicine chest to soothe her irritated skin. This was not the best time for anyone to be looking to her for understanding.

She scratched at the bodice of her dress, unable to hide her disbelief. "You mean he's never been late to pick you up? Ever?"

Phoebe went to the windows and stared down onto the barren playground. If possible, her voice sounded even smaller and less certain. "Maybe just a couple times."

"How many is a couple?" she asked, strangely disappointed to hear that she'd been right about Phoebe's father.

The child's silence was a poignant reminder of Eloise's past failures. Her recollection of the first few days after Phoebe's birth was fuzzy, but she remembered that Nathan's enthusiastic approach to parenting was one of the reasons she hadn't tried to force Janet into immediately doing her motherly duty. While Nathan and Phoebe Marie had bonded, Janet had become overly argumentative and indifferent. The only time the woman had seemed happy was when she'd been spending money or flaunting her wealth.

"Maybe your father had a problem at work or came home early and fell asleep."

Phoebe turned and shook her head. "Daddy never sleeps in the daytime. He's too busy bein' a policeman."

Beside the need to carry a gun and their propensity for dangerous situations, Eloise didn't know much about policemen, but she had heard they worked erratic hours with far from normal schedules. And what about Nathan's private life? Last night at dinner, he'd been forceful and focused, but he'd also been polite and attentive—positive characteristics any woman would feel drawn to. He was intelligent, attractive and single—surely he'd started dating again.

"Who watches you if he has to go out at night or on the weekends?" *When he's interviewing women for the position of new wife and mother?*

"Daddy's always there. We see movies or bake cookies, or play in our backyard with the dogs. Sometimes he sits with me while I go in my special drawer, the one where I keep the things Mommy left me, and we look at pictures. That's when he tells me how much she loved me and didn't want to leave."

The look of adoration shining from Phoebe's bright blue eyes made Eloise want to bash Nathan on his head for being late. Instead, she ran twitchy fingers under the collar of her dress.

Phoebe rubbed at her nose as she walked to the desk. "How come you keep scratchin' yourself?"

Eloise tugged down the offending neckline. "I think I'm allergic to this material. See, I'm all red. It's been driving me crazy."

Phoebe peered at Eloise's exposed collarbone and nodded knowingly. "Grammy has a pink lotion she puts on me when I get mo-skeeter bites. Does the dress itch at you like they do?"

"I wouldn't know, since I've never had the pleasure of being bitten by a *mo-skeeter*. What's the name of the lotion?"

"I dunno, but it works really good. I'll ask her tonight." Phoebe gave a megawatt grin. "Sometime, when Daddy has really important stuff to do, he asks Grammy to pick me up. Maybe we should call her. I bet she'd come get me."

She frowned at the childish logic. If Nathan knew he was going to be detained, didn't it stand to reason he would have already asked his mother to pick up her grandchild? When Phoebe's lower lip quivered, she didn't have the heart to argue.

"Oh, all right. Let's go see if Ms. Hewitt has her phone number on file." *And your home number, and your dad's work number. We might as well try them all.*

Phoebe skipped in front of her, then turned and walked backward to keep Eloise in sight. "I know Grammy's number by heart." She rattled it off to the tune of a children's song. "Her name is Rita Mae Baxter, and she lives upstairs from us in Georgetown. The house use to belong to my grandpa Breakwater. When he got old and really really sick, he died and *wilted* the house to my mommy. Now that she's gone to heaven, it belongs to me. But I let my daddy and Grammy live in it, 'cause when people love each other, that's what they do."

Impressed by the amount of information the little girl had just shared, Eloise thought about Janet. Nathan had been angry when she'd demanded he quit work so they could enjoy the money. He'd told her that Phoebe and his job came first and they could damn well survive on his salary or starve. After a time, Janet had stopped trying to make him see things her way and gone off on her own, almost in defiance of the requests.

He had played the part of an upstanding and conscientious man, but Eloise knew humans often hid their true personas. Nathan was still on the police force, which meant he hadn't given up his dangerous job. Now he was late to collect his daughter, after he'd made a big deal at their dinner conference about how he always tried to put Phoebe's interests first.

Did he really care about Phoebe or was he only saying what he thought people wanted to hear? Lost in thought, Eloise rounded the corner and barely avoided a full-body collision with Honoria Hewitt.

Grabbing at her cockeyed bun, the headmistress stiffened her spine as she collected herself. "Ms. Starr—Phoebe Marie. You're still here. Is there a problem?"

"No, of course not," Eloise answered, hoping to keep

things simple. "Phoebe's father is late picking her up, so we're going to call a few numbers and see if we can locate him."

"Oh, dear." Ms. Hewitt pushed a stray hairpin into her disheveled hair. "I usually stay until all the students have left, but I can't tonight. My car was giving me trouble this morning, so I had to take it to the repair shop again." She glanced at her watch. "If I don't leave now, they'll close and I won't have it for the weekend."

Eloise said the first thing that came to mind. "I'll see to it that Phoebe gets home safely."

A wave of relief washed over Ms. Hewitt's pale face. Indicating they follow, she walked into her office and went directly to a bank of files.

"Here's the list of contact numbers for Phoebe Marie. Except for the main entrance, all the school doors lock automatically at five. When you leave, go out that door and pull it firmly behind you, and it will lock as well. If you need anything, the janitor will be here for another fifteen minutes or so. Thank you for handling the matter, and have a wonderful weekend."

Seven

Eloise stood in the doorway leading out of her kitchen and watched Phoebe lick the icing from the middle of two chocolate cookies. She'd found the bag of cream-filled wafers her first night in the apartment, but had yet to try them. From the joyful expression on the child's face, she'd been missing out on a tasty treat.

She and Phoebe had walked to her apartment after it became apparent that Nathan Baxter was missing, as was the child's grandmother. She hadn't planned on bringing the little girl to her home, but her dress had become so intolerable, Eloise could no longer endure the torture. When Phoebe had recited her address, she'd thought to deliver her there in a cab, but with no one answering at the house it would have been pointless to arrive and be left sitting in the cold and dark.

"Give me a few minutes to clean up and change." She handed Phoebe the phone and sheet of paper given her by Ms. Hewitt. "While I'm gone, keep trying your number and the one for your grandmother. I'm sure someone will be home soon."

Munching diligently, Phoebe began to punch at the numbers as she swung her legs under the chair.

Eloise fled the kitchen and was out of the dress by the time she reached her bedroom. After dropping it in the wastebasket, she wrapped herself in a robe and rushed to the bathroom to check her medicine cabinet. Overjoyed to find a bar of soap meant especially for sensitive skin, she jumped under the warm spray, lathered her body and let the soap and terry washcloth relieve the worst of the itching.

She toweled dry as she thought about the child sitting contentedly in her kitchen. She'd called the personal phone numbers listed under Phoebe's name several times and left messages on each answering machine. Then she'd called the number for Nathan's job and left word there. Surely he or the child's grandmother were home by now. She intended to deliver Nathan his daughter and give him a stern talking-to on the duties of being a parent. All the better if Phoebe's grandmother was present, too, since it seemed both of the adults in the child's life could do with a serious scolding.

She dressed in a pair of snug-fitting jeans and a comfy black cotton sweater, then slid her feet back into her chunky shoes. Glancing in her bedroom mirror, she saw that her hair was a damp, tangled mess, so she brushed the mop behind her ears and used the butterfly clips to keep it in place. Certain she was presentable, she headed to the kitchen, where she found the girl still pressing out numbers.

"I keep tryin' my daddy's phone, but all I get is the answer machine." Phoebe's eyes filled with tears. "Where do you think he is?"

A fist of worry squeezed Eloise's heart and she couldn't help but imagine the worst. Had Nathan gone and done something stupid that might have put his life at risk? Where was Daddy dearest, the unthinking clod?

"I'm sure he's fine," she said brightly, not wanting to distress Phoebe further. "He's probably still at work, and the time just got away from him."

Phoebe sniffed as she ran a hand under her nose. "Are we goin' now?"

Eloise shrugged into the coat she'd left on a chair and grabbed her bag and keys. "If you're sure you know how to get home from here."

"I know how from the school," Phoebe mumbled. "It's

only a couple blocks. Sometimes, when the weather is nice, Daddy walks me there with Huey, Dewey and Louie."

Once on the sidewalk, Eloise stared at the dusting of stars barely visible in the slate-colored sky. Fast moving cars, taxis and buses clogged the street, their headlights casting distorted shadows, but the only true illumination came from street lamps set on the corner of each block. She was too new to the city to even begin to find her way to the Baxter residence. If Phoebe knew how to get there from the school, that's where they needed to be.

"You're sure you can get us to your house from the school?"

Phoebe looked left and right, then raised her confused gaze skyward. "I think so, but it's dark out," she said with a tremor in her voice. "I don't like the dark."

"It's not so bad," Eloise answered. Refusing to admit she felt the same, she took hold of the little girl's hand.

"Daddy sits on my bed and reads me a story if I wake up in the dark."

"Then we'll just have to find him. Now let's get you bundled up. It wouldn't do if you caught a chill and missed school." She squatted and zipped up Phoebe's coat, then tied her hat firmly under her chin. "How about if we head in the direction of the academy? Maybe once we get there things will look more familiar."

The chilly November breeze rustled the brittle leaves littering the walkway. Eloise shivered as they set off down the sidewalk. Once they turned on the street that led to the Hewitt Academy, the niggle of worry she'd felt earlier came rushing to the fore. In the distance she could see the flashing blue lights of a police car—make that three police cars—and it looked as if all of them were parked in front of the school.

They got closer and she noticed several uniformed policemen talking into handheld radios while a half dozen people wearing street clothes milled about. When she spotted Ms. Hewitt fiddling with the door at the top of the landing, she came to a halt. Phoebe tugged her hand free and began to run. It was then Eloise got a good look at Nathan, his hands stuffed into the pockets of his leather jacket, pacing the upper landing like a caged panther.

"Daddy! Daddy! You came!" Phoebe's cries rang out over the hubbub. A woman who'd been speaking to an officer at the edge of the crowd rushed to meet the little girl as she raced up the steps and ran to Nathan's side.

Assuming the woman was Phoebe's grandmother, Eloise waited to make eye contact and pass a friendly greeting, but a volley of curious gazes speared her like daggers, and she realized she was in trouble. And it was all Nathan's fault.

Nathan's expression flitted from panic to surprise to relief all in the space of a heartbeat. Bolting down the stairs, he swept Phoebe into his arms and swung her in a circle, then raised her up against him and squeezed.

"Ow, Daddy. Not so hard," Phoebe said, giggling. Pushing at his shoulders, she drew back and smiled. "I missed you. Ms. Eloise and me got worried when you didn't come pick me up."

Nathan clutched at his daughter the way a drowning man might cling to a life raft, then ran his hands over her tiny form as if checking for broken bones. "Oh, God, sweetheart. Are you all right?" Ignoring Phoebe's squeal of protest, he again pulled her close. "Where have you been? I'm so sorry I wasn't here for you. I was so worried when I thought—"

His anguished voice carried over the noise of the crowd, holding Eloise suspended. When Rita Mae enfolded both son and granddaughter in her arms, she observed the trio with an unsettling sense of detachment, almost as if she'd returned to her guiding angel form. Only this time, as she watched the scene unfold, something hurt deep inside her chest.

How often had she stood by while her charges had cried in despair or shed tears of joy? How often had she thought their actions overblown, or stupid or simply unnecessary?

How often had she hardened herself to their feelings and refused to acknowledge their pain or elation?

How many times had she witnessed something close to this very scene and never understood the depth of their emotions?

The ache in Eloise's chest grew, threatening her ability to breathe, but she didn't turn her gaze away until Ms. Hewitt, her hands fluttering, marched to stand in front of her.

"Ms. Starr, thank goodness you're here. Mr. Baxter was beside himself when he arrived and found Phoebe missing. What happened? I thought you were going to call him?"

"We tried," Eloise said softly, still in awe of the raw, new sensation swirling inside her body.

"You should have gotten hold of me," the principal said firmly. "I would have met you here and waited with Phoebe myself. Taking a child off of school property is against all rules. The school could be sued if anything had happened to Phoebe. Even so, Mr. Baxter is well within his rights to—"

"We did call. Phoebe and I left messages at her father's contact numbers and the house. We decided to go to my apartment where we could be more comfortable; then I realized that with no one at Phoebe's home it would be better if we returned here. If Mr. Baxter had been on time, none of this would be necessary."

"I understand your reasons for leaving school property, but you should have thought of the consequences. Mr. Baxter was in error, but he has a good reputation for being punctual, and has sworn he will never let it happen again. I hope the same can be said for your impulsive actions."

Eloise had no more answers. The discomfort of an itchy dress seemed small and irrelevant when compared to the soul-wrenching grief Phoebe's disappearance had caused her family. She couldn't think of another word in her defense. Gazing over the headmistress's shoulder, she saw Nathan hand Phoebe to his mother, kiss the little girl on the cheek and head their way.

Nathan clenched his jaw to hold back what he was certain would be a barrage of nasty words. "It's all right, Ms. Hewitt. I can take it from here," he said through gritted teeth.

Ms. Hewitt muttered another apology and sidled to the crowd still hovering around the police cars. Alone with Ms. Starr, he inhaled a breath. In his heart, he'd suspected Phoebe was safe, but that didn't help deaden the pang of utter inadequacy he'd experienced when he'd thought about how he had let his daughter down. Still, that didn't give the woman the right to abscond with his child. He'd come the second he found out Rita Mae had car trouble. Nothing like full-blown panic to give a man a heart attack.

And now, instead of looking contrite, Ms. Starr wore an expression he couldn't quite place. She didn't look angry, but she did look confused—or was it amazement peeking through her puzzling gaze? He felt a hand on his arm and turned to find Rita Mae holding Phoebe by the hand.

"This is entirely my fault," his mother began. Scooting around him, she shot Eloise a bedraggled smile. "I was at my bridge game when Nathan called. When I got in the car I found the battery had died and my cell phone with it. By the time I phoned a garage and Nathan, there was no answer at the school—"

"That was still no excuse for Ms. Starr to leave the premises with my daughter," he said sharply.

Rita Mae threw Eloise a commiserating don't-let-him-bully-you look. "Now, Nathan, don't go ballistic. Ms. Starr went above and beyond the scope of her duties just to make certain Phoebe was taken care of. She did what she thought was best."

Nathan suppressed a growl. If he didn't know better, he'd think the two women had just given one another some form of mental secret handshake. Still annoyed, he made a not-so-subtle suggestion. "Go home, Mother. Now. And take Phoebe with you."

Rita Mae gave a final half smile and drew Phoebe toward

the stairs. "Good night, Ms. Eloise," Phoebe said. "See you Monday."

Nathan waited until his mother and daughter were out of earshot before he bared his teeth in a grimace so threatening it was known to put the fear of death into the hearts of criminals and cops alike. He was willing to admit he'd screwed up big-time by leaving a message on his mother's phone instead of talking to her in person. Embroiled in a new case, he'd taken for granted that Rita Mae would do the job. When he'd received a message from the desk sergeant saying the school had called, he'd phoned there and gotten no answer; then he'd called Ms. Hewitt's house and demanded she meet him so he could inspect the grounds and get Eloise's exact address. The desk sergeant had made the decision to send over a couple of black-and-whites, just to be sure nothing was amiss.

Turning to Ms. Starr, he jabbed a finger in the air. "Stay here and don't move. We need to talk."

Instead of cowering like a sensible person, the teacher had the nerve to fold her arms and match his glare. Shocked at her audacity, he walked briskly to the patrolmen.

"Sorry, fellas, false alarm. But just to show how grateful I am for your concern, the next round at the Lights Out is on me. Have a safe night."

He took their good-natured comments in stride, well aware they understood his concern. Many of them had been his anchor after Janet's death; some had even become his extended family. They knew part of tonight's mixup rested with Nathan, but they didn't blame him for it. Family members of law enforcement officials understood the difficulties associated with keeping commitments; it was part of their life. This was his first day back on regular duty. Shit happened. A man did the best he could.

Inhaling, he swiped a hand through his hair. He'd received plenty of commendations that proved he was a good cop, but not a single award to show he was a competent dad.

He stunk to high heaven when it came to his personal life. He'd been a lousy husband and, try as he might, he was an equally lousy father—one who couldn't even do up his little girl's hair without the kid looking like she'd stuck her toe in an electric socket.

He'd eat crow, but only after he made it clear to Eloise that he was the person in charge of his daughter.

Hunching his shoulders against the wind, he decided to bluff his way through the next ten minutes. Turning around, he sucked in a breath, but Ms. Starr was nowhere in sight. While he'd been feeling sorry for himself for acting like a jerk, she'd had the good sense to leave.

Nathan sat on the side of Phoebe's bed and smoothed back her bangs with a clumsy hand. "I'm sorry I wasn't there for you today, punkin," he said for the hundredth time. *I'm sorry I let you down.*

"Don't be mad at Ms. Eloise, Daddy. She took me to her 'partment and gave me milk and choc'lit cookies. She even zipped my coat and tied my hat when we went outside. But she had'ta take a shower before she walked me home 'cause she was itchy all over."

Even though he knew it was against common sense, Nathan allowed his imagination to run wild. The idea of Eloise Starr standing naked under running water was so intriguing it almost erased the evening's debacle at the Hewitt Academy. Too bad he and the kindergarten teacher would never be able to experience the delights of sharing a bath. He'd made such a total jackass of himself, he seriously doubted the woman would ever consider another date with him, never mind a shower.

"Do you have to work tomorrow, Daddy?"

Phoebe's pensive tone brought him back to reality. "I do. It's the reason I was late tonight. I've been put back on full duty, punkin. That means I'll need to spend a lot more time at the station."

Phoebe bit her lower lip. "How much more?"

He tucked the covers securely under her arms. "Some nights and a few weekends. It will depend on the type of case I'm on. Just to make sure what happened today doesn't happen again, I'm going to ask Grammy to pick you up on a regular basis."

Phoebe worried a loose thread on her Barbie comforter. "Can't you find a different job?"

Nathan sighed. Janet had played the very same recording so often the tape had worn down and split apart, exactly like their marriage, and no amount of splicing had been able to put it back together. He'd never been able to give her the answer she wanted to hear.

"I love my work, Phoebe, not as much as I love you and Grammy, but my job is very important to me. Can you understand that?"

She wrinkled her nose, as if thinking hard. "Do you love it as much as Grammy loves to play bridge and do yoga?"

"More. My job earns us a living and helps to keep children safe. It's important to the community and, sometimes, it even saves people's lives."

Yawning, Phoebe snuggled under the covers, then turned on her side and clutched a miniature stuffed German shepherd to her chest. "Then I guess you have to keep doin' it. Can I go to sleep now?"

Standing up, he gazed at his daughter. "Sure. And how about you dream of what you'd like to do tomorrow night? I should be home for dinner. We can take in a movie, or go to the mall and look at Christmas decorations—whatever you want. Would you like that?"

"Uh-huh. But who's gonna make me breakfast? Is Grammy gonna watch me while you're gone?"

"If you're up before I leave, we'll eat together; otherwise she'll take care of you." Mentally crossing his fingers, he edged to the door and turned off the light. "Good night, sweetie. Sleep tight."

Nathan had left Rita Mae in the kitchen fixing a cup of herbal tea, and figured he'd better join her. Not only did he need to discuss the evening, he had to be certain she'd agree to baby-sit in the morning. If not, he'd have to make other arrangements, which wouldn't be easy at this hour.

He took the stairs slowly, cursing to himself when another vision of Eloise Starr, her satiny skin wet and glistening under a spray of pulsing water, appeared in his mind. Darned if the harder he tried not to think about the woman, the more she popped into his head. He had to get a grip and plunge back into work full force, then maybe she would find herself a nice quiet corner to hide in until he was alone in his bed at night. Because lately, his dreams seemed to be the only place it was safe to think about her.

Nathan stopped short of the doorway and took a breath, preparing a speech that would get him back into his mother's good graces. He could tell from the handful of disapproving looks she'd thrown his way at the school that she'd been worried sick over the screw-up and was probably sharing his guilt.

"You can stop hovering," came Rita Mae's voice from the kitchen. "I'm not going to bite."

Feeling like a little boy who'd been caught eavesdropping at his parents' bedroom door, he exhaled and walked into the room. "I wasn't hovering. I was thinking about tonight."

"Me, too. And I'm thrilled to know Captain Milligan came to his senses and returned you to full duty. I imagine you got so involved in your newest assignment you assumed I'd gotten your message. But it was an honest mistake, Nathan. You had no idea my battery would pick this afternoon to give up the ghost."

"That doesn't excuse what happened," he muttered.

"It wasn't your fault, but you did treat Ms. Starr abominably."

"Okay, seeing as you're such a know-it-all, what am I supposed to do next?"

Rita Mae stood at the stove and poured water from the teakettle into her mug. Turning, she propped her backside against the counter and dunked with determined precision. "Isn't it obvious? You need to deliver a heartfelt apology to her at your earliest convenience. It's the sensible thing to do."

"Thanks for the motherly advice," Nathan ground out, knowing full well she was on target. "I know I acted like an idiot, and I'm going to take care of it."

"Good for you." She set the tea bag in the sink and smiled. "I would have made you a cup of tea, but I know how much you hate the stuff."

"Will it help get me a good night's sleep?"

She opened a cupboard and took down a box. "Chamomile might make you relax. Care to try it?"

Nathan shrugged. "What the heck. I can't report to work tomorrow in this condition."

She fiddled with a cup and tea bag, poured water from the kettle, and set the drink in front of him. Bringing her own mug to the table, she settled into her usual chair. "I take it the new case is a tough one."

Frowning, he grabbed a napkin from the holder and folded it into a small square. "The workload's going to be as heavy as a trunk full of bricks."

"And just who is going to watch Phoebe while you're on this *heavy* case?"

Instead of answering, he slouched in his chair and took a swallow of tea. It would probably taste a hell of a lot better if he added a healthy dollop of whiskey.

Rita Mae raised a brow. "I'm playing tennis with Marcella Henderson tomorrow morning, then I'm scheduled for a massage."

"It's not often I ask you to rearrange your plans, Mother."

"I'm well aware of that, just as I know you're aware of my reasons for not jumping at the chance to spend more time with my granddaughter. I love Phoebe Marie more than life, but I won't become your crutch. She needs a mother and you need a wife. It's high time you realized that fact and acted on it."

"We've been down this road a million times. I'm not in the market for a wife." Nathan set his jaw. "I don't want another relationship like the kind I had with Janet."

"Janet was a spoiled little girl who never grew up. Her father gave her everything, and she married thinking you would do the same. When you stood your ground and refused her demands, she thought having Phoebe would get you to change your mind. When that didn't work, she went her own way and to hell with you or your daughter."

Unfolding the napkin, he quickly crumpled it into a ball. "Do you know how high the divorce rate is among law enforcement officials? I'd rather have no wife at all than one who left me because I refused to change professions. Phoebe couldn't take another loss, and after Phoebe police work is my life."

Rita Mae rolled her eyes. "Take a look around, Nathan. Not all women are out to change a man, and there are many who would understand your drive to serve and protect. You just have to find the right one."

He drained his mug and set it gently on the table. "I can take care of Phoebe myself."

Rita Mae shook her head. "You're being stubborn, selfish and incredibly short-sighted."

"I can give her everything she wants. She doesn't need a mother."

Snorting delicately, she stood. "Oh, really? Then maybe you'll fill me in on how you plan to grant Phoebe the wish she made when you took her to see Santa?" Walking to the door, she turned. "I'd be very interested to hear how you plan to give her a baby sister for Christmas."

Nathan sighed. "Very funny. Just let me know if you can

watch Phoebe tomorrow morning. I'm going to have to scramble for a sitter if you refuse."

"Don't worry," Rita Mae said, heading to the rear landing. "I'll take care of everything."

Eight

At the sound of the ringing telephone, Eloise stifled a groan. She'd spent a miserable night, tossing and turning while she dreamed about Nathan and his heart-wrenching reaction to Phoebe's pseudo-kidnapping. Never, even when he'd been arguing with Janet, had she seen him so upset or vulnerable. It made her queasy to think she'd been the cause of so much pain, but she refused to shoulder the entire blame. He'd been late. She'd done what she believed was best at the time, just like his mother had said.

She'd been willing to apologize, but he'd acted like such a jerk, glaring at her and Ms. Hewitt and bossing Phoebe's grandmother around, that she'd done the only thing that made sense at the time—run from the Hewitt Academy as fast as her legs could take her. She'd had no intention of humbling herself in the presence of his police buddies and whoever else was listening, especially when it hadn't been her fault—at least not entirely.

When the shrill ringing continued, she seriously considered ignoring it. Only Milton, Junior and Honoria Hewitt had access to this number, and she couldn't imagine either heavenly being sending her a wake-up call. That left the headmistress and after last evening's debacle, she was fairly certain what the woman would have to say. Ready to be removed from her teaching position, Eloise lunged at the receiver and steeled herself for her dismissal.

"Hello."

"Is this Ms. Starr? Ms. Eloise Starr?"

At the sound of the vaguely familiar voice, she struggled to sit upright on the mattress. "Yes. Who is this?"

"We met last night, Ms. Starr, in front of the Hewitt Academy. Unfortunately, things were a little too intense for us to be properly introduced. My name is Rita Mae Baxter, Phoebe Marie's grandmother. I apologize for calling at such an early hour, but I wanted to catch you before you began your day."

Swinging her legs over the side of the bed, Eloise sat at attention. Good grief, it was barely light outside. What in the world did the woman want?

"Is something wrong, Mrs. Baxter? Is Phoebe all right?"

"My granddaughter is fine. She's sitting beside me eating breakfast and dying to talk to you, as a matter of fact. We're trying to organize our appointments and I'm hoping you'll accept our offer."

"Your offer?"

"Phoebe's going to watch me play tennis this morning, then she's getting a manicure while I have my massage. We were hoping you could join us for lunch. There's a charming, child-friendly restaurant in the neighborhood, and I'd like to meet you there so I can thank you properly for last night."

Eloise remembered every second of the evening, before, during and after she'd returned Phoebe to the school. Unlike her son, Mrs. Baxter hadn't been rude, and she'd acted genuinely contrite for her part in the fiasco. Nathan, on the other hand, had made her head hurt and her stomach ache. She'd felt his pain like a blow and the sensation had sent her reeling. She'd been so upset when she'd arrived back at her apartment that she'd taken another shower just to calm down.

"Does your son know about this invitation, Mrs. Baxter?"

"Nathan? Why do you ask?"

"Because I got the impression he didn't want me spend-

ing any more time than necessary with his daughter. In all
honesty, I thought you were Honoria Hewitt calling to fire
me, and I fully expected to hear that she was doing so at his
request."

Her amused laughter forced Eloise to smile. "Nonsense.
Nathan was simply tired and upset. He takes his job and his
fatherly duties very seriously. The fact that his arrangements
for Phoebe didn't turn out as he'd planned embarrassed
him."

"Even so, I don't want to come home to my apartment
and find him here ready to place me under arrest." After last
night she wouldn't put it past him to clap her in handcuffs
the next time she did something he considered unlawful.

"That's not going to happen. Now hang on. Someone else
wants to talk to you."

"Please, Ms. Eloise," Phoebe added to the conversation,
"I really want you to have lunch with us. Grammy says it's
okay, and she's the boss of me when Daddy isn't around."

"Hear that?" Mrs. Baxter interjected, regaining control
of the phone. "I'm the boss when my son isn't here. And I
insist."

Eloise thought of all the reasons there were for her *not* to
get involved, then remembered what she'd been told by Junior. Befriending Nathan and his daughter was the key to
finding her way back to heaven. The sooner she accepted
that idea, the sooner she would reach her goal.

"Please, Ms. Starr. It would make Phoebe happy." The
older woman's sincerity pulsed through the phone line. "If
you must know, it would make me feel better, too. I'm
equally at fault for what happened. If I'd been more on the
ball, the entire incident could have been avoided."

Guilt, Eloise knew, was an emotion that led many humans on a path of self-destruction. It wasn't healthy and it
certainly never changed things. When a situation was finished, it was finished. Humans had to learn to grow from
the incident, forget it and move on.

"All right," she finally said. "Just tell me what time and where and I'll be there."

After hanging up the phone, she walked to her bedroom window and gazed through the frost-glazed glass. The forbidding winter sky reminded her of Nathan's expression when he'd glared at her on the school landing. How was she supposed to learn about faith, hope and love from a man who thought she was so irresponsible she was actually capable of endangering a child?

Milton had accused her of being unforgiving and not very understanding of her human charges and maybe, just maybe, he'd been correct. Until last night, she'd never known what it felt like to be a human in the middle of a crisis—worse, to be the one who'd caused it. From the look of it, Nathan truly did care more for Phoebe than his job, but was having a difficult time balancing the two.

And now Rita Mae Baxter was inviting her to lunch.

Eloise went to her closet and searched for something presentable to wear. She was sick and tired of dressing like a drudge. The jeans she'd worn last evening fit her well enough, but the sweater was dull, dull, dull. Surely she owned at least one dress, blouse or skirt that had a little color, a bit of style, a dash of pizzazz?

She snatched a blouse off a hanger and decided snowy white had to be better than funeral-parlor black. Then she realized she had the entire morning ahead of her. There were a few shops in the nearby area; maybe if she walked to the business district and did a bit of window shopping, she would find something presentable. She'd watched several of her charges use a checkbook, and it seemed simple enough.

It was time to do as Junior suggested and start living life as a human. Especially since it was the only way she was going to get back into heaven.

* * *

Smiling at a teasing remark Phoebe made to her grand-mother, Eloise swallowed the last of her grilled cheese sandwich. She had a shopping bag at her feet filled with new clothes, and she was having a fun time with the little girl and her grandma. It was turning out to be a nice day.

The affection the child and the older woman shared had come alive at the table, with Mrs. Baxter acting more like a friend than an authority figure. Dressed in tailored tan slacks, a black-and-tan-checked sweater and chic-looking leather boots, she looked almost young enough to be Phoebe's mother.

She had made Eloise feel welcome and comfortable from the moment they'd met, and right now Eloise was listening to her lunch companions tell stories about Nathan. Phoebe and her grandmother hadn't exactly been poking fun at him, but they had been enjoying a few laughs at his expense.

"One time, when I was helpin' Daddy train the German shepherds, I tricked him, and told him the squirt gun was empty, and you know what he did? He pointed it at his face and got himself all wet," Phoebe said with a giggle. "I laughed and laughed, and he said I was gonna get tickled. Then he chased me round and round the yard until he caught me."

"And where was I while all this soggy silliness was going on?" Mrs. Baxter asked, winking at Eloise.

"You were here and we were at the first lake house. Daddy says the second one is almost finished. He promised he'd take me for a visit over Christmas vacation."

Mrs. Baxter turned her attention to Eloise. "My husband built a modest cabin, the first lake house as Phoebe calls it, in the woods surrounding Lake Mary when we were newly married. After his wife passed away, Nathan got it in his head that he and Phoebe needed a larger, more mod-ern place to spend time together, so he started construction on a second house last year. I haven't been to see it yet, but from what Phoebe tells me it's impressive."

Eloise was familiar with each house but couldn't let on that she'd been to either one. "What's the new one like?"

"It's really really big and it's got lots'a windows. You can see the lake from Daddy's room and mine, too. There's another room for Grammy and two for guests, and about a hundred bathrooms." Phoebe dipped a French fry in her ketchup. "Daddy says I can invite a friend the next time we go there."

"That sounds like fun," Eloise said. "You and your friend could bring your Christmas presents and play with them there."

A look of frustration crossed Phoebe's face as she took a bite of crispy potato, chewed, then swallowed. "I don't think I'm gettin' any presents this year. Daddy told me this morning that I can't have what I wished for."

"Oh?" Mrs. Baxter sipped at her mineral water. "And what is it that you wanted?"

"You already know, Grammy. I don't wanna tell you again."

"Not tell me again? Then I suppose I'll have to guess." She tapped a red-painted nail to her chin. "Is it a pony?"

Phoebe squealed out a burst of laughter. "Not a pony. That's silly."

"Wait, I know. You want an elephant."

"Grammy! A'nelifant's too big to fit in Santa's sleigh. You got to guess again."

Mrs. Baxter reached out and poked the little girl in her tummy. "Didn't you want a dinosaur after you saw that last Disney cartoon?"

"No-oo. I keep telling you and telling you, I want a baby sister. Remember?"

"Oh, that's right." She folded her arms and sat back in her chair. "And what was the reason your father gave for Santa not being able to grant your wish?"

Phoebe swirled another French fry in ketchup and held it in the air. "Daddy said Santa isn't the one who brings babies to people. It's the stork that brings 'em, but only to mommies and daddies, not little girls. That's why I'm not supposed to expect a baby sister for Christmas."

"He said all that, did he?" The older woman's brown eyes twinkled as she glanced at Eloise. "Then I guess a clever girl would wish for something that would eventually get her what she wanted."

Phoebe's pale brows drew together in contemplation. Rubbing at her nose, she said, "Can't you give me a baby sister for Christmas? It's all I'm askin' for this year."

"Sorry, sweetie," quipped Mrs. Baxter. "Grammy's hormones are on permanent vacation. You're on your own in the baby sister department."

"What's hormones?"

She sighed. "Something you'll find out about all too soon, I'm afraid. Now, how was your grilled cheese?"

"I finished, see? And so did Ms. Eloise."

"You really didn't have to order off the children's menu," she offered, eyeing Eloise's plate. "I could have afforded to buy you a grown-up lunch."

"The sandwich was perfect. I don't eat meat."

"Ah, I see. Well, if you're sure you had enough—"

"How come you don't eat meat?" asked Phoebe. "Don't you like it?"

"Well," Eloise began, giving the only explanation she thought might make sense to a child. "I don't believe in killing animals. They don't eat us, so why should we eat them?"

"I like baloney sandwiches, but I like peanut butter and jelly better. That's not meat."

"There you go. Just think of all those chickens, cows and pigs that will live a longer life because you aren't going to gobble them up for dinner."

"I don't like pigs," said Phoebe, wrinkling her nose. "They're dirty and they smell yucky."

"So I've heard. But just because an animal smells bad

doesn't mean it should be killed," Eloise blurted. "I mean, I don't think a pig should be held accountable for his smell, do you? He is a pig, after all." Glancing from Phoebe to her grandmother, she realized she'd spoken without thinking and muttered, "If you believe in that sort of thing, of course."

Mrs. Baxter seemed to study Eloise as she spoke. "You have a delightfully simplistic way of explaining things. I take it you enjoy teaching small children?"

"Yes, I do," Eloise admitted with a nod. Not owning up to their opinions was one of the things that irked her the most about humans, and she was not going to follow in their apathetic footsteps. Besides, she really did like being with her students—most of the time.

"And have you always been a vegetarian?"

"For as long as I've been on earth," she said, pleased she was able to tell the truth.

"I've done some reading and I've heard vegetarians live long healthy lives. I imagine all those veggies and whole grains keep the system on track and . . . well oiled."

Averse to answering any more personal questions, Eloise pushed away from the table. "Thank you again for lunch, Mrs. Baxter."

"Please, call me Rita Mae. And what's your hurry? I thought we might sit and have a cup of tea together. Phoebe, would you like some dessert?"

"Nu-uh, I'm full."

"Well then, let me get the check." Rita Mae grabbed her purse just as her cell phone began to ring. "Excuse me." She flipped open the phone and glanced at the number. "Hello?" She chuckled at whatever the caller was saying, then bit at her lower lip. "I already told you I can't make our appointment. I have to watch Phoebe and Nathan has no idea when he'll be home . . . I did try a few friends this morning, but they were all busy. Don't you pick up your messages?"

Rita Mae's finely sculpted cheekbones turned bright pink

at her caller's answer. If Eloise had to guess, she'd think the woman was talking to a man.

"I'm, sorry. I simply can't," Rita Mae continued, "unless—" She gave Eloise a hope-filled smile. "Ms. Starr—Eloise. I hate to impose, but I'm in a bit of a bind and I need a favor. Would it be possible for you to take Phoebe to our home and wait for me there?"

Eloise felt hot and cold at the same time. It was one thing to be Phoebe's kindergarten teacher and rescue her from staying alone at school, but going to Nathan's house?

"Oh, no. I don't think I should—"

Phoebe began to dance around the table. "Please, Ms. Eloise. Please? I'll be really good. I won't talk a lot and I'll sit still and everything."

Rita Mae's expression was pleading. "I can give you the keys and the security combination and you can let yourself in. If it's a matter of money, I'll pay you. And I promise I won't be more than an hour or two."

"Please," asked Phoebe once again.

"I would never take your money," said Eloise. But the fact that the woman offered her cash meant it had to be serious. And she didn't have anything planned for the afternoon, except to go home and try on her new clothes . . .

"When did you say Nathan would be home?"

"Late. Very late. I'll do my best to return long before he gets there. Word of honor."

Eloise sighed. Phoebe's grandmother had been so nice, and it sounded as if she truly did have a problem. "All right. If you're certain—"

Rita Mae gave her a grateful smile, then informed her caller she'd join him shortly. Phoebe jumped up and down beside her chair. "Yeah! Yeah! Yeah!"

Eloise only wished she could feel so elated.

* * *

"I hope I showed the proper appreciation for your being so prompt with that phone call this afternoon," murmured Rita Mae. "It was perfect timing."

"Your timing's pretty damn good too. I just wish I knew what you had up your sleeve, leaving me that message on my answering machine this morning with an exact time to call."

"Never you mind," she responded. "I promise you'll be the first to know if my idea works out."

Joseph Milligan settled the woman in his arms closer to his chest. "If you say so." Sighing contentedly, he shifted to face her. "I'm tired of sneaking around, Rita Mae. It was a real pain in the rear having to put on a poker face the other day when Nathan invited me over to sample your cooking. Damn near made me laugh out loud."

Rita Mae stretched contentedly on the king-size mattress, basking in the afterglow of several hours of fantastic sex. With his steel gray hair, black eyebrows and broad-muscled chest, Joe was a man any woman with a pulse would be drawn to. The idea that her son wanted her to prepare a meal for him was almost ludicrous, seeing as she and the police captain had been busy sampling each other for the past six months.

"I need a little more time, Joe," she said, snuggling comfortably into his side. "Phoebe still misses her mother, and even though Nathan and Janet weren't getting along, he's grieving the loss as well. I just wouldn't feel right leaving them when they're so . . . unsettled. Especially since you returned Nathan to full duty."

Joe turned so that Rita Mae was completely enfolded in his embrace. "Don't blame your refusal to commit on me. No matter our personal involvement, it was high time Nathan got back on the street. Now that I've convinced you the age thing is no big deal, I want us to be together in every way. I think we should get married."

Rita Mae felt her cheeks warm. Joseph Milligan was an unattached male who, after his performance in bed this afternoon, had proved himself as capable as any twenty-year-old in the whoopee department. He'd hinted at a permanent relationship in the past, but this was the first time he'd actually brought up the subject out loud, and she wasn't sure whether to act pleasantly surprised or thoroughly annoyed. If this was the man's idea of a marriage proposal, it was sadly lacking in the romance department.

"Are you proposing to me?"

Joe blinked, as if he just realized what he'd said. "Well, yeah. I guess I am."

His simple statement put Rita Mae's stomach in a tangle. She'd admitted to herself months ago that she was head over heels in love with him, and she knew in her heart Joe felt the same about her—even if he'd never said the words. At times like this, she wondered why she'd resisted him for so long, but then her common sense took hold and she admitted she knew the reason. Even though she'd been completely taken with his charm and never-take-no-for-an-answer attitude, the fact that he was her son's senior by a mere fourteen years still rankled.

She was the older woman, and would be so forever. No matter whether they married or not, Rita Mae would always feel as if she had robbed the cradle.

"I'm not sure I'll ever be able to marry you, Joseph Milligan," she said with an indrawn breath. Though she'd considered the next words from time to time, she had never thought there would be a need to say them. "But I might be persuaded to move in with you."

"Move in with me?" His sexy mouth quirked up at the corners as he warmed to the idea. "And live with me in sin? Wow, I really have corrupted you."

Frowning, she poked him in the ribs. "Don't be cute. It only reminds me of how young you are."

"I'm forty-seven, Rita Mae. Last time I did the math, we were only about five years apart in age."

"When you were in the eighth grade, I was a senior in high school," she lectured. "I could have been your baby-sitter."

His gray eyes twinkled under waggling eyebrows. "And the games we could have played—"

"Would have been illegal," she snapped.

"And all the more fun." He dropped a kiss on her temple. "Stay for a while and let me cook for you."

"Are you telling me you're free tonight?"

"If you can stay, I can be free."

Rita Mae sighed. They had met at Janet's funeral. When he'd first asked her out about a week later, she'd danced around what she'd known to be the real issue and told him it was too soon—that she had to be available for Phoebe and Nathan. After he'd persisted, she'd taken great pains to point out the difference in their ages. It was then he'd informed her that he was well aware of how old she was because he'd already quizzed her son. After that revelation, she'd refused his phone calls for six months, then made him grovel to get back in her good graces.

They'd had several private dinners out of the area, until their fifth date when she'd let herself be coerced into going to his house for a quiet lunch. Six hours later, after the most intense-yet-tender sex she'd ever experienced, they'd eaten the meal in bed. Since then, provided he could slip away from work, they'd met once or twice a week, always in the afternoon at his home, when she knew Phoebe was in school and Nathan was on duty.

"Thanks to your phone call, I have someone to watch over Phoebe, so I suppose it could be arranged," she said with a lazy smile. She needed someplace to be for a few more hours. Where better than in Joe's arms?

"Yeah? So who did you get? And why do I have the feeling that if Nathan knew about it, there'd be hell to pay?"

Rita Mae tugged at his chest hairs, smiling when he muttered a wounded *ouch*. "Don't be so certain I'm up to no good. Once Nathan sees that I've found him the right woman, he's going to thank me."

Joe drew a sharp breath. "Oh my God. You fixed him

up?" When she didn't answer, his nicely corded belly began to rumble with laughter. It took a full minute before he said, "Son of a gun—Nate is dating. Who's the woman? Do I know her?"

"No, but you will if I have anything to say about it. And if you even hint that I was matchmaking, this is going to be our last time together."

Joe shook his head. "Honey, there isn't a person in the world who wants Nate to be happy more than me." He chuckled again. "So how are things going?"

"Unfortunately, they're not, but I'm doing my best."

"Hot dog. That means if it works out, he and Phoebe will be someone else's worry and you'll be free to take care of me for, oh, say the next thirty years or so."

Over the course of their relationship, Joe had proved himself to be considerate and caring, but still very much *a man*. Even so, Rita Mae enjoyed the idea of being needed in a way that made her feel like a woman instead of a housekeeper.

"I was thinking maybe we could take care of each other," she said hesitantly. The passion she felt for him was so remarkable, it sometimes frightened her. She only hoped she'd found the woman who would make her son feel the same. "If your serious about that proposal."

His smile started slowly, then built to a face-splitting grin. "You just tell me what I have to do to get Nathan married off and it's a done deal, sweetheart. Now how about we go back a couple of years? You be the baby-sitter and I'll be the bad little boy you've been hired to watch. I can think of about a dozen different games I'd like to play, if you're interested."

Suddenly feeling like a schoolgirl, Rita Mae giggled. Despite her age, the police captain had a certain charm she found completely irresistible. "You are a naughty boy, Joseph Milligan. A very naughty boy."

Nine

Eloise stood in the entryway of the Baxter house and tapped out the numbers Rita Mae had given her to disarm the security system. "Are you sure I'm doing this right?"

"Uh-huh," answered Phoebe, nodding her head. "I've watched Daddy do it lots'a times. See—the green light is blinking. That means we're safe."

Noting the light, Eloise felt better. It would be just her luck for the alarm to sound at police headquarters, which would send squad cars screaming to the house. If that happened, Nathan would have her arrested for certain.

After setting down her packages, she gazed around the foyer. A gilded oval mirror and cherrywood table graced one side of the foyer, while a spindle-backed bench with a floral seat cushion rested against the stairway wall. Turning to the right, she peered into a charming room framed with windows and filled with gleaming dark wood furniture. Matching love seats with yellow-and-blue-flowered upholstery flanked a fireplace faced with shiny brass doors. Glossy hardwood floors peeked from beneath a plush navy blue area rug. Through a large archway farther down, she could see a sparkling brass-and-crystal chandelier hanging above a polished table; yellow-and-blue-striped wallpaper covered the wall over a white-painted chair rail, while a huge china cabinet sat against a far corner of the dining room.

The classy interior had to have been Janet's doing, because Eloise couldn't imagine Nathan as the decorator.

Both rooms were perfect and untouched, like pictures from a magazine.

"What'cha lookin' at?" asked Phoebe, standing by her side.

"That's a very pretty room. Do you play in there?"

"Nu-uh. Daddy says it has'ta stay neat for company, but we don't get too many visitors. When my friends come over, we play in the den."

"And where is that?"

"Next to the kitchen in the back. I'll show you, but first you gotta put your pocketbook and shopping bag on the foyer table, then you have to take off your coat and hang it in the front closet. Mine goes in the mudroom in back."

Phoebe took off her mittens and opened a door under the stairs. As commanded, Eloise deposited her bags on the table, hung up her coat and closed the closet door. "Now what?"

"We go to the kitchen," answered Phoebe, continuing down the hall.

They walked past a small-but-elegant powder room and what Eloise assumed was a pantry, under an archway and into a spacious kitchen. Light oak cabinets covered two walls; dark green counters and brilliant white appliances ringed the room. A table and four chairs in the same wood as the cabinets snuggled into a niche complete with a bay window, matching draperies and chair pads. Compared to the living and dining areas, this room, with its lingering aroma of freshly baked cookies, felt warm and inviting.

"I have to hang up my stuff," pronounced Phoebe.

Eloise propped herself against a counter while Phoebe struggled out of her coat and hat. Someone, probably Nathan, had mounted a series of hooks at kiddie level so the little girl could put away her clothes. She spotted Nathan's more manly outerwear on the upper row: a heavy brown jacket on one peg, a matching scarf and gloves on another, and next to them an olive-drab rain slicker.

Phoebe stepped into the kitchen and went to the table. "I'm gonna make hot chocolate. Do you want some?"

Curious, Eloise raised a brow. "You know how to make hot chocolate? Aren't you a little young to be using the stove?"

"Grammy taught me how to work the microwave, so it's okay." Phoebe dragged a chair across the shiny black-and-white tiles, situated it next to the counter and climbed up, then took down a box of cocoa mix. After opening another cupboard, she retrieved two yellow mugs. "Do you want to help?"

"Sure," Eloise said, fascinated by the five-year-old's competency. Phoebe had been acting like a cross between General Patton and Miss Manners since they'd come through the front door, but Eloise didn't mind. She was totally out of her element in a kitchen. "What do you want me to do?"

Phoebe handed her the mugs and packets of chocolate. "Open these and dump one into each cup, then fill 'em with water, but not all the way."

Again, Eloise did as she was told. "Now what?"

After shoving the chair to the microwave, Phoebe scrambled up and opened the door. "You need a spoon—they're in the drawer right there." She pointed. "You have to stir until everything is mixed really good; then give me the cups and I'll do the rest."

Eloise followed orders. Phoebe set the mugs inside the oven, closed the door and pushed buttons until the machine began to hum.

"Are you sure it's all right for you to do this by yourself?"

"Grammy says so, but she told me if I did it in front of Daddy he might get sad. I'm supposed to let him be useful and make hot chocolate when we're together, so he'll feel important." She peered into the window of the still-running appliance. "You're company, so it's okay."

Eloise grinned. Rita Mae was teaching her granddaughter to be competent and feminine at the same time, something Eloise was aware she still needed to learn.

The timer rang and Phoebe removed a mug and handed

it over. "Be careful, 'cause it's hot. You need to stir some more while I get the milk from the refrigerator. If you pour a little in the cup, the chocolate gets cool and creamy."

Five minutes later, they were enjoying their drinks at the kitchen table. Eloise sipped the dark, rich taste slowly while Phoebe swallowed the mixture in a few long, greedy gulps.

"Do I have a mustache?" The little girl held out her chin for inspection.

"No," Eloise answered. "How about me?"

Phoebe checked while Eloise turned her face from side to side. "Nu-uh. Wanna come upstairs?"

Eloise took both mugs to the sink and rinsed them. She'd never watched a child before, but she knew it was a full-time job. Phoebe was old enough to be on her own for part of the time, but the most caring humans never left children her age alone for long. The better ones even *played* with their kids. And she was determined to be one of the better ones.

"What's upstairs?"

Phoebe slid off the seat, then pushed her chair and Eloise's neatly into the table. "Besides my room, there's a guest room and a couple of bathrooms and Daddy's bedroom, plus a room that was mine when I was a baby, but it's empty now. I have dollies and games and books for us to play with. Come on." She walked to the front hall. "I want to show you something special."

Phoebe's room was the first one on the right at the top of the stairs. She took Eloise by the hand and walked her to the dresser. She dropped to her knees and Eloise did the same; then she opened a bottom drawer and rummaged until she found what she was looking for.

"This was my Mommy's perfume." She took out a cut-glass bottle with a dribble of yellow liquid in the bottom and inhaled a big breath. "Do you like it?"

Good question, thought Eloise. As an angel she'd never had to worry about smells. Now that she was human, she could experience hundreds of different scents. She sniffed the almost-empty bottle. The aroma was pungent and exotic, not a scent she would feel comfortable wearing.

"It's not exactly what I'd put on," she said, careful of hurting Phoebe's feelings.

The little girl capped the bottle and set it back in the drawer. "What kind'a perfume do you like?"

"I'm not sure. Maybe something light and fresh, like rain on a warm spring afternoon or the scent of grass in a meadow full of flowers. I don't wear a lot of perfume."

"Me neither," Phoebe echoed. "Grammy says I'm too little, but I can use it to remember."

"You should listen to your grandmother. She's a smart lady." Where the heck was Rita Mae, anyway?

Phoebe dug deeper and pulled out a photo album. "This is a picture of Mommy and Daddy when they got married." She gazed at the glossy snapshot of Janet in her wedding veil and dress, smiling for the camera. "Sometimes I need to stare at her for a really long time, just to remember what she looked like."

Eloise closed her eyes, unable to speak. How much more of Janet's life was she supposed to endure before she could excuse herself? If she'd known what she was getting into, she never would have said yes to coming upstairs.

Leaning into the drawer again, Phoebe brought out an ornately edged picture frame. "Here's me and Mommy right after I was born."

The lump that had lodged in Eloise's chest the moment she'd sat down began to swell. Janet had complained that her stitches hurt and she wanted to sleep, but Nathan had insisted on taking the photo.

She stared intently at the image of the human whose soul she had thrown away. Attractive and dark-haired with her lips set in a petulant smile, Janet was holding a tiny bundle swaddled in pink. Maybe, if she hadn't given up on Janet so soon, the woman would have found the strength to be a real mother to her daughter, if only for a short while. If she'd been able to turn Janet around before she'd been called back to heaven—

"I was only one day old when Daddy took the picture," said Phoebe, as if Eloise hadn't the brains to figure it out. "He said I was perfect."

And you were, Eloise thought. *You still are.*

"Where's your mommy?" asked Phoebe, breaking the spell. "Does she live around here?"

Eloise blinked. "What? Um . . . no. I don't have a mother."

"Do you miss her?"

"I try not to think about it," she managed, avoiding the need to tell a lie.

Phoebe set the photo back in the drawer and brought out a gold locket hanging from a chain. Before Eloise knew what she was up to, Phoebe draped the chain over Eloise's head and onto her neck. "Here, you can have this."

She started to take it off, but the unhappy expression on Phoebe's face stopped her short. "I can't accept this."

"But it's just jewelry. Don't you like jewelry?"

"I don't think your dad would approve if he knew you were giving your mother's things away."

"It's mine and I can give it to whoever I want," Phoebe answered in a soft but stubborn voice. "You can take out the pictures and put one of your mom and you inside. It will remind you of her and then you won't be sad."

Eloise snapped open the locket and her heart gave a flip-flop. On one side was a picture of Janet, on the other a photo of Phoebe as a spun-gold, bright-eyed toddler.

"You can use it when you have a little girl of your own."

"I . . . um . . . it takes two people to get a baby. The stork only brings them to mommies and daddies, remember?"

"So how come you haven't found a daddy, so you can have a baby?"

Eloise shifted on the floor and rose to her knees. "I

haven't really looked for one. It's not easy finding the right daddy—I mean man to marry, you know."

Phoebe closed the drawer and stood, as if the matter was settled. "My daddy isn't married. I think you should—"

Nathan held back a curse as he watched the late afternoon sky turn a deep gunmetal gray. Storm clouds had rolled in and the scent of snow hung heavy in the air. He'd spent the day investigating a robbery that had taken place early in the morning at a neighborhood convenience store much too close to Georgetown for him to be comfortable.

Young men, barely out of their teens according to witnesses, had committed their third heist in as many weeks, and this one had ended in a death. He was going to have to remind Rita Mae to stay out of that type of establishment when she took her morning walk, just in case the perps widened their scope of operation.

Bone weary, Nathan parked his SUV and walked up the steps to his home. His mother's car was nowhere in sight, which meant she and Phoebe were out shopping for groceries or walking a local mall. If he knew Rita Mae, they'd overhauled Phoebe's Christmas wish and were visiting one of those Santa-suited fat men to make sure whatever her new request was went to the top of the list.

It had almost killed him when he'd tried to make Phoebe understand that her wish for a baby sister was not going to happen. She'd shed a few tears, but in the end she'd said okay. Except it wasn't—not really. She was lonely and he and Rita Mae were no replacement for a sibling.

He shuddered at the thought of having to explain the whole facts of life—birds and bees thing—to his daughter, but maybe it was time. As much as he'd like to push the chore onto Rita Mae's shoulders, it was his responsibility as her father. If Phoebe learned that it took two committed parents and not one ham-handed dad to make a baby, maybe she'd stop pestering.

He unlocked the front door and took care of the alarm, then walked to the back of the house to hang up his jacket. Spotting Phoebe's coat on its usual peg, he figured she and Rita Mae were upstairs. His mother had probably parked in the alley behind the house, as she did when she had to bring in groceries. He guessed she and Phoebe were in her third-floor apartment doing whatever they did to amuse themselves when he wasn't around.

He had time for a shower, maybe even a quick nap before dinner. He was beat. In between filling out paperwork and talking to witnesses, he'd done nothing but think about what had happened last night at the Hewitt Academy. Somehow, he had to find a way to apologize to Eloise and still get his point across.

Phoebe was his kid, and the kindergarten teacher had to stay out of their lives. She'd pretty much given her word she would remain in her teaching position until the end of the year, and that was all he wanted from her. The attraction he felt toward Eloise was purely physical and he had to control it. Getting involved on a personal level had been a dumb idea from the get-go. He didn't need another woman in his life and neither did his daughter.

Back in the foyer, he spotted a large black purse and shopping bag on the hall table. He'd been too preoccupied to notice the items when he'd come through the door, and now he wished he had. The handbag was all too familiar.

The sound of giggles and muted conversation carried down the stairs and he fisted his hands. He'd already made up his mind to apologize to Eloise for his earlier rash behavior, but he'd planned to do it at the school on Monday morning, not here in his own home. He was going to strangle his mother for allowing the woman in his house.

Silently counting to ten, Nathan headed up the stairs. He didn't want to frighten Phoebe by bursting into the room, but he did want to make his feelings clear once and for all. Eloise Starr may have infiltrated his fantasies, but he'd be damned if she was going to do the same with his life.

The stair runner muffled his footsteps as he arrived on the upper landing. He reached ten and start counting all over again, just in case he felt the urge to shout. Phoebe's room was on the right. His gut clenched at the sound of her wistful voice.

A sharp rap on the door saved Eloise from what she was certain would have been a very un-Kodak moment. She whipped her head around just as Phoebe jumped up and ran to her father.

"Daddy! You're home!"

Nathan swung his daughter in his arms and held her tightly against his chest. The blatantly protective gesture made Eloise want to scream. How dare he think she would hurt his child?

"Hi, punkin. Where's Grammy?" His dark eyes raked Eloise with a glare. "I thought she was going to be with you the whole day?"

Phoebe squirmed and he set her down. "We had lunch with Ms. Eloise, until Grammy got a phone call. She had to meet somebody, so she asked Ms. Eloise to stay with me."

"Lunch, huh?" Nathan stuck his hands in his pockets and propped himself against the door frame. "Who was the call from?"

"I don't know," Phoebe said. "I'm hungry. Are you gonna take us out to dinner?"

Eloise tucked the locket inside the collar of her blouse. She could return it to Phoebe at school, when they had more time to talk. Standing, she tried to shoulder her way past Nathan while she mumbled a good-bye. "I'll be leaving now. Excuse me."

"Hold on a second."

Nathan grabbed her by the arm. His touch was electric. She stopped in her tracks, but refused to meet his gaze.

"I want to have a word with Ms. Starr, punkin. How about you straighten up in here, then wash your face and hands. I'll call you when we're finished talking."

Bristling, Eloise headed into the hall and down the stairs with Nathan on her heels. Walking to the closet, she found her coat and shrugged it on. "I get the message," she hissed, staring at him. Watching her from the foyer, he looked as unmovable as a roadblock. "You don't want me spending time with Phoebe, and you're angry I'm in your home."

He sighed and ran a hand over his clenched jaw. "Look, I know I'm acting inhospitably, but seeing you in my daughter's room was a surprise. What were you doing having lunch with her and Rita Mae today?"

"Your mother was trying to make up for last night's fiasco. I met her and Phoebe at a restaurant she chose and we had lunch, then she got a call. Someone needed her and she begged me to baby-sit. She'd been so pleasant, I found it hard to refuse."

The flicker of a smile passed over his face. "Yeah, Rita Mae can be pretty persuasive when she wants."

"Besides, she promised she'd be home before you got here."

His knowing gaze pinned her in place as surely as if he'd nailed her feet to the floor. "So you were hoping to avoid me?"

"Well, duh! Just listen to yourself," Eloise huffed. "I'd be an idiot not to. You're practically tossing me out on my— my fanny. And don't think you fooled Phoebe with that 'Ms. Starr and I have to talk' line. She's more perceptive than you give her credit for."

"Don't try to tell me about my own daughter. You don't know a thing about her."

"I know more than you think. I'm her teacher, remember? I see her every day and I probably spend more hours with her than you do."

Nathan moved forward, his voice ringing in the air. "You know something? I think I *am* gonna throw you out."

Eloise sidestepped his looming bulk and grabbed at the doorknob. "Don't bother. I'm leaving. You—you—"

"Stop! Don't fight!" Phoebe's voice carried ahead of her as she raced down the stairs. With her sapphire blue eyes leaking tears, she stood on the bottom step and glared at her father. "Why are you yellin' at Ms. Eloise?"

Nathan's flustered gaze ping-ponged between them. "We weren't yelling. We were talking."

"You were shouting and you sounded mean." Sniffing, she swiped at her nose. "I like Ms. Eloise. I want her to have dinner with us."

"That's not necessary," Eloise said, resisting the urge to offer Phoebe comfort. "Besides, your father worked all day. I'm sure he's tired, and it's too late to cook. I'll just go home and—"

Nathan raised a hand. His voice lowered in pitch as he made an effort to be pleasant. "Phoebe's right. You were nice enough to do Rita Mae a favor, and I'm acting like a boor. Let me buy you dinner. Please?"

Torn between his surly attitude and Junior's haunting prediction for her future, she had nothing to say.

Nathan grinned at his daughter. "Why don't you get your coat and hat, while I try to convince Ms. Starr to join us?" The little girl skipped happily to the kitchen, and he gave Eloise a feeble smile. "I promise not to shout."

Surprised by his change of attitude, she closed her eyes and nodded. By the time Nathan retrieved his coat and she gathered her shopping bag, Phoebe had returned and taken her hand. Together, they walked out the door and down the stairs to the car.

Eloise walked beside Nathan and his daughter, pulling her coat tighter around her. They'd parked up the block from an

Italian restaurant that was supposed to be one of Phoebe's favorites. The restaurant, about a mile from the house, was in
a converted town home on a quiet side street, and if not for
the blustery weather Eloise might have suggested they walk.

After climbing a flight of stairs, Nathan held open a door
marked simply *Mama Lucy's,* and they went inside. Once
they hung up their coats, they were seated at a table covered
in a cheerful red-and-white-checked tablecloth.

Studying the menu, Nathan seemed more relaxed in the
muted glow of candlelight, softer somehow, which had
Eloise breathing a sigh of relief. Totally absorbed in coloring her place mat with the crayons provided by the hostess,
Phoebe seemed oblivious to their conversation.

"Besides being kid-friendly, this place serves good food.
I would have brought you here the other night, if you hadn't
wanted to try Chinese."

"I'm sure it will be fine," she said, pretending to be engrossed in the specials listed on a blackboard on a side wall.
"But I have money. You don't have to pay."

"Hey, I owe you. Besides, it makes my daughter happy."

Eloise ran a finger over the condensation on her water
glass. "My guess is we were both taken in by someone's
good intentions today. I get the feeling Rita Mae didn't
show up before you came home on purpose."

"Gee, whatever gave you that idea?" he asked, flashing
his first real smile of the night. "Don't let yourself get
scammed by my mother. She only wants you to *think* she's
innocent. In her heart, she's a meddler and a busybody and
I—"

"What's a dizzy-body, Daddy?" asked Phoebe, who was
still coloring diligently.

Nathan rolled his eyes. "A *busybody* is someone who
likes to stick their nose into things that don't concern them.
Your Grammy is an expert. Now tell me, what did the two
of you do this morning?"

"I watched Grammy play tennis, then she took me to the

place where she gets massages. I got a manicure." Phoebe tore her gaze from the place mat and held up her pink-tipped fingers. "See?"

"Very nice." He turned to Eloise and gave a lazy grin. "What did you have for lunch?"

"Ms. Eloise and I had grilled cheese 'cause we don't eat meat. We're *bed*getarians."

"Is that so?"

"Uh-huh. We don't eat animals 'cause they don't eat us."

"I see. Well, I guess that means no more pepperoni pizza, or hot dogs, huh? We'll just have to survive on macaroni and cheese, or—"

"Peanut butter and jelly." Phoebe slid to the floor and pointed to a huge glass fish tank near the rest rooms. "Can I go look at the 'quarium?"

"After you tell me what you want."

"I'll have whatever Ms. Eloise is having," she said. "Now can I go?"

"Sure, but stay in sight. And don't stick your hand or anything else in the water."

The waitress came to take their order, and Eloise asked for pasta primavera.

"Make that two," said Nathan, "and I'll have the veal special with a glass of the house red." He nodded at Eloise. "Would you like something to drink, maybe a glass of wine?"

"Just water, thank you."

He leaned back and folded his arms across his chest. "I suppose you're going to lecture me on the health hazards of eating meat."

She shot him an expression of infinite patience. "If I didn't lecture you at the Chinese restaurant, I'm certainly not going to do it now. Everyone has to make their own choices in life. Mine just don't involve killing animals for food."

"What about eggs? The kind we get from the grocery store are unfertilized."

"Then I eat eggs."

"Milk?"

"Cows were put on earth to feed calves and humans alike."

"Look, Eloise—"

"It's Ms. Starr to you, and do not even think of berating me for my beliefs in front of Phoebe, or anyone else."

"Nope. Not me. Just the opposite, in fact."

"Go on."

He cleared his throat. "I'm sorry for the way I reacted last night at the school."

Not quite sure of his meaning, she arched a brow. "Don't you mean *overreacted?*"

His expression grew sincere. "Okay, overreacted. The thing is, I'm sorry. Sorry for being late to pick up my daughter, sorry for flying off the handle—What the hell, I'm sorry for being me, okay? I jumped to conclusions and I was wrong."

A strange tingling of warmth spread upward from Eloise's chest to her cheeks. Nathan was apologizing? She'd never apologized to anyone, ever, even when she'd suspected she might be wrong. Remembering how she'd hurt last night, when she realized the pain she'd caused him, she thought that maybe it was time she did. After all, it was the *human* thing to do.

"I'm sorry, too," she answered, sucking in a breath.

"You are?"

"I shouldn't have taken Phoebe off school grounds. I should have exercised more patience and figured you would show up eventually. Which you did." She fiddled with her napkin. "I caused you a great deal of worry, and I'm sorry."

His eyes crinkled at the corners. "Hey, no problem. Rita Mae has promised to be there for Phoebe, and barring unforeseen trouble, she's dependable as a rock."

"That's good. Children need stability in their lives."

"I'm glad to hear you say that, because I have to—I need

to ask you a favor." He gazed first at her, then over to Phoebe, who gave him a cheery little wave from the aquarium. "I want you to promise me something."

She clenched her hands together in her lap, squeezing her fingers until they ached. "If I can."

The waitress returned with Nathan's red wine and a glass of milk for Phoebe. He furrowed his fingers through his hair. "Look, if I promise to never again bring up what happened last night, can we start from scratch and be civil to each another?"

Eloise secretly breathed a sigh of relief. She needed Nathan to get back to heaven. Junior had said they were supposed to interact, get involved and become intimate in the most human of ways. The concept was suddenly more appealing than ever before.

"We can try."

"Phoebe likes you, but I don't want to see her hurt again. You said you were only going to stay until the end of the school year. Promise me that if you have to leave, you won't just disappear from her life. I don't want to be left holding the pieces of her broken heart, like I was when her mother died."

It will happen, she wanted to say. *It's what I'm going to have to do in order to return to heaven.*

She gave him a hesitant smile. "Don't worry about Phoebe. If I leave, I'll try my best to make sure she understands why."

Ten

"It's snowing!" Phoebe ran out the restaurant door and down the stairs onto the sidewalk, where she danced a little slip-and-slide. Spinning in place, she shouted, "Yeah! I love snow!"

Following right behind her, Eloise gave a silent cry of delight when she saw the fat cottony flakes. Raising her face skyward, she giggled when the fluffy white stuff tickled her nose and cheeks. Whirling in a circle of happiness, she closed her eyes and imagined she was floating in a mist high in the mountaintops, just as she'd done in her life as an angel.

The puffy white flakes swirled and drifted in the glow of the streetlights, blanketing whatever they touched in a protective covering of clean and calm. Everything looked pure and bright, as if the world were being given a fresh new start. She knew snow was cold, but it was wet too, and it smelled amazing—like frozen sunshine.

A flake stuck to her eyelashes and Eloise brushed it away. As an angel, she'd had no substance. More and more since becoming human, she realized the benefits of a body. She could smell, she could taste, she could feel. Why hadn't she thought about those exhilarating senses sooner?

"Careful," Nathan called when Phoebe skated to the edge of the walkway. "Don't go into the street."

Phoebe flashed a brilliant smile. "Can we make a snowman when we get home?"

Nathan took her hand. "Not tonight, but probably tomorrow. How about we listen to the radio and hear what the weatherman has to say."

He scooped Phoebe up in his arms and headed to their parking space. Eloise walked behind them, watching the little girl raise her hands over his head to capture snowflakes. Other pedestrians stepped lively on the slippery walk and she did the same until they arrived at the car. When Nathan ducked into the back to make sure Phoebe was buckled into her safety seat, Eloise couldn't resist sticking our her tongue to catch a cluster of frozen flakes. Smiling at the cool crisp taste, she shifted her gaze and found him staring at her over the roof.

"When was the last time you were in a snowstorm?"

"Not that long ago," she stammered.

"Then you didn't move here from down South?"

"I've been lots of places." She climbed into the front seat and he slid behind the wheel. Adjusting her seat belt, she kept her focus straight ahead. "Just drop me at the corner near my apartment building. I can manage the shopping bag by myself."

Nathan started the car. "Bear with me while I check out something first." He turned on the heater, then the radio and fiddled until he found a station giving the latest weather report. The prediction was iffy, but at the very least four inches would be on the ground by morning. If the storm hit full force, it might dump up to fifteen inches by tomorrow night.

Rubbing his hands together, he said gleefully, "Did you hear that? We could be in for a blizzard."

"I've heard blizzards can be dangerous."

"Not if people use their heads and stay off the road. Last winter we got hit with two feet in less than twenty-four hours. Phoebe and I made hot chocolate and built a snow fort in the backyard." He glanced in the rearview mirror. "Remember that one, punkin?"

Receiving no answer, he turned and found his daughter

slumped against the door fast asleep. Chuckling, he quirked up a corner of his mouth. "I should have figured. When she was a baby and she had a hard time falling asleep, all I had to do was get her inside a warm car and it was lights out. And from the sound of it, today was especially busy." He adjusted the heater and turned on his windshield wipers, then snapped his seat belt into place. Before putting the car in reverse, he pressed a button on the center console.

"What are you doing?"

"Turning on the four-wheel drive. I don't use it much in the city, but it comes in handy when I'm on our property at Lake Mary. I expect the roads are only going to get worse as the storm moves in."

After backing out, Nathan concentrated on his driving. Once he eased into traffic, he found a station playing classical music and lowered the volume. The quiet strains filled the car, taking the edge off the tension of the drive.

Now toasty warm, the inside of the SUV felt like a haven amid the swirling cocoon of white. Traffic was moving at a slow but steady pace. Glare from the overhead pole lamps cast bands of shadow and light into the car, alternately illuminating and shading Eloise's face.

She shifted in her seat and the light reflected off the glittering snow, washing her with a silvery glow. Nathan couldn't help but smile when he saw that her eyes were closed, just like Phoebe's. He had always thought her an attractive woman, but until now he had never studied her. She was lovely with delicate, clearly formed features. Her brows were dark over heavily-lashed eyes and her nose was small and straight. Her full mouth sat in a tempting line above a finely carved jaw.

He realized he was ogling and shook his head. He'd been thinking of Eloise in the most basic of terms practically since the day they'd met, and this was the first time he'd been able to appreciate more than her voluptuous figure. Because of the robbery-homicide that morning, he'd been swamped all day, but she'd managed to slip into his thoughts at odd moments, even when he was working full-tilt.

Since Janet's death, he'd done his best to protect Phoebe and keep her safe from future loss. On the way home tonight, he'd been more than ready to give up his idea of ever having a relationship with the kindergarten teacher, all for the sake of his daughter. Even if he discounted Rita Mae's meddling, he had to acknowledge the fact that Eloise Starr had managed to wriggle her way into Phoebe's life.

And, he suddenly realized, his.

Well, maybe not his *life*. He was a cop, after all, with a full caseload, a bossy mother who sat on top of him like a hen on a nest, and a child who needed him. Most of the time, Eloise only finagled her way into his thoughts when he allowed himself to daydream. Or when he lay alone in his bed at night. Or times like now, when he was so close to her he could smell her soap-scrubbed scent.

"Daddy? I got to go to the bathroom."

The words hit him like a bucket of ice water, drowning his fantasies and steering him back on track. "Can you hang on for a few more blocks? It's going to take a while to get home."

"Uh-huh," came the tiny voice from the backseat. "But hurry."

With her last pronouncement, Nathan made a decision. Coming from this direction, they had to drive past their street to get to Eloise's apartment building. It would be foolish to make Phoebe wait, when he could get her to the bathroom first. He took a side street, hoping the snow had kept most of the other vehicles on the more heavily traveled main road, and managed to save a few seconds.

"Daddy? I got to go now."

He'd waited to buy the luxury SUV until he was certain his daughter was potty-trained. Now he wondered how the leather seats would hold up under kiddie fire. "Can you cross your legs and hang on another minute?"

"I'll try."

He took the corner and felt the four-wheel drive gain traction on what could have been a dicey turn. After pulling into his driveway, he whipped open the door and jumped out. Phoebe had already unsnapped her belt and was scrambling from the backseat.

"I got you. Keep your legs together, okay?"

He picked her up and shut first her door, then the driver's door with his foot. Sliding along the walk, he shuffled up the steps as he fumbled for his keys. Once he made it to the landing, he undid the lock and deposited her in the front hall powder room before he turned on the light.

Phoebe wriggled as she tried to shed her coat and pull down her pants at the same time. Staring up at him, she frowned as she slammed the door in his face. "Don't look, Daddy. I can do it by myself."

"Okay, okay, but I'm here if you need me." Catching his breath, he saw the security system blinking like a one-eyed sentinel and quickly punched in the code before the silent alarm had a chance to register at headquarters.

A car door opened and closed and he waited for Eloise's knock. When it didn't come, he peered through a side window and caught her in the light from a street lamp removing her shopping bag from the rear of the SUV. What the hell did the woman think she was doing?

He heard the toilet flush and knocked on the door. "Phoebe? Honey, I have to run outside for a minute. Wait here, okay?"

He stepped onto the front porch and immediately began to slide on the snow-covered bricks. Skittering like a hockey puck on ice, his arms pinwheeled as his feet did a cartoon-like scramble. Cursing his smooth-soled wing tips, Nathan grabbed at the railing in time to halt his tumble. Advancing down the stairs like a geriatric without a walker, he made it to Eloise's side just as she shut the rear door.

"Where do you think you're going?"

She gazed up at him, her eyes alight with mischief. "You need to take care of Phoebe. I can walk from here."

He brushed the snow from his face. "It's too cold and slippery to walk that far."

"So I noticed."

She grinned and he got the distinct impression she'd caught his clumsy attempt at ice dancing.

"I'll drive you home. Just let me get Phoebe bundled up again and—"

"Don't be silly. She's inside where it's warm, which is where you should be. Besides, I have on my Ms. Hewitt shoes."

He took a step back and stared at her feet, encased in boxy black granny shoes. He hadn't noticed them earlier, but he silently agreed that they were just this side of ugly.

As if reading his mind, she quipped, "I think the soles are made of recycled tires."

"Just get in the car. Please?"

Instead of answering, her eyes flicked over his shoulder and he heard a familiar voice. "Nathan? What in the world is going on out there? I came down when I heard the front door open, and now I find Phoebe crying in the bathroom and you outside shouting in the middle of a snowstorm."

Well, hell! He grasped Eloise by the elbow just in case she dared make a getaway, and turned to find his mother standing on the porch. "What's wrong with Phoebe?"

"Nothing a set of dry underwear won't fix. Hello, Eloise. Did you and my granddaughter have a pleasant time?"

Eloise tugged free and scooted around him. "I had a wonderful afternoon, Rita Mae. How was your appointment? Did you meet up with your friend?"

"I did." The older woman gazed at the falling snow. "It's starting to get nasty. Would you like to come in for a cup of something warm before you head home?"

"No, thank you. I'm—"

"For the love of Mike!" Nathan shouted.

"Who's Mike?" Eloise asked.

He sighed. "The man in control of my patience. Look, if you won't come inside and you won't let me give you a ride home, just wait one minute while I change shoes. Can you do that?"

"You don't have to walk me home."

"The hell I don't."

"Of course he does. I raised my son to be a gentleman."

He jumped and spun on his heel. Somehow, Rita Mae had spirited herself from the porch to the car, and was standing behind him holding his hiking boots. Raising his gaze, he saw Phoebe waving from the open front door.

"I changed my clothes, Daddy. Can I come with you and Ms. Eloise?"

"No you may not, now get inside." Shaking his head, he speared the women with a frown. "You're both nuts, you know that?" He snatched the boots from Rita Mae's hands and propped himself against the rear of the car, then bent and changed shoes. Giving his mother a frozen smile, he thrust the wing tips into her waiting arms. "You'll stay with Phoebe?"

"Of course." She smiled graciously at Eloise, as if she were saying farewell to a guest at one of her bridge games. "Take care and be safe." She brushed a pile of fat wet flakes off his coat lapel. "I'll see to it Phoebe gets to bed. Don't worry about a thing."

Nathan picked up the shopping bag. "Can you manage all right?"

"I'm fine." Walking backward ahead of him, Eloise waited until he caught up. "Isn't the snow wonderful? It reminds me of fat fluffy clouds someone ran through a paper shredder and blew down to earth."

Nathan scowled as he glanced into the invisible sky. *Shredded clouds?* The woman was certifiable. The flakes were falling faster now, and they'd changed from big and wet to small and dry. Not a good sign.

"Why are you so grumpy?" She adjusted her steps as she settled alongside him. "If I didn't know better, I'd think you hated the snow."

"You don't know better. You don't know anything about me," he muttered, annoyed that she had him pegged.

"You'll never get to heaven if you tell lies. I heard the excitement in your voice when you reminded Phoebe about building that snow fort last year. Admit it. You love the snow."

He tried to remain stern, but the corner of his mouth hitched into a grin. "Okay, I do like snow, but usually while it's outside and I'm inside toasting my feet in front of a roaring fire." They were on the corner waiting to cross the street. "Not when I'm freezing my butt off walking a nutcase home at ten o'clock on a Saturday night in the middle of the first snowstorm of the season."

He was halfway into the intersection before he realized Eloise hadn't followed. Turning, he saw her standing under the streetlight, her expression a mixture of anger, disbelief and dismay.

"In case you haven't noticed, we're about to be swallowed up by a blizzard. Think you could move it along?"

"You think I'm crazy?"

He heaved a sigh. "Not exactly. But you are different."

"Different?"

He nodded, knowing it was true. "Yeah. But in a good way." That was true too, and it was probably time he told her so.

"Oh? And what does that mean?" she snapped, stepping off the curb.

He waited for Eloise to get to his side, then he took her free hand and tucked it in his elbow before leading her across the street. Surprisingly, she didn't pull away, and he felt the warmth of her fingers through his heavy topcoat.

"It means just what I said. You're not like Phoebe's last teacher, or my mother." He almost added Janet to the list, but thought better of it. "You're not like any woman I've ever met before. Different."

They walked arm in arm through the swirling flakes. Glancing out of the corner of his eye, Nathan could tell by her furrowed brow that she was thinking. He only hoped he wouldn't have to explain himself in more detail, because he had no idea how to voice his feelings out loud. They turned right, then crossed another intersection. Eloise held back and he realized they were on her street.

"Don't tell me I'm not going to be allowed to walk you to your door again."

She let go of his arm and brushed the flakes off her face. "I'm not sure—"

"It's something a friend would do for a friend," Nathan reminded her. "Besides, the sooner I know you're safe inside, the faster I can get home."

Accepting his logic, she nodded, and he stopped himself from breaking into a victory dance. Following her up the block, he climbed the stairs to her brick-and-stone apartment building, stopping on the generous porch protected by an overhang.

Eloise reached into her purse for her keys. Avoiding eye contact, she opened the door and stepped into the lobby.

Nathan brought her bag inside and waited.

"This is where I live," she mumbled, her voice a breathy sigh. "I can take it from here."

"If you don't mind, I'll see you to your door."

He sidled closer and she walked quickly across the tiled lobby to a sturdy looking door marked with attractive brass lettering. After sticking her key into the lock, she turned and focused on his chest.

"Thank you for tonight. I meant what I told your mother. I had a wonderful time with Phoebe—and dinner."

"You're welcome."

Without warning, the forbidden thoughts he'd been fighting against crept into Nathan's mind, making his fingers itch. Unable to resist, he pressed closer. The melting snowflakes dotted Eloise's hair and cheeks, sparkling like liquid diamonds. When she finally raised her chin, he caught the look of longing in her smoky blue eyes and felt the jolt all the way to his gut.

"Nathan. I—"

Unable to resist, he lowered his head. "I'm going to do something I've wanted to do almost from the day we met."

"You are?"

He flattened his palms against the door on either side of her head. "I can't stop thinking about you, though God knows I've tried. No matter what way I add it up, I find myself attracted to you, and I think you feel the same."

"I do. I mean—I don't."

"I hope that's your stubborn side talking, because it's not the message I'm getting from that trembling mouth of yours." He leaned closer, until he could see his reflection in her eyes. "I think we owe it to ourselves to see where this is going."

Eloise held her breath. The insane idea that Nathan might kiss her frightened her, but the thought that he might not was infinitely more terrifying. She concentrated on his face and every feature drew sharply into focus. The woodsy tang of his aftershave mingled with the aroma of fresh snow and a scent she knew was his alone. A rogue lock of hair tumbled boyishly onto his forehead. Flecks of gold danced in his tobacco brown eyes, telegraphing his curiosity.

Leaning toward her, his mouth grew taut. His breath fluttered against her face, warming Eloise to her toes. He inched closer and the pounding in her chest accelerated until she thought her heart might burst. She felt hot and tingly and cold and damp all at once, just as she had the first time she'd made the free fall from heaven to earth.

Slowly, he feathered his lips over hers in a gentle but demanding caress. Sighing, she closed her eyes and mimicked his sweet, hungry motions. Nathan's body shifted as he cupped her jaw. Sucking and tasting, he teased her bottom lip with his teeth and she thought he might try to swallow her whole. A blink of sanity fluttered through her mind and she shoved at his chest to push him away, then rose on tip-toe to offer more. Threading her fingers through his hair, she tugged him down so they were joined more fully. As if waking from a dream, her body came alive under his touch, every nerve ending screaming to be ministered to in the same heart-stopping fashion.

Deepening the kiss, he thrust his lower body against hers, shocking her with the force of his desire. Swamped by a tidal wave of emotion, she whimpered and heard Nathan give a satisfied groan low in the back of his throat. Slanting his head, he took possession of her mouth. The pressure of his body coupled with the demand of his lips was more than she could bear. She burned wherever his hands touched. Her mouth ached with the need to taste him all over.

Eloise thought her blood was on fire, or maybe it was her brain. How else could she explain this raw, mindless wanting, this compelling desire to melt into him so they could be one?

Junior had said she would need to dive in feetfirst, do what humans did and feel what they felt in order to be allowed back into heaven. If that were the case, she should be sitting in Milton's office right now, because she'd already gone above and beyond the directive. If humans experienced this same all-encompassing heat from a mere kiss, it explained a lot more than their multitude of stupid thoughts and even dumber actions.

It explained everything!

Gasping for air, Nathan drew back from the most seductive lips he'd ever had the pleasure of kissing and reluctantly ended their union. *Wow* was his first thought—*amazing,* the second.

Shaken from head to toe, he rested his forehead against

Eloise's brow in an effort to regain his equilibrium. He couldn't recall the last time he'd been this primed for sex.

Eloise trembled in his arms, and he felt as if he could climb Mount Everest barefoot. Who was he kidding? He'd *never* been this ready.

"Well. That was . . . interesting," he said, hoping to gauge her reaction. Meanwhile, he'd grab hold of his self-control and make a move for her apartment door. If she was half as hot as he was, they needed a fire extinguisher and a bedroom. Fast.

Eloise blinked back to reality at the sound of Nathan's raspy voice. *Interesting?* What was that supposed to mean? Frowning, she studied his face, hoping to find a hint of understanding, a flicker of awareness that would show he'd been as overcome as she had by the kiss. But he looked the same as he always did when he appraised her: amused and just a little too smug.

When she didn't speak, he released a breath. "You're worrying me," he muttered, his hands still wrapped around her waist. "Say something."

"Sorry, I don't seem to have your clever way with words."

"What did I say?"

Refusing to be taken in by his little boy-lost expression, she arched a brow. "It's what you didn't say that has me concerned. I was hoping for a more expressive comment than merely *interesting.*"

Nathan paled at her sarcasm. "I didn't mean it in a bad way. It's just that I didn't expect there'd be so much chemistry— so much—Let's just say you took me by surprise."

The mutinous look in her eyes warned that he was only digging the hole deeper. "Oh, hell. I probably should have quit when I was ahead."

"Pardon me," she said with a tilt of her chin, "but at what point did you think you were ahead?"

"You kissed me back, so I figured I was doing okay."

Focusing on the center of his chest, her cheeks flushed pink. "It was all right."

Jeez, since when did a simple *all-right* kiss make your eyes cross, or cause your partner to plaster themselves against you so tight it felt as if they'd been dipped in Crazy Glue? The woman had practically sucked the air from his lungs and left him blazing like a runaway forest fire, and she called that just *all right?*

Nathan tucked his hands in his pockets. There was no way she could be serious. She had to be yanking his chain—or fishing for a compliment. "That's not what it felt like to me."

A spark of something he couldn't place flashed in her eyes. She bit at her kiss-swollen lower lip and damn if he didn't want to devour her sassy mouth all over again.

"I'm sorry if I disappointed you," she said on a whisper.

"You did fine. But I'm sure you've heard that before."

She squared her shoulders and sidled to the door, her voice still breathy but stern. "I'm not exactly an expert, if you want to know the truth."

Now he knew she was fishing. No woman who kissed the way she did could be so naïve. "Come on, a girl with your looks? You've probably had plenty of practice."

Eloise stared down at her shoes. When she raised her head, he read the message she'd been trying to convey and his insides snaked into a knot. Hell on roller skates. So much for hoping to keep things light and have a harmless fling with the teacher. *She was a virgin.* And if not, she was the closest thing to it a woman could be in this day and age. He shook his head.

"Look, I'm sorry if I came on too strong. It's just that you—I—It's been a long time for me—since Janet's death, if we're going to be honest with each other. Your response made me think you were—"

She opened the door and shoved her shopping bag and purse over the threshold with her feet. The hurt radiating from her eyes made him cringe inside.

"Eloise. Please."

"You thought I was—let me think—what do they call it? You thought I'd be easy, didn't you?"

Nathan ran his hands through his hair. The night was sledding downhill at breakneck speed and it wasn't his fault—at least not all of it. "Not easy, just experienced," he said, now on the defensive. "Let's face it, you didn't push me away or say no."

Her shoulders heaved with the force of her sigh. "No, I didn't. And that was my fault."

The door closed with a hollow sounding thump. He heard the dead bolt slide home and knew it was useless to try and coax her back into the hall or finagle his way inside. Turning, he walked to the lobby and peered through the entry door's leaded glass onto the street, where the snow was falling hard and fast.

Nathan hated when he acted like a jerk. Since Janet's death he'd tried his damnedest to be a compassionate and sensitive man, mostly to show Phoebe that regular guys could be that way. He didn't want his daughter to grow up thinking men never listened when a woman talked, or only thought about watching sports on TV while downing a cold beer. He wanted her to know there were men who were capable of being considerate of a woman's needs, so that when the time came for her to start dating, maybe when she was thirty or so, she'd listen to her head—not her hormones.

He didn't want Phoebe to marry the kind of man he'd just shown himself to be.

How was he supposed to know Eloise was an innocent? She'd responded like a woman who'd kissed more than her fair share of men, never once signaling that he'd crossed the line. Hell, she'd been so eager he'd been positive she was going to invite him into her apartment to finish what they'd started.

He gave a mirthless chuckle. Just his luck he'd been lusting after a woman for the first time in two years and she was turning out to be untouchable. He found a pair of leather gloves in a pocket and jammed them onto his hands. Pushing open the heavy front door, he headed out into the building storm.

He had a lot to think about. He just wished he knew where to begin.

Eleven

Eloise leaned against the apartment door, half expecting Nathan to pound it down. When he didn't, she wasn't sure whether to be relieved or miserable. After taking a few calming breaths, she decided miserable was the way to go.

She touched her still-tingling lips. From the moment Nathan had confronted her in Phoebe's bedroom, she'd known something was going to happen between them tonight. Dinner had been relaxing, full of lighthearted fun, mostly because his apology had sounded so sincere. But she couldn't ignore the tension arcing between them during the quiet moments at the table. It was the reason she'd tried to gather her purchases and escape the minute he'd rushed Phoebe out of the car and into the house.

His accusing words rang in her ears, and she conceded he had every right to think she was willing to jump into bed with him. She'd acted shamelessly and enjoyed every second of their kiss. He'd used her for his pleasure because she'd given the impression she was doing the same. But the idea that she was willing to be intimate, as he supposed she'd been with other men, was way off the mark.

Nathan would have been her first . . . and her last.

Eloise removed her coat and hung it on the coatrack. Shivering, she rubbed her upper arms and headed into the bedroom. Sitting in the chair beside her bed, she leaned back and closed her eyes. Finally, she could put a name to the disquieting feelings that had coursed through her from the first moment she'd met Nathan all those years ago.

She now knew that it was lust, desire, longing—even jealousy of Janet that had seared her to her soul as a spirit. Tonight, in a body composed of flesh and bone, the urge to take Nathan inside of her and make them one being had nearly overwhelmed her. Junior had warned her, but he'd neglected to mention that she was going to feel so deeply— that she would ache this much.

He had never explained what becoming involved with a human would do to her heart.

Blinking, she gazed around the room, hoping the smart-mouthed angel-in-training would pop in as he usually did and give her a clue. Unfortunately, the bedroom remained empty. She was on her own.

Closing her eyes again, she thought about Nathan's assessment of their kiss. He'd used the word *interesting*. Did that mean he'd enjoyed it, or hated it? Or something in between? She'd felt his arousal when he'd pressed against her, but she knew it didn't count for much. Years of complaints from her female charges had taught her that men's erections were often a completely physical reaction that required little heartfelt thought.

But the piercing way Nathan had stared with his hungry, gold-flecked eyes—eyes that seemed to see deep into the most hidden part of her—that was another matter.

Pressing her fingers to her temples, she willed away the beginnings of a headache. She forgot the exact statistics, but she remembered hearing that over the centuries more pain had been inflicted in the name of love than any other emotion.

Gee, didn't that sound like fun? The pain was already here and she hadn't even experienced the *L* word yet. Not that she ever intended to fall *in love,* of course. Junior had never said anyone would be measuring, so it was probable all she needed was a taste of the silly emotion, one tiny drop of the *L* word, and she'd be fulfilling the order she'd been given to experience it.

Her fingers massaged in little circles as she tried to remember the other improbable conditions the angel had cited.

She was supposed to use Nathan to get the full human effect. The thought skittered through her brain, overtaking her senses. A relationship with Nathan . . .

If he hadn't broken away, they probably would have been in this very room right now. Nathan would have been holding her, touching her in places she'd just realized existed, making her crazy all over again. And she would be kissing him—she'd really liked the kissing part—caressing him, running her hands over his broad, muscled shoulders, down his chest and—

Her hands stilled. Sweat beaded her upper lip and she felt light-headed. What in the world had happened to her common sense? Why was she having such a hard time controlling her body and aligning her thoughts? Where was a guiding angel when you needed one?

Eloise sighed. It wasn't fair to blame Milton or Junior for her predicament. She'd gotten here all on her lonesome. Even if she discounted the confusing mix of emotions Nathan had mired her in, she'd already begun to obey another dictate. She truly cared for Phoebe.

The little girl had sneaked into her heart when she wasn't looking and now sat there like a forgotten promise. She'd felt the tug the second she'd entered Phoebe's bedroom. Phoebe had given her a gift, made more precious because it belonged to her mother. Nathan had barged in on them before she'd answered what she knew would be the child's pointed question, but it wouldn't be long before Phoebe posed it again.

Phoebe was hoping for a substitute mother, and she'd chosen Eloise to fill that void.

What a disaster it would be, for her, a guiding angel

who'd disposed of more souls than grains of sand in the ocean, to be put permanently in charge of a human being in a parental manner. Eloise had seen the hurt, felt the grief of mothers who lost children. She never wanted to be in that horrible position. Being their guiding angel had been difficult enough. Being one of their mothers would be more than she could bear.

She walked to her bathroom. Maybe a warm shower and a few pills from her overflowing medicine cabinet would help. She had no idea how to cure the rest of what ailed her. The quiver in her stomach and the wobble in her knees would pass, she supposed, as would the throbbing tucked high between her damp thighs. But her heart was another matter. When would it stop pounding whenever Nathan walked into a room? When would it cease to tremble at the sight of his smile or the teasing gleam in his eyes?

Minutes later she was ready for bed. Just as she suspected, the shower had washed away the queasy flutterings. It had even helped soothe the parts of her that were throbbing. But it didn't do a thing to drown the feelings she was developing for Nathan and his daughter.

"Breakfast was very tasty," Rita Mae said, grinning at her granddaughter. "Thank you for inviting me."

"Tell me again what part you liked best, Grammy," demanded Phoebe, her eyes bright as she handed her grandmother used silverware to load in the dishwasher.

"Haven't we already had this discussion?"

"Uh-huh. But I want to tell you what I did again. What part of breakfast did you like best?"

"Hmm." Rita Mae tapped a finger to her chin "Well it wasn't the orange juice or the scrambled eggs, so it must have been the blueberry muffins. What bakery did you say they came from?"

Phoebe jumped in place, tickled they were playing the

silly game. "No bakery. I made them," she said proudly. "Daddy let me hold the mixer while he poured the milk, then I stirred in the blueberries and spooned the batter into the muffin pan. I didn't get to put them in the oven or take 'em out, 'cause he said I might burn myself, but he let me put 'em on a plate when they got cool."

"You did a wonderful job, sweetie," Rita Mae said as she closed the dishwasher door. "What do you and your father have planned for the rest of the day?"

"I wanna go outside and build a snow fort."

"Really? That sounds like fun. And when you're through, I know a place where you can get a cup of hot chocolate and some fresh-baked cookies."

Nathan listened to his mother and daughter's babble with half an ear, while his mind wandered to where it had been for most of the past twelve hours—in the hallway of Eloise's apartment building. Last night, after an angry walk through a serious snowstorm, he'd arrived home wet and frozen. Thanks to the virginal Ms. Starr, he'd spent most of the night tossing and turning while he relived every second of the time they'd spent pressed up against each other like two hormone-riddled teenagers.

Eloise had turned to liquid heat in his hands, and he'd responded in kind. Then she'd acted as if he'd been the bad guy. Could any woman her age—he guessed her to be in her late twenties—truly be such an innocent?

He hid behind his newspaper when a distasteful idea that had been lurking for a hefty part of the morning hit him full force. What if it had been an act? What if Eloise Starr wasn't a first-timer or even a slightly experienced novice, but a fortune hunter bent on setting a trap? Everybody thought he had money; this house alone was worth close to a million dollars. Only his best friends knew it all belonged to his kid.

What if Eloise Starr was setting him up in hopes of marrying a wealthy man and was using his daughter as bait?

The idea sat in his stomach like a lump of uncooked muffin batter. Washington was full of people with their own agendas. He'd read plenty of profiles on predatory women, even investigated and arrested a few who had done in their husbands for the cash. But disguising oneself as a kindergarten teacher? That was above sneaky. And to use a child? She would have to be heartless, morally bankrupt, a felon—

"Can we, Daddy? Can we build a snow fort?" asked Phoebe, breaking into his thoughts.

Trying for cheerful, he folded the Sunday *Washington Post,* stood and walked to the sink, where he set his coffee cup on the counter. "I don't think there's enough snow for that, punkin, but we could probably build a snowman."

"Not a snow*man.* I want to make a snow daddy."

He ran a hand over the back of his neck and shot Rita Mae a grin. "We could try."

"An' a snow mommy and baby sister too," she called over her shoulder as she skipped to the front hall. "I'm gonna find my snow pants and parka in the upstairs closet. You get dressed too. I'll be right back, okay?"

Nathan didn't say a word, even after he heard his daughter's feet pound up the stairs. When he'd returned from walking Eloise home, Rita Mae had looked pointedly at her watch and smiled, then pecked him on the cheek and left for her apartment. Now, with Phoebe searching for winter clothes, they had a few minutes to get into things on a more personal level. Bracing himself, he waited for the questions he knew his mother had been dying to ask.

Rita Mae kept her back to him as she wiped down the granite countertop. "So, does the paper say we're going to get more snow? Pity it stopped at five inches."

"Could be," he muttered. Shuffling to his chair, he sat with a thud and slouched, pouting like a twelve-year-old.

"Really? That's nice. Maybe we'll have a white Christmas this year. It's been ages since we—"

Damn. Why wouldn't she look at him? "Nothing happened last night, Mother."

Rita Mae didn't break stride. Instead, she went to the cupboard and took down a fresh tea bag, then walked to the stove and turned off the gas under the screeching kettle. Nathan envisioned the oh-so-wise smile on her perfectly lined lips as she puttered. He heard the laughter in her voice when she said, "Too bad. Maybe next time."

He scowled. She was such a smart-ass, especially when she echoed his sentiments with dead-on accuracy. "Don't you ever get tired of meddling?"

The sudden stiffening of her spine told him he'd set her back a peg. "Me? Meddle?" She sniffed. Taking her seat at the table, she dunked her tea bag with vigor. "Really, Nathan, I'm hurt by your accusation."

He curled his lip into a condescending grin. "Do not insult my intelligence by trying to tell me you didn't set up yesterday's scenario. You never did say who made that important phone call that took you away from lunch."

Rita Mae stopped dunking, scooped out the tea bag with her spoon and twirled the string to wring out the last of the brew. "A friend. And it was an emergency."

Familiar with her precise actions, he shook his head. His mother could say more with the assembly of a single cup of tea than most woman did yapping volumes. "You're telling me the lunch thing with Eloise wasn't a setup? That you asked her to join you out of the goodness of your heart, and then got a *surprise* phone call that required you to hand my daughter over to a stranger?"

"Don't be ridiculous. Eloise Starr isn't a stranger. She's a kind and caring woman. She's a kindergarten teacher, for heaven's sake."

"So she wants us to think."

"What's that supposed to mean? I told you I was the one who had the previous engagement. Eloise tried to say no, but I insisted."

"Ah-ha!" Nathan jabbed a finger in the air. "You admit it. It was a setup."

Rita Mae *tsked,* her expression that of a woman fast losing patience with her child. "I needed a favor and Eloise obliged. It was as simple as that. Honestly, I know policemen are suspicious by nature, but you're taking this too far."

"I'm a simple man, Mother. Forgive me if I keep getting the details mixed up in my feeble male brain."

She tapped the side of her teacup, then smiled at him, and Nathan knew they were okay. But how in the hell was he supposed to get his point across? There had to be some way to show his mother the havoc a busybody could create, even with the best of intentions. If his suspicion about Eloise turned out to be true, Rita Mae would be furious to learn she'd been part of the woman's dastardly plan.

"It's just that I like Ms. Starr," she finally said, after sipping her tea. "And Phoebe adores her. Eloise is lovely, so fair and statuesque. So not—"

"Like Janet?" he suggested.

"Exactly."

That was true. Janet had been petite and dark-haired. Eloise made him think of Marilyn Monroe, Jayne Mansfield—He swallowed at the thought. Hadn't he heard on the news about some curvy, blond bimbo who'd been accused of marrying a randy old geezer in order to get his money? He was years away from collecting a pension, but he was definitely randy where Eloise was concerned, and the part about marrying for money—

"So, did the three of you enjoy yourselves last night?"

Hell, yes, he almost snapped. Especially in Eloise's hallway. Stabbed by the Devil's pitchfork, he suddenly thought it might be fun watching his mother sputter and blush when he told her in graphic detail how he and Eloise had dived on each other like sex-starved gerbils. It was no less than she deserved for—Nah, he couldn't be that mean, especially with this new idea taking root in his brain.

"It was fine."

She nodded. "Well, that's something then."

It had been *something*, all right. "I want you to give me your word that you'll stop interfering," he said in his best law enforcement voice. "I also want you to promise that you and Phoebe won't take anymore early-morning strolls to the corner deli. There's a gang on the loose knocking off convenience stores. Yesterday they killed someone."

Before Rita Mae could answer, footsteps tapped in the hall. Phoebe scampered into the kitchen, outfitted for a trek in the wilds of Alaska. Taking in her father, who was still sitting in jeans and a T-shirt, she gave a stricken look. "You can't go outside like that, Daddy. You got to put on your coat and earmuffs and hiking shoes." She held up a crumpled ball of brown leather. "I found your gloves at the bottom of the stairs."

Exactly where he'd left them last night, after he'd stripped them off in a fit of temper. "Okay, okay, just give me a minute." Nathan took the gloves and set them on the table. "You, young lady, need to find your boots."

"I know. But I haf'ta have help getting them on."

Rita Mae stood and took Phoebe by the hand. "How about we look for your boots while your father goes upstairs to change?"

Nathan pushed from the table and headed to his bedroom, thinking he'd put on a sweater and drag a pair of sweats over his jeans. Maybe if he spent the afternoon in the freezing cold, he'd stop thinking like a cop and accept what had happened between him and Eloise for what it was—a man, a woman and a whole lot of heat.

Yeah, right.

Nathan drove Phoebe to school on Monday morning with his SUV's four-wheel drive in the ON position and his mind in the throes of a meltdown. Even though he hadn't heard a word from Eloise on Sunday, he couldn't shake the idea of her being a gold digger. He should have called her, but instead he'd spent the day amusing his daughter and hanging the Christmas decorations his mother had dragged up from the basement. Thanks to his adolescent attitude, he felt like a coward, but he'd have to be ten times stupid to make it easy for Eloise Starr to get to him.

Later that night, after he'd tucked Phoebe in bed, he'd spent some time in front of a blazing fireplace. Sitting with his feet up on the coffee table while he sipped a glass of red wine, he mellowed a bit when he reminded himself that if the kindergarten teacher were truly trying to trap him, she'd be doing her best to wheedle her way into his life. Rita Mae had been the one who'd invited her to lunch and insisted she baby-sit Phoebe, not the other way around. It was possible his suspicions were out of line.

He parked the SUV and helped Phoebe out of the car, then took her hand as they went up the steps of the Hewitt Academy. Maybe if he stuck his head in the classroom and said a polite hello, he'd be able to read Eloise's reaction and figure out where to go from there.

"Come on, Daddy," ordered Phoebe, tugging him toward the kindergarten door. "I want to tell Ms. Eloise about the snow family we built."

She let go of his hand and raced down the hall while Nathan measured his steps, still leery of approaching Eloise in her classroom. Before he reached the door, Ms. Hewitt rounded a corner, saw him and nodded.

"Mr. Baxter. Good morning."

"Ms. Hewitt." His gaze moved automatically to her clunky shoes and he hid a smile. Eloise had been so on target about the headmistress and those shoes.

"I was wondering if I could speak to you for a moment," the woman continued. "In my office?"

Curious, Nathan followed her to a door marked *Private, Staff Only.* Once inside, he saw that the room was divided into partitions, but they were all empty. He couldn't help but notice the lack of computers or any type of modern office convenience. The room was spartan, with utilitarian gray metal desks, matching chairs and wastebaskets.

They entered another door with the word *Principal* stenciled in plain black letters. Ms. Hewitt waited until he sat down, then took her own seat across from him behind an overladen and untidy desk of mammoth proportion.

"Mr. Baxter," she began, adjusting her Coke-bottle lenses. "I must first ask you to give your word you will keep what we're about to discuss in confidence. Can you agree to that?"

Nathan caught the hint of a blush staining her cheeks and decided Honoria Hewitt wasn't bad looking, just buttoned-up and a little on the frumpy side. Rita Mae had registered Phoebe at the school, and Nathan hadn't spent much time in the woman's presence. She looked to be a lot younger than he'd first thought, not much older than Eloise as a matter of fact.

"Sure. No problem." He sat forward in the uncomfortable chair when a worry crossed his mind. "This isn't about Phoebe, is it? She's not having a problem or anything, is she?"

Ms. Hewitt straightened her spine further, if that was possible, and shook her head. "No, of course not. Phoebe is a lovely child—a joy to know. She's above average in verbal skills and socializes happily with the other children. I find her to be quite well adjusted for a little girl who recently lost her—Who has only one—" She flushed a deeper pink. "I'm sorry. I'm not explaining myself very well. It's obvious you're a fine parent."

Nathan knew what the headmistress was trying to say. "Thanks for the compliment. So, if not Phoebe, then what is it you and I have to talk about?"

Ms. Hewitt seemed relieved to move off the topic. "It's Ms. Starr that we need to discuss."

Holy hell. Had Eloise told her about his ham-fisted Saturday night pawing? Had he been such a clod he'd caused her to go running to her employer? Was there some unwritten rule at the Hewitt Academy that frowned upon fraternization between parents and the staff?

"Ms. Starr?" he said with what he hoped was a blank face.

"I'm still a bit upset over Friday's incident, and I wonder if you might be willing to do me a favor."

Friday's incident? "Oh, you mean the confusion over who should have picked up Phoebe?" He leaned back in the chair. "I already told you, I don't intend to hold the school responsible. My mother convinced me that she and I were as much at fault as you were. I can promise it won't happen again."

Ms. Hewitt picked up a pencil and began drumming an end on the one bit of space on the desk not covered in papers. "Thank you for that. But there's something else that came to my attention when I was doing paperwork, and I was hoping that someone with your pull—" She forced a tepid smile. "Sorry, this is a sensitive issue and I don't mean to make more out of it than it is." Sighing, she continued. "You are an officer of the law. As such, you have connections which I, an ordinary citizen, do not. To accomplish what I feel I must, I would have to find a private investigator, which might become public knowledge, thereby causing negative publicity for the school, something I would hate to see happen."

"Okay," said Nathan, curious. "Go on."

Ms. Hewitt stared at the pencil, realized she'd been tapping out her own special brand of Morse code and stopped. "It is the policy of this school to call the references listed on all applications submitted by teachers seeking employment. In the case of Eloise Starr, an error was made."

"An error? I'm sorry, but I'm not following."

Her pensive expression shifted to one of embarrassment. "Miss Starr's application has no references. I cannot find anything more in the file than a pitifully brief sheet of personal facts. I have no idea why I didn't call her on it, or insist she furnish the other documents I would normally want in her folder, but I imagine I was in a panic about covering Ms. Singeltary's hurried departure so I let Ms. Starr's lack of documentation slide." She turned her hands palms up. "I'm swamped right now, and I don't have the time to do anything about it, so I was wondering if you could use your connections to run some sort of background check on the woman. For my own peace of mind and the good of the school, I must have those forms in the file."

"Why haven't you just asked Ms. Starr to furnish the references and other paperwork you need?" he asked. "Seems simple enough to me."

"I did ask her, this very morning. Her answer was vague and a bit . . . dismissive. It's close to the Christmas holiday and we're all a little frazzled, I'm afraid. I thought it would be easier if you took care of it, that's all."

Nathan folded his arms, revved by the request. It sounded like Eloise had answered Ms. Hewitt's questions about her past the same way she'd answered his—not at all. What better way to do Ms. Hewitt a favor and sort out his own gnarly suspicions at the same time?

"This would be on the QT, of course," he said, just to double-check. "You'd keep the information strictly between the two of us?"

Ms. Hewitt met his pointed gaze with one of her own. "I wouldn't have it any other way. It's for the files, you see, just to make certain they're complete. Apart from removing Phoebe from the premises, which I feel was done solely for the benefit of the child, Ms. Starr hasn't attempted anything that would make me suspect she's untrustworthy. Even though her teaching methods are a bit . . . unorthodox, I'm satisfied, but as my grandmother used to say, it's always better to err on the side of caution." She folded her hands on top of a pile of papers. "Don't you agree?"

Hell, yes, Nathan wanted to blurt out. Instead he said, "I'd like a copy of the information you have. I need some place to begin the search."

Removing a single sheet of paper from a manila folder, Ms. Hewitt stood and took it to a desktop copier. With her ramrod-straight back to him, she set the paper on the glass and pushed a button.

Nathan blew out a breath. Talk about coincidence. He'd been toying with the idea of checking up on Eloise, but he had yet to decide if it was the right thing to do. He could have figured out her entire history simply by going on the Internet. People had no idea how much information was available about them online. But the idea had stuck in his craw. Unless he had strong suspicions of a crime, he didn't think it was fair to invade anyone's privacy. Ms. Hewitt had just handed him a gift. He was free to run a check with a clean conscience.

Turning, she gave him the single page. "This is all I have. I hope it's enough."

He scanned the form, noting a social security number and a few details about Eloise's education, along with her current address. "It might be faster if we had fingerprints, but I don't want to go there unless I turn up something unusual."

Ms. Hewitt walked him to the door. "There's no hurry. It's more for my peace of mind than anything else. Thank you."

Twelve

Thanks to her up close-and-personal encounter with Nathan, Eloise had tossed and turned for the past two nights. She did her best to look alert and professional this morning by dressing in a new skirt and blouse. She'd even tamed her hair into a soft knot on the top of her head, a compromise between her usual flyaway mess and the head-mistress's scraped-back bun.

She arrived at school hoping to find refuge in her charges, and instead bumped into Ms. Hewitt. The principal had given her a disapproving once-over, then immediately begun to ramble about some paperwork that was missing from a folder. The woman went on for so long, Eloise wanted to scream. In the end, she'd simply excused herself and raced into her classroom.

What was she supposed to do about the missing papers? Ask Milton or Junior to write her a recommendation?

Glancing up from her desk in time to see a trio of bright-eyed students dressed for winter coming through the door, Eloise stood to greet them. She knew exactly how they felt. She'd drifted off near dawn on Sunday and slept late, then walked to a corner store and ordered breakfast. After eating her sweet roll and milk, she'd spent the rest of the day avoiding Nathan's street while she strolled the neighborhood, marveling at the beauty of the snowfall. By late afternoon, most of the fluffy stuff had been shoveled and left to melt in piles at the curb, but she still remembered that first euphoric moment when her heart had taken flight at the sight of the fat flakes falling from the sky.

Just then, Phoebe trotted in, all pink-cheeked and chatty. "Where were you yesterday, Ms. Eloise? I kept hopin' you'd come over to play. Daddy and I built a snow family, and I wanted you to see it."

Eloise clutched at Janet's locket hidden under the buttons of her blouse. Maybe she should have found the courage to stop by, not to see Nathan, of course, but to speak with Phoebe about her generous gift and explain the reason she had to return it.

"I had some personal things to take care of." She peered around the door frame. "Did your grandmother drive you this morning, or was it Na—your father?"

"Daddy. But he's talking to Ms. Hewitt. Grammy's gonna get me after school."

Eloise refused to believe that the hollow, achy feeling centered in her chest had appeared because Nathan was avoiding her. But he could have stopped in to say hello. "That's nice. Do you think Rita Mae will come inside to visit?"

"Maybe." Phoebe hung up her coat and hat. "Can you come over for dinner tonight? Daddy said he'd make us macaroni and cheese."

Us? She dashed the collective word from her mind. *Us* meant the Baxter family—Nathan and Phoebe, maybe Rita Mae. Not Nathan, Phoebe and Eloise Starr. As much as she enjoyed being with them, she had to remember that fact. Her goal was to find her way back to heaven, not become part of a family.

"I don't know. I have a lot of stuff to take care of for school. There's the play and lesson plans and—"

"Good morning."

Nathan's voice, as dark and steamy as hot chocolate, warmed her from the inside out. Turning, she found him propped in the doorway, teasing her with his too familiar grin.

"You're welcome to come to dinner, if you don't mind mac and cheese."

"Oh, well. I'd have to check my schedule. I have things to do for the play and—Has Phoebe told you what an important part she has?"

"I think she might have mentioned it a few hundred times." He patted the little girl on the head and she flitted off to join her friends. "I'm still not sure what she's supposed to wear for a costume."

Me neither, thought Eloise, and added that chore to her mental things-to-do-so-I-won't-be-fired list. "I'll be sending home a note in a few days, informing the parents of what they need to know."

His gaze swept from her hair to her form-fitting, bright red blouse and knee-length navy blue skirt. "I like what you're wearing." He quirked up a corner of his mouth. "Has Ms. Hewitt seen the outfit?"

Eloise nodded, pleased someone besides the sour-faced Honoria had noticed. The clothes were tasteful and tailored yet colorful. Like her hairstyle, they signaled a compromise between what she'd wanted to buy and what she thought Ms. Hewitt would accept as proper schoolteacher garb. Besides two other blouses and a cream-colored skirt, she'd also purchased a lime green jacket and splurged on a pale pink sweater that reminded her of cotton candy.

"She did, but I don't think she approved. I'm never sure if I'm doing the right thing around her, but I do know these shoes are the next to go."

Nathan's intimate gaze slid to her feet and back up her body. When he stopped to stare at her mouth, Eloise swore her lips began to tingle.

"Yeah, I can see why you'd want to get rid of them. What made you buy them in the first place? I don't remember the staff here being required to wear uniforms. Or did you have to sign a form promising to adhere to the Ms. Hewitt code of dress in order to get hired?"

Responding to his joke with a tentative grin, she swallowed and said the first thing that came to mind. "They were a part of what I'd been sent here with, but they're not the real me."

"Thank God for that," he said with a chuckle. "So, we'll see you for dinner?"

"I don't know—"

"Look." He tucked his hands in his pockets. "I get the feeling I'm supposed to apologize for what happened between us the other night, but to tell you the truth I don't think I did anything to be sorry for."

He wasn't sorry that he'd kissed her? The thought turned her feeble smile joyous. "You didn't. And I apologize if I made you feel that way."

His serious expression softened to one of relief. "I think we need to talk. I get the idea you weren't—that you hadn't kissed too many men before me. Am I right?"

Eloise felt herself blush as two students ran through the doorway calling out a good morning. If Ms. Hewitt or one of the parents heard what Nathan was asking, she'd be fired for sure. "I don't think this is the proper place to discuss it. The children—"

"Then come to dinner. I may not make it because the case I'm covering requires a lot of my attention, but I know Rita Mae and Phoebe would like the company."

"I—"

"If I don't show, just page me about a half hour before you're ready to leave and I'll do my best to get there in time to walk you to your door."

Mary Alice Murphy took that moment to barrel between them. "Mith Eloweeth! Mith Eloweeth! Look what I brought." She held up a plate piled high with cookies and shoved it into Eloise's hands. "Our houthkeeper baked Chrithmath cookieths with real frosting. Aren't they nith?"

"Yeth—I mean—yes, Mary Alice. They're lovely." Grasping the plate firmly, Eloise met Nathan's amused gaze. "Sorry, I have to get the class started. And I'll think about the dinner invitation."

"If I find out you walked home alone, I swear I'll come to your apartment and bang on the door until I wake up the neighbors. Page me." With that, Nathan turned and sauntered out the door.

The man is too cocky, thought Eloise. *Definitely full of himself.* But her stomach quivered at the way he'd as much as confessed that he'd enjoyed kissing her and, from the inflection in his voice, planned to do it again . . . tonight, when he walked her home. And though she hadn't exactly said yes to dinner, she was tired of eating alone.

She shook her head. Five minutes of bantering with Nathan and her palms were sweaty, her lips itchy and her heart beating faster than a runaway train. No wonder humans never had their priorities straight. Good thing he wanted to continue their relationship, because the sooner they got their personal interaction over with, the sooner she'd be back in heaven, where she most definitely belonged.

Nathan sat at his computer terminal, inputting the data from Ms. Hewitt. He'd traced hardened criminals with less information than he had on Eloise, and he'd still managed to receive fairly comprehensive reports. If nothing else, the search would give him answers to a few of his questions.

"You get any leads on that gang yet?"

At the sound of his captain's voice, Nathan sat upright in his chair. Joe Milligan didn't come out from behind his desk to patrol the squad room very often, but this string of robberies had everyone nervous.

"Nothing concrete. They strike at random so it's hard to pin down an MO. We've alerted all the chains to be on their toes, but it's the mom-and-pop establishments that have me worried. The last hit was almost too easy. The store had no surveillance cameras or alarm system, and the owners barely spoke English. Whoever's in charge of the gang does a thorough job with their homework."

"Okay. See to it Hawkins and LaRue do a store-by-store canvass; talk to the owners and warn them what they're up against. And take care of it today."

Nathan was on the homicide detail, while the other men were in charge of the robberies, but they were working side by side on the case. "It's as good as done." The captain grimaced and he asked, "Anything else bothering you?"

Joe rubbed a fist across his chest and shook his head. "Just do me a favor and kick me the next time I even think about eating a pork-and-bean burrito, will you. Had the damn thing for dinner last night and the sucker still feels like it's eating a hole in my gut."

For the first time Nathan noticed that the captain looked a little worn around the edges, his normal ruddy complexion pale, his energetic attitude a bit off. Usually a natty dresser, it was clear from his unknotted tie, wrinkled dress shirt and creased suit pants he'd pulled an all-nighter.

"No offense, but you look like hell. You getting enough sleep these days?"

Joe gave a grin that didn't quite reach his eyes. "I'm fine. It's this damn job that needs an overhaul. Sometimes I think I'm too old to be working twenty-hour days. And I guess it wouldn't hurt to change my diet from fast food to something a little more nutritious." He glanced at Nathan's computer. "Looks like the data you requested is trickling in. You searching for anyone important?"

Nathan knew it went against protocol to do the background check on Eloise from work, but he had no choice. The police line gave him free entry into a myriad of investigative avenues, funneled him past a reel of red tape and took him directly to the appropriate sites.

"Uh, no, not exactly," he admitted. "I'm doing a favor for the woman who runs my daughter's school."

"The Hewitt Academy?"

"Ms. Hewitt hired a teacher, then neglected to collect all the appropriate paperwork. She asked me for help in covering her bases."

"Interesting." Captain Milligan peered at the computer. "It doesn't look to me as if the woman has a past. Does the principal suspect fraud or misrepresentation?"

Swiveling his head to check the screen, Nathan winced inwardly at how little had come through. "Not really. She's just a stickler for detail."

"Well, good luck. Looks like you're going to need it. By the way, I'm still waiting for that dinner invitation you promised." Joe's grin stretched from ear to ear. "I'm a bachelor, remember. If you're really concerned about me, you'll make sure I get a home-cooked meal every so often. It'll go a long way in improving my attitude."

"Sorry, I forgot. I'll check with Rita Mae and let you know when. Maybe this weekend, if I get a break in the case."

The captain raised a bushy brow, a hint of his old take-charge personality lighting his haggard face. "Who says you have to be there for me to enjoy your mother's cooking? Once I'm alone with Rita Mae, I can take care of myself." Someone called to him from across the room and Joe waved. "Let me know the day and time and I'll show with bells on."

Nathan watched the captain swagger away. It was hard to imagine Rita Mae with a man like Joe Milligan or any man, for that matter. She was his *mother*, for shit's sake. Growing up, he hadn't even liked the idea of his mom and dad in bed together doing what married couples did. Now here he was, fixing her up with a guy who seemed to practically lust after her. But Rita Mae deserved to be happy, and it just might be enough of a diversion to get her to stop meddling in his and Phoebe's lives.

Turning back to his desk, he ordered the computer to print out Eloise's data while he stewed over his morning. Flirting with her in the doorway to her classroom while he had the abbreviated details of her life hidden in his coat pocket had cranked up his guilt quotient. No matter how many times he told himself he was merely assisting Ms. Hewitt, he knew the investigation was for his own peace of mind.

The printer burped out a page and Nathan breathed a sigh of relief when he saw that Eloise had no fingerprints on file and no outstanding warrants—no criminal record of any kind. After scanning the information, he reached for the phone and dialed the number listed for her high school.

"Centerville Catholic Academy," a female voice answered.

"This is Nathan Baxter, Washington, D.C. Metropolitan Police. I'm running a check on one of your graduates and I need to speak to someone in charge of past records."

"Hold, please," said the voice.

Nathan read through the single page while he waited, noting the pathetically sparse information. Eloise had been born on Christmas Day, nineteen-seventy-three, in a small town in Illinois. Her mother and father were deceased, she had no siblings or relatives and no past employment record. How in the hell had she been supporting herself?

"This is Sister Mary Catherine. How may I help you?"

"Nathan Baxter here, Washington, D.C. police. I'm running a background check on one of your former students, a Ms. Eloise Starr, class of ninety."

"What is it you wish to know?"

The woman's well-modulated tone carried Nathan back to his elementary school days, making him feel like a seventh-grader again. "She's teaching at a private school in the District and they neglected to get references. I'm doing them a favor with the paperwork, and I was hoping you could tell me something about her."

"We usually receive this type of request through the mail, Mr. Baxter, in the form of an official communication."

Nathan thought he'd better make a stronger case if he was going to get anywhere. "We're not looking to arrest or fire her, Sister. We just need the basics."

"I see. Well, give me a minute, please. It may take a while to locate her file."

Nathan could envision the woman's stiff demeanor, just from the tone of her voice. It took some time, but Sister Mary Catherine finally returned.

"What is it you wanted to know?"

"Was Ms. Starr a good student? Did anything unusual happen to her while she was at your school?"

He heard the rustle of papers before the sister spoke. "I'm afraid there's not much in her file. She attended Centerville Catholic from September of nineteen-eighty-six until her graduation. I wasn't principal then, so I must admit I don't remember anything about her."

"And her grades were good?"

"She graduated with honors. Her excellent SAT scores allowed her to go on to our sister school, the Catholic College of Teachers, a short distance from here."

"And who might I call to check on her credentials there?"

"That would be Sister Eileen, Dean of Admissions. You may tell her we spoke."

Still curious, Nathan had to ask, "I couldn't help notice that Ms. Starr lost her parents at an early age. Does it happen to say who she lived with while she attended your high school?"

Sister Mary Catherine didn't hesitate to answer. "The records indicate that she resided here. She was enrolled in our postulant program."

Postulant program? "As in the—the novitiate?" he stuttered, too surprised to say more.

"That is correct. It is a program we run for young women who are trying to decide whether the life of a servant of God is their proper path."

"Thank you." Feeling poleaxed, Nathan hung up the phone. Eloise had been in a program that would have led her to become a nun? *Holy shi*—He stumbled over what Phoebe always called one of his "bad words." Somehow, the curse just didn't fit this scenario.

Leaning back in his chair, he scanned the paper again. Nowhere on the sheet did it say Eloise had actually become a nun. Had she taken her final vows? If so, why had she left the convent?

He furrowed his fingers through his hair. If what the sister said was true, and he had no reason to doubt the woman, it explained a lot about the evasive answers Eloise had given to his questions. Growing up in a small rural town and entering a nunnery at thirteen wouldn't have allowed her much time to learn about fashion or eat Chinese food. No wonder she'd been so revved about buying new clothes. She'd spent the better part of her life wearing sackcloth and granny shoes.

He recalled their hot-as-hell encounter in her apartment hallway and suddenly realized that her shocked expression made perfect sense. Her confusing response to their knock-your-socks-off lip lock had been genuine. If she'd truly been sequestered in a convent for the past fifteen years, he was probably the first man she'd ever kissed.

Unfortunately, even with this latest bit of information he had no choice but to finish what he'd started, and not just for Ms. Hewitt's sake.

He dialed the college and was connected to Sister Eileen. After introducing himself, he learned that Eloise had earned a master's degree in child development, as well as a degree in elementary education, which would please Ms. Hewitt.

"I just need to know one more thing, Sister. Did Ms. Starr take her final vows? Was she ever a full-fledged nun?"

"I don't see how that fact would hold much weight with her current employer, Mr. Baxter. You did say she already had the job? This is just a check on her references?"

"That's a part of the problem. She failed to give references. I—that is—Ms. Hewitt was wondering why."

"The records show that she got along well with children, especially the little ones, when she taught at the convent grade school. She left here of her own accord about a month ago. If you want to find out about her religious calling, you're going to have to ask her yourself."

"Did you know her, Sister? Did you ever spend any time with her?"

"Actually, I've only just arrived at this college. I'm sorry, but that's all I can reveal without a court order or official request of some kind."

Nathan hung up the phone. Short of inventing a reason for a more in-depth query, he'd just received all the information he was going to get.

The kindergarteners sat in groups of three or four, each child with their own copy of the same book. It was Eloise's job to listen as they read out loud, make certain they understood the words and monitor their progress. She'd followed Ms. Singeltary's guidelines and clustered the students according to their ability. There was one group of exceptional readers, Phoebe among them, three tables of students with average skills and one table of children who were less proficient, mainly because they were the offspring of visiting diplomats and therefore unfamiliar with English.

She'd started with the better readers and left them answering questions in their workbooks. The average children had taken up a bit more of her time, but they too were now diligently writing. With most of the class on assignments, she could give more of her attention to the foreign students.

Amelia Santiago and Zeman Metumba were coming along nicely, she noted, sounding out the words and working hard at their pronunciation. But Sebastian Beauchamp was definitely having a problem.

She listened to the little boy struggle with the most simple of words before she spoke. "Sebastian, can you stay after school today? I really think you need extra help with your reading."

The child's eyes grew wide and, dare she think it, frightened. "Ulimar has orders to bring me home right after school. I don't think he will let me stay."

"Nonsense," she answered, smiling encouragement. "I'm sure your father would want you here if he knew it was for a good reason. Doesn't he want you to learn to read?"

Sebastian stared at the book in his hands, his face a mask of insecurity. "He says I must learn to read English, the common language of the free world, if I want to attain a position of power in our country. He says a great ruler must understand the written word to communicate at all levels."

"I see." Eloise frowned. "Then you need to read well, and I want to help."

Tucking his chin against his chest, the boy swiped at a tear. "I understand from looking at the pictures, Miss Eloise. Why can't that be good enough?"

His defeatist attitude stabbed at her heart, and she placed a hand on his shoulder. "Because pictures don't tell the whole story. And when you get older and go to college, many of the books you'll need to read won't have pictures. Wouldn't you like to know what the words say?"

"Maybe I won't have to go to college," he mumbled, dashing away another tear.

"How about your own language? Can you read books written in your native French?"

"I try. Mostly my nanny reads to me."

"I see. And does your nanny read to you in your own language or English?"

"Veronique doesn't speak English, but she knows the best stories." He smiled through his unhappiness. "If you tell my father I cannot read, he will be most displeased with me. As the oldest son, I am the one he relies on. I am to follow in his footsteps."

A disturbing idea formed in Eloise's mind and she forced herself to ask, "Sebastian, what would your father do if he found out you were having difficulty with your studies?"

The little boy glanced at his classmates, who were now

listening to the conversation with great interest. "He would frown and then he would yell. Sometimes, when I do something I shouldn't, like spill my milk or fight with my brothers, he yells a lot."

"He just raises his voice? Nothing else?"

"I get sent to bed without supper when he is very angry."

"And Ulimar?" she prompted.

The name coaxed a glimmer of a smile. "Ulimar plays ball with me and my younger brother, but mostly he watches over us. Father says he must remain a figure of authority."

Relieved that the child wasn't being physically abused, Eloise sat back in her fairy-size chair. "Maybe if you told me the problem, I could help? What if I point to the letters and you tell me the sounds?"

The little boy shrugged, but did as she asked. They went through the vowels together, then Eloise tackled the consonants. "So far so good," she pronounced "Let's move to the next step."

After a few minutes, she determined the child definitely had a learning disability. His understanding of individual letters was fine, but when they put the letters together to form words, he got them all turned around. She'd heard humans discuss the topic of dyslexia and thought it very likely that might be his problem. Shame on Ms. Singeltary for not recognizing the child's disability and taking care of it. Even sadder was the fact that Sebastian felt so cowed by his father he couldn't ask for help.

The clock inched toward dismissal time and she sighed. "All right, we're through for today. Everyone put away your books and come back to your seats."

"When are we gonna have another play practice?" asked Shawanna. "I can't wait to be the baby Jesus' mother."

"And what are we gonna wear?" asked another student.

"I wanna wear a vest like I saw on a Brittany Spears video," said Missy. "My big sister said it was heavenly."

"Angels don't wear vests, you stupid head," sassed Adam.

Not really, thought Eloise, but now was not the time to give them a lesson on the ethereal form of heavenly beings.

"Adam, no matter what you might think of Missy's idea, calling her a stupid head is impolite, now apologize."

He shot Missy a glare. "I'm sorry you're a stupid head." Turning back to Eloise, he continued his argument. "But angels have wings and halos. At least that's the way they look in all the pictures."

"I don't think anyone on earth knows what angels wear or what they look like. The pictures you've seen are all from artists' imaginations." Eloise smiled inwardly at her clever explanation.

"Then why can't we use our 'maginations and decide what to wear for ourselves?" asked Billy.

"Because—" Eloise wrinkled her brow. Okay, so why couldn't the children have free rein with their imaginations? Would it be so bad if they created their own costumes? She didn't remember reading anything about wardrobes in the lesson planner she'd inherited from Ms. Singeltary. Why did they have to follow a rule when one didn't exist?

"Billy, I think that's an excellent suggestion." When the students cheered, she propped her backside against the desk and gave an impromptu speech. "Listen up, everyone. For tonight's assignment I want each of you to draw the costume you'd like to wear in the pageant. Tomorrow, we'll review the pictures and decide what of each design stays and what has to go."

Hands rose to the ceiling in excitement.

"Can I use crayons?"

"You may draw the picture with anything you like."

"Can I cut mine out of a magazine?"

Eloise found it hard to believe Lucy was going to find a shepherd's costume in any of the magazines lying around the Chen house, but who was she to say no to the request?

"Sure, if you can find one that fits your part."

"Can my big sister help?"

"Nope. It's got to be your idea and your sketch. No help from anyone else allowed. In fact, I think we should keep the costumes a secret until the day of the play."

All children loved a secret, didn't they?

Thirteen

Eloise stood at the base of the stairway leading to the stately town home and let her gaze roam the tidy street. Signs of the upcoming holiday were evident up and down the block of tall, elegant houses. Douglas fir and Scotch pine trees covered in lights, tinsel and ornaments peeked from behind satin-draped windows. Gaily ribboned wreaths and swags decorated every door. The smell of wood smoke hung heavy in the air, a pungent reminder that Christmas would soon be here.

Focusing on her destination, the Baxter house, she noted the electric candles in each window emitting a cheery, inviting glow, along with the impressive circle of pine boughs wrapped in twinkling lights that graced the front door.

Closing her eyes, Eloise imagined living here on this street, in the house she was about to enter. She remembered the foyer and its highly polished floor, the living and dining rooms' tasteful decor and the kitchen's homey warmth. Many humans resided in more luxurious houses, but none, she was sure, had a home as comfortable and welcoming as this one.

"She's here, Grammy! Ms. Eloise is here!" Phoebe swept open the front door, shouting loud enough to stop a taxi in the street. "We've been waiting for you. Grammy and I are cooking. Come in and hang up your coat while I go get her."

Touched by the little girl's enthusiasm, Eloise climbed the steps and walked into the center hall. Glancing around, she noted that someone had taken the time to decorate for the upcoming holiday on the inside as well as out. Bright red bows were tied to the base of the spindles on the banister. A ball of mistletoe, its berries a pristine waxy-white, hung from the brass chandelier; a basket brimming with pinecones guarded the foot of the stairs, while the invigorating scents of pine and cinnamon permeated the air

Following the instructions Phoebe had given on her last visit, Eloise placed her handbag on the foyer table, then took off her coat and dutifully hung it in the hall closet. At the sound of footsteps, she spun around to see Rita Mae heading from the back of the house.

Taking Eloise's hand, she leaned close and kissed her cheek. "I was so pleased to hear you would be joining us. I'm sorry I didn't stop by the classroom when I picked up Phoebe, but I was running late."

"I hope my being here isn't any trouble." Eloise tucked a stray curl back into the knot of hair on her head. After she'd promised Phoebe she would come to dinner, she'd hurried home from school, then changed into jeans and her new pink sweater. In a rush, she'd neglected to redo her hair. "I'm afraid Phoebe has taken it upon herself to adopt me."

"Well, how lucky for us. We love the company, especially on nights when my son has to work. Come into the kitchen. We can have a glass of wine and talk while I finish supper."

Wine? Eloise shrugged away her skepticism. Junior said she needed to do what humans did, and many of them enjoyed alcohol. She'd been tempted to try a glass of red wine when Nathan had drunk his at dinner the other night. If Rita Mae was having a glass, surely she could do the same.

She walked into the kitchen and found Phoebe putting the finishing touches on the table. Quilted place mats decorated with a jolly Santa and his sleigh circled a center display of fat red candles that sat in the middle of a wreath of twigs covered in small red berries.

"You sit here. I got to help Grammy."

Phoebe pulled out a chair and Eloise noticed her red-and-white-striped apron, a miniature replica of her grandmother's. Marching to the stove, the little girl climbed onto a stool and began stirring a pot with a long-handled wooden spoon.

Rita Mae turned from the counter. "Be careful, Phoebe Marie. Remember what I told you about getting too close to the burner, and do not touch any part of that saucepan but the handle." She carried over a glass of pale gold liquid and placed it on the table. "I hope you like sauvignon blanc. It's one of my favorites."

Eloise picked up the drink and held it to the light. "It looks lovely."

"Happy holidays." Rita Mae raised the glass, then brought it to her lips.

Mimicking her actions, Eloise took a sip. The fruity liquid slid down her throat and she imagined cool spring water quenching her thirst on a hot summer day. A bubble of surprise tickled from the inside out and she giggled.

"Hic!" "Oh, my. Excuse me." She giggled again. *"Hic!"*

Rita Mae gave her a motherly smile. "Not used to alcohol, are you?"

Eloise shook her head. "Is that bad?"

"I'd hardly call it bad, but it is refreshing. You don't have to finish, but if you decide you like the taste, I'd advise you to sip slowly."

"Grammy, the cheese is getting all thick and gooey," called Phoebe. "What should I do now?"

Rita Mae set down her drink. "Nothing until I get there. We're having macaroni and cheese and a tossed salad," she informed Eloise, "along with something Phoebe's dying to try—vegetarian hot dogs. I found them in the supermarket today, and they look quite promising."

"It sounds wonderful," Eloise said. How kind of Rita Mae to go to all that trouble, just to cater to her and what might be a whim for her granddaughter. Eloise doubted Phoebe would stay on her vegetarian kick for long—especially once her teacher was out of the little girl's life.

Rita Mae hoisted her granddaughter from the stool and set her on the tiles. After giving the pot a stir, she handed Phoebe a crystal bowl and the child carried it to the table.

"This is our salad. I shredded the lettuce, but Grammy won't let me cut tomatoes or anything. What kind of dressing do you want?"

"What kind are you having?" asked Eloise.

"We like Italian."

"Then that's what I'll have."

Rita Mae served plates piled with food. Phoebe set a bottle of dressing next to the salad bowl, then climbed onto a chair. "Can I say grace?"

"Maybe Ms. Eloise would like to, since she's our guest," suggested Rita Mae.

Before Eloise had a chance to decline the offer, Rita Mae and Phoebe bowed their heads. She wasn't sure what form of belief system was in place at the house and didn't want to offend, so she decided to do her generic best.

"Thank you God, for the gift of sustenance," she said, letting the words flow from her heart, "and thank you for allowing me to share in Phoebe's life." As soon as the last phrase left her mouth, Eloise felt heat scald her cheeks. What in the world had made her utter such a sentimental statement?

Rita Mae raised her head and stared at her intently. "That was lovely, Eloise. We're happy you've come into our lives, too. Now let me know if you like those hot dogs."

A short while later, after a round of lively dinner conversation and a tasty supper, Rita Mae sat back in her chair while Phoebe carried their plates and silverware to the counter. "I was surprised to hear that my granddaughter has homework tonight. She says it's a big secret and she doesn't want help, but I must admit she has me curious."

Phoebe rubbed at her nose as she returned to the table. "I

haf'ta do it all by myself, just like Ms. Eloise said. I'm gonna go to my room 'cause I need quiet so I can concentrate."

Rita Mae's blue eyes crinkled, but she kept a straight face. "You do that, sweetie. I'm sure we'll find something to talk about while you work."

Eloise waited for the little girl to leave before she spoke. "Wasn't I supposed to give the students homework?"

"I don't remember Phoebe having any before tonight, but I don't see the harm in it. Besides, she seemed very proud of the fact that she had a special project."

Eloise envisioned the Hewitt Academy's answering machine shorting out with the flood of angry phone calls it was sure to receive and shuddered inside. "I guess that will give Ms. Hewitt one more reason to fire me."

"Don't be silly. I hear you're doing a marvelous job, much better than Ms. Singeltary. I can't imagine what you've done that would make Honoria let you go."

Holding up her fingers, Eloise ticked off a personal litany of offenses. "I left my students alone on the second day of class, I took Phoebe off school grounds without permission, and for some reason there are important papers missing from my file. I never seem to wear my hair in an appropriate manner, and I have a strong suspicion my new clothes don't pass approval. Now I've handed out a homework assignment when there aren't supposed to be any." Raising her shoulders, she sighed. "I'm just not living up to Ms. Hewitt's expectation of a responsible teacher."

"None of those things sound very serious to me. Besides, I think the final judge should be the children and their parents. From what Phoebe's told me, you have the students' approval one hundred percent. I sometimes overhear gossip from the mothers, and I know for a fact that several of them think you're doing a good job."

"Really?"

"Really. Honoria wouldn't dare hold that evening you took

Phoebe home against you. Nathan's already made a point of letting her know you did what you thought was best."

"He did?"

"Of course." She propped an elbow on the table and rested her chin in her hand. "I'm so happy to see the two of you getting along. My son and granddaughter need another woman in their lives."

Eloise frowned. "I hope you don't think—That is—I didn't purposely set out to push my way into—"

"I'd hardly call it pushing when I practically had to drag you to lunch the other day. And you're doing me a favor when you make yourself available to sit with Phoebe." She raised a brow. "Nathan is grateful too, you know, even if he doesn't always show it."

"But Nathan—"

"Needs to stop being such a hard-ass."

Eloise wanted to slap Rita Mae a high-five. Instead, she swallowed the last of her wine to hide her grin.

The older woman placed a finger over her smiling mouth. "Oh my. I can't believe I said that out loud." She gave a polite cough. "You do like my son, don't you? He hasn't done anything to frighten you away?"

Eloise searched for the words to describe the heady blossom of need, the exhilarating rush she felt whenever Nathan gazed at her through his deep-set brown eyes, touched her with gentle fingers or placed his lips on hers.

"Oh, no." She realized she didn't sound convincing and added, "Not at all."

"That's good. He's been so hurt, you see. And I'm at a loss as to how I should help him." Rita Mae shook her head. "All a mother ever wants is to see her children happy."

Eloise could only imagine the intense, self-sacrificing emotions that drove a parent to want the best for their child. So many of her past souls, both mothers and fathers, thought only of themselves.

"Janet didn't want children, not really," said Rita Mae. "When that truth finally registered, it almost killed Nathan."

Eloise shifted in her seat. The memory of one of her many failures cut deep, much more so now that she was being bombarded with all these unsettling human feelings. "I can't fathom anyone not wanting Phoebe," she said, hoping to steer Rita Mae from the topic of Janet. "She's such a bright little girl."

"With an abundance of love in her heart. She positively pines for a younger sister, but what she really wants is to make her family whole. It pains Nathan, knowing that he isn't enough for his child."

"Nathan has nothing to be ashamed of," Eloise began. "I've seen the way he cares for his daughter, protects her . . . loves her. It's beautiful to watch."

"I agree. And my sincerest hope is that someday he finds someone as giving as he is to do the same for him." Rita Mae leaned back in her chair. "May I ask you a question?"

Doubting it would stop the woman if she said no, Eloise simply nodded.

"I get the impression you've never been married."

"That's right."

"And you *do* like men?"

"Like men?" Eloise felt her face warm as the pointed query sunk in. "I . . . um . . . "

It was Rita Mae's turn to blush and fumble for her words. "I know it's a terribly personal question, but one just never knows for certain these days. I'm sorry if I've overstepped my bounds, but you do understand what I'm asking, don't you?"

"I think so. And yes, I like men." *Especially tall, broad-shouldered ones with attitude, who desperately love their little girls.*

"Then why is it you've never married?"

"I haven't had much time for interaction with members of the opposite sex." Pleased she'd managed to describe her situation without lying, Eloise smiled. "And before that, well, my other position wouldn't allow it."

"Really?" Rita Mae scoffed out a laugh. "From the sound of it, one would think you'd been living in a cave."

Or on a cloud, thought Eloise, hoping to change the subject again. "I really should be going."

The older woman acted as if she hadn't heard. "Phoebe chatters about you constantly. She told me she'd shared her special drawer with you."

Eloise rested her hand over the locket tucked under her sweater. "Phoebe gave me something the other afternoon—something that belonged to her mother. I've been waiting for the proper time to return it, but so far—"

"Phoebe gave you something that belonged to Janet? What was it?"

Eloise tugged at the chain until the treasure sat in the palm of her hand. Tears formed in Rita Mae's eyes when she said, "Nathan gave that locket to Janet the day Phoebe was born. Unfortunately, it didn't meet her Cartier-inspired jewelry criteria, so she rarely wore it."

"Even so, I can't accept it. It's too precious," murmured Eloise. "But I don't want to hurt Phoebe's feelings."

Rita Mae reached out and closed Eloise's fingers around the heart-shaped nugget of gold. "Then keep it, please, at least until the end of the school year. It would pain Phoebe more if you returned it so soon."

"But if Nathan found out I had it—"

"He might be angry, at first, but he would eventually understand. Janet wasn't the right woman for him and he's come to accept that."

The ache Eloise had pushed aside at the mention of her dead charge's name swelled in her chest. It was clear Rita Mae's opinion of her daughter-in-law was skewed. Yes, Janet had been headstrong and spoiled, but deep down she'd been a good person. When Eloise saw that Janet wasn't about to change, she'd removed the woman from her list of souls. She'd died a short while later, leaving behind a husband and child who needed her.

"Besides," Rita Mae continued, "the locket is Phoebe's now. It's her right to do whatever she wants with it."

Eloise clutched at the gift, a symbol of regret that would be with her always. "But I still don't think—"

The phone rang and Rita Mae crossed the kitchen to answer it. "Hello? Yes, this is she . . . Yes, I know him . . . What? Oh, no . . . I mean, yes, of course . . . Tell them I'm on my way. I'll be there in five minutes."

She hung up the receiver and whirled toward the back door. "Eloise, please, stay with Phoebe. See to it she gets to bed. There's been an emergency. I have to go out and I'm not sure when I'll return. I'm just going to get my jacket and car keys. Tell Nathan . . ."

Her words faded as she disappeared. Footsteps hammered up the rear stairs and back again, telling Eloise that Rita Mae's handbag and coat had been sitting near the door. Seconds later the outside door opened and slammed shut. A car engine revved; tires squealed. Then there was quiet.

She heaved a sigh. Nathan had asked that she page him when she was ready to leave, but now she had no idea when that would be. Rita Mae had assumed she would stay with Phoebe. And why not? Friends did that kind of thing for one another.

She stood, pushed in her chair and cleared the table of glasses and napkins. She would have to break the news of her grandmother's emergency and make sure the little girl went to bed. Should she notify Nathan and let him know what was going on, or take her chances and hope that Rita Mae returned soon?

She headed to the front of the house. Right now, Phoebe needed her, so that was her first priority.

* * *

By the time Eloise arrived upstairs, Phoebe had finished her homework and dressed in her pajamas. She didn't seem to care one bit that her beloved Grammy had taken off and left her teacher in charge. Instead, she decided to show Eloise more of her treasures and she began with her hair baubles.

"Daddy still has a hard time fixin' my hair, so I try to do it myself," Phoebe said with a sigh. "Even though I practice on my Barbie doll, I can't ever get mine to look like hers."

"Are you talking about that skinny mannequin sitting on top of the toilet?" Eloise pointed to a well-endowed yet anorexic-looking piece of plastic with an empty expression on its face.

"Uh-huh. I want to grow up to look just like her," said Phoebe. "She's beautiful."

"She has a head the size of a marble."

Phoebe's expression turned doubtful. "You think so?"

"I know so. Just look at her body. No real woman is built that way."

"She has lots of pretty clothes," said Phoebe, sticking up for Barbie.

"And those feet," countered Eloise. "It's a wonder she doesn't fall flat on her face."

"But I like Barbie," Phoebe said, her lower lip quivering.

"It's fine to like her," Eloise stated, "just don't grow up trying to resemble her or what she stands for. You're a very pretty little girl, just the way you are. And you're too smart to have a doll for a role model. Reach for the stars, find someone important to copy, like a—a woman senator or doctor, even a teacher."

Wrinkling her nose, Phoebe gazed at her from the mirror. "Our hair's almost the same color. Do you like being blond?"

"What's not to like?" Eloise picked up a hairbrush and began to work the tangles out of Phoebe's hair.

"People make dumb blonde jokes all the time. Want to hear the one Billy told me the other day?"

"Sure."

"What did the dumb blonde say when she looked inside the box of Cheerios?"

"I don't have the foggiest idea. What?"

"Oh look, donut seeds."

Eloise stopped brushing and fisted a hand on her hip. "Well, duh!"

Phoebe rolled her eyes. "See what I mean?"

Together they broke out in a fit of giggles. Eloise sat on the commode while Phoebe doubled over with laughter. Finally, Eloise said, "You know what?"

"What?"

"How about you ignore the jokes? People who say nasty things about the color of someone's hair or poke fun at how they talk, or make them feel bad about their weight are usually jealous or just plain mean. We—you don't need that type of person in your life. If you try to be their friend and they can't be nice, you say 'good-bye.'"

Phoebe gave another giggle. "You sound like that lady on *The Weakest Link*."

"Don't know her, but I'm an expert at doing my best until I figure it's hopeless."

"Grammy says it's never hopeless. That's why I keep asking for a baby sister." She turned to Eloise. "But I think I should change my wish and ask for a mommy instead. That way, when God answers my prayers, I'll get the sister too."

The low blow slammed straight to Eloise's heart. "Time for bed," she declared, giving Phoebe's hair a final stroke with the hairbrush. "Off you go."

"Okay, but I have to say my prayers first." Phoebe walked to her bed and turned down the covers, then dropped to her knees at the side of the mattress. "Hi, God, it's me, Phoebe Marie Baxter. I don't have much to say tonight, just the usual stuff. First, tell Mommy I miss her and I tried really hard to be good today. Please keep my grammy safe because I love her so much, and keep my daddy safe, because I love him best. And please, please, please find a way to bring me a new mother." She stood halfway, then glanced at Eloise and got back on her knees. "Oh, yeah, and keep Ms. Eloise safe, too. She's my teacher and I love her almost as much as I love Grammy. Amen."

Eloise opened and closed her mouth, too choked up to speak. Smiling weakly, she held back the tears threatening behind her eyes. "Thank you, Phoebe, that was very thoughtful."

"I figured since you don't have a little girl, someone should put in a good word for you." She climbed under the covers and snuggled a stuffed dog in her arms. "Will you stay with me 'til I fall asleep?"

Eloise took a seat in the rocking chair next to the night-stand. "If you want me to."

Moonlight, as pale and shimmering as Phoebe's hair, danced across the floor and crept over the little girl's pensive face. She let out a sigh. "Ms. Eloise, why do you think Mommy died?"

Eloise grabbed at the arms of the rocker to keep from bolting into the hall. *Oh, please, no. Anything but this.* "I don't know why, but I'm sure God had His reasons."

"But I thought God gave people angels to keep them safe."

She heaved a breath. "Phoebe, I'm going to tell you a little secret about how God works, but you have to promise not to repeat it. Can you do that?"

"Why is it a secret?"

Good question. Eloise closed her eyes. "Because if everybody knew, there wouldn't be any more mystery and life would get very boring."

Eloise could almost hear Phoebe's mind pondering the notion before she said, "How about I keep it secret just because you asked me to?"

"That'll work. Are you ready for me to tell you?"

"Uh-huh."

"Angels are sent here to guide people along life's path

and keep them from making stupid mistakes. That's the entire scope of their job."

"You mean they're supposed to keep us from eating too much ice cream 'cause it might make us sick, or not jump from the top step 'cause we could break something?"

Eloise smiled into the darkness. "Sort of."

"So why do people have to die?"

"Only God knows the answer to that one, and He's not talking. But when He calls a soul home, there isn't a thing anyone, not even an angel, can do to prevent it."

"So my mommy had to go?"

"She didn't have a choice, because I'm sure if she did, she never would have left a wonderful little girl like you."

It became so quiet, Eloise was certain Phoebe had fallen asleep. Then she heard a sigh.

"Good night, Ms. Eloise."

Eloise bit hard on her lower lip to keep from crying at the knot that had formed in her chest, but it didn't help. Somehow, when she hadn't been looking, Phoebe had grabbed on to her heart. She could feel each finger, each grip of love as it flowed from Phoebe to her, forming a bond as unbreakable as tempered steel.

"Good night." *I'll be here watching over you.* "Sleep tight."

Fourteen

Nathan and Isobel Romero pulled up to the house in one of the city's many generic patrol cars. The slate gray automobile hummed like a top, but all anyone who bothered to look would notice was the parade of dents from too many close calls and fender benders dimpling the car's sides, rear and front end. He and his partner were through for the night. Since Isobel had picked him up that morning after he'd taken Phoebe to school, they'd agreed she would drop him off and return the car to the communal lot, where her own vehicle was waiting.

The air was blustery with the scent of snow. Nathan left the car and followed Isobel up the steps. His pager hadn't gone off for anything other than police business all night. If Eloise had walked home alone, he was going to throttle her. That gang was still on the loose; their last hit had been mere blocks from her apartment. It was the reason he was so late getting home. This time, they'd struck in the afternoon.

"Nice place," muttered Isobel, judging the upscale neighborhood through keen brown eyes. "Pretty fancy digs on a detective's salary."

"We get by." Nathan shrugged the simplistic reaction. Isobel's measuring look was identical to the many he'd received from his police buddies the first time they saw the house, and he'd learned not to explain.

Unlocking the door, he waved a hand to usher her inside. Peering into the darkness, he listened for the sound of the television from the rear of the house. That was usually where Rita Mae waited when she baby-sat. He checked out the den, noted all was quiet and headed for the dimly lit kitchen with Isobel on his heels. He grinned when he saw the dishes of a dinner for three sitting on the counter. Every once in a while, as a special treat, his mother took Phoebe to her apartment. She, Phoebe and Eloise should be there now, because Eloise hadn't called him for a ride home.

"Can I make you a cup of coffee or tea?" he asked. "Or do you want to get going?"

Isobel propped herself against the counter. "Nothing at my house but a cantankerous cat and an unmade bed. Tea would be nice. Something soothing. You got any peppermint?"

He opened a cupboard door and removed the box of assorted teas. "Orange Spice, Earl Grey, Raspberry Mist—Yep, here's Peppermint." He filled the kettle, set it on the stove and turned on the gas, then took down a mug and placed it next to her. "I have to let my mother know I'm home. Go into the den and I'll be back in a minute."

"Will do," the petite detective answered.

Nathan climbed the rear steps two at a time, but when he entered the apartment he realized it was empty. Only mildly concerned, he went back downstairs. Thoughts of Eloise, here with his daughter, had consumed his day. Even though she hadn't called him, he'd assumed she had come to dinner. Would she have left without telling him?

He glanced into the empty guest bedroom, then crossed the hall. Stepping through the doorway to Phoebe's room, he stopped in his tracks and released a pent-up breath. Moonlight spilled from the window, casting a pale glow over his sleeping child, who was curled up tight around her stuffed German shepherd.

He scanned the room, expecting to find his mother, and instead spied Eloise dozing in the antique rocker next to the nightstand. The incoming light skimmed the top of her head, shadowing her features, but the darkness couldn't hide the candy pink softness of the sweater caressing the curves of her ample breasts.

Treading carefully, he went to his daughter and tucked the blanket over her inert form. With a gentle hand, he smoothed her bangs, noting that someone had taken the time to untangle her hair so that it fell in curling spirals over her thin shoulders. He shook his head, silently thanking God for the miracle of Phoebe Marie.

Still surprised at finding the teacher here instead of his mother, he sat at the foot of the bed. With Eloise resting so peacefully, he had the opportunity to study her again and this time he couldn't help but notice the features she and Phoebe shared. His daughter's face was heart shaped, while Eloise's was a perfect oval, but they had the same silvery wash of hair, the same stubborn chin and dark, slanted brows. It was only Eloise's mouth, wider, with more generous lips, that differed from Phoebe's childlike cupid's bow.

He still couldn't fathom that she'd been a nun. No woman as beautiful as Eloise would have willingly hidden herself away in a convent. No woman who responded to his kiss the way she had would have been content living such a singular, celibate existence. He wouldn't believe it until he heard the words from her. She simply couldn't have been a nun.

Eloise shifted in her chair and Nathan found himself captured in her wide-eyed gaze. "Good evening," he whispered.

Blinking, she sat up straight and glanced from him to Phoebe and back again. He stood and held out his hand, offering to help her from the rocker. She stared at his fingers for a long second before she took them in her own. Standing, she let him lead her from the room.

Nathan shut the door and turned to see that Eloise had already moved to the top of the stairs, far enough away that they could talk without waking Phoebe.

"Where's my mother?" he asked, walking toward her. Rita Mae rarely went out at night, and when she did, was always back by this time.

"She got called out on an emergency. I told her I'd stay here until you got home."

He leaned against the wall, hoping to prolong the private moment. "What kind of emergency?"

"She didn't say, but it sounded serious."

"So that's why you didn't page me."

"You said to page you when I was ready to leave. As you can see, it never happened."

Eloise started down the steps and he took her hand again. "Hang on a second. There's someone downstairs. I'm going to ask her to stay with Phoebe so I can take you home."

Staring at their entwined fingers, she tugged. "I don't need an escort. It's only a few blocks."

Nathan refused to let go. He couldn't help notice how graceful and feminine her hand looked encased in his larger, more masculine one. Her fingers were long and slender and smooth with short unpainted nails—untouched just like her.

Fighting the urge to cradle her against his chest, he sighed. "This conversation's getting old. I appreciate your taking care of Phoebe and I want to drive you home. It's freezing out. I think we're in for more snow."

"Really?" Her eyes shined a brilliant blue. "That's great news."

"Yeah, well, tell it to the Roads Department." He released her hand. "My partner's in the kitchen. Let me talk to her for a minute."

Eloise heard the frustration in his voice and decided it might be better to acquiesce than argue. It was late and she was tired. The brush of his shoulder as they rounded the landing reminded her that if he brought her home, he might kiss her again. Not necessarily a bad thing.

In the kitchen, they were greeted by a doll-size woman with sparkling ebony eyes and a shining ponytail of straight black hair pulled back to rest low against her slender neck. Eloise immediately felt like a giant crow towering over a wren. Something foreign sparked in her chest, an unidentifiable emotion she wasn't comfortable with, but couldn't push away.

"Isobel Romero, Eloise Starr." Nathan rubbed at his nape. "I need a favor. I have to make sure Ms. Starr gets home safely and there's no one to watch Phoebe. Do you think—"

"Maybe Ms. Romero could give me a ride," suggested Eloise.

Isobel and Nathan spoke at the same time.

"I'd be happy to—"

"That's not necessary—"

Isobel snorted out a laugh. "No problem. I can hang here a few more minutes. Take the heap. It should still be warm." She tossed him a ring of keys.

Nathan caught them midair. "Ms. Starr and I have things to discuss, but I won't be long." He took Eloise by the arm and propelled her out of the kitchen. "Feel free to turn on the TV and help yourself to whatever you can find in the fridge," he called over his shoulder.

He held open the front door and they walked to the car parked across the street.

Just as Isobel had predicted, the car was warm. Though not as luxurious as Nathan's vehicle, it was also spacious and clean. Eloise buckled her seat belt into place and he did the same. He put the car in gear just as a snowflake hit the windshield.

"You were right," she said, unable to contain her joy. "It's starting to snow."

Peering at the lone flake, Nathan eased out of the parking space. "Yeah, it's a regular blizzard out there."

She inched forward in the seat and concentrated on the circles of light from the overhead street lamps. "Have you heard a weather report?"

He stabbed at a button on the dashboard and the radio shot to life "... *with overnight temperatures in the twenties and that low-pressure center moving in, be prepared for at least ten inches, folks. Now back to our regular programming."*

A blare of salsa rhythm filled the car. Nathan quickly changed the station to classical and turned down the sound. "Sorry, Romero is into her ethnicity these days. Says it takes her back to her roots."

"She's very pretty," said Eloise. "How long have the two of you worked together?"

"Little over a week." He took the corner slowly, as if he wanted to prolong their time together. Falling snowflakes could now be seen crowding the glare thrown by the headlights. "Why?"

"No reason. I just wondered."

He gave her a sideways stare. "There's nothing between us, if that's what you're asking. We're just coworkers trying to do our jobs."

"I didn't mean to imply anything to the contrary," she said with a little sniff. "But she is attractive."

"If you like the type."

"Pretty and petite? Isn't that the *type* most men want?"

"Some, not all. Take me for instance—"

"Let's not." She focused straight ahead.

"I like my women with a little meat on their bones."

"I see."

"And I'm partial to blondes."

Eloise showed no reaction. Janet had been dark-haired and delicately built, just like Isobel, and Nathan had found her attractive enough to marry. Sadly, she didn't think there would ever be an appropriate time to discuss the differences between her and his dead wife.

"Did you hear what I said?"

"I heard."

"Sure you're not jealous?" His voice sounded confident and all too smug.

"Hardly." She cringed inside. The indefinable emotion had

just been given a name, and now that she knew what it was, she wanted to crawl under a rock. "Turn right at the corner."

"I know where I'm supposed to turn," he said with a decidedly happy lilt. "Eloise, I think we need to talk."

"Isn't that what we're doing?"

He pulled to the curb and shifted to face her. "I mean really talk. I have a few questions I need to ask and you're the only one who can answer them for me."

"It's late. You shouldn't keep your partner waiting." She opened the car door and made it all the way to the porch before he reached her side. "I can let myself in. You need to go home. Rita Mae might call you or—"

Nathan snatched the key from her shaking fingers. "You are the most obstinate woman I have ever met." Pushing the door open with one hand, he placed the other on her back and scooted her into the foyer. Once they were at her apartment, he propped himself in front of her. "Invite me inside."

Eloise shuffled to the right and he stepped in her way. She zigzagged to the left and he followed. Finally, she stopped dancing and glared. "Why should I invite you in?"

He met her glare with a challenge of his own. Grabbing her upper arms, he bent and kissed her hard on the lips.

Eloise melted against him and he growled low in his throat.

When he loosened his hold, she wound her arms around his neck. The kiss took on a life of its own, demanding and giving at the same time. Eloise raised herself on tiptoe to meet him more fully and Nathan took every advantage, molding himself to her thighs, her waist, her breasts.

He moved his hands inside her coat to her sweater and flattened his palms against her back. Eloise arched into him, wishing she'd taken his hint and let him into her apartment. She needed privacy to explore these new and exhilarating feelings that seemed to assault her at every turn.

An ache of need formed in the pit of her stomach. Human desire took command of her body, telling her to press against him and surrender. To find a way to stay in his arms forever.

Breathing heavily, Nathan pulled back and gazed at Eloise's flushed face. Her eyes were closed, her lips swollen. The kiss was everything he wanted it to be and more. So much more.

"I swore the next time we did this, it wouldn't be in a hallway. Not again."

Her eyes fluttered open. "You don't want to kiss me?"

"Kissing you is all I've been thinking about for the past few days. I vowed the next time it happened I wasn't going to go about it like some hormone-driven teenager trying to get to second base."

"Second base?"

"Eloise, don't look at me like that."

She worried her lower lip. "Like what?"

"Like I'm the only man you've ever kissed."

Her eyebrows drew together as she asked, "Is that bad?"

He sighed. "Not bad. Just—"

"If you say 'different,' I swear I'm going to stomp so hard on your instep you'll need a cane to walk out of here."

"Okay, okay." He thought before he spoke. "Not different. But I think I've figured out your secret."

"Secret? You think I have a secret?"

"I know you have a secret. Several, in fact."

"I have to go inside."

"And I have to get back home, which means we're going to talk later. Are you sure you don't know where Rita Mae went?"

"Positive. She just got the one phone call and raced out the door." Eloise disengaged her arms from around his neck and took a step back. "Why?"

"Because I worry about her. She's been alone for the past five years, ever since Dad died. She has her bridge pals and her yoga buddies, but she devotes most of her time to the care and feeding of me and Phoebe, and it doesn't seem fair."

He unlocked her door and handed her the key. "If she's not home by morning, I'm going to send out a search party."

Eloise sidled over the threshold and gazed up at him. "Let me know if there's anything I can do."

Reaching out, he cupped her jaw and gave her a soft sweet kiss, very unlike their last one. "I will. And I was serious when I said we have to talk. Maybe you'd go to dinner with me one night this week, just the two of us?"

"I think I'd like that."

"So would I."

She closed the door and he waited until he heard the locks click in place. Jamming his hands into his pockets, he recalled the look on her face after their kiss. He didn't know one damn bit more about Eloise than he did when he'd first met her, not really. But he was more certain than ever of one scary thing.

Not only did he have the hots for his daughter's teacher. He was lusting after a nun.

Eloise stumbled through the hallway without hanging up her coat or setting her handbag on the foyer table. Still enthralled by the possessive touch of Nathan's lips, she didn't want to spoil the amazing sensation by speaking or thinking too hard. She knew beyond a shadow of a doubt that he wanted her. For now, she would concentrate on that disarming fact and ignore the rest.

Waltzing into her bedroom, she twirled toward the dainty side chair and sat with a plop. Drawing a deep breath, she let her mind cloud over as she relived every second in his arms. Heat filled her from the inside out, as if a bed of hot coals burned low in the very center of her body. The warmth radiated outward in waves, up to her chest and face, and down to her pelvis and thighs.

If this was desire, no wonder humankind acted so silly and stupid when gripped by it. Such an overwhelming emotion could be frightening, even dangerous if put in the wrong hands. People who had a hard time containing their ordinary everyday feelings would certainly have trouble keeping this more disturbing and pervasive one in check.

She tried to get hold of her thoughts, but one overlying observation shone clearly in mind. If Janet had truly loved Nathan, how could she not have wanted his child? How could she not have wanted him?

The idea caused her to brighten. From the moment she'd met Nathan when she'd been an angel, she'd been fighting her reaction to his presence, worried she had overstepped her responsibilities. If Janet hadn't cared for Nathan, maybe it was all right for her to use him as her return ticket to heaven.

"Now you're on the right track," an amused voice shot out of the darkness, slapping her back to the present.

"Junior." She sagged in the chair. "Where did you come from?"

He sat cross-legged on her bed, tossing a tennis ball-size circle of light from side to side. "You know better than to ask that question."

"I didn't mean it like that," she chided. "I only meant, where have you been? It's taken you long enough to check back with me."

He threw the brilliant sphere to the ceiling, where it vanished in a golden shower of angel dust. "There wasn't anything to get back to. You're not moving very fast here, El."

She opened and closed her mouth. "Not moving fast? What are you—blind? Haven't you been keeping tabs on me? Haven't you seen the way Phoebe and I are bonding? The way Nathan and I have been—"

"I saw what happened between you and Phoebe tonight." He leaned back on his elbows and gave a quirky grin. "I also saw you and Nathan. And from my vantage point you're moving like a snail in reverse."

She clutched at the arms of her chair. "I'm doing the best I can. It's only tonight that I got some of it sorted out. I let Nathan kiss me, didn't I?"

"You're frightened. You just thought it a minute ago, so don't try to deny it."

"I am not frightened. I merely told myself I now understood why humans *might* be frightened . . . and . . . and confused when faced with such overwhelming emotions." She brushed a curl from her forehead. "Besides, it's impolite for you to read my thoughts."

Junior shook his head. "Aw, come on. Don't be such a party pooper. What do you care if I'm nosing around inside your head? You don't have anything to *hide* from me, do you?"

She folded her arms across her chest. "On that rude note, I think I'll change the subject. How are my charges?"

"My . . . er . . . your charges are doing just fine. This guiding angel thing is a piece of cake."

She arched a brow. "Oh, really? Then I guess Tina and Dan Bingham are pregnant?"

"Tina? Well, no . . . I mean maybe—" Sitting upright, he tucked his thumbs under his suspenders and gave them a snap. "Sure she—they is—are."

"Ah-ha! Trick question and you failed. Tina's had a hysterectomy, and she and her husband were contemplating adoption." Grabbing the hair at her temples, she raised her gaze to the ceiling. "Some great job you've been doing."

Junior stood and began to pace. "Okay, okay. I'll look in on the Binghams tonight. But I swear to you, I'm doing my best. Nothing bad has happened to any of them."

"You're telling me none of my souls has done anything stupid?"

"Define stupid," he said, his expression a bit less cocky.

"Oh, like . . . say . . . falling in love with the wrong person, or maybe being cruel to their children or worse, indifferent to the people they care about. You know how the Big Guy feels about apathy."

Spinning on his heel, Junior stuffed his hands in his pockets. "Okay, I'll look into it. Now let's get back to you."

"Do we have to?" Eloise sighed. "My neurons are sort of overloaded right now."

"Maybe you're just too caught up in the small stuff. Try to concentrate on the big picture here, El. You have a goal—"

"I know. Faith, hope and love. I've been working on it."

"You kissed Nathan Baxter."

"He kissed me." She closed her eyes, not wanting to remember with Junior in the room. "I believe kissing is one of the first steps humans take in having an intimate relationship. You did tell me I was supposed to have one with him, didn't you?" *And please say yes,* she thought silently.

"I heard that." He grinned. "Yes."

"Fine."

"Good."

"Don't you mean good night?"

"Not just yet." He buffed his nails on his white cotton shirt. "So, tell me, how do you feel about Nathan?"

"You are so exasperating." Eloise pinned him with a glare. "What does Milton have to say about all of this?"

"Milton is thrilled. He told me to tell you to *go for it.*"

"That doesn't sound much like the heavenly Doughboy to me. Are you sure those were his exact words?"

Junior had the decency to look askance. "Um . . . no, not exactly, but I know it's what he meant. He wants you to succeed, El. He wants you to be the best you can be."

She narrowed her eyes. "Isn't that the U.S. Army recruiting slogan?"

"Catchy, isn't it?"

Eloise had enough of Junior's verbal fencing. His presence only reminded her of how much she missed her old life . . . her life without Nathan and Phoebe. Suddenly, she didn't like the road her thoughts were traveling.

"I have a busy day tomorrow. I think you should leave," she said in her best schoolteacher voice. "Drop by sometime next week and maybe I'll have something new to report."

"See what I mean—a snail's pace."

Before Eloise could send him off with a more emphatic edict, Junior disappeared from the room.

Fifteen

Sometime overnight, the low-pressure system stalled over western Virginia. The leading edge of the storm was now sitting just outside the District, sending errant snowflakes and weak winter winds stumbling through the city at odd intervals during the day.

Eloise had hoped there would be no school so she could ponder the time she'd spent with Phoebe, Nathan and Junior, but it was not to be. Like Honoria herself, the Hewitt Academy was a stickler for duty. No snow meant class was in session.

The students were clustered at the bookshelves putting away their readers when Ms. Hewitt literally tripped through the doorway. Several of them stared in concern as she fell forward, then righted herself and, frowning, scanned the room. Eloise kept her gaze focused on her desk while she watched the scene unfold through half-raised eyelids. What did the prissy woman want now?

"Who's boots are these?" demanded the headmistress, shoving at one of the offensive objects with the toe of her granny shoe.

A few of the children shuffled quickly to their seats without answering, while a group stood like fawns caught in oncoming headlights.

The principal folded her arms and nodded to the row of pegs on the back wall. "And those coats need to be hung properly."

No one moved.

"I asked who owned these boots." She tapped a foot with impatience. "And I expect an answer."

Finally Brent shuffled over and picked up his boots. Taking them to the stack of cubicles, he stuffed them inside one of the boxes, then walked to his seat.

Ms. Hewitt glared, her face verging on tomato red. "The coats, if you please."

Billy, Miles and John sidled to the pegs, removed their bunched-up jackets, shook them out and set them back in place.

Eloise heaved a sigh. The rabid look in Honoria's eyes made her think the principal had again found the words *Ms. Hewitt sucks the big one* scrawled on the mirror in the eighth-grade rest room, or that she'd come across another dead mouse in her desk drawer. Either way, whatever was annoying the woman couldn't possibly have anything to do with her students. The show of terror had to stop, before someone—namely Honoria Hewitt—got hurt.

"Is there something I can do for you, Ms. Hewitt?" asked Eloise, rising from her chair.

Ms. Hewitt pierced Eloise with a glare, and the children quivering in her presence took the opportunity to scamper to their seats. Tight-lipped, she nodded regally. "If I may speak with you in the hall?"

Eloise gave the students a grin of reassurance. They'd been pestering her all day about when they would be allowed to go over their homework. "I'll only be a minute. When I return, we'll work on your assignment for the Christmas pageant. If you need to put any finishing touches on your ideas, now's the time to do it."

Eager whispers and excited giggles echoed in the room. Pleased her assignment had been a success, she walked to the hallway and found the principal pacing in front of a bank of lockers. Eloise firmed her resolve to not let the woman bully her. She needed to chill, as Billy had said the other day.

"Ms. Hewitt, is there a problem?" she asked, pasting a serene smile on her face.

Standing ramrod straight, Honoria held her ground. "The children are supposed to be in the auditorium at this very moment, practicing for the play. May I ask why they are still in the classroom?"

Eloise crossed her fingers behind her back. "We aren't ready to go live yet."

"Go live?" Ms. Hewitt scoffed. "The play is only two weeks away and I have yet to approve the costumes or staging."

She has yet to approve!? Oh-oh. Eloise hid behind an innocent look. "I wasn't aware that the staging and costumes needed your approval. It wasn't in Ms. Singeltary's instruction manual, and you never said."

Ms. Hewitt removed her oversize spectacles and pinched the bridge of her nose between two fingers. For a second, Eloise sympathized with Honoria and her world-weary expression. The few times she'd been in the teacher's lounge, she'd heard the staff grumbling about the school's precarious financial state, and wondered if it was all too much for the young headmistress. Unfortunately, Eloise had problems of her own to consider.

Reseating her glasses, Ms. Hewitt expelled a breath. "I didn't want to say anything in front of your students, but there have been phone calls, Ms. Starr. At least four. You gave the children homework."

The woman's words rang like a pronouncement of doom. "Is that a problem?"

"For a few of the parents, yes. They feel, as do I, that a five-year-old is too young to have such responsibilities."

Eloise had a suspicion that if the headmistress knew the homework was a lesson in using their imaginations to come up with costumes for the play, there would be even more trouble. "It was a simple assignment—a drawing. We're going over it this afternoon, then we're going to practice lines from the play."

Drawn back into the spirit of the pageant, Ms. Hewitt nodded. "That sounds promising. And there will be no more homework?"

"Not that I know of," admitted Eloise. "But I'm curious. What exactly did the parents object to?"

"I think it was the fact that the youngsters insisted they work on the project in secret. Some of the parents were worried their children were being asked to do something inappropriate."

"Inappropriate?" Eloise cringed at the distasteful word. She was an angel. How dare anyone suggest such a thing? "That's ridiculous. I'd show you the assignment, but it's part of a surprise. They'll be thrilled. I promise."

Ms. Hewitt folded her arms in contemplation. "I sincerely hope so, because frankly, my patience is wearing thin. I don't normally listen to gossip, but there have been rumors of conduct unbecoming a teacher, Ms. Starr. That is a charge I don't take lightly."

"Rumors of unbecoming conduct?" Eloise had an idea what that might be but wanted it spelled out in capital letters at least a foot high. "Well, don't keep me in suspense. What are the charges?"

"You and Mr. Baxter have been seen together in public on several occasions. It's also being said that you're closely involved with Phoebe Marie. Is this true?"

Eloise squared her shoulders as she stepped toward the lockers. "I went to dinner with Mr. Baxter to discuss his daughter. He wanted to be sure I understood Phoebe's home situation."

"So you haven't gotten personally involved with the child or her father?"

Angels do not lie, Eloise reminded herself, but there was no time like the present to answer a question with a question. "Are you telling me I can't have a private life and teach here at the same time? That my friendships must be approved by you?"

Ms. Hewitt narrowed her gaze. "I'm only saying that when said friendships affect the reputation of this school, it might be more prudent of you to think twice. The last thing the Academy needs is another incident of the type it had with Ms. Singeltary."

"I can assure you I do not plan on getting pregnant any time in the near future," Eloise snapped. "Now if you'll excuse me, I need to get back to my charges." She turned and headed for her classroom, furious the woman had stuck her nose where it didn't belong.

It dawned on her as she swept through the doorway that she had just called the children her charges, exactly as she'd so often referred to the souls in her care. Slowing her steps, she stopped at her desk and turned to gaze at her students. Trusting faces, expectant and full of what she now recognized as hope—in her—stared back, waiting for her to say something profound.

Suddenly, the idea that she held their minds and hearts in her inexperienced hands made her stagger. She propped herself against the desk. Smiling feebly, she patted at her hair.

"Why was Ms. Hewitt so angry?" asked Lucy.

Eloise shrugged. "Sometimes, when adults have a problem they're worrying over, they take it out on the people around them. I think that's what was wrong with Ms. Hewitt today."

"I didn't mean to leave my boots in the middle of the floor. They got there by themselves, honest," Brent said with a sniff. "Am I gonna get detention?"

"I hardly think so," Eloise said. "But the next time any of you see Ms. Hewitt in the hall, I want you to say a polite 'good morning' or 'good afternoon' and give her a big smile. Is that understood?"

"You mean I can't tell her to chill out?" asked Billy. "'Cause she really needs to take a pill."

Unable to help herself, Eloise grinned and the children

brightened. "No more dawdling or feeling down. Who wants to show their costume first? Raise your hand."

Nathan parked in the lot behind Georgetown University Hospital and turned off his SUV. Resting his hands on the wheel, he digested the two strange but similar incidents he'd been involved in today.

This morning, just as he'd pulled in front of the Hewitt Academy to drop off his daughter, his pager had chirped. It was the first he'd heard from Rita Mae since last night's mysterious disappearance, so instead of walking Phoebe to her classroom, he'd stood in the entryway and watched her skip down the hall while he picked up the voice mail.

His mother's message had been so vague and disturbing, he forgot to stop off and say good morning to Eloise. All Rita Mae told him was that she'd been at this very hospital sitting with a sick friend, and wouldn't be available to get Phoebe after school. She planned to slip home for a quick shower and change of clothes and go right back to her friend's bedside. What the hell was up with that!

Once inside the station, he'd been informed that Joe Milligan had been taken to this same hospital sometime last night with chest pains, and the doctors had deduced that he'd suffered a mild coronary. Nathan had been put in charge of the day shift until the top brass could decide who they were going to get to take the captain's place while he recuperated.

He'd done some fancy talking to convince the chief that he wasn't ready to fill Joe's shoes, then finagled time off to visit the captain. After cleaning up a few reports and getting a promise from Isobel that she would handle the investigation on her own, he'd hightailed it to the hospital. If he was lucky, he'd get to see Joe and find Rita Mae at the same time.

He stopped at the gift shop on the way to the coronary care

unit. The men had taken up a collection and given him the okay to buy flowers, balloons, gag gifts, even porno videos, whatever he could find to cheer up their leader. It took a mere three minutes to choose a vase of fresh flowers and a bunch of gaudily decorated helium-filled balloons. The rest of his time was eaten up picking out gifts guaranteed to set Joe to laughing.

He was pretty pleased with both presents: a bedpan painted on the inside with a bright yellow happy face and a six-inch plastic nurse doll with a button on her rounded fanny that read "pinch me." When you pressed the button, the amply endowed healthcare professional gave a sexy shriek of glee. Between the gifts and the half-dozen get-well cards and assorted computer-generated messages he carried in his jacket pocket, he felt like the friggin' Ambassador of Tacky Taste.

He got off the elevator on the CCU floor and received instructions from a woman at the desk. After giving him the rules—family members could visit anytime, but everyone else was limited to fifteen minutes—she directed him to Joe's room.

Striding down the hall, Nathan had to admit that hospitals creeped him out. He'd spent time in this one as a teenager, when his last grandparent had died, and again several years ago when his father had lost his battle with stomach cancer. Rita Mae had been stoic, only breaking down when his dad had breathed his last, but he'd been a regular crybaby.

Joe wasn't old enough to be his father—hell, the man was still in his prime—and he certainly wasn't old enough to die, but Nathan's gut still quivered when he thought of the captain and his brush with death.

Juggling the balloons, flowers and bedpan, he tucked the bag holding Nurse Naughty under his arm and shouldered his way into the room. Prepared to call out a hearty "what the hell happened to you?" he stopped short and gazed at the bed—or rather the woman perched daintily on a chair at the side of it.

"Mom?"

Rita Mae raised a finger to her lips. "He's just dozed off. Don't you dare wake him."

Nathan searched the room, found an empty chair and dumped his parcels, being careful to balance the vase between the chair's back and seat cushions. It gave him time to form questions to which he wasn't sure he wanted the answers. He turned to see his mother straightening the covers over Joe's chest with an almost loving expression on her makeup-free face.

Wires ran from under the sleeve of his standard issue hospital gown to a bank of monitors behind Rita Mae's chair. A stack of romance novels and two thrillers sat on the side table, along with a trio of paper cups dangling tea bag strings, and a half-eaten plastic container of fruit.

It was obvious she was here for the duration.

For want of something better to do, he ran a hand over his nape. "So, Mom. Eloise told me you had an emergency, but I never thought—"

"Please use your inside voice," Rita Mae said with a hiss. "Can't you see Joe needs his rest?"

Feeling about seven years old, Nathan finally found the wherewithal to inspect the man in the bed. The captain's face looked haggard, the whiskered skin so pale it faded into the sheets. Suddenly, the conversation the two of them had shared the other morning when he'd been running the background check on Eloise shot to the fore. The man had been having chest pains while they'd been talking and neither of them had the good sense to notice.

"Sorry. I—" Dropping his voice ten decibels, he stuffed his fists in his pockets. "What are you doing here?"

Rita Mae moved to the foot of the bed and waited. When Nathan met her there, she took his arm and pulled him toward the door. "I'm sorry I didn't give you the details in my voice mail, but Joe thought it best to keep things quiet."

"You've been with him the whole time?"

"I went home about an hour ago, while Dr. Pearle was examining him, to shower and change, but yes, I've been here since right after he was brought in last night."

Nathan still couldn't put the pieces together. His mother and Joe Milligan? Rita Mae had treated the guy like rat poison from the moment they'd met, and now she was considered family?

"I'm sorry, but I'm just not getting this. The nurse at the front desk told me the only people allowed in here for more than a few minutes at a time are relatives. How is it you've managed to take up residence?"

What he really wanted to ask was *why are you here at all?* but the look on Rita Mae's face said she wasn't up to fielding stupid questions.

She sagged against the wall and folded her arms across her chest. Dressed in sneakers, jeans and an oversize black sweater, it was clear his mother had already decided comfort was a priority.

"Joe asked for me when they brought him in. Once he was coherent, he listed me as next of kin on the forms and the hospital officials notified me immediately." She sighed as she furrowed a hand through her tousled hair. "I was so worried I was going to lose him."

"Are you trying to tell me that you and Joe—That you and the captain are—That you two have been seeing each other?"

Her expression smug, Rita Mae raised a brow. "I'd say that sums it up quite nicely."

"But—but when? How?" Nathan stuttered. "I mean, you're always at home, or playing bridge or taking a yoga class. I don't get it."

Smiling as if she had a secret, which she obviously did, she said, "We manage to find the time. Yoga class is over in an hour, and the spa isn't the only place one can go to get a massage, you know."

Nathan felt himself blush. From the sound of it, his mother and the captain had been intimate for a while. Christ, they'd been having an affair.

"I've embarrassed you." Rita Mae continued to smile. "How nice for me."

"I'm a little more than embarrassed," he squeaked out in a tone that sounded childish even to his ears. "I'm in shock."

Rita Mae pushed away from the wall. "We're in love, Nathan. We'd planned to tell you at Christmas. Joe had it all worked out. You were supposed to feel sorry for him because he didn't have anyone to spend the day with, and he was going to push to be invited over for our holiday dinner. Then we were going to spring the surprise. We're getting married."

"Married?"

"That's right."

Nathan spun on his heel as Rita Mae raced to the bed. "You're supposed to be sleeping," she chided, smoothing her hand over Joe's forehead.

"Who in the hell can sleep with you two butting heads?"

She threw Nathan an I-told-you-so glare. "Are you feeling better?"

"Better?" The captain struggled to sit up. "Hell, yes. At least I will when I get out of here." He turned and gave Rita Mae a naughty-little-boy grin. "Maybe if I tell those know-it-all doctors you've agreed to move into my place and dispense a little private nursing, they'll discharge me today."

Nathan hadn't heard his mother giggle in years, not even when she played with Phoebe, but she giggled like a lovestruck teenager when she heard the loaded suggestion.

He raised his gaze to the ceiling. *Well, hell.*

"Are those flowers for me?" Joe asked while Rita Mae cranked up his bed. " 'Cause I was hoping for something a lot more interesting than frilly girl crap from the boys at the station."

Refusing to comment, Nathan retrieved the gifts. He passed the vase of flowers and Mylar balloons to his mother and she set them on the nightstand, then he handed Joe the bedpan.

The captain snorted. "Cute, real cute. I may actually have a use for this someday." He eyed the paper sack. "You wouldn't happen to have a pastrami on rye in there, would you?"

"Uh, not exactly," Nathan muttered. It was bad enough he'd been thrust into this uncomfortable situation without warning. There were some things a guy just didn't need his mother to see.

Joe held out the hand not connected to anything mechanical. "So hand it over."

He set the bag on the bed and headed for the door, hoping to make a quick getaway.

Eeek! Eeek! Eeek!

The captain's laughter bounced off the walls.

"Nathan Jerome, do not leave this room." Rita Mae's tone was tight with disapproval.

Nathan stopped in his tracks and rolled his eyes. Caught red-handed, he turned.

"Thanks for the visit," Joe said with a chortle. He raised Nurse Naughty in salute. *Eeek! Eeek! Eeek!*

Smiling full-out, his mother walked over and took his hand. "I know this has come as a surprise and we should discuss it, but now simply isn't the best time."

"You can say that again," muttered Nathan.

Rita Mae pecked him on the cheek. "Thank you for coming, and for bringing the gifts. I'll call to let you know when I'll be home."

Eloise sat at the miniature table between Sebastian and Phoebe. They were the last students to be picked up, but she wasn't worried. She'd already asked Ulimar to give them a few minutes so she could tutor the boy in his reading skills. And she suspected Nathan was in the process of making arrangements for his daughter in case Rita Mae was still involved in her emergency.

"Raa—bit," said Sebastian, repeating Eloise's precise pronunciation.

"Very good. What this?" Eloise pointed to a picture of a raccoon.

"Ar—ar—" the child stuttered, struggling with the word.

"Raa—" she prompted.

At the sound of shuffling feet, she turned in her chair. Ms. Hewitt stood in the doorway wearing a terrified expression, while behind her loomed Ulimar, complete with his snow white turban and forbidding scowl.

"Phoebe, will you help Sebastian while I speak to Ms. Hewitt?"

The little girl pushed her book aside and nodded.

Eloise tugged on her lime green jacket as she approached the door. Immediately after she'd informed the chauffeur that he would need to wait, he had disappeared. From the look of it, he'd gone to fetch the principal. The dirty rat.

"Is something wrong?"

Her face pale, the headmistress said, "This gentleman is Sebastian's father's right-hand man. I believe he wants to bring the boy home."

Eloise gave a toothy grin. "Of course, Mr. Ulimar." She picked up an envelope from her desk, then walked to the row of pegs, grabbed Sebastian's coat and went to the table. "It's time to go. And I want you to give this letter to your father. Will you do that for me?"

The child shifted his gaze to the doorway, then back to Eloise. "Yes, ma'am." He slipped the note in his book bag and shrugged into his jacket. Ms. Hewitt stepped aside and they watched as he followed his driver from the room.

The principal heaved a sigh. "I want to apologize for my

surly behavior earlier this afternoon. I have a lot on my mind at present and, well, I'm sorry." She fixed her gaze on Phoebe, who had gone back to reading her own book. "Mr. Baxter called to inform me that he's on his way. Apparently he's having sitter problems."

"I see," said Eloise.

"He and I have a small matter to discuss, so he's coming to my office before he picks up his daughter. If you don't mind staying with Phoebe, I'll send him to you as soon as we're through."

"That's fine. Oh, and Ms. Hewitt?"

The principal spun on her heel. "Yes?"

"Everyone has a bad day once in a while. I accept your apology, but next time you need to growl at someone, don't let it be my students, okay?"

Honoria nodded. Eloise waited until she rounded the corner to her office before coming back to sit with Phoebe. This morning, when Nathan hadn't stopped in to say hello, she'd thought he might be preoccupied with Rita Mae's defection; now she was certain of it. Was he going to ask the headmistress to recommend a sitter?

What was she—chopped liver?

Phoebe's question brought her back to the here and now. "Are we gonna get to the rest of the homework tomorrow, Ms. Eloise, because a lot of us didn't get to show our costumes."

Several of the children, Phoebe being one of them, had been polite and let others go first when the time had come to discuss the pageant. "I know. We'll get to them tomorrow afternoon, I promise." She remembered some of the more outrageous ideas and asked, "What did you think of Shawanna's drawing?"

Phoebe wrinkled her nose. "I don't ever remember any pictures where Mary wore a turban or a dash—dish—Whatever it was Shawanna wants to wear, do you?"

"I believe it's called a dashiki, a traditional African tribal garment," Eloise explained. "You were supposed to use your imagination, remember?"

Phoebe closed the book. "Do you know when my grammy's gonna get here?"

"That's why Ms. Hewitt stopped by. She wanted to let us know that Rita Mae is still caught up in last night's emergency, so your dad is coming instead. He's got to stop in and talk to Ms. Hewitt, then he'll be here to take you home."

"Can you come home with us?"

"I . . . um . . . maybe your father wants to spend some time alone with his best girl. Besides, I thought I'd walk to the mall and buy some shoes."

"We could come with you. If it starts to snow, you're gonna need a ride."

From the corner of her eye, Eloise spotted Nathan walking past their door to make his appointment with Honoria. What Phoebe said was true, and maybe while they were together she could convince Nathan to let her substitute for Rita Mae.

Substitute for Janet, she amended silently.

"Come on, let's get our coats. Maybe you can talk your dad into shoe shopping."

Sixteen

Nathan faced Ms. Hewitt across her piled-high desk, sympathizing with her expression of amazement. Between Joe Milligan's heart attack and finding Rita Mae at his bedside, he felt as if he'd been pummeled up, down and sideways. This business about Eloise being a nun was still more than he could accept, and from her open-mouthed, wide-eyed stare, it seemed as if the principal agreed.

"You—you're sure?" Honoria asked in a voice that was little more than a squeak.

He chose his words carefully. "I said it looks as if she might have been a nun. There's no reason for the convent to reveal the information without a court order, and even with one I doubt they have to. I'm not familiar with any law on the books stating it's a felony to leave a religious order if you change your mind."

"But Ms. Starr did attend their high school and college affiliate?"

"According to the sister I spoke with, yes."

"And she obtained a degree from—" Ms. Hewitt opened a file, "The Catholic College of Teachers?"

Nathan held up two fingers in the universal sign for victory. "Two in education, one of them is a master's. And the head sister said she got along especially well with the little kids. She has the credentials to teach kindergarten."

"Well, that's certainly a weight off my mind. What better reference than that of a Mother Superior? I just don't understand why Ms. Starr never said anything about being in a convent."

Nathan had been wondering the same thing, but hearing it voiced out loud by Ms. Hewitt ticked him off. Eloise had every right to a personal life, no matter how unconventional. So what if she'd left it to start over? He couldn't fault her for that.

"What did you expect her to say? Oh and by the way, I was a nun but I'm not anymore? I thought it was her teaching ability you were worried about, not her search for an alternate lifestyle, if that's what you want to call it."

"It's just so unbelievable." The principal folded and unfolded her hands on the desk. "Ms. Starr seems so self-confident and together—so—so—un-nunlike."

Un-nunlike, he could buy, even with her convoluted animals-don't-eat-us-so-why-should-we-eat-them attitude, but confident and together? The woman pinned butterfly barrettes in her hair, didn't own a car and had never tasted Chinese food until a few weeks ago. Since he couldn't imagine using those adjectives to describe Eloise, he truly hoped they were discussing the same person.

"I have to get going. It's late, and I'm in a bind. My mother's suddenly found herself in the middle of a crisis, so I have to hunt for someone to pick up Phoebe after school and stay with her until I get home from work." Standing, he nodded at the report. "I hope you're satisfied with the information, because I don't think you're going to learn more unless you ask Ms. Starr yourself."

"Thank you, Mr. Baxter. I'll think about what you've said. And I do appreciate your help."

Nathan let himself out of the office and headed down the hall to pick up Phoebe. Speaking to Ms. Hewitt just now had cleared his head. Eloise was entitled to her past. He only hoped he could find a way to work it into the conversation, so he could hear the explanation directly from her.

The second he stepped in the doorway and saw Eloise and Phoebe together, their pale blond heads bent in concentration over a book, he knew what he needed to do. Suddenly, everything seemed so right. Eloise was the perfect person to baby-sit his daughter. All he had to do was convince her. He rapped lightly on the classroom door.

"Daddy!" Phoebe jumped from her chair. Dressed in her jacket and ready to leave, she took his hand and tugged him toward the hall. "Come on. We gotta drive Ms. Eloise to the mall. She needs to go shopping."

"Oh, we do, do we?" He swung Phoebe up and into his arms. Glancing at Eloise, he raised a brow. "I guess we could give her a lift."

"Can we eat at the food court?" Phoebe begged.

Eloise hoisted her bag over her shoulder. "I think it's my turn to treat for dinner. And if you don't mind, I'd be very grateful for the ride."

Nathan's primitive male brain automatically thought of about seven different ways she could show her appreciation. Nope, scratch that! He had to find out the truth about her past before he could concentrate on their future. Funny, but the idea of Eloise being divorced or widowed, or even a reformed felon, was something he could take in stride. Yet the thought that she was an ex-nun needed special handling.

"No problem. Besides, there's something I need to talk to you about. Let's go."

Though it was only a short walk from her apartment, Eloise had never been in Georgetown Park. It had taken her so long to choose new clothes from the limited selection at a small specialty shop that she'd found the idea of patrolling an entire mall daunting. As an angel, she'd wanted for nothing. Humans needed stuff, and plenty of it. They had to make choices in apparel, cars, food, housing—even buying shampoo or picking the right television show or movie could be a frightening task.

She'd started life here with a funded checking account,

which she assumed represented her salary as a teacher, but she wasn't sure how much her job actually paid. She figured her rent was taken care of until the first of the year. Just this morning, she'd withdrawn money at an ATM machine for groceries and personal spending. She hoped it was enough for a new pair of shoes and dinner for three.

Nathan had parked in the underground lot and taken them up by elevator. Now on the main floor, Eloise couldn't believe how beautiful and open the shopping area was. People bustled from store to store, their arms laden with packages as they strode with cheerful purpose through the walkway. Oversized brass trumpets and wreaths wrapped in gold and burgundy ribbon hung from the three-tiered structure's dramatically domed ceiling in a glittering display. The mall's centerpiece, a miniature toyland complete with mechanical elves, shared a common area with an overstuffed Santa sitting on a throne while he listened to children whisper their heart's desires.

She strolled with abandon, alternately dawdling behind Phoebe and Nathan to stare at the window displays or racing ahead of them in an effort to take in every sight and sound.

They arrived at their destination and Eloise, with Phoebe as her assistant, took charge. She glanced at the array of food stalls and restaurants ringing the seating area. "You sit while we take care of dinner," she instructed Nathan.

After paying for their order, she let Phoebe carry the tray with food, while she toted the one with drinks to their table. Once seated, she began to sort out the meal. To make small talk, she asked, "I don't mean to pry but I am curious. What was Rita Mae's big emergency?"

Nathan helped hand out utensils. "She was called to the hospital. A friend we both know had a minor heart attack."

"Is your friend all right?"

His lips thinned to a frown. "He will be soon."

Eloise opened her mouth to ask another question and Nathan shook his head as if to say now wasn't the time to discuss it.

"Do I know Grammy's friend?"

"You might. Do you remember my captain, Joe Milligan?"

Phoebe sipped at her drink, then set it aside. "Is he tall with curly hair and a big smile? Did he come to the house once after Mommy died?"

"That's him."

"I remember because he told me not to be sad, then he read me a story in the den. Grammy sat with us while you talked to people in the living room. He was nice." She blinked her big blue eyes. "Is he gonna die, too?"

Eloise's stomach clenched at the pointed question. Nathan still glowered, and she wondered if it was because his child was obsessing about death or because Rita Mae had left him adrift.

Leaning forward in his chair, he took hold of Phoebe's hands. "People go to hospitals to get better, punkin; that's why the captain is there. Besides, Grammy is staying with him, and she'd never let anything happen to someone she cared about."

"Was Grammy with Mommy when she died?"

"No," Nathan said, "but Mommy wasn't sick. She died because of an accident."

"Ms. Eloise told me she died because God called her home."

His face pale, he gave Eloise a sidelong glance. "That's right, He did. And we have to hope He isn't calling the captain just yet." Eyeing their plates, he smiled. "Now how about we eat our dinner? This burger looks great, and those cheese-and-broccoli potatoes look good, too."

Phoebe gave Eloise a halfhearted grin and scooped up a bite of dinner. "Are you gonna come with us to shop, Daddy?"

"And here I thought I was just the chauffeur. You mean I actually have to participate in this little adventure?" Nathan teased.

"Of course." Eloise dug into her potato, relieved they'd changed the subject. "I need all the help I can get choosing a pair of shoes." She laughed when she caught the cross-eyed look he threw their way. "We'd come with you if you were buying fishing gear."

Women's shoes? Nathan's palms began to sweat. With Eloise's help, he'd just talked himself out of one quagmire and into another. He knew of at least a dozen different forms of torture, each of them less painful than helping a woman buy shoes. He'd rather strut through the lingerie department modeling panties and a bra or wait for the last tree in Rock Creek Park to drop its final leaf than help a woman find the perfect pump. He'd probably turn to stone and grow moss before Eloise picked out a single pair.

He mentally crossed his finger. "How about I look for a Christmas gift for Rita Mae while you two scope out the shoe stores?"

"But I wanna help pick out a present for Grammy, too."

"A present for your grandmother is pretty special, don't you think?" said Eloise.

Phoebe wrinkled her brow. "Can't we shop for Grammy first, then go look for shoes with Ms. Eloise?"

Nathan rolled his eyes. "I was a good guy today. I visited the captain and caught up with my paperwork. Why do I have to be punished?"

"**Daa-dee.**" She exaggerated the word. "Shoe shopping isn't the same as time-out."

"I'd say it's more like time served," he muttered. Neither of them took the bait, so he finished his burger. "Why don't you go with Ms. Eloise? We can come back another night to shop for Grammy. How does that sound?"

"Okay." Phoebe made a gurgling noise with her straw as she downed the last of her milk. "Now can I have dessert?"

Nathan sat back in his chair. "Is that the proper way to ask for a treat?"

She stuck out her lower lip. "Please may I have dessert?"

"Hmm." He scanned the food court. "How about frozen yogurt or a cookie?"

"How about both?"

He raised his index finger. "One."

"What do you want, Ms. Eloise?"

"Why don't you choose first? I'll get what you don't pick and we can share."

"Do you like strawberries?" Phoebe asked.

"Do you?"

"They're my favorite. If Daddy lets me have yogurt with strawberries on top, you could get a choc'lit chip cookie."

Nathan was already standing when Eloise said, "I'd like to pay for the desserts."

"You bought dinner; dessert's on me."

"Please, Daddy, let me get the yogurt." Phoebe scrambled from the chair. "I know how to ask for it myself. Honest."

He noted that the stand in question was only about ten feet away and he had a clear view. "Okay, but stay in sight." He handed her a five-dollar bill and took his seat. "We'll watch from here while you order."

Phoebe marched to the counter looking very much like a competent young lady. Until tonight, he'd thought she was over her worries about death, but from the comments she'd made about Joe and Janet it was clear she was still fixated on loss and dying.

"Thanks for telling Phoebe what you did about her mom," he began. "Sometimes she still can't believe that Janet is gone."

"I was worried you might not approve of the two of us discussing her mother."

"It's a part of life she has to learn to accept. I appreciate your trying to make it easier for her. I don't always say the right things when we reminisce about her mother."

"Do you miss her? Janet, I mean."

Nathan watched his daughter hand her money to the person behind the counter as he answered. "Janet had left my life long before she died. We stayed together for Phoebe's sake, but I was beginning to realize it was a mistake. Before I could talk to Janet about the two of us separating, she was gone."

Happy to get that part of his past out into the open, he remembered he had yet to ask Eloise an important question.

"Um . . . about Rita Mae."

Eloise kept her gaze on Phoebe.

"With her committed to spending time at the hospital, I'm kind of in a bind. I was wondering if you might consider lending me a hand?"

Turning, she stared in disbelief. "You want my help?"

"Well, yeah. I'm going to need a sitter, and you live close. Besides, Phoebe enjoys your company. I was wondering if maybe you could bring her home after school or over to your place some nights? I know it's an inconvenience, but competent sitters are hard to find, especially—"

"Yes."

"I'd want to pay you—" The warmth of her smile touched him from across the table. He realized she'd already given her answer and grinned in return.

"And no payment is necessary. Maybe we can work out a schedule—a day or two at my apartment, a day or two at the house. I'm sure Rita Mae's friend—Captain Milligan, was it?—will be released soon and she'll be back to her regular duties."

Recalling his last conversation with Rita Mae, Nathan shrugged. "I don't think I can count on my mother anymore. She and Joe are planning to get married."

"Married?"

"Hey, I'm still having trouble coming to grips with the fact they've been dating. And Joe owns a pretty nice house on the other side of town. If they decide to live there, it's going to be difficult for her to take care of Phoebe."

"Rita Mae's been alone for several years. Surely you didn't expect her to feel fulfilled caring for her son and granddaughter for the rest of her existence?"

"I never really thought about it," he muttered, knowing

full well Eloise was right. His mother was warm and giving. She deserved happiness. He'd just never realized what a hole it would drill in his life when she found it.

"I respect Joe and I want him to recover, now more than ever, but it's hard to imagine them as lovers, going at it like two—" He clammed up right before he embarrassed himself with a crude analogy. "Well, you get the picture."

A flicker of a smile passed over Eloise's lips. "Don't worry about Phoebe. I'm sure she'll understand if Rita Mae remarries. She's a lot like her grandmother, you know. She has a great capacity for love and understanding."

Nathan waited while his baby walked back to the table, a cup of strawberry-covered yogurt in one hand, crumpled bills in the other. Eloise was right. His daughter was a caring child. He only hoped, if the time came, she could handle another loss.

"Looks like the storm finally moved in," commented Nathan as he turned the SUV onto M Street.

Eloise craned her neck to watch the snow swirl in the light from the street lamps. "Maybe we won't have school tomorrow."

"Guess we'll need to listen to the radio, or the class mothers will call. What's the Hewitt Academy's procedure for handling a snow day?"

Until the minor skirmish she and Honoria had fought today, Eloise had to admit she'd been told precious little about the running of the Hewitt Academy. Sometimes she thought the prissy principal might be making up the rules as she went along.

"I'm not sure. Ms. Hewitt and I have argued about so many things we've yet to get around to school policy."

"How about the superior you worked under at your last job? Did the two of you get along?"

If she stretched the truth until it was as thin as the skin on an onion, Eloise thought, then yes, she and Milton had gotten along better than she and Honoria were right now. "My last supervisor was easier to work for."

"And where was that?"

"Where was what?"

After stopping at a traffic light, Nathan turned to face her. "Where did you teach before you came to this area?"

"I worked in a lot of places." Not a lie. She did have souls to watch over in almost every city around the world, and taking care of them was hard work. "I really don't think we should be having this conversation in front of you-know-who," she whispered.

Nathan checked his rearview mirror. "You-know-who is already fast asleep. And you're avoiding my question."

"I don't see why where I taught before I came to D.C. has any relevance. I'm here now and that should be all that matters." Staring straight ahead, she sniffed at the indignity of his cross-examination. "The light is green."

He crossed the intersection at a snail's pace and headed up the hill on Wisconsin Avenue. "I don't get it. What's the big secret? It isn't a felony to be a member of a religious order, so why don't you just come right out and admit it?"

A religious order? "Excuse me, but would you mind clueing me in on what you're talking about? What religious order?"

Nathan heaved a sigh. "I know all about where you were before you came here, Eloise, so you might as well stop dancing around the truth. I know you were a postulant at that high school in Illinois, and I know you lived in the convent while you went to college and afterward, when you taught at a Catholic grade school."

Lived in a convent! Eloise caught herself before she burst out laughing. From the sound of it, Milton had done one smart thing when he'd sent her here. He'd given her a past with the safest cover possible. Short of her heavenly existence, what could be more innocent or more private than living life as a nun? But how did Nathan know where she was supposed to have been before the Hewitt Academy?

"And you found this out—how?"

He took a corner at a crawl, then braked at a stop sign. When he finally spoke, his voice was flat and matter-of-fact. "Honoria Hewitt asked me to run a background check on you."

"She did what?"

"A background check. Apparently there were some papers missing from your file—references and work history she needed. She knew I was a cop with access to various ways to—"

"Spy on people?"

The car behind them honked and Nathan grumbled out a few choice words as he moved into the intersection. "I wasn't spying. It was a professional courtesy for the principal of my daughter's school."

"I see. Well, now that you know all about me, why the interrogation? You've already learned everything you need to." Which, she figured, had to be pretty dull and nonspecific. Nuns were saintly, or so she'd heard. She'd never had one in her charge, but from what other guiding angels had said, sisters were truly the easiest of humans to care for.

"Because I wanted to hear it from you." He pulled in front of her apartment building. "I guess I was hoping you'd trust me enough to tell me you were an ex-nun."

Eloise heaved a sigh. If *someone* had dropped a little hint before she'd been sent here, she might have come up with a way to let him know about her supposed past. Just wait until she got another visit from Junior.

"It's not something I feel comfortable talking about." Again, not a lie. "Besides, it's over and done with. I haven't gone mucking around in your past, have I?"

The moment she made the comment, Eloise knew she'd skated a little too close to the edge. She didn't have to muck. She'd been mired in the thick of Nathan's life from the moment he'd met Janet until just before she died.

"Not that I know of, but it wouldn't upset me if you had. A woman can't be too careful these days when she first starts to date a guy."

Eloise shivered at the tremor of awareness that rippled up from inside her. Nathan had just said they were dating, which usually signified the beginning of a relationship. Continued dating led to more intimate exploration, some of which they'd already started, which would lead to the most personal intimacy two humans could have with one other. It was a thought that worried and thrilled her at the same time.

He unbuckled his safety belt and glanced into the rear seat, and Eloise did the same. Phoebe was slumped sideways in her car seat, her baby-doll face relaxed and serene. She and Nathan turned back toward each other at the same moment and found themselves inches apart.

Gazing into his dark brown eyes, she imagined his thoughts. Guilt mixed with insecurity and a heady dose of desire swirled in his mind like a building snowstorm. How could she fault him for doing Honoria a favor, when she'd made it so difficult for him to find out anything about her? It was part of his makeup to be suspicious. Nathan had risked their friendship by telling her about the background check, but he was too honorable a man to hide it from her.

"So, now that my past is . . . out of the way, are you still going to let me watch Phoebe after school?"

His voice dropped to a whisper. "I wouldn't dream of asking anyone else."

"That's . . . good." The warmth of his breath feathered across her lips. Her heart beat with the anticipation of his mouth touching hers.

"You know what I want?" A spark of mischief lit his eyes.

"What?"

"A whole night of just you and me, alone together. No more sitting in a crowded restaurant or overheated car while we fence words in front of a precocious five-year-old, and no more walking to your apartment in the middle of a blizzard so I can grope you in a hallway."

She smiled. "And you want that because?"

"Because I want to kiss you more than once, and I want to touch you in places you've never been touched. I want to be with you in the most intimate way two people can be so I can show you everything that's physically possible between a woman and a man." He ran a thumb across her lips. "Does that frighten you?"

Caught in his hypnotic stare, she held her breath, afraid if she exhaled she would spoil the moment. The time had come to be honest with herself and admit to things she'd swept from her mind the day Janet had first met Nathan in college. Now, after years of envying the woman her humanity while Eloise wondered what it would be like to be held in his arms, Nathan was offering to do that very thing.

"Not frightened." She leaned into his caress. "But I am nervous. I've never had a man say anything like that to me before."

"I'm honored to be the first." He moved closer. "It's late. I'd walk you inside but—"

"It's okay. I wouldn't want you to leave Phoebe alone in the car for a second. I only have my handbag and shoes. You can watch from here until I'm inside."

Sliding closer, he enfolded her in his arms. "You are something else, you know that?"

Enveloped in warmth, Eloise nestled into Nathan's chest and raised her face to meet his seeking mouth. Gentle yet demanding, he kissed her until her body puddled like candle wax. He nibbled at her lips and she opened to him fully, finding his taste sweeter than anything she'd yet to savor as a human.

Nathan took control of the kiss, knowing it would have to sustain him until he could make good on his wish to get Eloise alone. She was as eager and responsive as he remembered, and the thought of their future time together spurred him on. Slipping his hands to the front of her coat, he fumbled with the buttons. He moved his hands to her waist and slid them under her sweater, inching his fingers to her breasts so he could take possession more fully. Cupping a swelling mound, he grasped a distended nipple with his fingers and rolled it through the fabric of her bra.

Her soft sound of acceptance made him feel ten feet tall. He answered Eloise's whimper of pleasure with a moan. It took a second before sanity intruded and he realized they were sitting in a car with his daughter sleeping in the backseat.

Tearing his mouth away, he hissed a ragged breath. "I swear to God this is the last time we do it this way."

Drawing back, Eloise opened her eyes. "I'd better go in."

Nathan heard the disappointment in her voice and nodded. "I'll stay here until I can't see you anymore. Be careful on the sidewalk. It might be slippery."

Disentangling herself from his arms, she slid to the door and opened it. After a final smile, she slung her handbag over her shoulder, picked up her shopping bag and made her way to the apartment steps. Once inside, she turned and waved. Then she was gone.

Nathan sat staring through the windshield, overcome by a rush of loneliness—something he hadn't felt for several years. Tonight was the first time in a very long while he'd played the part of a man with a whole family, and the experience made him remember all the good stuff he'd been missing. Being cared for by a woman besides his mother was nice; hearing his daughter share secrets and discuss her insecurities out loud was refreshing. And shoe shopping with Eloise as if they were married had been comfortable—almost fun.

He shook his head. Damn Rita Mae for putting the *M* word out there. After Janet's death, he'd promised himself he'd never think of marriage again, and here he was imagining his life as a husband for a second time.

He put his car in drive and pulled away from the curb. It was going to be a long night.

Seventeen

The storm that hovered at the edge of the city had fizzled overnight, leaving nothing more than a light dusting on the frozen ground. Eloise stared out the schoolroom's frost-glazed windows with her chin propped in her palm, reluctant to admit she'd found her thoughts straying time and again during the day to what had occurred when she and Nathan last said good-bye.

She knew it was only human to get lost in the thrill of a soon-to-be consummated relationship. As a woman, it was natural to have Nathan constantly at the forefront of her mind. But this intense desire to be with a man, to see him everyday and hear him laugh or whisper an intimate thought, to feel the touch of his hands or the brush of his lips, made her restless and edgy, as if she'd lost all control of her already confusing human self.

She glanced at the envelope Phoebe had handed her earlier, which held the combination to the security system and a key to the Baxter home. Nathan's message was polite and informative, but she'd been wishing for more. Now, with only minutes to go before the end of class, she looked forward to a little solitude instead of the constant chatter of five-year-olds. In the midst of the chaos, Missy Jenkins ran to Eloise's desk and bounced on the balls of her feet.

"Ms. Eloise, Ms. Eloise. Can I give out the invitations to my sleepover? Please?"

She focused on the stack of small white envelopes on her

blotter. "Please tell me you've invited all the girls, because it wouldn't be polite to exclude anyone."

"Uh-huh. But no dumb old boys allowed. They'd only spoil our party," Missy said with a pout.

Dumb old boys, indeed, she thought, watching Missy hand out her envelopes. In another ten years every one of them would be singing a different tune. She waited while Phoebe, her eyes wide with joy, walked to the desk clutching the colorful piece of paper like a treasure.

"Look what Missy gave us. We're all invited to a sleepover at her house. I'm gonna bring my Harry Potter DVD."

Eloise saw that the invitation was for the coming Friday night. The guests would leave directly from school with sleeping bags, pajamas and games in tow, and stay at the Jenkins's home until the following afternoon. As they had throughout the day, the seductive words Nathan whispered in the front seat of his car echoed in her brain. If he'd meant what he said about wanting them to spend time alone, Friday would be their chance, provided his job didn't interfere.

She glanced up as Honoria barreled into the classroom. Ulimar strode behind her and, like a mighty oak, took root in a back corner, his gaze piercing as he stabbed them both with a glare of disapproval.

The principal nodded at Ulimar, then said to Eloise in a quiet but firm voice, "What exactly was in that note you sent home with Sebastian yesterday?"

"I merely asked Mr. Beauchamp to allow his son to stay after school a couple of afternoons this week so I could give him private reading lessons," Eloise answered. "Was that a problem?"

"Not as far as I'm concerned, but he called a few minutes ago and threatened to remove his son from the Academy if you don't let him come home as scheduled. You are, and I quote, 'a mere female meddling with the education of his child.'"

Eloise frowned. "I'm his teacher. It's my duty to meddle.

Besides, I'm almost positive Sebastian has dyslexia and should be evaluated by a professional. How dare the man not want what's best for his son?"

Honoria folded her arms across her chest in a take-no-prisoners gesture. "I told him I would answer his demand once I spoke with you. Now that I know what you're doing, I'll hold the driver off for as long as possible, but we'll have to comply if he tries to remove the boy bodily."

Relieved the principal finally saw her side of things, Eloise decided to let Ms. Hewitt turn her impressive will on Ulimar while she and Sebastian continued with the lesson they'd worked on earlier. She'd thought Ulimar was unable to speak English, but from the sound of his and Honoria's heated words, he had a good enough command of the language to make his message clear. Mr. Beauchamp was not a happy man. He did not believe his son needed special assistance, and to suggest the boy was not intelligent enough to grasp a concept so simple as reading was tantamount to a slap in the face.

Thirty minutes passed while they struggled through the workbook. Finally, she felt a tap on her shoulder and turned to find the principal waiting.

"I think I've done all I can for today." Honoria held Sebastian's coat in her hand. "Mr. Ulimar is honor bound to adhere to his employer's orders. He says Mr. Beauchamp will be furious they aren't home by now." She helped the little boy into his jacket and led him to the door.

Eloise slipped the letter from Nathan into her bag and she and Phoebe headed for the street hand in hand. "How would you like to take a detour before we go to your house?"

"Where are we going?"

"To a shop I sometimes visit. I thought we could bring dessert home."

They strolled through the waning daylight to a small corner store. The store had a magazine rack, shelves holding food staples and a coffee stand for neighborhood commuters on the go, along with a back counter and deli case.

When they entered the store Mr. Belgradian's face creased with the force of his smile.

"Eloise, is good to see you. Where were you this morning? I had your hot chocolate and sweet roll waiting."

Eloise felt her face flush. She'd been so busy daydreaming about Nathan, she'd completely forgotten to stop in for her usual morning fare. "I had to get to school early." She glanced at Phoebe. "This is Miss Phoebe Marie Baxter. I'm going to be watching her for a few days."

Mr. Belgradian fisted his hands on his hips. "Such a beautiful little girl." His gaze darted back to Eloise. "You are related, no?"

"She's one of my students." Eloise warmed at the comparison. "And we want to bring home some of your baklava for tonight's dessert."

"So, Miss Phoebe, you like Greek food?" He leaned forward on the counter.

"I don't know. What's black-lava?"

"Bahk-lah-vah," he said, slowly straightening, "is food for the gods—honey and nuts and—" He raised a finger and winked. After fussing at the rear counter, he turned and handed her a sheet of waxed paper holding a square of the sticky treat. "This is baklava."

Giggling, Phoebe held the paper in her hand.

"Eat, eat. Before I let Eloise pay good money, I must know if you like it."

She took a bite, chewed and rolled her eyes. "It's dee-lish-us."

The old man grunted his pleasure. "I make you a box."

"Four pieces, please," said Eloise. She grinned at Phoebe, who was enjoying the pastry. "One each for you and me and one for your father, plus an extra in case Rita Mae comes home."

Phoebe set the empty paper on the counter and turned, taking in the scattering of small wrought iron tables and chairs adjacent to the front window. "Maybe we could bring Daddy here sometime."

"Maybe we could." Eloise took the box and said good-bye to Mr. Belgradian. Together, she and Phoebe walked home.

"What are we having for dinner?" Phoebe asked, after Eloise unlocked the door and disarmed the security system.

"Are there any more of those hot dogs your grammy made the other night?"

"Uh-huh. And there's leftover macaroni and cheese too."

"Then that's what we're having." She shuttled Phoebe into the kitchen. "You can show me how to use the microwave to heat it all up, okay?"

Less than an hour later, Eloise stood beside the open dishwasher. She'd counted on Phoebe to know how to operate the daunting appliance as well as she'd worked the microwave, but they were still struggling to finish the task when the back door opened and a voice called out, "Hello! Anybody home?"

"Grammy! You're here."

Rita Mae bent to give her grandchild a hug. "Of course I am. How could I stay away from my favorite girl?" Standing, she grinned her approval. "Eloise, hello. Nathan told me he asked you to take care of Phoebe. I'm so glad you said yes."

"We have baklava," Phoebe informed her. "We're gonna have some as soon as we load the dishwasher. There's enough for you and Daddy, too."

"How wonderful." She took off her coat and hung it on a top peg. "Eloise, why don't you sit while I make a pot of tea to go along with dessert?" Rita Mae filled the kettle, then finished with the dishwasher. Once everything was assembled, they ate while they talked about Joe Milligan. "He's doing much better," she confided. "Dr. Pearle may release him on Friday."

Phoebe jumped from her chair. "I got something to show

you. I'll be right back." She ran from the room and up the front stairs.

Rita Mae raised a brow. "What's that all about?"

"She received an invitation to a sleepover for Friday night," said Eloise. "All the girls will be there."

The older woman's eyes filled with tears. "She's growing up so fast."

"She's going to miss you when you marry the captain."

Rita Mae sat back in her chair and dabbed at her eyes with a napkin. "Then Nathan's already blabbed the good news?" She rested her elbows on the table. "Was Phoebe upset?"

"She was more upset about the possibility of the captain dying." Eloise wished she could share her feelings about Janet with someone. "Nathan did a good job of convincing her it wouldn't happen."

Rita Mae sighed. "Thank goodness the boy is beginning to use his head. His asking you to baby-sit was a huge step." The phone rang and she remained seated. "You're in charge. Why don't you answer it?"

Eloise crossed the room to pick up the receiver. "Hello."

"Hi. How are things going?"

Nathan's deep voice sent a tingle all the way to her toes. "Fine. We had dinner and cleaned the kitchen. Your mother just got here."

"Did she say how Joe is? I've been too busy to call the hospital."

"He's doing so well he may be released this week." Before Eloise realized what she was saying, she asked, "When are you coming home?"

She heard him huff out a breath and imagined him running a hand through his hair. "Too late for you to hang around and wait for me. But I might be able to call in a favor and have a black-and-white take you home."

She ignored the disappointment tugging at her middle. "I don't want you to go to any trouble. I can walk or call a cab."

Rita Mae appeared at her side. "Nonsense. Phoebe and I will drive you."

"Is that my mother?" Nathan asked.

"Yes, and she's going to take me home, so don't worry."

"Okay, but I really wish I was going to be the one to see you to your door." He waited a beat before saying, "How about you put Mom on?"

"Hang on a second." She gave the phone to Rita Mae as Phoebe darted into the room holding the invitation.

"Is that Daddy?"

Rita Mae assured Nathan that Captain Milligan was recuperating nicely and handed Phoebe the phone. After a few seconds of chitchat it became obvious she and her father were discussing the sleepover.

"That means you got to help me bring my overnight stuff to school . . . Missy Jenkins . . . her address is on the invitation . . . okay." She offered Eloise the phone. "He wants to talk to you."

"Yes?" said Eloise, fairly certain she knew what Nathan wanted.

"Who are these Jenkins people? Do you know them?"

"I've met Missy's mother and she's a lovely woman."

"Yeah, but will they keep a close watch on the kids? And Phoebe doesn't like to sleep without her stuffed dog, and the—"

"Nathan, I'm sure they'll take care of everything."

"What night was it again? 'Cause I can try to wrangle time off to chaperon or—"

"It's this Friday."

"As in two more nights Friday?"

"Uh-huh."

"I see." He paused and Eloise could almost hear him thinking. "Well then, I guess I need to be free for a different reason, unless they invited you to the sleepover too?"

"Very funny. Are you sure you don't want to chaperon."

"I guess I sounded like a real dope for a second, huh?"

"You sounded like a caring parent. And are you asking me out on a date?"

"Hell, yes."

"Then I accept."

Eloise breathed a sigh of relief. It had taken a half-dozen trips by several of the mothers, but the girls had finally left the Hewitt Academy for Missy's slumber party. All she had to take care of was her session with Sebastian before she could go home to get ready for her date.

She joined the little boy at the table, while Ulimar stood in his usual spot in the corner, as unreadable as ever with his arms folded across his massive chest. Sebastian had improved, but Eloise was certain he needed special help. She'd written a second letter and instructed him to deliver it to his father. In it, she asked Mr. Beauchamp for permission to have Sebastian evaluated. Even though she didn't think he would agree, she had to try to make the man see the light.

Since Joe Milligan was better, Rita Mae had been able to watch Phoebe, but she'd made it clear that she was moving over the weekend. This morning, Phoebe had handed Eloise a note from Nathan, reminding her that he would pick her up at seven. She supposed that, among other things, they would talk about her taking care of Phoebe on a more permanent basis.

The thought sat like lead in her midsection, and she forced herself to admit that she was finally coming to understand why humans had so much trouble handling the flood of complex feelings that must assault them daily. For one short, sweet moment, when Phoebe had waved good-bye and left with the other girls, she'd known a mother's worry at seeing her child off on her first big adventure. Later, she was going to spend time alone with Nathan in order to experience more human emotion, a thought that had her tense with anticipation as well as fear.

Junior had told her it was her best route back to heaven, but she was still leery of what might happen. Emotions, she'd come to realize, were tricky, often confusing and painful. Since coming to grips with her own, she was willing to admit that maybe Milton had been correct after all.

Maybe she had needed a dose of human reality in order to be a more kind and caring guiding angel.

She walked home in the dusky twilight, alone with her thoughts. What if, after tonight, she never saw Nathan or Phoebe again? What if she were transported back to heaven and simply disappeared from their lives? Would they remember her, or would Milton make arrangements for someone else to take her place in their minds, for someone else to help Sebastian learn to read or encourage her students to use their imaginations?

She rested her palm over her breastbone and felt the weight of Janet's locket. Would another woman come along who enjoyed brushing Phoebe's hair or thrilled to the sound of Nathan's dark, steamy voice?

Ignoring the ache building in her heart, she pushed the thoughts aside. She was an angel, not a human. And when she was back where she belonged, doing what she'd been created to do, none of the puzzling questions would apply.

She showered and changed into her pink sweater and navy skirt. After slipping into her stockings, she put on her new navy pumps with three-inch heels and strappy sling backs. The shoes made her legs look long and shapely, her size-nine feet almost dainty in form. Pinning her hair in a cascade of curls, she added the butterfly clips because she knew Nathan enjoyed seeing her wear them.

Her stomach fluttered at the sound of the outside buzzer. She pressed the button that opened the foyer door and waited until he knocked, then pasted a smile on her face. When she opened the apartment door, her smile froze in place.

"Miss Eloise Starr?" The dark-skinned man towered over

her, no small feat considering Eloise's height in her pumps. Dressed in an expensive-looking gray suit, matching tie and snowy white shirt, it was obvious he thought himself important.

"Yes?"

"May I come in?" His slightly accented tone was clipped, the words precise.

She peered around his shoulder and saw that he was alone. "Who are you?"

The man tugged at the knot in his tie. "I am Xavier Beauchamp. Sebastian's father."

Eloise inched the door closed as she spoke. "Did you get my note?"

He placed a large hand flat against the door, and the hairs at the nape of her neck stood on end.

"I did."

"Do you have questions?"

His smile seemed more of a leer. "No questions, but I do have something to say to you."

"Then please call the school and make an appointment." She leaned her weight into the door and found it wedged in place. "This isn't a good time to talk."

Mr. Beauchamp pushed into the apartment, foiling her attempt to hold her ground. His measuring gaze roamed from her mouth to the front of her sweater and back up again. His gaze smug, he reached out and stroked her cheek with the back of his hand. Eloise flinched. His black eyes held her suspended and the eerie sensation made her recoil. Taking full advantage, he used the opportunity to crowd her into the wall.

She tried to scream, but the sound was blocked by the lump in her throat. His very expression violated the space around her. She was being threatened in the most primitive way a man could threaten a woman and it made her feel helpless and small. Taking one more step, he loomed over her.

"Please leave," she managed to squeak. She stiffened her spine to keep from shaking. "Now."

He caged her between his arms and pressed against her suggestively. "Not until we get better acquainted. I think it is time I explained how the men in my country treat a woman. We have found that it puts them in their place quite nicely."

Before Eloise could answer, the man jerked backward from the foyer and disappeared into the hall. She realized he hadn't left under his own power when she heard a familiar voice.

"And what place might that be, bud?"

She stepped into the doorway, her heart beating like a jackhammer. "Nathan. This is the father of one of my students. Mr. Xavier Beauchamp."

"Oh yeah?" Nathan kept his left hand on the jerk's shoulder while he gripped his gun with the right. When he'd realized there was a man in Eloise's apartment, his gut had tied itself into a knot. Then he'd heard the guy's threats and his first instinct had been to spin him around and pop him one, but common sense held him in check.

The man shrugged free and straightened his jacket. "This is not your concern," he snapped. "You have no business here."

Nathan ignored the posturing comment and glanced at Eloise. "Did he hurt you?"

She stuck out her chin. "No. But he did try to intimidate me. I'm fine now that you're here."

Mr. Beauchamp turned to leave and Nathan caught him by the arm. "I don't know how you treat women in your country, fella, but this is America. Apologize to the lady."

The man stretched to his full height. "Do you know who I am?"

Nathan had noticed the block-long stretch limo with official plates and national flags on the front fenders when he'd pulled up to the building. He'd wondered what high-ranking diplomat would have reason to be in the neighborhood, and now he knew. Too bad it was Beauchamp, because even if Nathan arrested him, the jerk would be able to hide behind his status and claim diplomatic immunity.

He shrugged. "A bully?"

Spinning on his heel, Beauchamp strode away, and Nathan saw red. He followed down the hall, intent on dragging him back to apologize. When he clasped the diplomat on the shoulder, the guy rounded on him, fists raised. His first punch slammed Nathan hard against the hallway wall.

Nathan sprang upright and attacked with a solid blow to the man's jaw. Beauchamp staggered backward, spun around and shot out his leg, scoring a kick to Nathan's midsection.

Huffing out a breath, he crouched, but Eloise ran between them and held up her hands as if to protect him from the next punch. Nathan was so surprised by her stupid-but-endearing gesture he had just enough time to move her aside before the guy hauled back and clipped him on the cheekbone. Dazed, he assessed Beauchamp's fighting stance and prepared to fight dirty.

Suddenly, Eloise shot between them again. Stabbing a finger in the guy's chest, she pecked at him like a woodpecker. "You are a bully, just like he said. You'd better leave or—or—I'll call the police!"

Nathan shook his head. He *was* the police. Unfortunately, thanks to the immunity glitch, he'd have to act like an ordinary citizen and take advantage of her diversion. Doing a little fancy footwork of his own, he faded to the right, then locked onto the diplomat's wrist and twisted, jamming the man's arm tight up against his back.

Locking the fingers of his other hand around the guy's neck, he pushed the creep toward Eloise. "I said apologize."

Eloise folded her arms across her chest. A second passed before she gave a surprisingly angelic smile.

Nathan shook the bum hard enough to rearrange a few brain cells. "Excuse me? I didn't hear you."

"I am sorry to have intruded in your home, Ms. Starr," he

muttered. "I will make an appointment to speak with you at the school, as you suggested."

"I'll look forward to it. Good night."

Nathan marched him to the foyer and shoved, sending the man crashing into the front door, but Beauchamp never looked back. Instead he straightened and walked into the night.

Nathan helped himself to a fourth piece of veggie pizza from the box sitting on Eloise's coffee table. He had to use his left hand, because his other one was holding a washcloth filled with ice against his right eye.

After he'd gotten rid of the rat bastard bully, Eloise had insisted he come into her apartment so she could examine his bruises. He'd shed his holster and suit coat, then unbuttoned his shirt so she could check for damaged ribs. He'd been fantasizing about her soft, warm fingers stroking his body for weeks. It was almost worth getting the shit kicked out of him to finally live the dream.

When she'd assured herself he had no internal injuries, she'd made him an ice pack and led him to the sofa. The exchange with the creep, along with his rapidly swelling eye, had taken away their desire to go out to dinner, and he'd suggested pizza, which had made Eloise smile. And oh how he loved to see her smile.

Now, seated on the floor next to her, he chewed slowly. If he didn't know better, he'd swear the bum had knocked loose a few molars.

"Does it still hurt?" Eloise's voice was grim with concern.

"Nah. Just aches a little. I'll be fine." He set down the pizza and took a swig of beer. "I still can't believe the nerve of that guy. Who the hell did you say he was?"

"Xavier Beauchamp. He's some sort of big deal government official from some French-speaking island."

"And what stick did he have up his butt?"

She grinned. "I've been tutoring his son, but Sebastian needs professional help. I think he's dyslexic."

"Well, he sure wasn't thanking you for calling it to his attention, now was he?"

"It seems I insulted him by suggesting his child was less than perfect. Stupid human."

Nathan had to admit the guy was stupid—but human? Only in the basest of terms. "Think he'll make trouble for you with Ms. Hewitt?"

She set her crust in the box and leaned against the sofa. "I don't think he can. Honoria is on my side about getting the boy tested, and I certainly didn't invite the man here." She reached out and took the ice pack from his face. "You're going to have a huge bruise. Your eye is already closing."

Ignoring the pain, he waggled his eyebrows. "I know a way to make it feel better."

She rose to her knees and moved closer, as if eager to do whatever he suggested. "How?"

"When I was a little kid, Rita Mae used to kiss the ouchies away. If my mother could make it better—"

Eloise caught on quickly. *Tsking,* she shook her head. "I guess what they say is true—all men are little boys at heart."

She raised a hand and cupped his cheek, and Nathan felt an important body part turn to stone. He'd planned to make his big move tonight, but only after he'd wined and dined her—not half dressed on her living room floor looking like a prizefighter.

"Is that what the nuns used to say about us?"

"I don't want to talk about nuns or convents or anything else but the here and now," she countered. "This is supposed to be *our* time together."

Nathan clasped her wrist and placed a kiss in the center of her palm. "I was hoping you'd been thinking about what I said before." He twisted to face her and came to his knees. "You're sure—about us being together tonight?"

Eloise brought her hands to his jaw, holding him gently. His shirt hung open, giving her a generous view of his corded abdomen and well-muscled chest. Earlier, when she'd checked for bruises, her hands had trembled when they'd caressed the dusting of crisp dark hair that arrowed to his waist. She'd known from the fit of Nathan's slacks that he'd been ready to make good on his promise to do more than kiss her, but instead of pushing he'd joked and ordered the pizza.

Now that they were alone, with the entire evening ahead of them, the thought of her returning to heaven seemed small and insignificant. It was her turn to show him that she was ready to move to the next step in their relationship.

"I've never been more sure." She leaned forward and placed her mouth on his cheekbone, fluttering her lips like the wings of a butterfly. "I guess we'd better get the ouchies out of the way, so we can move off the topic of your mother."

She ran a finger over his puffy lower lip and bestowed another kiss. "Does it hurt here?" she whispered.

"Sort of."

Pressing harder, she opened her mouth and made a little sucking motion. "How about now?"

"Better," he rasped.

Eloise couldn't believe the way her heart pounded. Nathan tensed, and she felt a rush of power at the idea that she was holding him captive in her hands. Only minutes ago, he had rescued her with an impressive show of strength. Now she was the one in charge, the one in control.

She moved her hands to his hair, threading her fingers through his curls. Slanting her head, she kissed him fully and he moaned into her mouth.

"You're making me crazy. I think I need to lie down," he muttered. "Preferably in the nearest bed."

Drawing back, she rose to her feet. "What a coincidence. I know where you can find one."

Nathan stood, a lopsided grin on his face. "Sweetheart, you have no idea how much I was hoping you'd say that."

Eighteen

"You are so beautiful." He brushed tendrils of hair from her cheeks, then cupped her jaw. "I love the way you look at me, all wide-eyed innocence, as if you've never been given a compliment before."

Eloise touched his hands to assure herself that Nathan was standing here in her bedroom, solid and real and waiting. "No one before you," she said truthfully.

He leaned down and kissed her, lingering over her lips as if savoring their taste. She clasped his wrists with her shaking fingers. Heat pooled low in her middle and seeped between her legs, staggering her with its intensity. When her knees turned liquid, Nathan caught her in his arms.

"Maybe it's time we moved to the bed." He sat her down on the mattress and took a step back. His gaze settled on her face as he quirked up a corner of his mouth. Before she could speak he shrugged out of his shirt, undid his belt and tugged on the zipper of his slacks.

The glow from a street lamp cast smoky shadows, giving Eloise enough light to see his tanned skin, broad shoulders and tapered waist. A rush of warmth bubbled in her veins. "What are you doing?"

His coffee-dark eyes crinkled at the corners. "Getting ready to make love to you."

Placing a hand against her heart, she sucked in a breath.

Frowning, he zipped up his pants and folded his arms across his chest. "If you're having second thoughts, I'll understand. But I should warn you that waiting might send me to the nearest emergency room."

"Are you in pain?" The right side of his face was turning an interesting mix of colors. "Is it your eye? Or your ribs?"

He gave a mirthless chuckle. "I don't believe any man's ever died of my particular ailment, but it is dammed uncomfortable."

"I don't think we're talking about the same thing."

"And you'd be right." His hands fell to his sides. "So, do you want me to leave?"

Eloise forced her mind to empty of all but one thought: Nathan was her ticket to heaven. If he left now, it could delay her return—or postpone it altogether. And getting back to heaven was her only goal—wasn't it?

"It's just that I've never—I mean, I haven't—"

"That's what I thought." His voice sounded weary as he reached for the shirt he'd tossed on her chair. "Though it kills me to say so, maybe it would be better if we chose another time and place."

The thought of heaven disappeared from her mind. There was no other time or place. There would never be another man. Here and now, with Nathan, was all there could ever be.

She shot to her feet and grabbed at the shirt. "Stay," she whispered. "I want to be with you. I want you to show me how to be a woman."

The fabric slipped from his fingers. Turning, he took her in his arms. Eloise gazed into his eyes and he exhaled.

"Don't look at me like that."

"Like what?"

"Like I'm a knight from one of Phoebe's fairy tales or someone who's about to save you from certain death. I'm nobody special, Eloise. Just a guy who wants to get you into bed more than he wants to breathe. I can't make any promises past tonight. You understand what I'm saying?"

She nodded and Nathan's heart turned. He was a jerk

with a capital *J.* She'd been a nun, for God's sake, and here he was, ready to jump her bones. He was about to tell her this was all wrong when she struck the lowest of blows.

"I know there won't be anything more between us when this is over, and I'm willing to accept it. But I still want to make love with you. Please."

A single teardrop beaded, tracing a path down her cheek, and Nathan lost himself in her plea. Crushing her to his chest, he slanted his mouth over hers, determined to devour her sadness and make it his own. They could worry about tomorrow later. Right now, each of them needed what the other had to give.

He let her go and tugged off every stitch of clothing in a few quick motions. Her full lips puckered to an O as she stared at his chest, then lowered her gaze to his erection. Until that moment, he'd never thought himself better endowed than average, but the expression in Eloise's eyes made him inordinately proud of himself.

She struggled with her sweater and he helped pull it over her head. When she undid her skirt and it fell to the floor, all the air escaped from his lungs. Reaching out, he opened the front closure of her bra, then stepped back as she shrugged it from her shoulders. Standing before him in nothing but white cotton panties and sheer hose that went to the tops of her thighs, she resembled a goddess formed to tempt him alone. Her full breasts glowed alabaster, her nipples shimmered rose-petal pink, her belly dipped and curved to shapely, flaring hips.

Hesitantly, she placed her arms across her body. Caressing her with his eyes, he dropped to his knees and touched her with trembling hands. Words formed in his mind, but his mouth grew too dry to speak. Slipping his fingers to the waistband of her panties, he slid the cottony material over her hips and thighs and let it puddle at her ankles. Then he worked his way up the backs of her calves, to her knees and thighs, delighting in the way she quivered under his palms.

When he felt the lacy band of her hose, he moved to her belly and feathered his thumbs over her triangle of golden curls. "Let me," he begged, hoping to fulfill a fantasy he'd been living over and over in his dreams.

Gently brushing her mound, he felt her tremble. The scent of her arousal enveloped him and he sighed, fluttering the fine hairs. He peeled the first stocking down to her dainty ankle. "Balance on my shoulders and lift up your foot."

She did as he asked.

"Now the next one."

Tossing the panties and stockings on the chair, he sat back on his heels and removed her hands. Entwining their fingers, he placed his lips on the plump flesh between her thighs.

She gasped and he stood. "If I do anything you don't enjoy or frightens you, I want you to tell me."

Eloise licked at her lips. "What you did just now—"

"Did you like it?"

"I think so."

"Good, because there's a lot more I plan to show you." Cuddling her close with one arm, he turned down the covers with the other, then sat and drew her onto his lap. He groaned when her naked bottom and hip brushed his swollen shaft.

Eloise stared at his flagpole-size erection. "Did I hurt you?"

"Only in the best way a woman can hurt a man," he assured her. "Just in case you don't know, this is what a fully aroused male looks like."

She raised her head and he saw a spark of amusement flash in her eyes. "May I touch you?"

"You can do whatever you want, but be forewarned I'm ready to—Well, let's just say *I'm ready.*"

Eloise ran a finger down and back up again. He shuddered at the exquisite sensation, and she enclosed him fully in her palm. "It's soft and hard at the same time," she murmured, moving her hand. "Like velvet over steel."

He made a strangled sound in the back of his throat. She slid her fingers over the sensitive tip and his body tightened in response. A few more strokes and he was going to embarrass himself for sure.

"Do you want to touch me?" She continued to explore his throbbing shaft with keen interest.

Holding on to her wrist, he stilled her pumping and turned to lay her on the bed. Instead of talking, he answered the question by skimming his hands and lips over her generously formed body. She opened her mouth and he delved inside, hoping the sensual motion would prepare her for what was to come. Capturing a breast in his hand, he tugged a hardened nipple between his fingers, then bent and took it in his mouth, sucking gently at first, then harder when she gave a soft mewl of encouragement.

He moved to her other breast and drew it into his mouth until she arched against him. He caressed her rib cage, dipped into her navel, massaged her rounded belly and slipped his hand between her legs. When he slid a finger into her tight, wet cleft she clenched her thighs together like a vise.

"Open for me, sweetheart. I promise you'll like what happens next."

Eloise blindly followed his command. When he fondled a spot she had yet to touch, she clutched his upper arms and rode the shock wave zinging through her body.

"Nathan, I can't—I want—"

"You can, sweetheart, you certainly can," he crooned. "That's it, let me do all the work. Just let it happen . . . let it happen."

Bright lights flashed behind her eyelids. She opened her mouth to scream and he plunged his tongue inside, stroking her in rhythm with his fingers. Trailing kisses downward from her mouth to her chin, he bit at her nipple and she cried out her pleasure. Moving her hips, she matched the pace of his hand, rising higher and higher until she thought she would float off the bed. A final tremor shook her as she crested above the clouds to the very edge of heaven itself.

Panting heavily, her body a pliant-but-sated mass of blood, muscle and bone, she barely realized Nathan had left her. Every nerve in her system felt newly awakened, each of her senses ready for the next step. This is it, her mind registered. This was what she'd been sent to earth to experience.

Before she could take the thought further, Nathan returned and settled between her thighs. She furrowed her fingers through the hair on his chest, ran her palms over his rippling abdomen, and his lips curled in satisfaction. His skin quaked like living marble, cool yet pulsing under her hands.

"What's going to happen next might hurt a little, so I want you to hang on to me and relax, okay? I've never been any woman's first before, and I don't know how else to prepare you."

She nodded, too consumed by passion to comment. He parted her slick folds and entered her in one swift thrust, then waited for her to accept him inside. She convulsed around his shaft, pulling him into the heart of her and time stood still. He filled her with his flesh, his mind, his heart, until there was nothing else in her world but the two of them, joined as one.

Resting his weight on his elbows, Nathan rocked his hips until she caught his rhythm and met him stroke for stroke. Increasing the pace, his breath rasped in her ear. As she soared toward heaven again, she raised her eyelids and drank in his determined expression. When he met her gaze and smiled, Eloise saw a moment of what could be mirrored in his eyes.

In the space of a heartbeat, the world exploded around

her a second time. Giving herself to Nathan, she clutched him to her breast as he shouted his triumph.

Weightless, Eloise stretched and snuggled deeper into the cloud. She couldn't remember the last time she'd had this wondrous feeling of complete and perfect contentment. Though she'd expected her entrance to heaven to be a bit more dramatic, she appreciated the rest. Returning to guiding angel status was going to be a snap after the hard work of being a human.

Though she couldn't put her finger on the exact moment she'd been transported back, she knew it hadn't been after the first time she and Nathan had been intimate. Or the second.

So when?

The cloud shifted and made a rumbling sound, and she frowned. If a plane had passed by close enough to buffet the cloud, the noise would have been much louder, and thunder would have jolted her into space. What had made the racket?

Suspicious, she opened her eyes and stared at an all-too-familiar ceiling. Glancing to the side, she found Nathan snoring softly, his head turned toward her, one hand tucked under his poor battered face. His eye had swollen shut during the night, and just looking at it made her wince.

He'd been so heroic, coming to her rescue, then taking pains to make certain she wanted to go to bed with him. The things he'd done with his mouth, his hands. His tongue! The memory sent a shiver racing toward her toes and back up again. She tugged the covers to her chin, ready to snuggle into him, when the reality of the situation slapped her fully awake.

She was not in heaven. Not even close.

What the heck had happened? Had she missed something important in this man-woman business? Skipped a vital part of the lesson—or failed completely?

Slowly, she recounted every moment of the night. Nathan, saving her from Mr. Beauchamp and showing him the door. Nathan, letting her examine his injuries, then caring for her welfare by ordering pizza for their dinner. He'd even offered to leave when she'd appeared insecure. Then he'd kissed her senseless, stroked her in all the right places and made her cry out in human satisfaction.

No . . . she'd done everything she was supposed to. She was sure of it.

So why was she still here?

Without warning, Nathan rolled toward her and enclosed her in his arms. His chest was inviting, his legs warm as they wrapped around her and pulled her near.

His erection throbbed against her thigh and she puddled inside, recalling all the pleasure that one rigid muscle had supplied for them both. When she'd thought about sex as an angel, no part of the act had interested her. She'd never understood the fascination humans seemed to have with something as silly looking as a penis.

Last night had made everything clear.

"You awake?" He snuggled her tightly against him.

Eloise smiled, amazed that the mere sound of his voice had the ability to make her wet and wanting. "Uh-huh."

"Did you sleep okay? How do you feel?"

"Umm . . . fine. How about you? Does your eye hurt?"

His chest vibrated with laughter. "My eye is a little on the achy side, but the rest of me feels just fine."

"That's good." What else was she supposed to say?

He pulled back his head and tipped up her chin, kissing her quickly. "How do I look?"

Raising a brow, she gave him a more thorough inspection. "Like a squashed eggplant."

He grimaced. "That bad, huh?"

She nodded.

"Okay, don't move. Just give me a minute."

Before she could answer he crawled out of bed, and the

sight of his naked backside sent a fresh tremor coursing through her. How could anything be wrong, when being here with him felt so right? If something had gone haywire, the idea that she might get another chance to fix it was fine with her.

Maybe Junior would show up to explain. If she could just talk to him, she was certain he could set her straight or—

The absurd thought made her go cold all over. Right now, the last thing she needed was to have Junior in the room. In fact, she wasn't sure she could ever look him in the eye without blushing. Nope. The next time she talked to him, she was going to be wide awake, fully clothed and staring at the ground.

Nathan sauntered into the room, a cocky grin on his multihued face. She ducked deeper under the covers, mostly because she had no idea what to do next. He'd asked her to stay put and not move. Maybe there was more she needed to do to regain heaven—another part to the man-woman ritual she'd never heard about.

He slipped under the blanket and drew her to his chest. She caught the minty scent of his breath and realized he'd used mouthwash, or maybe brushed his teeth.

"How are you feeling, really?" He tucked her head under his chin.

"I'm fine. Honest."

"Then you're not sore or . . . anything?"

"No, but thanks for asking." What was he getting at with all these questions?

"Well, in that case—" He slid down until they were eye to eye and waggled his brows. "I have another condom."

"You have another—"

"Optimism is one of my better qualities."

He nestled closer and she felt the impressive proof of his desire prod her hip. Heat flooded her cheeks.

"Oh."

He quirked up a corner of his mouth. "Is that a good 'oh' or a bad 'oh'?"

Eloise sighed. Her stomach was starting another crazy roller coaster ride and she was too confused to put on the brakes.

"It's this shiner, isn't it? It makes you want to hurl."

She bit back a giggle. He sounded like a little boy who'd been told he had to leave the room. She stroked his cheek, then placed a gentle kiss under his swollen eye. "It isn't that. It's just—Are you sure you want to do this again—with me?"

"You're joking, right?"

Morning sun peeked through the windows, affording her a better view of his beaten face and puzzled expression. Junior's words echoed in her brain. *You've got to dive in feetfirst—act and feel like a human woman.*

Maybe she'd misunderstood his instructions. Maybe she was expected to interact with Nathan more than once or twice. Maybe she had to do it again and again before she got the hang of it and was given the okay to return.

Closing a hand over her breast, Nathan teased her pebbled nipple. The exquisite sensation tremored through her system and spiraled between her legs, blocking all common sense. Moving with him, she rolled to her back and opened her thighs in automatic reaction to his presence.

Maybe this time she would get it right.

Eloise gazed out the classroom window, waiting for her charges to arrive. Errant snowflakes whirled and eddied, matching the fragmented thoughts swirling in her mind. She hadn't heard from Nathan since Saturday afternoon, when he'd left her apartment to pick up Phoebe, and the fact chewed her up from the inside out. She'd heard many of her feminine charges complain that men never called when they said they would, but she'd never expected it would happen to her.

She recalled their night of passion in detail, remembered every kiss, each intimate touch and tender gesture as if it had just occurred. When Nathan left, he'd held her to his chest and kissed her like a nomad drinking a final glass of water before setting off to join a desert caravan.

Had he meant the sweet words he'd uttered, or was he more like the rest of the male population? Were men so alike in their thinking that none of them ever meant what they said? Even Junior hadn't showed his face, and she'd been positive that at some point the wise guy angel-in-training would appear to set her straight.

In between pondering their night together and worrying about why she hadn't returned to heaven, she'd spent the rest of the weekend trying to get a handle on everything she had to do to fulfill her responsibilities as a kindergarten teacher.

There were only a few days left until Christmas and the play, and she wasn't ready for either occasion. She hadn't even thought about the presents her students were supposed to make for their parents. Ms. Hewitt had reminded her this morning and told her everything she needed could be found in the art supply cabinet in her classroom, but that did nothing to lower her anxiety level.

Before today, all she'd ever touched in the cabinet were the crayons and colored paper. After Honoria left, she'd glared at the cupboard again, hoping a clever idea would simply pop out fully formed. So far, nothing wonderful had taken place.

She walked to the cabinet and opened the double doors. To her great surprise, the supplies were neat and tidy. Some of the boxes were labeled and many of them were in cartons or envelopes. Bottles of glitter in all colors of the rainbow, boxes of crayons and pots of paints and brushes filled one shelf. Containers holding sticks, plastic straws, toothpicks, spoons, sequins, blunt-tipped scissors and something called pipe cleaners filled another. Stacks of cardboard, colored paper and sheets of a thin, spongy material were stacked on a third. Glass jars held multihued beads of varying shapes and sizes; skeins of yarn, plastic string and stringy string overflowed another.

She walked to the window again and rested her chin in her hands, hoping her angel brain would find a way to think like an arts-and-crafts maven. What tricks did Martha Stewart use to combat cutesy-block?

Her students began to trickle through the door in groups of two and three. Phoebe walked in and sidled to the window ledge, a grin splitting her pixie face. "Ms. Eloise. Daddy told me to tell you he was gonna pick us up after school, and he wants to take both of us to dinner."

Her heart skipped in her chest. Before she could answer, Felicia Rathbone walked to Eloise's other side and imitated her teacher's thoughtful pose.

"What are you staring at, Ms. Eloise?"

"The snow. It's so clean and white. Sometimes looking at it helps me to think."

"My father says it never helps to stand and stare. If a body wants to get anything done, they need to act," said Felicia.

Easy for your father to say, thought Eloise, biting back a sharp retort. *He's merely a high-ranking diplomatic attaché. Let's see how he'd handle my life for a day or two.*

"I love the snow," said Lucy, taking a spot next to Phoebe.

"Me too," said John, who then made room for Adam.

Soon the entire class, all except for Sebastian, Eloise noted sadly, was lined up and gazing out the window like sparrows on a telephone line.

"Do you think we'll have snow for Christmas?" asked Shawanna.

"I hope thso," answered Mary Alice, her sigh frosting the glass. "Iths the besthest thing in the whole entire world."

Eloise raised up her head and glanced at the supply cabinet, then back to the window, peering at the fluffy flakes that stuck to the windowpanes. She smoothed the lapels of her lime green jacket, grateful she'd thought to wear a new outfit. She had hours to go before she saw Nathan. Fortunately, there would be plenty of work to keep her busy.

"I think it's time we used our love of the snow to make a few presents," she decreed. "All of you march to the arts and craft cupboard. No pushing!" she shouted when they left the window at a trot. She grabbed at a stack of Lilliputian-size aprons hanging on a peg inside the door. "Everyone needs to put on an apron. Then get in line so I can hand out the rest of the supplies. We have a full day ahead of us."

She sat the students in groups of four and handed each child a pair of blunt-tipped scissors and a sheet of the thin, white foam. Then she took down king-size bottles of glue and containers of glitter and set them on each table.

"Does anyone know what we're going to make?" she asked the room in general.

"Pillows?" guessed Adam.

"Clouds?" asked Amber.

"Sheep?" suggested Felicia.

"I know, armored tanks," shouted Billy.

Eloise smiled. "Snowflakes. Beautiful, glittering snowflakes that can be hung from a window or ceiling, or small, delicate snowflakes you can use as tree ornaments. You each have one sheet of foam to use whichever way you want. You can make as many small snowflakes as you like, or make a single huge one. The choice is yours."

It was fun to see how each child reacted to the task. Some were quiet and industrious, carefully cutting intricate patterns of lovely detail. Others, like John and Zeman, chopped their foam as if hacking through the jungle with a machete. Lucy's and Shawanna's designs were artistically unique, more closely resembling sculptures than snowflakes, while Billy decided to cut with a manly flare, shaping his foam to look suspiciously like a fighter jet and a gun.

After slipping into her apron, Eloise walked from table

to table offering advice, but she let each child use their own creativity. When Phoebe asked if she could make other designs, she said, "Of course, but it might be nice if whatever you chose was related to Christmas. What did you have in mind?"

"Angels," she announced solemnly. "I'm gonna make a guiding angel for Grammy and Daddy and one for me. Then I'm gonna make some snowflakes."

"Guiding angels?"

"Like the ones you told me about. So me and Grammy and Daddy won't do any more dumb things."

"Good, that's very good," Eloise mumbled, resting a hand on Phoebe's head. *And when I get back to heaven, I'll make sure all those angels know what you've done.*

Once the cutting was finished, she handed out plastic spoons and wooden sticks. "Next, I want you to squirt some glue on the ornaments and use the sticks to spread it around, then scoop out the color glitter you want and sprinkle it onto the glue. And share," she reminded them. "There's enough for everyone."

"I want the red glitter," said Brent, "and the white and blue. I'm gonna make my snowflakes look like the flag."

"I need silver," Lucy demanded. "Everyone knows snowflakes glow silver in the light."

The students chattered as they worked, commenting on their own and their tablemates' efforts. Things were running smoothly until Missy Jenkins began to cry.

"Ms. Eloise! Billy dumped green glitter on my snowflake. Make him wipe it off."

Before Eloise got to their table, Billy raised his foam gun in defense and began to make menacing machine gun noises. *"Ak-ak-ak-ak-ak.* Stay back or I'll shoot."

"Billy, that is not nice!" shouted Eloise. "Guns are not ornamental."

John and Adam started to fight over the blue glitter at the same time. Suddenly, Adam let go and shot a spoonful of the sparkly stuff straight at John's head. Blue glitter rained down on their table. Grabbing at their ornaments, the girls sitting near them scooted backward, screaming. Brent fell off his chair and toppled a desk, dumping glue and glitter on himself, the floor and anyone near enough to get caught in the flutter of debris.

From the corner of her eye Eloise saw Adam and his spray of sparkles. "Adam, stop that!" She raced over in time to get shot with a retaliatory scoop of gold. "John! What are you doing!" she snapped, brushing at her apron.

"Ee-uuu! Zeman's sucking on his glue stick. That is so gross. Ms. Eloise, make him stop," screeched Amelia.

Eloise turned in time to see Zeman stand, glue stick in his mouth, and race around the desks with Amelia on his heels. They crashed into the watercooler and sent it toppling. Water sloshed onto the linoleum, running in rivers to the center of the room.

Depending on the disaster, the children began to shriek or cry or threaten. Eloise raced to upright the cooler and felt her feet slip out from under her. When she landed with a splat in the center of the mess no one noticed. Chaos and misery ruled.

She skittered to her feet, noting that at least she'd managed to soak up some of the water with her slacks. She let the children wail while she stood the plastic water bottle upright, then hefted the cooler to a stand. Straightening, she ran a hand through her hair and winced when her fingers stuck to the curly strands.

She tugged her hands from her hair and turned to find Honoria Hewitt standing in the doorway, her mouth open and her eyebrows raised to her hairline.

Rubbing her hands on her apron, Eloise gave her a weak half smile.

"Ms. Starr. What do you have to say for yourself?" Honoria demanded.

Eloise shrugged. "Merry Christmas?"

Nineteen

After leaving Eloise on Saturday afternoon, Nathan retrieved Phoebe from her sleepover, then helped his mother pack. Rita Mae watched Phoebe while he checked in at the station and worked far into the night to catch up on his caseload. The next day, he and a few men from his division moved his mother into Joe's house. He'd rented a truck, directed the effort and, when the guys were finished, treated everyone to lunch. He also managed to swallow a lot of ribbing on the condition of his face before he managed to half-convince everyone he'd won a run-in with an ill-mannered kitchen door.

By the time the moving crew left, Rita Mae's personal touches had turned the captain's house into a home. She installed her treadmill and yoga mat in a spare room and announced that Joe was going to use both regularly, then she rearranged the furniture in the den to accommodate her favorite chair. Joe even displaced a few of his police thrillers to make space on the bookshelves flanking the fireplace for her library of romance novels. Before dinner was on the table her kettle sat on the kitchen range, while her imported china tea service with matching cups and saucers graced the sideboard in the formal dining room.

After dinner, Nathan watched the happy couple clean up side by side, as if they'd done so for years. When they started casting each other meaningful glances, he and Phoebe got the message and said good-bye.

He'd thought about calling Eloise a dozen times over the weekend but failed to act on the idea. Last night, after wrestling his overtired daughter into bed, he'd convinced himself it was too late to phone her. This morning, he wanted to kick himself. He'd thought about Eloise while they packed, had seen her face while he filled out reports, wished she'd been with him while they moved furniture and dreamed of making love to her during the night. Thanks to his pathetic excuses, he'd awakened with a guilty conscience a mile long and a hard-on stiff enough to pound nails.

Now, on the way to pick up Phoebe from school, he longed to hear the sound of Eloise's voice more than he wanted to think or sleep or eat. He'd been an idiot not to call her, and he knew why.

He'd been afraid.

Nathan shook his head. Amazing. The big bad cop had just admitted he was frightened of phoning a woman. And not just any woman, but the woman he loved.

The idea scared the shit out of him.

He should have seen it coming the first day he'd laid eyes on her, but he'd been too stubborn to acknowledge what he knew to be true. Now that he'd finally taken Eloise to bed, he was still avoiding the next step. Telling her how he felt.

Pulling in front of the school, he blew out a breath. He'd given himself permission to take a few hours off for dinner, but that was all. He had more work than he could handle in a twelve-hour day, including the murder committed by the teenage gang. He was hoping Eloise would agree to bring Phoebe to her house and keep her overnight, because he had no idea when he'd be able to break free.

He climbed the stairs at a trot and hurried down the hall. Greeting several of the mothers, he noticed the kids carrying packages wrapped in gaily colored paper and guessed they were presents. Eloise had never mentioned what she'd been planning for the children to make as gifts, probably because she didn't want to ruin Phoebe's surprise.

Stepping through the doorway, he stopped short. He'd expected to find his daughter and Eloise, but not Honoria, and certainly not the three of them hunched over a table giggling. The glint of gold caught his eye and he gave the classroom a quick scan. If he didn't know better, he'd think the glittering ball dropped in Times Square every New Year's Eve had exploded right where they sat.

The room had been transformed into an iridescent winter wonderland. Shimmering snowflakes of all shapes and sizes hung from the windows and ceiling; a subtle dusting of gold, silver, green, blue and red washed the desks, floor and walls. He squinted at the glitter dotting Phoebe's ponytails and Eloise's top knot. Even Ms. Hewitt's bun sparkled.

"Daddy! Don't look!" Phoebe shouted, diving on top of the package she was wrapping.

The women turned, both of them wearing huge smiles. The principal stood and frowned at his face before saying to Eloise, "I'll ask the janitor to come in a bit earlier tomorrow morning to give the room another cleaning."

He stepped aside to let Honoria pass and noted the sparkly sheen on her nose and cheeks. From the corner of his eye, he saw Eloise help Phoebe wrap her gift. He waited until they were finished before he came fully into the room.

"What happened in here?"

"We made presents." Clutching the packages to her chest, Phoebe walked to a wall peg, took down her backpack and stuffed the gifts inside. Then she shrugged into her coat. "They're for Christmas."

Eloise came to his side, her pale hair shimmering, her blue eyes shining. "That's not quite all that happened, but it was the way things started and ended. The middle's the part that got a little crazy."

He brushed a spray of glitter from her cheek, letting his hand linger. "Are you sure Ms. Hewitt isn't going to reconsider and fire you tomorrow?"

"I thought she might at first." Eloise pressed her cheek

into his palm before pulling away. "But the children were so contrite that Honoria got into the swing of things and decided to make a few decorations of her own." She twirled in place. "Isn't it pretty?"

"It's beautiful. I take it the project was your idea?"

"Uh-huh. But I can't tell you exactly what we did, because it's a surprise."

Phoebe nodded in agreement then, in a gesture as natural as breathing, put one hand in his and the other in her teacher's. "Where are we going for dinner?"

Sucker-punched, Nathan cringed. How could he have been so blind? How could he have been denying something that was so obvious his five-year-old child had known it for weeks?

Something so simple and right he'd been an idiot not to have acknowledged it sooner.

Not only was he in love with Eloise. They were a family.

Eloise glanced up and found Nathan grinning, his gaze a caress, and her insides turned to ice. Even though his face was a rainbow of bruises, she recognized his soft, sappy expression instantly, not only because she'd seen it on so many of her charges, but because she'd often belittled them for it.

Nathan was in love with her.

Clamping her teeth together, she smiled politely while she climbed into his SUV. This could not be happening. Yes, she'd been sent here to learn about love, but no one had said Nathan was going to fall in love with her. She didn't want his love. All she wanted was to return to heaven.

Before they pulled from the curb, she suggested they pick up dinner at Mr. Belgradian's and eat at her place. Afterward, she could send both Baxters home so she could think.

Nathan turned to her and spoke softly. "I don't want Phoebe to hear me ask in case it's not a good idea, but I'm in a bind tonight. Would it be all right if she slept over?"

He was in a bind! "No problem," Eloise muttered, staring at her fingers. So much for finding time to think.

He tipped up her chin and peered at her from under raised brows. "You okay?"

"Fine," she answered, but the words came out tinny and overly bright.

They went to the house and he and Phoebe hurried inside to pack an overnight bag. Closing her eyes, she took several measured breaths. Her time here was supposed to be simple and uncomplicated. Become human—learn a lesson—return to heaven. Short and sweet with no strings attached. Why were things suddenly spiraling out of control? She pressed at her temples to stop their pounding. Maybe if she found a different job and another place to live, then figured out another way to get back, everything would fall into place.

Nathan maneuvered into a parking space in front of her building and they scrambled from the car. Like a luminous pearl dangling from a diamond necklace, a polished quarter moon hung high in the star-studded sky. The lingering scent of wood smoke filled the air, a pleasant reminder of the holiday to come.

"Christmas will be here before you know it," he said, gazing at the heavens. "I hope you'll join us at Captain Milligan's for a family dinner. Rita Mae mentioned it and I promised I would ask."

"Please, Ms. Eloise," pleaded Phoebe. "Captain Joe said it will be lots'a fun, and Grammy told me there'd be presents for everybody and Christmas cookies and everything."

Say no, Eloise's common sense commanded, but the word yes stumbled from her lips before she could stop herself.

She hung up their coats while Nathan and Phoebe went into the spare bedroom with her overnight bag. With her mind a muddle, she walked to the kitchen and began to assemble their meal. A minute later Phoebe skipped in, her big blue eyes wide. Eloise caught the adoring gaze on the little girl's doll-like face and choked back a sob. Phoebe's expression was so identical to Nathan's she thought she might burst into tears.

"I've come to help you set the table. After Daddy leaves, we can read a story, or maybe play a game."

"Yeah, well don't plan on getting too comfy." Eloise hated the way the harsh words rose from her throat. "I don't have many little girl things lying around the apartment."

"That's okay." Phoebe ignored the tone and opened drawers until she found the silverware. "I'll help you clean up, just like I do at home. I know how to wash dishes." She set the utensils on the table. "We can pretend you're the mommy and I'm your little girl. It'll be fun."

No! No! No! Eloise wanted to shout, but didn't get the chance. Nathan sauntered in and took down plates from the cupboard, exactly as if they'd always lived here together. The microwave chimed and he removed their supper and brought it to the table.

"This looks great, doesn't it, Phoebe? Let's serve Eloise first since she's being so nice having us over for dinner."

Eloise fisted one hand on the counter and placed the other over the locket hidden under her blouse. A dull ache began to throb through her veins and seep straight into her heart. Why hadn't someone warned her that there would be pain?

Why hadn't Junior told her what to do when love entered her life?

Eloise woke the next morning groggy and disoriented. She'd done her best to distance herself from Phoebe, but doubted she'd had much success. They'd spent the evening reading from a book of fairy tales Phoebe found in her bookcase, then she'd tucked the little girl into the bed in her spare room. And this time, when Phoebe said her prayers, she made her wish crystal clear. She came right out and asked God to make Eloise her mother.

This morning, they had packed lunches and walked to the corner store, where they ate a breakfast of hot chocolate and sweet rolls. For a few fanciful seconds, while chatting with Mr. Belgradian, she'd forgotten about her life as a guiding angel and allowed herself to believe she was Phoebe's mother. Then she'd faced the truth.

Phoebe deserved more than a pretend parent who was sure to break her heart. She needed a very special and forever mother, one who would always be there to love and guide her. And Nathan deserved a woman who could love him without fear or restraint. No way could she fill either of those roles.

She'd promised Nathan that if she left, she would tell him so he could prepare his daughter, but she had no idea when that might be or how she could warn him. Surely leaving them now, before things got further out of hand, would be kinder than popping out of their lives as if she'd never existed.

Seated at her desk, Eloise admitted that before she went away there were responsibilities she couldn't ignore. First and foremost was the play. The children and Honoria were depending on her to see to it things went smoothly, and she wasn't about to let them down.

Once all of her charges arrived, she marched them to the auditorium. After assembling them onstage, she surveyed the set and gave each child a task. Honoria arrived with a few of the high school students and they moved props, set the stable in place and arranged bales of hay until the stage resembled a nativity scene.

Their practice went better than she'd hoped. Afterward, she forced herself to ask the headmistress a question, even though she already knew the answer. "Sebastian is still absent, Honoria. Has his father taken him out of school?"

The principal stared at her toes before speaking. "I'm afraid so. I meant to tell you the day we made the snowflakes, but things got a bit out of hand and it slipped my mind. Mr. Beauchamp left a message on the answering machine informing me that his son would no longer be attending the Hewitt Academy."

Eloise tamped back a rush of tears. Not only was she a lousy guiding angel, she couldn't even do a decent job as a human being. She wouldn't be surprised if, when she got back to heaven, she'd be the one to replace Junior at guarding the polar ice caps. Then again, given the chance, she'd probably ruin that job too.

"What if I called him and promised I wouldn't press the issue of Sebastian's dyslexia or—"

"No," Honoria said firmly. "The boy needs help and it would go against Hewitt Academy policy if he were enrolled here and we didn't give it to him."

"It's all my fault." Eloise heaved a sigh. "If I hadn't insisted he be tested or just forgot that he had a problem—"

"Please don't do this to yourself, Eloise," Ms. Hewitt began, sounding more like a confidant than a superior. "I'll admit I had my doubts when you first came here, but you've turned into a capable and caring teacher. You did the best you could for the boy, and that's all anyone can ask."

This was all Mr. Beauchamp's fault, Eloise decided, and when she got back to heaven, she was going to find the man's guiding angel and tell him so. Most of the humans she'd met were kind and understanding. Even Honoria had changed her prissy ways and was now treating her like a friend. And friends deserved the truth from each other, no matter the cost.

"I have something else I need to discuss with you, and there may not be a better time." She lowered her voice. "I won't be coming back to the Hewitt Academy to teach after the holiday break."

Honoria's eyes grew concerned. "Oh, no. Eloise, please don't tell me you're—"

"Pregnant?" Eloise sighed. The idea of having a child with Nathan filled her with a frightening calm. She raised her head. "Of course not. It's just that things here have gotten complicated and I can't stay."

"I see." The headmistress folded her arms and raised a brow. "It's Mr. Baxter, isn't it? He's making things difficult for you and you can't deal with it. Just like a man to be so—"

"It isn't Nathan. Or Phoebe. Or anything to do with the school or you. It's personal and that's all I can say, except to apologize for leaving on such short notice."

Honoria pushed her glasses up the bridge of her nose, her smile calculating. "Then I'm afraid I can't accept your resignation. If it's personal, it can be worked out, and I intend to help."

"But—"

"No buts. Now let's get on with rehearsal. We have a play to put on in two days' time."

Lunch and afternoon lessons passed quickly, until it was time for her and Phoebe to walk to the Baxter house. Eloise girded herself for heartache and wasn't disappointed. Every second spent in Nathan's home, whether cooking dinner with his daughter, reading to her before bed or simply warming herself in front of the family-room fire, was like an arrow to her heart; every moment a painful reminder of what it would be like to live here and partake of a life that could never be.

That evening, Nathan came home exhausted, but he wouldn't let her walk home alone. He'd already made arrangements for Detective Romero to stay with Phoebe so he could see Eloise to her apartment. Pressing up against her in the doorway, he caged her between his arms and murmured into her hair, "Do you have any idea how much I want to come inside so we can have a few minutes alone? God, I wish I could wrap up this lousy case." He hugged her to his chest. "I miss being with you and Phoebe."

Though every syllable he uttered was a mirror of her own thoughts, Eloise refused to answer. It was better this way. Once she was gone, Nathan would fall out of love with her. After she returned to heaven, she wouldn't have to worry about breaking his heart.

He kissed her soundly and she shivered from head to toe. Running his palms down her back and around to her front, his breath rasped in her ear. "Eloise, we have to talk. I need to tell you—"

She placed her fingers over his mouth. "I have to go in. We can talk later."

He stepped back and smiled through eyes overflowing with passion and love. "Soon. Promise me it will be soon."

She slipped through her apartment door and sagged against the frame. It was then she realized that losing Nathan would haunt her long after she went back to heaven, possibly until the end of time.

Walking to her bedroom, she sat in her comfy chair. "Junior, where are you?" she demanded with just enough bite to let him know she meant business.

Shrouded in silence, she ran her hands through her hair.

"Junior, please. I'm so confused. If you can hear me, come and talk to me for just a minute."

When nothing happened, she changed out of her clothes and climbed into bed, sinking deep under the covers. Overcome with grief, she thought about all of the charges she'd discarded and the pain each of them must have experienced during the course of a lifetime. Why hadn't she tried harder to understand their turmoil and sympathize with their feelings? Why hadn't she listened more and judged less?

She could accept the fact that she would be in pain for the rest of her angelic existence, but somehow she had to find a way to leave here without hurting the people who loved her.

The day of the Christmas pageant dawned crisp and clear. Eloise walked to her classroom lost in thought until, one by one, her charges arrived and she checked them over carefully, taking the time to adjust ribbons and buttons while she made sure each of the children was costumed properly.

Dressed in bib overalls, Zeman had hung a miniature hammer and saw from his belt to remind everyone that Joseph was a carpenter. Shawanna, the very picture of a world-mother figure, had swathed herself in a dramatically patterned dashiki of brilliant swirling colors. Amber, the lone wise woman, decided to borrow the graduation gown, tassel and mortarboard her older sister had used when she'd graduated from kindergarten two years earlier.

The shepherds had chosen more standard garb, pants and ponchos and walking sticks that resembled modern canes, and Lucy had brought her dog Darby, because everyone knew shepherds used sheepdogs to guard their flock. Luckily, the black-and-white Aussie mix was well trained and loved children.

"Mths. Eloweeth, Mths. Eloweeth." Mary Alice, her face alight with joy, ran through the door and straight to Eloise's desk. "Thse coming. My mother canthseled her hair appointment and thse's coming to my play."

"That's wonderful." She gazed fondly at the little girl, a sight to behold in a tailored, navy-and-yellow dress, lustrous rope of pearls and high heels twice the size of her feet. Wearing her mother's jewelry and clothing, Mary Alice would be the most modern of all the angels. "Just remember to do your best and, no matter what, she'll be proud of you."

Parents, grandparents and friends poked their heads in the room to wish the children well. Rita Mae escorted Phoebe inside and gave Eloise a warm smile. "I'm cooking dinner at Nathan's after the play. Please join us. I want you and Joe to get better acquainted."

"I'm not sure that will be possible," Eloise stammered. How could she have forgotten about Rita Mae and the kindness the older woman had shown? "I may have things to take care of here."

"No problem. We'll wait for you." Rita Mae kissed Phoebe's cheek and headed out the door.

Clothed in the traditional billowing white robe of a heavenly being, Phoebe stared up at her, a satisfied grin on her hope-filled face. Inspecting her for the first time, Eloise took a closer look at the girl's topknot of curls.

Phoebe wore butterfly clips in her hair.

Eloise swallowed her joy and her sorrow. "Who fixed your hair this morning?"

"Grammy. She and Captain Joe came over early, 'cause Daddy had to leave before breakfast, and I told her I wanted to wear it just the way you do."

"I see. And where did you get the barrettes?"

"Grammy and I went to a store last week and bought 'em. I told her we had to find some 'zackly like yours," she answered with a toothy grin. "I'm gonna be a kindergarten teacher when I grow up, just like you."

Honoria's timely arrival gave Eloise a chance to breathe through the haze of sadness caused by Phoebe's remark. Pushing her way through the cluster of adults and children, the principal clapped her hands and spoke in her usual no-nonsense tone. "All parents and friends need to find seats in the auditorium while we prepare for the pageant. Please plan to stay after the play and enjoy the refreshments."

Minutes later, the kindergartners trooped up the stairs of the stage's rear entrance. Eloise made a final inspection of the scenery while the children gathered around the curtain to check out the audience. Raising her gaze, she found Honoria giving her the high-sign from across the stage and knew it was time to begin. Honoria helped the angels climb the bleachers while Eloise guided Phoebe up to her perch and strapped her into her harness.

"Now remember, stay very still until the spotlight hits you, then speak loud and clear, okay?"

"Uh-huh." Phoebe's eyes filled with tears. "I saw Grammy and Captain Joe, but I didn't see my daddy. I don't think he's gonna make it in time."

"Your father is a wonderful dad." Eloise cupped Phoebe's

face in her hands and brushed away the tears. "Have faith and believe hard enough, and he'll be here."

Phoebe sniffed. "Okay."

Eloise backed down the ladder and stepped to the stable. "You two ready?" she asked Mary and Joseph, adjusting the baby doll in Shawanna's arms.

They nodded in unison.

The shepherds and Darby began to fidget and she ran to stage left. "Let the angels announce the birth; then walk in slowly, no pushing. Do you remember what you're supposed to do after that?"

"Uh-huh," said Lucy. "We drop to our knees in front of the stable and wait for the wise men, then Phoebe says her part. When we hear the music, everybody sings 'The Little Drummer Boy.'"

"Good. That is so good," beamed Eloise. "You're going to do great."

She raced to stage right and lined up the wise men. Earlier in the week, she'd decided to let them each bring a gift of their own choosing to the stable instead of the traditional boxes of gold, frankincense and myrrh. "After the shepherds file in, it's your turn. Tell me what you chose to bring."

"I'm giving the baby Jesus a cell phone, so he can always be connected to the world," said Brent removing a phone from his pants pocket.

Miles held up a model airplane. "And I'm givin' him a jet, so he can get wherever he needs to be in a hurry."

Amber flashed a small rectangle of plastic. "It's my father's platinum card. I borrowed it, so the baby Jesus will have money to buy whatever he wants."

A corner of her mouth lifted as Eloise imagined the reaction of the audience. "Make sure you speak clearly and explain your gift before you give it. After that, Phoebe will do her thing, then everyone is going to sing and we're finished. Is anyone nervous?"

Miles raised his hand. "I haft'a go to the bathroom."

"Oh, Miles, can it wait?"

He shook his head and she turned to one of the high school boys assigned to move props. "Think you can escort Miles to the rest room and back in the next three minutes?"

"Sure, Miss Starr, no problem," the young man assured her.

Crossing her fingers, Eloise stepped farther back into the wings and waved to Honoria. The principal slipped through the opening in the curtain and welcomed the visitors to the pageant, then ducked back inside and cued the music. The janitor raised the curtain. An older student brought up the stage lights and signaled the angels to begin.

Eloise held her breath and prayed.

Twenty

Nathan scaled the front stairs of the Hewitt Academy two at a time. Just his luck he'd gotten caught in the middle of a strategy planning session with the big brass. The meeting had wrapped right about the time he thought he'd have to sneak out the side door. Good thing, too, because leaving this type of priority think-talk would not have sat well with the chief. But he'd been prepared to take the heat. No way was he going to disappoint his daughter or Eloise today.

He stood in the auditorium doorway and peered into the cavernous room. Rita Mae had promised to save him a seat, but it was dark as Hades inside. Squinting at the stage, he recognized a few of the little girls from the slumber party and realized he'd made it in the nick of time. The angels had just announced the news of a brilliant star shining over Bethlehem. Music spilled from the speakers; a group that he guessed were shepherds filed in, one of them leading a dog on a leash. The music grew louder and the shepherds fell to their knees.

Skulking against a far wall, he inched his way down the aisle, happy to be in the dark. His battered face had garnered all the disparaging looks he could handle for one day. Sure enough, there were Rita Mae and Joe in the front row, saving a seat as promised.

Nathan hunched down and duck-walked to his place. His mother clasped his hand and smiled. "You made it."

"Of course I did." He nodded at Joe, then scanned the stage. "Where's Phoebe? I thought she had a special part?"

"Shh." Rita Mae squeezed his fingers. "Watch."

A little girl wearing what looked to be a cap and gown led the parade of wise men marching in from stage left. The music dropped to a whisper and the trio turned to face the audience. One by one, they announced their gift to the Christ child. By the time the last little boy raised a small airplane, said his piece and handed the toy to Mary, the crowd was in stitches.

Rousing applause filled the auditorium. He checked out the angels and spotted Missy Jenkins dressed in hip-hugger jeans and a feather boa, tarted up like a mini Brittany Spears. In fact, only one little girl was dressed in what he'd always thought of as traditional angel garb, though a few of the other kids sported silvery halos.

He grinned at the eclectic group of heavenly beings. Leave it to Eloise to give the kids free rein with their costumes. Besides, who knew what angels really looked like? Phoebe had been telling him for the past few weeks that guiding angels—and she'd been very careful to use the word *guiding* instead of guardian—were everywhere, watching over people so they wouldn't do anything dumb.

If angels did exist, who said they couldn't resemble the human race?

A pale blue spotlight shot to the top of the stable and Nathan about swallowed his tongue. Perched on a platform over the nativity, her tiny face glowing with an inner light, was his daughter.

He moved to bolt from his seat, but Rita Mae held his arm. "Eloise would never allow Phoebe up there if it wasn't safe. Now sit back and enjoy the show."

"Yeah, you're right." Eloise loved his daughter and Phoebe loved Eloise, of that he had no doubt. It was one of the reasons he'd decided to take the plunge and ask her to marry him. Phoebe needed a mother and, though he never thought he'd say it, he needed a wife. To be more specific, he needed Eloise. Ever since their hot and heavy night together, he'd realized he didn't want to live without her.

All eyes were trained on Phoebe. Nathan spotted Eloise in the wings giving his daughter the high-sign and his heart quickened. He quirked up a corner of his mouth. Damn if they didn't look like twins. Phoebe's hair was done up on top of her head with little pink butterfly clips in her curls, just like Eloise's. The audience settled while Phoebe smiled sweetly, the picture of a benevolent heavenly being.

"Born unto you this day in a stable in Bethlehem is the Lord, our Savior," her clear voice rang out. "And He shall bring the world great joy." She raised her arms to heaven. "Come let us adore Him."

Still grinning into the crowd, Phoebe waggled her fingers, a sure sign that she'd spotted her dad.

Phoebe finished her lines and Eloise gave her a thumbs-up. The child's angelic expression so transcended time and place, she thought her heart would burst. Phoebe had every right to be proud. She'd done a great job, as had all the children.

The strains of "The Little Drummer Boy" echoed through the auditorium. The children sang softly at first, then with more fervor as the song crescendoed to a finish. The curtain closed to cheers of "Bravo" and another bout of fervent applause. Eloise hurried onto the set and the students gathered around her, all of them talking at once. A high school helper unhooked Phoebe's safety belt, led her from the platform and escorted her to the circle of children. Honoria hissed out a warning and they held hands to form a line across the stage.

The curtain rose and the line bowed as one.

Three curtain calls later, Eloise and her students moved to the manger and sat down Indian style. The first grade filed onto stage and began the carols. Most were traditional, but their teacher had added a song or two in celebration of Hanukkah, which turned the songfest into an international event. On the final tune, "We Wish You a Merry Christmas," everyone joined in. Honoria announced that refreshments were being served in the gymnasium and the students marched single-file into the hall, where family and friends waited to congratulate them.

Eloise thought this was the perfect time to slip away and head to her classroom, but she didn't get far. While the crowd lumbered into the gym, she was confronted by a trio of smiling women.

"Ms. Starr?" A tall, attractive African-American woman spoke first. "I'm Ruth Roberts, Shawanna's mother, and this is Claire Taylor, Adam is her son. Karen Chin is Lucy's mom. We hope this isn't a bad time."

Eloise pasted a smile on her face. She'd seen each of the mothers at one time or another when they'd picked up or dropped off their children. Until now, not one of them had bothered to give her more than a nod or mumble a polite hello. What did they want?

Claire Taylor took a step closer. "I'm sorry I haven't been able to stop by and talk with you before this, but Christmas is my busy time. I run a gift and craft shop in the District and we do a booming business between Thanksgiving and the new year. I just wanted to thank you for all you've done for the kindergarteners."

"Thank me?"

"Adam loves school, especially art class. He says it's because you let him use the colors he likes and you never tell him his drawings are childish or immature. He's talking about going to design school when he grows up. I just wanted you to know how much that means to his father and me."

"And Lucy says it's thanks to you that she loves to read," added Mrs. Chin, a small slender woman with a cap of shining black hair. "She's already thinking medical school. She used to go on about being a nurse, but she says you convinced her she could be a doctor. Considering no one else in our family has more than a high school education, it's a fine ambition."

"High school education?" Eloise repeated. "But I thought all the children here had parents who were—are—Um, I'm sorry, I guess I'm confused."

Ruth Roberts smiled. "The Hewitt Academy has a long-standing reputation of granting scholarships to children like Lucy who have the ability to learn but lack the funds. The school accepts a limited number of less privileged kids when they begin kindergarten and nurtures them right through their senior year. Honoria even sets funds aside for college. Thanks to the generosity of some of the alumni, about a hundred children a year get a quality education, but the school bears the bulk of the financial burden."

"I didn't know," Eloise said honestly. "Ms. Hewitt never mentioned it."

"That's just like her to keep it a secret," said Karen. "Honoria's not an easy person to open up to. Now that you're more aware, I expect you'll understand a little better where she's coming from. Then again, after watching the play we assumed the two of you were rolling along like wheels on a wagon. She never would have allowed this type of non-traditional pageant to take place if she didn't trust you."

"Here, we wanted you to have this." Claire Taylor handed her a brightly wrapped package and a card. "A few of us chipped in and got you a little something. It's not much, but it's from the heart."

"We, that is, all of the kindergarten parents, are so happy you replaced Ms. Singeltary," chimed Ruth. "We haven't had the chance to speak to every one of them, but we're sure they agree." She winked as she said, "And from what we've heard, we know Mr. Baxter thinks you're special."

Eloise held the gift to her chest and watched the women continue down the hall to the gymnasium. Overwhelmed by what she'd just learned, she was more determined than ever to leave this place. Phoebe loved her. Nathan loved her.

Everybody loved her! The parents were depending on her to guide their children; they were even giving her presents and thanking her for doing her job.

Leaving here today—now—was best. Honoria would find another teacher over the holiday break, the children would start fresh the first of the year, and she and Junior could devise an alternate route to return her to heaven. The students and parents at the Hewitt Academy would forget her, as most humans did when faced with change.

She arrived at her classroom and sat in her chair. Gaily wrapped packages addressed to "Teacher" and "Ms. Starr" covered her blotter, more symbols of her students' appreciation and love. Fingering her books and pencils, then her teacher's manual, she gazed out at the miniature desks that had so terrified her that first day. This room and everything in it had come to signify more than she'd ever thought possible. There had to be one small reminder of her time here, one tiny memory she could keep and hold close to her heart.

Opening a bottom drawer, she removed a folder and looked at the pictures she'd had the children draw as their first assignment—pictures of their vision of heaven. Stuffing the folder in her handbag, she walked to a wall peg and shrugged on her coat.

Turning, she stepped out the door, straight into Nathan's open arms.

Nathan caught Eloise by her elbows. "I've been looking everywhere for you. Phoebe was fantastic. All the kids were. Everybody in the gym is talking about the great job you did, but the party's breaking up. Rita Mae and Joe are taking Phoebe to the house, so I thought maybe this would be a good time for us to talk."

She shrank from his touch, and he took in the exhaustion in her eyes and the ghostly pallor of her skin. "Is something wrong? You're not sick, are you?"

"No. It's just that I—I'm not coming to the house. I have things to do at my place."

"What kind of things, because I'd be glad to help." He stepped closer and nuzzled his lips in the crook of her neck. She smelled like vanilla and spice, good enough to eat, but she felt stiff and unyielding in his arms. "We could stay at your apartment for a while, take a little break. I don't think Mom or Joe would mind."

She pulled from his embrace. "That's not a good idea."

"Sure it is. I've been waiting all week to get you alone and this is a perfect time." He took a deep breath, then plunged into his speech. "I thought I could wait until Christmas to give you your surprise, but it's burning a hole in my pocket." He dug into his coat and brought out a small, velvet-covered box. "It doesn't take a genius to figure out what's inside."

She placed her hand on her chest. "Nathan, no. I—"

He cupped her cheek in his hand, willing what he felt inside to telegraph straight to Eloise's heart. "I meant to do this in more romantic surroundings, but the school is just as good a place as any to tell you how I feel. I—we—Phoebe and I—" He shook his head. "I'm sorry if I'm going about this all wrong, but I never thought I'd be proposing again."

He snapped open the box and tipped it toward her, exposing a brilliant round diamond in a classic gold setting. Perfect and shining, he'd thought of her the moment he'd seen it in the jeweler's window.

"I love you, Eloise, and I want to spend the rest of my life with you. Will you marry me?"

Jerking her head up, she stared at him. She bit at her lower lip as tears filled her eyes. "I'm sorry, Nathan, but the answer is no. I can't marry you."

Nathan blew out a breath. Great. Maybe he ought to be taking a bow for another stellar, ham-handed performance. She was probably still trying to get used to living outside the convent walls and here he was, pressing her into a new life exactly the way he'd pressed her into bed.

He gave her an understanding grin. "Sure you can. It's easy. All you have to say is 'yes,' then let me slip this baby on the fourth finger of your left hand. We don't have to get married right away. There's plenty of time to tie the knot."

Panic and a glimmer of sorrow flashed across her face. "You're not listening. I said I can't marry you. End of discussion." Clutching her bag to her chest, she stepped to the side. "Excuse me, I want to leave."

Nathan swallowed. "I'm sorry if this comes as a surprise, but I thought our feelings for each other were the same. I know I should have told you how I felt the morning after we slept together, but it took me a few days to get my head on straight." Clasping her shoulders, he pulled her to his chest. "I love you, Eloise. We belong together. If I'm moving too fast, at least tell me you'll think about it. I can wait for you, sweetheart, for as long as it takes."

She brushed at the tears now falling freely down her cheeks. "I don't love you, Nathan. Now let me go."

Raising his hands in a gesture of surrender, he backed off but followed her into the hall. Before he could speak, she slammed into Rita Mae and Honoria standing side by side at the lockers. When he called to her, Eloise spun in a circle and plowed down the corridor without a backward glance, then ran out the main door.

Nathan closed his fist on the box and snapped it shut. Stuffing it in his pocket, he blew out a breath. Damn, what the hell was that all about? Scowling, he turned to Ms. Hewitt and his mother. "What do you two want?"

Rita Mae fidgeted with her handbag. "I'd hoped to find you before you found Eloise. There's something important you need to know." She tossed Honoria a pleading smile. "Go on. Tell my son what you just told me."

Wringing her hands, Ms. Hewitt began to pace. "I don't know, Rita Mae. Eloise spoke to me in confidence. I don't feel I can—"

Crossing his arms, Nathan growled out a curse. "After

what just happened in this room, I doubt there's anything you can say that will surprise me. Now spit it out."

"Oh, all right. But I was hoping to change Ms. Starr's mind before anyone found out." She heaved a sigh. "Your mother and I started discussing the kindergarten class, and it just slipped out."

"Yeah, Mom has a knack for that sort of thing." He ran a hand through his hair. "Now what the hell are the two of you talking about?"

"Eloise quit her job, and she won't be back after the holiday," Rita Mae blurted. "You have to do something, Nathan. Right now."

Brushing at her tears, Eloise ran from the building. The loving expression on Nathan's face, the beautiful ring, his heartfelt proposal—All of it was too much for her to absorb. Someday she would learn to live without his touch or the sound of his voice. *Without him.* At the moment, all of it was more than she could bear.

Sorrow scratched at the back of her throat, mixing with the lump that had risen from the pit of her stomach. For the good of everyone, it was time to make a fast, clean break. As if on automatic pilot, she headed for Mr. Belgradian's. She could sit and drink a calming cup of cocoa while she thought about her options. If need be, she'd stay until Mr. Belgradian locked up for the night, then slip into her apartment unnoticed. She would pack and be gone by morning.

Dark clouds scuttled across the afternoon sky, bringing an early dusk. Ignoring the *Closed* sign hanging on the window, she pushed through the door to the small shop and was enveloped in warmth. Marching past the young man filling the entryway, she set her handbag on a table and searched for the shopkeeper's welcoming smile.

When a rush of goose bumps tripped down her arm, she stopped short and took stock of the room. Three men, their faces covered in knitted ski masks, glared at her. The man nearest the counter was pointing what looked to be a homemade weapon at Mr. Belgradian, who was standing behind the cash register with upraised hands and a terrified expression.

"Good goin', Scooch," said the guy with the gun. "I told you not to let anyone in."

"I tried to stop the bitch, but she charged right into me. Wasn't my fault," Scooch whined.

"Get over here." The gunman gestured to Eloise. "Where I can keep my eye on you."

Eloise looked at each man in turn. Were these the three robbers she'd heard about from Nathan? She remembered him warning Rita Mae, but she'd never thought they would end up in Mr. Belgradian's store. Lost souls, they'd chosen a darker path in the world. Lucky for them, she was an angel with eons of experience.

Throwing back her shoulders, she dug in her heels. "Mr. Belgradian, are you all right? Have these boys hurt you?"

"Eloise, please. I am fine. Just do as they say."

She sniffed in indignation. "I will not." Fisting her hands on her hips, she stalked to Scooch and peered up at him. "Excuse me, but what do you think you're doing?"

Openmouthed, Scooch gaped at her. "Look, bitch, just do like Weed says. Go stand next to the old man and nobody will get hurt."

"I'm not talking to you." Eloise squinted at a spot over his shoulder. Where in the world was the man's guiding angel? How could competent heavenly beings allow their charges to get involved in something this wrong? "I was hoping to speak to someone else."

"What you talkin' 'bout—speak to someone else?" Scooch took a step back. "Don't you be givin' me no evil eye or nothin'."

The second robber pushed from the wall and grabbed her

by the coat sleeve. "This way, bitch. And shud'up. We don't got no time to mess wif you."

Wrenching her arm free, Eloise rounded on him. If these boys had been pink-slipped by their angels, maybe she could guide them. Then again, if this was the way she was meant to return to heaven, she wasn't about to leave her human life with Mr. Belgradian in danger.

"Eloise, please," shouted the shopkeeper.

"Don't worry about me, Mr. Belgradian. It's these young men who have a problem." She glared at each robber in turn. "Their guiding angels have more than likely given up on them, and they're lost. They just need a bit of help to find their way." Walking to the robber with the gun, she arched a brow. "Looks to me like you're the man in charge."

"Yeah." He leered at her through the slit in his mask. "You got that right."

"There's still time, you know. You can walk out of here and promise never to do this again. When I get to heaven, I'll ask your angel to take you back."

Weed spit out a rusty chuckle. "Hear that, fellas? She wants us to reform."

Scooch snorted. "Aw, ain't that nice?" His buddy merely shook his head.

The gunman jabbed his weapon in the air. "You are a piece of work, you know that."

"I'm a teacher and a former guiding—uh—guidance counselor. I know all about lost souls—er—students like you."

"Look, lady, we ain't your students and we sure ain't lost." He waved the gun in her face. "Stop messin' with us and get behind the counter."

Eloise narrowed her eyes. If she blocked their way out the door, she might be able to distract them long enough for someone to arrive and stop them.

"I think I'll stand right here, thank you very much."

Weed bit out a nasty curse, then nodded at the second man. "Get her outta the way. Now!"

Twenty-one

Nathan stalked onto the sidewalk, still in shock over what he'd just learned. Eloise was leaving the Hewitt Academy—leaving Phoebe. Leaving him! And from the sound of it, she hadn't planned on letting him know. Unfuckin'believable!

He stared up one end of the street, then the other, too furious to think straight. Recalling something she'd said to him a few weeks ago, he kicked a discarded soda can so hard it landed across the street.

Eloise had promised that if she ever decided to quit her job he would be the first to know, so he could be the one to explain it to his daughter. She'd stood there and lied to his face. He'd been a chump, thinking she was different from other women, hoping she would stick around, when all the while she'd been playing him for a fool. Using him to—to—

He sucked in air. Furrowing fingers through his hair, he fought to contain his temper. Using him to what? Get a few free meals? Baby-sit his daughter until all hours—without pay? Lose her virginity?

Checking out the sidewalk a second time, he shook his head. Talk about acting like an idiot. He loved Eloise, and she loved him. Something was bothering her—maybe it was Honoria, or the play, or maybe she really was sick and didn't want him to know.

All he had to do was get her to talk to him and everything would be okay. When two people loved each other, there was nothing so bad it couldn't be worked out. That's what the problem had been in his first marriage. Neither he nor Janet had loved each other enough to want to make it work.

It was different with Eloise. She was different. And he wasn't going to lose her without a fight. Hell, he wasn't going to lose her—period.

Walking at a trot, Nathan headed toward her apartment. She'd left in a hurry, but she'd been on foot, so she couldn't have gone very far. Once he convinced her to let him in, he'd change her mind or die trying. Turning a corner, he spotted the convenience store where they'd picked up dinner earlier in the week. Phoebe had told him Eloise liked it there, so maybe she'd stopped to get supper. It would only take a minute to check.

He sauntered to the curb and slowed his steps. Funny time to have a Closed sign on the window, he thought. Then again, he wouldn't put it past Eloise to flip the sign over just to throw him off track. If she was inside, it might be better if he waited for her to come out. The last thing he wanted was to grill her in front of the old man.

A sudden knot of suspicion coiled in his stomach. Hoping to assuage his fear, he ducked down and pressed against the side of the building and cased the interior of the store. Something about that Closed sign didn't sit well . . .

The knot drew taut as he surveyed the scene inside. Just as he suspected, something was wrong. Very wrong.

Three men wearing ski masks—Eloise standing with her chin notched into a mutinous pout—Belgradian behind the counter with his hands in the air.

Whoever said gut instinct was a waste of time didn't know cops.

Nathan skittered backward and rose to his feet, scanning the sidewalk. The leaden sky and a chill wind had pushed the afternoon into darkness. Except for a few taxis, the street was empty, not a patrol car in sight. His brain went into overdrive. Pulling out his cell phone, he called for backup, then took his gun from its holster and placed it in his pocket.

Inching to the edge of the window, he checked the store again. If he was reading the situation correctly, Eloise was actually holding a conversation with the thugs. She seemed to be lecturing them, shaking a finger at the guy with the zip gun as if he were one of her students. It would be stupid to charge in if she had them on hold. He had to think.

Straightening his shoulders, he calmly slid a hand over the gun in his pockets. Until the cavalry arrived, finesse was the key. That and protecting Eloise.

He opened the door to the sound of arguing. When the overhead bell rang, everyone turned mute.

"Hey, honey, I'm glad you waited for me." Nathan headed for Eloise's side, but thug number one blocked his path. The kid was tall and wiry, with dark frightened eyes and a nervous twitch to his hands.

"Stay back, man." He shoved Nathan in the chest. "Don't want no trouble wif you."

Eloise blew a curl from her forehead. "What are *you* doing here?"

"Meeting you, like we discussed." He raised his left hand in surrender. "Sorry for interrupting, fellas. How about you let us go? We didn't mean to screw up your plans."

Eloise took a step toward him, but thug number two grabbed her arm. "Hang on, bitch. Nobody said nothin' 'bout lettin' you leave."

"Who are you calling a bi—a female dog?" she asked with a huff. "And if that's your attitude, I don't blame your angel for abandoning you."

Angel? Abandoning him! What the hell was she babbling about now? Nathan gave himself a healthy mental kick and got back on track. "Hear that, buddy? Let the lady go and we're outta here. You'll get your cash and no one will get hurt. What do you say?"

"Eloise, go to your man, please." Mr. Belgradian's voice broke. "I will give them the money."

Thug number three, the one with the zip gun, darted his gaze from Mr. Belgradian to Eloise to Nathan.

"Remember what you said, Weed, about taking folks out. We don't want no trouble like the last time." This from thug number two, who sounded twitchier by the second.

Considering, the gunman pointed at Eloise and waved her toward Nathan. "You two. Stand over there where I can keep an eye on the both of you."

Eloise did as he asked and Nathan pushed her behind him.

The gunman sidled to face them and gestured to thug number two. "You and Scooch go over to the old man and help him unload the cash drawer. Go on! Time's wastin'!"

The robbers shuffled to the counter and Scooch opened a paper sack. "Here, Pops, load this up and don't be stingy."

Mr. Belgradian moved to fill the bag.

Eloise stepped from behind and poked at Nathan's shoulder. "I really think you need to get out of here. I can handle this fine by myself."

Nathan ground his back molars. "You can handle it? Now I know you're coming down with something." He slid his gaze to the window. Where the hell was his backup?

Thug number three raised a shaky arm and shot Nathan a sneer. "What you lookin' at?"

Nathan shrugged. "The weather. Looks like we're in for one mother of a snowstorm."

The gunman took a step closer. "Quit being such a wise ass and get away from the window."

He jerked his arm and Nathan made his move. Stepping in front of Eloise, he whipped out his gun.

"A cop! He's a fuckin' cop!"

The thugs waiting for the money turned. Quick as a striking snake, Mr. Belgradian reached under the counter and pulled out a baseball bat.

Eloise shrieked as the old man clobbered Scooch flat on the back of his head. The blow threw him into his pal and both men stumbled to the floor.

The gunman whirled, his eyes glittering with rage.

"Drop the gun," Nathan commanded. "Now!"

Was he crazy? Eloise scuttled to his side, but Nathan pushed her back.

The gunman took aim. *No!* she screamed, but the word stuck in her throat. She vaulted between them. "Get back. Phoebe needs you, you stupid man. Get back!"

Nathan shoved Eloise behind him and fired, hitting the gunman's arm. The zip gun exploded, and Nathan staggered to his knees.

Falling backward, his world went black.

Eloise opened her eyes and frowned. Something was wrong, but she couldn't quite put her finger on the problem. She turned in a semicircle and recognized heaven, so why didn't it feel as if she were home?

"Hey, El. You finally got it right."

Junior's cheery voice grated like nails on a blackboard. She swung around and found him standing behind Milton, who was seated at his white marble desk, grinning as only the senior angel-in-charge could.

"Welcome back," said the dimpled Doughboy. "We've been waiting for you."

Eloise took another look around. "I can see that. What I want to know is, how did I get here?"

Shaking his head, Junior folded his arms. "Now there's an intelligent question. This is heaven, remember? What does it matter, so long as you're back where you belong?"

Eloise felt a throbbing in her chest and glanced down at her coat. If she was in heaven, why was she still wearing human clothing? Her fuzzy pink sweater peeked out, but it was bloody and torn, as if she'd been injured.

"What happened to bring me here, if you don't mind my asking."

"Holy smoke, El, why do you care? Just be happy—"

Milton raised a hand and Junior had the good sense to button up. "Faith, hope and love." The senior-angel-in-charge steepled his fingers and tapped them on his chin. "You've been practicing the virtues all week. You risked your job to teach a child how to read. You made your students joyous, gave them purpose, taught them how to have fun. And mere seconds ago, you were willing to give up your life for a friend. You even tried to reform the unreformable and save Nathan at the same time. Your faith in him and your love for Phoebe showed Us you learned a lifetime of important lessons. You've finally earned the right to make your choice."

"My choice?" Why was her head so muzzy? And why did her chest hurt? "Wait a second. What happened to Nathan?"

Milton's smile turned upside down. "I'm afraid there's been a little accident we still have to get sorted out. But not to worry. We have a few minutes to get it under control."

"Accident? What do you mean—accident?"

Milton glanced down and Eloise followed his lead. Gazing into the desktop, she got an overview of the store. Nathan was prone on top of her human body and the two of them were surrounded by a pool of blood. Her blood, she realized. And Nathan's.

Clenching her fists to her chest, she met Milton's sympathetic eyes. "You call that *under control!* Nathan is dying. You have to fix this. Fix it now!"

"It's not up to me to fix, dear child. It's up to you."

Eloise pressed her fingers to her temples. Why wasn't anything the way it was supposed to be? Her head was pounding, and angels never felt pain. They never felt anything, and she was aching from the inside out.

"What do you mean, it's up to me?"

"You have to choose. Either you go back to earth and

Nathan comes up here, or the other way around. Only one of you can remain on earth. It's the rule."

"No! Stop! Don't let him die." She clutched at the edge of the desk. "Nathan has to live. Please, you have to let him live."

Milton stood. "So you're telling me you would rather stay here and give up human life, than reside on earth?"

Eloise inhaled a breath. "Not if Nathan won't be there with me. And besides, Phoebe needs him. That's all that matters. He can't die."

"Do you love him?" Milton folded his arms. "Or were you merely toying with the idea of love?"

"No! Yes! No!" She tugged at her hair. "Is there a right answer to that question? Give me a hint, because I'm really confused. Can't you just put things back the way they were?"

The senior angel raised a bushy brow. "Back the way they were? And what way would that be, exactly?"

"Nathan alive, watching his daughter grow up happy and well adjusted. And me there with him—with them—guiding Phoebe in her choices while Nathan and I share our lives." She brushed at her cheeks and felt the wetness. How could she be an angel and still be crying? Now she was positive something was wrong.

"Are you telling me you want to go back, Eloise? You want to remain human?" Milton lifted his hand and a gavel appeared. "Or do you love Nathan and Phoebe so much that you would sacrifice your chance at earthly happiness, so they could have each other? Tell me now, because the choice is yours."

"Don't you hear what I'm saying? Without Nathan beside me, I won't have earthly happiness, so yes, I want them to have each other." She sobbed, unable to stop the tears. "I'll be a better angel. I won't give up on my charges, ever again. Just let Nathan and Phoebe stay together. Please."

Milton tossed Junior a sage expression. "Now do you understand what I've been getting at?"

"Uh, yeah. I guess so." Junior shrugged. "She's willing to sacrifice her happiness for that of the humans she loves. Right?"

"Correct."

"Works for me," Junior said. "I guess."

Milton turned to Eloise. "You have yet to answer my question, Eloise. Do you love Nathan Baxter as much as he loves you, with all your human heart and soul?"

Did she have a human heart and soul? Was that the reason she'd been aching inside, hurting so much that she wanted to run back to heaven? Did she love Nathan the way he loved her?

Suddenly, everything became clear as crystal.

"Yes, I love him. More than I ever imagined was possible."

"And?" Milton prodded.

"And I want to marry him, bear his children and share a life with him. I want to watch Phoebe grow up and have babies of her own. I want every second of the pain and joy of being human. For as long as He allows it."

"If that's what you want, then I'm pleased to tell you it's yours." Milton smiled, his face beaming. "And because you love Nathan, the rule can be rewritten. Love is the reason you were sent to earth in the first place. That and to find your true path. If you want to live that path on earth, He certainly won't stop you."

Eloise closed her eyes. "Then send me back. It's where I want to be. It's where I belong."

She waited, but nothing happened. Cracking open one eye, she sneaked a peek. Junior and Milton were grinning like a pair of fools.

"I'm waiting." She smiled. "Oh, and Milton?"

"Yes?"

"Thank you."

* * *

Nathan groaned. Rolling to his side, he touched the ache high in his right shoulder. Wincing when his fingers came away sticky with blood, he bit back a curse. Damn, that hurt. Idiot kid with the zip gun got him good.

Raising his head, he saw policemen swarming the store. Isobel was hovering, her expression dour as she knelt over the body lying next to him.

"Eloise!" He fumbled to his knees, almost retching with the pain. "Aw, no! Aw, hell!" He reached down to help her, but Isobel pushed his hand away.

"She's hurt bad, Nate. The bullet that hit you went right through your shoulder and straight into her chest. Don't move her. The ambulance is on its way."

Nathan choked back a sob. He'd warned her to stay back, but the little dope just wouldn't listen. He should have used better sense and waited outside. Maybe none of this would have happened.

"Eloise." He leaned over her, fighting the lightning-hot stab of pain. She was so pale, so quiet. Cupping her cheek, he whispered, "Hang on, honey. Just hang on."

"Nathan?" Eloise's eyes fluttered opened. "Is that you?"

"It's me, sweetheart. Don't move. Just lie still. Help's coming."

"Hurts," she mumbled, flattening her lips. "Never thought being human could hurt so much."

"Pain is good, honey." *Even though you're delirious,* he thought to himself. "If you're in pain, it means you're alive."

She struggled to sit up and he pressed her back, but she batted at his hands. "I'm okay. Just want to breathe. I'll do it better sitting up."

He locked gazes with Isobel, who nodded her approval.

"You sure you feel good enough to move?"

Still struggling, Eloise rose up on her elbows. "I'm sure." He used his left arm to lever her into a sitting position.

Eloise patted at the bloody fuzz that used to be her sweater. Her hands moved to her neck and tugged.

Nathan helped her with the task until they pulled the locket out from under her clothes. He held it in his palm and his eyes opened wide. Lodged in the battered lump of gold was a bullet-shaped piece of metal.

"Is this what I think it is?" he asked, his voice reedy and thin. "The locket I gave Janet when Phoebe was born?"

"Phoebe gave it to me. I meant to give it back to her, but the time just never seemed right." Eloise leaned into his chest. "It saved my life."

Nathan shook his head, wanting to say more, but unsure of the words. Two medics pushed through the door with a gurney. "Okay, who's first?" the rescue worker asked Isobel. "Which one of them is worse?"

Isobel stood. "I'd say they're both in pretty good shape at the moment. How about you see to the perps and give these two a little room?"

Eloise waited until the medics were gone before rubbing at her chest. "I'm going to have one heck of a bruise." She turned to Nathan and ran a finger over the blotchy colors decorating his face, then grimaced at the wound in his shoulder. "You sure you're okay?"

Nathan caught her fingers in his hand. "As long as you're with me, I'm better than okay." He settled back against the wall and pulled her closer into his good side. Together, they watched the excitement while their breathing slowed and synced. One set of medics worked over the gunman, another loaded Scooch onto a gurney. A patrolman cuffed the third boy and led him out the door. Mr. Belgradian sat at a table, talking to a detective.

Finally, Nathan asked the question that had been nagging at him for the past few minutes. "Eloise, do you believe in miracles?"

She whipped up her head. "What?"

"You know, things that happen for no earthly reasons. Stuff like what just happened with Janet's locket? Miracles."

How did she tell him that until now her entire human existence had been a miracle? That loving him and Phoebe and being allowed to live out her time on earth with them was the biggest miracle of all?

"I don't think there's any other answer. If I hadn't been wearing it, I probably wouldn't be here right now." That was the truth, or as close to it as she wanted to get. "I need to thank Phoebe for giving it to me."

"So maybe it's a sign from heaven?"

"A sign?"

"That there's a higher power telling us we belong together. I asked you a question a little while ago. Do you remember what it was?"

"Let me think a minute." He grinned and bent his head to drop a kiss on her nose. "Oh, yeah," she teased. "You proposed."

"And you turned me down."

"I did?"

"You did. I heard you."

"Oh, well, I must have misunderstood the question. Ask me again and I'll do better."

Nathan maneuvered her upright and dug for the ring box, then nestled her back against his chest. Opening the box with one hand, he set it on the floor and removed the ring.

"Wow, that thing is blinding." The ring was so bright it brought tears to her eyes. "You sure you want me to wear it?"

"Let me ask the question, first, okay? You can wear it if you give the right answer."

She gazed up at him, her blue eyes dancing. "Before you do, I think it's important you know that I love you. More than I ever thought I could love a human being. I wanted to make that clear before you said something you'd be sorry for later."

He grinned. Between Eloise, Phoebe and Rita Mae, he was going to be in way over his head. And Phoebe wanted a little sister. If he played his cards right, he was going to be surrounded by meddling, bossy women. He was a lucky guy.

"Eloise Starr, you are my heart and my soul and the joy of my life—"

"I am? You didn't say all that the first time. Maybe if you had—"

"I didn't think of it the first time. It all just came to me a second ago. Now let me finish before I forget the most important part." He nuzzled his lips against her ear. "I love you. Will you marry me?"

"Does that include 'until death do us part'? Because I think those words are important."

"It does." He held her tighter with his good arm. "And beyond, if that's possible."

Eloise held out her hand and he slipped the ring on her finger. "It's possible. In fact, it's more than possible."

Epilogue

"So this is a wedding." Perched on the edge of a pillar high above the choir loft, Junior assessed the church, decorated in Christmas colors of red, green and white and overflowing with happy people. "I've never been to one before."

Milton sighed. He really was a sucker for a joyous occasion. If this were a christening, he'd be positively beside himself. As it is, an angel finding true love and choosing to remain human was one for the record books. But he'd always known Eloise was unique.

"Remember your first, my boy. It's special. This one just happens to be more so than most."

"Nathan seems content." Junior nodded toward the groom, who was standing patiently next to Captain Milligan at the altar. The detective's grin, which Eloise had finally told him was beyond sappy, seemed firmly etched in place. "Good thing, since he's had so much chaos in his life."

"Nathan is a smart man," said Milton. "He loved Eloise the moment he saw her. It's so nice when things work out for the best."

The organist started the processional and the two angels watched as Eloise's students marched up the aisle two by two. Then came Phoebe, scattering rose petals like thistledown. Her Grammy had told her earlier that she'd have the baby sister of her heart by next Christmas, and

Phoebe believed it to be true. She had, after all, her own personal guiding angel and mother all rolled into one.

Honoria followed Phoebe down the aisle, wearing a stylish gown and fashionable shoes. The fact that she'd gotten Eloise's word she would stay on to teach kindergarten for as long as she was able had lightened the principal's heart. Eloise was the very best teacher she'd ever been smart enough to hire.

Junior peered so far over the railing he slipped off the edge. Milton *tsked* his disapproval as the angel-in-training floated back to his side. "You'll have to learn decorum, my boy, if you want your very own charges to care for."

"But I wanted to see Eloise when she stepped inside. She looks like an ang—uh—an apparition. She's wearing a long, satiny white dress, white veil with a ten-foot train and a little white circle of daisies in her hair. And she's got those butterflies Nathan likes pinned to the flowers. I don't know how she managed to arrange everything in forty-eight hours, but she is gorgeous."

"Yes, well, let's just say she had a little help and leave it at that, shall we?"

"We can do that?"

"When the situation warrants."

Eloise, a vision in white, passed under them on her way to the altar. Milton couldn't see her face, be he imagined it was glowing. She'd made the right choices, passed with flying colors and He was satisfied.

Nathan reached out a hand to help her onto the altar and his expression said it all. His eyes held tenderness and joy, and he seemed completely captivated by his bride.

"So, what's next?" asked Junior.

"Why babies, of course. Several lovely little ones. And absolute happiness for—"

"I meant for me. Where do I go from here?"

"Shh. This is the part I enjoy the best," Milton hissed. "Vows, written from the heart and filled with meaning are so—so—" The senior angel waved a hand. "You know what I mean."

Eloise and Nathan kissed and he heaved another sigh. They turned as one and he saw their radiant smiles, felt their utter happiness and rose a few inches above the choir loft. "Ah, now there's a romantic sight."

"Yeah, sure is." Just as the new Mr. and Mrs. Baxter passed below, Junior tossed a shining ball of angel dust toward them, inordinately proud when it rained glitter and good luck on the happy couple. It was his gift, small but potent, to ensure their future.

Milton watched the ball disappear in a flash of gold and sent an approving nod Junior's way. "That was a very nice gesture. Perhaps you'll make a compassionate guiding angel after all."

"I was hoping you'd think so," Junior said, eager to get on with his new task. "So, when are you gonna tell me what's next on my agenda?"

Dimpling, Milton brushed a finger to the side of his nose. "All in good time, my boy. All in good time."

About the Author

JUDI McCOY is living her dream. Not only does she get to write about romance each and every day, she also resides on the tip of Virginia's beautiful eastern shore in the tiny-but-quaint town of Cape Charles. When not writing, she gardens and tends to her orchids, or watches the hummingbirds sip at the feeders in her backyard. Thanks to the care and support of her loving husband Dennis and her two spoiled dogs, she is a happy woman. Judi enjoys hearing from her fans and promises to answer every query. Please visit her website at: *www.judimccoy.com* or e-mail her directly at: *judi1022@earthlink.net*.